PENGUIN BOOKS

THE RECORDING ANGEL

Evan Eisenberg writes about music, culture, and technology for *The Nation*, *Saturday Review*, *The Village Voice*,
The Whole Earth Review, and other publications. He
studied philosophy at Harvard and Princeton and has
worked professionally as a synagogue cantor.

Acknowledgments

For their comments on drafts or parts of drafts, and for thoughts shared with me over the years, I wish to record my heartfelt thanks to John Aniello, Alan Bernstein, Gerald Cohen, David Hamilton, Ted Klein, Maria Margaronis, Ann Marlowe, Erik Murkoff, Adam Narva, Elizabeth Pochoda, Paul Sanford, Steven Sater, Victor Shargai, Joan Warner, Charles Weinstock, and other friends too numerous for this 45-r.p.m. page. But there are some performances to which recording cannot do justice. Let the patience and warmth of my editor, Cynthia Merman; the toughness and marginalia (themselves works of art) of my deeply literary agent, Joe Spieler; the generous candor of my interlocutors in Chapters One, Three, Nine, and Eleven; the faith, understanding, and marathon typing of my parents, Arlene and Howard Eisenberg, and of my sisters, Sandee Hathaway and Heidi Murkoff; the unsecured loans and infinite capacity for *shepping nachus* of my grandparents, Millie and Harry Scharaga; and the love, courage, and grace of my wife Freda live on only as legend.

E.E.
New York City
Bastille Day, 1986

EVAN EISENBERG

THE RECORDING

 ANGEL

The Experience
of Music from
Aristotle to Zappa

PENGUIN BOOKS

For my father, my mother, and my wife

PENGUIN BOOKS
Published by the Penguin Group
Viking Penguin Inc., 40 West 23rd Street,
New York, New York 10010, U.S.A.
Penguin Books Ltd, 27 Wrights Lane,
London W8 5TZ, England
Penguin Books Australia Ltd, Ringwood,
Victoria, Australia
Penguin Books Canada Ltd, 2801 John Street,
Markham, Ontario, Canada, L3R 1B4
Penguin Books (N.Z.) Ltd, 182-190 Wairau Road,
Auckland 10, New Zealand

Penguin Books Ltd, Registered Offices:
Harmondsworth, Middlesex, England

First published in the United States of America by
McGraw-Hill Book Company 1987
Reprinted by arrangement with McGraw-Hill, Inc.
Published in Penguin Books 1988

1   3   5   7   9   10   8   6   4   2

Copyright © Evan Eisenberg, 1987
All rights reserved

LIBRARY OF CONGRESS CATALOGING IN PUBLICATION DATA
Eisenberg, Evan.
The recording angel: the experience of music from Aristotle to
Zappa/Evan Eisenberg.
p.   cm.
ISBN 0 14 01.1338 X
1. Sound recordings—Social aspects.   2. Sound recording industry.
3. Music and society—20th century.   I. Title.
ML 1055.E35   1988
303.4'833—dc19   88–17449

Printed in the United States of America by
R.R. Donnelley & Sons Company, Harrisonburg, Virginia
Set in Souvenir

Contents

ONE   Clarence   1
TWO   Music Becomes a Thing   11
THREE   Tomás   35
FOUR   Ceremonies of a Solitary   43
FIVE   The Social Record   69
SIX   The Cyrano Machine   87
SEVEN   Glenn Gould   101
EIGHT   Phonography   109
NINE   Nina   161
TEN   Canned Catharsis   175
ELEVEN   Saul   209
TWELVE   Deus Ex Machina   227
Index   257

Chapter One

Clarence

From the outside Clarence's house looks like the others in this part of Bellmore, Long Island. The tiny plot of crabgrass may be a shade browner than average, but there is nothing remarkable until you step up to the door, which has a hole stuffed with rags where the lock should be; ring the doorbell, which does not ring; knock; and see materialize, behind the small square of glass, a face. A navy-blue watch cap is pulled down to the eyes, whose lashes glisten with rheum. The square Yankee jaw, peppered with a rash, expands in a smile, and the high-pitched harried voice calls for you to come around the back.

Clarence opens the kitchen door and you enter, but just barely. Every surface—the counters and cabinets, the shelves of the oven and refrigerator, and almost all the linoleum floor—is covered with records. They are heavy shellac disks, jammed in cardboard boxes or just lying in heaps; crowning one pile is a plate of rusty spaghetti. In the far corner are four shopping bags full of sugared doughnuts. There is a stench.

1

"The toilet is stopped up," Clarence apologizes. "I have to go to the public library to defecate. I urinate in a pail." He gestures toward a closet in the corner. "I'm sorry about the cold. They won't fix the furnace. I shave every morning with cold water." The rash, it is now clear, is a vast collection of shaving cuts.

"Look at this place! Can you believe this? And that bastard Healey tells everyone what a good Catholic he was to do all this for me." Healey, a lawyer whose name I have amended, bought the lien—legally, his secretary bought the lien—on Clarence's ancestral home in Roslyn Estates, Long Island, a fourteen-room manse assessed at $48,000. Clarence had inherited it and some $70,000 from his father, a celebrated Cadillac salesman, in 1970; but within a few years he had given away all the money, and then all he had left was the house—unheated, unlit, so crammed with trash that the door wouldn't open—and three quarters of a million records. Hobbled by rheumatoid arthritis, and never one for gainful employment anyway, Clarence went on welfare. As he couldn't pay the taxes on his estate, he lost it to Healey's secretary. This place is Clarence's booby prize.

In some ways, things are better for him here. He has electricity, and if his fingers are too stiff to change the light bulbs at least he can play his records. In Roslyn he had to use a third-hand battery-operated gimcrack, a kid's toy really, and after a time even that went out of service. Now he has a good thrift-shop plug-in portable in the kitchen. Oddly, there is another on top of the records on what must be the dining-room table, and also a scruffy transistor radio; leading me to them Clarence says, "These are for you. Because you said you didn't have any music where you're housesitting. I got them at the thrift shop, but they work okay."

So Clarence is a saint, though he stinks to high heaven. The stories of his magnanimity ($10,000 tipped to a cabbie who wanted to open a bar) are not apocrypha. He even gives away records.

"You said you love Gershwin, and Fred Astaire? I have all the old Brunswicks from *Shall We Dance* and *A Damsel in Distress*. They're yours. Here, they're somewhere on the Frigidaire": and Clarence spends the next hour excavating, each record caked with history, anecdotes shaking off like clotted sand. "Oh, this is very rare: one of Jolson's first. You like Jolson? It's yours. Here's a very rare Ethel Waters, 'Frankie and Johnnie were lovers,' you should have that. Here's one of the first Astaire records"—Clarence sings: "'*S wonderful, 's marvelous* . . . you like that? It's yours. No, take it. You love Gershwin more than I do. Do you have . . . there's a Twentieth Century-Fox double album, about twenty dollars, Ira sings; and did you get the Frances Gershwin album? I want to dig it up. I have a very rare song sheet Ira autographed for me at the Museum of the City of New York. Yeah, I met him, he's a very sweet man. If I can find it you're gonna die. 'Dawn of a New Day': that was the theme song of the nineteen thirty-nine World's Fair and it's George and Ira Gershwin on the Brunswick label. Now obviously Gershwin died in thirty-seven, so they had to write it two years prior unless George wrote the music and then Ira. . . . Did you hear Joe Franklin on the radio, he said 'George Gershwin's wife Ira'? I swear. Oh, here's another Fred Astaire! You'll have the whole set. Here's *another* Fred Astaire!"—the sweet, tinny radio voice is now a treble—"You hit the jackpot! You'll have all the originals, the whole set that's on the Epic album!"

The records are heavy and cold, like black ice: as though, should the furnace miraculously start to work, they would thaw into some kind of music fluid. "Cold won't hurt the records," Clarence assures me, "only heat. As I told Irv Molotsky"—the *New York Times* reporter who wrote about Clarence some years back—"records are inanimate until you put the needle in the groove, and then they come to life."

*   *   *

Clarence Browne grew up in the Depression. "Momma didn't buy a new dress for twelve years. Poppa had a job with the Cadillac company; that was it. Well, I used to go to the Port Washington Five-and-Ten and buy those Big Little Books (now they go for fifty dollars each). I had Jackie Cooper, I had . . . I still save them. Oh, I would get one Big Book and I was happy. I was always satisfied.

"But then I started getting these records. I started getting more and more, as you see. I used to schlepp all around New York City. I might get five hundred records at a shot—they were a penny or a nickel each in those days, secondhand." By now the Depression was over, and adolescent Clarence found his wallet full. His collection grew. "Finally Momma and Poppa said, 'We don't want you to have any more records unless you make something of them.' Now my idea originally, long before that, was to share my collection with everybody. You see, collectors—take collectors of oil paintings—they don't do that; they only share with themselves. Share it with everybody!"

Clarence got his chance in the late forties, when Jerry Lawrence was doing the Wax Museum program on WMCA. "His records had big hunks out of them, as if they were worm-eaten—not bookworms, recordworms." So Clarence called in and offered the use of his collection, about ten thousand records at the time. "Lawrence said I was manna from heaven."

This was the beginning of a long amateur dalliance with show business. Clarence not only furnished records for but also appeared on numerous radio and TV programs, often in the company of Pegeen Fitzgerald, who co-hosted a popular talk show with her husband Eddie. It was through her that Clarence came to know most of the stars whose autographs spangle his records. He met her when he was twelve. "Poppa was head of the Cadillac division for the World's Fair in nineteen thirty-nine, and Eddie was the Voice of the World's Fair.

WOR was broadcasting from the Jersey pavilion, and I went in there with Momma. I was going around collecting all this literature—'Clarence Collector' I call myself—and Momma was yelling at me: 'Don't take all that junk!' Then Pegeen came up and introduced herself and said, 'I think you're doing the young man a great injustice. He has a very inquiring mind.' That's how I met her, and she was the door to everyone else."

The mound of records on the doorless refrigerator does not seem to be shrinking, though the cold weight in my arms (there is no place else to put the records Clarence has gone through) is growing. "Groucho Marx: now this is rare. He was a gentleman. I'm sorry he had that mess with the nurse; yet the son was on her side. My Southern Fried Mammy used to say anybody over fifty ought to be shot. She always said you can't beat Father Time." When we meet, Clarence is fifty-three. Recently, he confides, he bought a bottle of poison.

"Billie Holiday. The last time she was in the Women's House of Detention, right before the end, I got her out. But she couldn't sing anymore.

"My friend Paul always said when I die they ought to put all my records around me, like the Egyptians did. They had a song in 1922, when they opened King Tutankhamen's tomb, called 'King Tut.' I gave it to Wilfred R.; he loves Egyptian stuff. Wilfred has at least two hundred thousand classical records I gave him to keep for me. Paul's got at least ten thousand of my records. But most I keep myself. The fellow from the church—he brought the spaghetti—said it looks like a record store in here." Clarence takes me outside to see the shedlike garage, which is packed with records. Bricks are piled against the doors. "Some kids came around and jimmied the lock. They steal the records. And the movers broke thousands of them. They did it on purpose. It makes me want to cry.

"They call me crazy. I never do anything to hurt anybody. I've always loved my fellow man more than myself; that's why I'm in the shape I'm in now. You see, Poppa left me all this money when he died. I helped everybody, thinking it would last. Now they wake me up in the morning throwing stones against the wall. It hurts me so. And most of the people I helped avoid me now. I never asked anything back from them, but they just throw back their heads and cross to the other side of the street."

The basement, too, is packed with records, but in a more industrial way. Cardboard cartons are stacked within inches of the hanging ranks of bare-bulbed light fixtures, of which there are an astonishing number. In the far corner, gleaming, the furnace sits like a dormant dragon. Clarence tries to explain the legal intricacies that are keeping it asleep; apparently Healey, or his secretary, will repair it only if Clarence concedes some factual point or other, and Clarence will not concede. He has a lawyer from the Legal Aid Society, about whom he has no complaints; but he still has no heat.

The stairway to the second floor is terraced with cartons, and the climb is not expedited any by Clarence's arthritis. At the top is a shallow hall narrowed by cartons. A door on the right presents the congested latrine and a reflux of the funk I had almost gotten used to. The first room on the left is Clarence's office. Between boxes are a desk, strewn with jig-saw bits of paper, and several homemade filing cabinets. "I try to catalogue everything. Index cards are too expensive now, so I get deposit slips from the bank or tear up election flyers."

In the next room there is a bed behind the boxes, and a dresser. There are no sheets or blankets on the bed, just some old overcoats; also bowls of cat food and of water. "This is Baby's feeding station. He sleeps under my armpit—you should hear him purr! He always hides when people visit. A long time ago I had a dog, Chicky. When I was on TV, Channel Four, and I was watching the broadcast at home, Chicky was in my arms, and when I came on she started licking the screen. Smart? You don't think that dog was smart?"

Among the odds and ends on the dresser are some Edison

cylinders. "Oh, I've got a bunch of those. You know what Pegeen has in storage out in California? Barrels of Edison cylinders they used to record bar mitzvahs. So I bought them for five dollars a barrel." Someone had recorded my bar mitzvah, too, but the cassette fell apart. "Your luck and my luck," says Clarence, "it's wild!" Not sure how to take this, I observe that recording bar mitzvahs was just the sort of job Edison had in mind for the phonograph. "I should show you," says Clarence, "some of these things I made up: I call them the family phonograph album. An old rococo ornate velvet-covered thing, with records by a husband and wife, a mother and daughter—show-biz families."

Old, ornate arms rise from the dresser to hold a mirror. Its receding surface is taped over with letters and mementos. In black script on yellowed vellum is a note of condolence on the death of Clarence's mother, signed by Pegeen Fitzgerald.

For all his diligent filing, the record world Clarence lives in is a quirky place. "I collect anything with 'Clarence' on it. I don't like rock and roll, though I think the names are fabulous, but there's a Negro rock and roller named Clarence and I have all his records. Pegeen loves 'Bye Bye Blues': I've given her over two hundred and fifty versions. There's a record collector, name is Caminatti, he lives on Disk Lane. (No, really, and there's a guy in the phone book named Record!) All Caminatti collects is 'Nola.' He has about four thousand versions.

"Ethel Waters. I gave David B. an Ethel Waters album, autographed; he's been offered about fifteen hundred dollars for it. Dave's the sweetest guy. He writes like an angel. He autographed his book for me. You'll autograph your book for me, won't you? Dick Sudhalter inscribed his Bix book for me. 'For Clarence, with love and respect,' he wrote. Now isn't that sweet? I went to his concert at Carnegie Hall, and there was a guy next to me in a pink corduroy suit who kept jumping up and down. You know how the seats are. He made me seasick." That sort of thing rarely happens when you listen to a record, unless of course the record is played at a concert. "The band segued into the original recording of 'Back in Your Own Back Yard.' It didn't work. The record was flat."

So much listening, so much mingling with musicians: has Clarence ever wanted to be a musician himself? "I took piano lessons when I was a kid. Momma never forced me. I had a wonderful teacher named Elwood Branch. He had a repertoire in his mind of at least twenty thousand songs. His fingers would scratch the finish of the piano above the keys, so he put a strip of glass there to protect it. He used to accompany the old silent films. . . . But if you want to play an instrument you have to keep at it. Oh, I could play Christmas carols and all that jazz. But I used to pay him maybe ten dollars extra just to sit and play for me. I went to art school, though. With Norman Rockwell's son." Clarence went to college, too: Bard, a venerable enclave of independent study on the banks of the Hudson. But nothing in his schooling proved vocational. He has only one calling. Living on $270 a month, Clarence is still buying records.

"I bought some in a thrift shop the other day. The little old Jewish woman who ran the shop said, 'So vat do you do vith them?' I said, 'I get mozzarella cheese, I get tomato sauce and slather it all over the records.' She said, 'So vat do you do vith it then?' I said I put it in the oven. She finally realized I was pulling her leg." Actually he does put them in the oven, but only for storage.

Clarence helps me pack my presents—the very minimum he will allow—in several of his toughest plastic bags, amid cardboard, and secures them all in a great blue vinyl thing with leather straps. He walks me to the station in the wretched wet and we stop at a diner nearby. Clarence barely lets me treat him to soup, concerned that I won't have money for my ticket. The waitress is astoundingly courteous, given Clarence's smell and runny nose.

Time is running out, and still I find it impossible to ask the question I came with: Clarence, you give records away prodigally, unasked. If you were to sell a certain number of the more valuable ones you could live reasonably well. You could strike a balance. Why don't you?

Here is my chance. Clarence is not talking, he is sipping split-pea soup. But the words will not come out. I can taste them, and they taste of betrayal. Besides, the answer to my question is clear and becomes still clearer, like hard tap water resolving (look closely: see your fingertips pressed against the far side, the swirling grooves and ridges magnified, lucent?) as Clarence tells of a fellow collector in Brooklyn.

"He lives on Sixteenth Street. He's old now. Sweetest guy that ever lived. Oh, he has a collection that I'd love to get. He started in the twenties. He wrote the liner notes for Ruth Etting on Columbia; those were his records they used. He'd probably want two hundred thousand for that collection of his. In my heyday I used to carry a thousand dollars with me, which was silly, but you never knew what you'd find when you went down to Dayton's."

The thing about this collector in Brooklyn. He's deaf.

Chapter Two

Music Becomes a Thing

I give you wings. You'll soon be lifted up
Across the land, across the boundless crests
Of ocean; where men dine and pass the cup,
You'll light there, on the lips of all the guests,
Where lithe, appealing lads will praise you, swelling
Their song to match the piper's sweet, shrill tone.
At length, my boy, you'll enter Hades' dwelling,
That black hole where departed spirits moan,
But even there your glory will not cease,
Your well-loved name will stay alive, unworn;
You'll skim across the mainland, over Greece,
Over the islands and the sea, not borne
By horses, Kurnos; you'll be whirled along
By violet-crowned maids, the Muses; yours
Will be each practiced singer's finest song
As long as light exists and earth endures.

When Theognis made this claim, all of Greek tradition backed him up. It was no secret in the sixth century B.C. that the poet could grant immortality. He kept the file on heroes, on sages, on beautiful women and boys, and so gave excellence a great incentive. But although the poet had always controlled immortality, it was only recently that he had gotten a share in it. The work of the oral bard had been anonymous, a thread in tradition's embroidery. Writing corrected this, since it could preserve not only the actors and argument of a tale but the teller's special arrangement of words. Now the poet's words really were winged and would fly, in strict formation, indefinitely.

The irony is that writing, even as it perfected poetry's wings, clipped them. It tied poetry down to paper. It turned poetry into a thing. Poetry listeners became poetry owners, who could hoard scrolls or keep them as talismans. A good example might be Alexander the Great, whose armies gave wings to Greek culture and who (legend has it) kept the *Iliad* under his pillow wherever he encamped. Later, in the eponymous city he founded on the Nile delta, there arose a stupendous library and museum. Timon of Phlius, the Skeptic philosopher, called it the birdcage of the Muses.

The irony is in the facts, the contradiction only in the metaphor. Wings mean giving the slip to earthly conditions, one of which is mortality. That is why we picture our angels with wings and why the Greeks saw their gods, including the Muses, airborne. In reality, though, winged creatures are not known for longevity. The really durable things (tortoises, stones) are precisely the most earthbound and inert, the most thingly. So in reality, the best way to set something intangible safely beyond time is to reify it.

The Greeks did not manage to preserve the musical ingredient of their poetry. Their pitch accents and rude alphabetic notation tell us little, and anyway the scores, except for a fistful of fragments, are lost. But in the European Middle Ages a system of musical notation arose of which ours is a refinement, and to which an unbroken tradition connects us. So it would seem that the music on the extant staves of the past seven or eight centuries has been preserved; but we should not be too sure. Average pitch has risen about a semitone since Mozart's day. As to tempo, for music that antedates the metronome, we have only some vague Italian phrases to guide us. And matters of expression and style—ornamentation, double-dotting, rubato, and so on—are sometimes anybody's guess.

Isn't this nitpicking? By these standards, is our literary heritage any better preserved? After all, we can only guess how Milton spoke his verse (except for *L'Allegro* and *Il Penseroso* he doesn't even indicate tempo). Somehow, though, it doesn't seem to matter. Holding my Odyssey Press edition, first published in 1935, I hold *Paradise Lost* itself. As long as I have a good idea of what the words meant in the author's day and a rough idea of how they sounded, I can appropriate the poem. This is *our* conception of poetry, anyway; a culture that connected verse and song might conceive otherwise. For us, the book is the work.

Perfect preservation is a matter not simply of technology, but of ontology as well. A defect of preservation is a defect of reification, and this is the trouble with clefs and quavers. They aren't music; they just represent it. The music itself is sound.

"I just bought Beethoven's Seventh." Hearing this, you don't expect to be shown the Eulenburg score, not unless you're a musician or you think I am; for in our passably literate society only musicians can read music. And even for a musician, silently reading a score does not provide the full aesthetic experience of a work, the way silently reading a novel does for littérateur and layman both. A musical score is a set of instructions, useful to those who can carry them out. So scores have been collected by musicians, by the patrons who retained them, and sometimes by investors. For the listening public at large, in every century but this one, there was no such thing as collecting music. The enthusiast might collect art and literature—even, in a weak way, drama—but not music. This circumstance could be seen as good or bad; from the point of view of the philistine it was very bad.

*   *   *

To the early-nineteenth-century German writers who gave
him that nickname, the philistine was an enemy of the spirit.
He was someone, usually someone with money, who took the
assumptions of capitalism with him into the realm of culture.
One assumption was that anything of value could be understood as a commodity to be bought and sold. The fact that
most art took the form of objects was convenient. It implied
that culture, too, could be had for a price. A rigorous liberal-
arts education was not really necessary, and neither was any
application of mind to works of art; all you needed were the
objects. If there were paintings in the parlor no one would ask
whether you'd looked at them—you weren't blind; some
bumpkin might ask if you'd read all your books, but you had
only to reply, as Anatole France (for subtler reasons) once did,
"Not one tenth of them. I suppose you use your Sèvres china
every day?"

Music was inconvenient. The piano, because it cost a small
fortune, became the prime status symbol of the bourgeois
home. Scores could be collected; but they had to be piano
music, or piano and voice, or four-hand reductions of orchestral music, and they had to be playable by the daughters of the
house. A stack of difficult scores would fool nobody, since the
ladies were expected to exhibit their skills after dinner. Some
rich men's daughters played so well that their teachers fell in
love with them, but that was not what the rich men had in
mind. They would rather have bought the music in bulk and
kept the musicians away.

It was partly this resistance of music to philistine appropria-
tion that made it the darling of the romantics—especially the
early German romantics, who ranged themselves as *Davidsbündler*, in Schumann's phrase, against the philistines of all
the world. "How melancholy a thing it is," wrote Friedrich von
Schlegel, "to see a collection of the most interesting works of
art heaped together merely as an assemblage of costly treas-

ures! The void then stretches before us comfortless, ...
unfathomable. Man is beggared—art and life are rent asu...
der!" Repelled by commerce and commodities, the romantics
became wary of things in general. Repelled by what we have
come to call materialism, they lashed out at at materialist science, at the analysis of the lived world into objects and more
objects. Music seemed to resist that analysis.

Hegel, who without quite being part of romanticism came
to dominate it, put music near the top of the hierarchy of arts
erected in his *Lectures on Aesthetics*. Music was superior to
architecture, sculpture and painting because it was not embodied, but ideal and subjective. It took second place to poetry, though, for where music was essentially sensual, poetry
was a product of reason. Here Hegel shows his unromantic
side. For the true romantic, music's apparent ability to bypass
reason and go straight to the soul was as great a merit as its
incorporeality. Writers like Tieck, Hoffmann and Jean Paul
considered instrumental music the supreme art, to whose condition their own aspired. For the first time since the Renaissance, poets called themselves singers; they called their books
Lyrical Ballads, *Hebrew Melodies*, *Buch der Lieder*. They were
eager to have their words set to music—a humble attitude
that encouraged a humble hybrid, the art song. "I can neither play nor sing," wrote Wilhelm Müller, "yet when I write
verses I sing and play after all. If I could produce the tunes,
my songs would please me better than they do now. But
courage. A kindred soul may be found who will hear the tunes
behind the words, and give them back to me"—as Schubert did when he set Müller's *Die Winterreise* and *Die Schöne Müllerin*. It's hard to imagine Alexander Pope talking that way.

There was no hostility to literature among the romantics,
only melancholy about its necessary form. "Books," said
Emerson, "are the death of literature." "True art is never
fixed, but always flowing." Here was another motive for the
romantic suspicion of reified art: if life is flux, fixity is death. By

this logic improvised music and folk music were the ideal; but composed music, as its playing allowed of spontaneous expression, also passed muster.

In 1877 music began to become a thing. The process took several decades, because the early phonograph allowed only a thumbnail impression of timbre and because Edison, who was partly deaf, turned his device to nonmusical and painfully unmusical uses. He meant it mainly for the business and family voice-recording chores that cassettes now handle, and when the public demanded music he gave them vaudeville ditties. In America the critical moment, the moment at which one might pinpoint the reification of music, was 1906. In that year the Victor company introduced the Victrola, the first phonograph designed as furniture, a console in "piano-finished" mahogany that retailed at $200. In the same year Victor's Red Seal line had its first real flowering, with Caruso and Patti heading the list. These one-sided records cost as much as seven dollars, which in 1906 could get you a full suit of clothes. Victor told its dealers: "Not all your customers can afford to purchase a seven-dollar record, but the mere announcement of it will bring them to your store as a magnet attracts steel." Even the less expensive Red Seals, being operatic, did not sell nearly as well as Victor's brass-band and vaudeville releases. But in Victor's advertising (and Victor was one of the first big advertisers in any industry) opera singers were glitteringly featured. As the firm explained to the trade, "there is good advertising in Grand Opera." The outcome of this strategy was that, to quote Roland Gelatt's *The Fabulous Phonograph*, "a collection of Red Seal records established one as a person of both taste and property. Along with the leather-bound sets of Dickens, Thackeray, and Oliver Wendell Holmes, Victor Red Seals become the customary adjunct of the refined American parlor, to be displayed with becoming pride to impressionable guests and relations."

There had been musical snobbery before this. But whereas dances, recitals, and soirées remained slippery ground for the bourgeois, records brought music to his home turf, which was acquisition.

The collecting of cultural objects can satisfy any number of needs, among which snobbery may not be the most important. Here is a tentative list.

1. The need to make beauty and pleasure permanent. As beautiful sights and sounds go by one tries to grab them rather than trust them, or others as beautiful, to come around again. This indicates a mistrust of the world, a mistrust that goes back to the Greeks (at least) and helps explain why they made and preserved so much art. What is the sense of mimesis, after all? There will be other springs, other heroes, other hetairai. Why pin and press these specimens when others, alive and just as lovely, will surely flutter by? The Greeks might have answered, in part, that the latter will not be as excellent as the former. Hesiod saw things going downhill, the standards slipping, from gold to any old alloy. The Greeks had no faith in nature's abundance, or the Muses'. The marketplace might teem with poets, but when would there be another Homer?

Arguably this mistrust is as old as man, and was Adam's true motive for seizing the apple. But in modern times it has gotten narrower, so that the concern is less for posterity than for one's own next few weeks. The paradox was seen most clearly by Blake:

> He who binds to himself a joy
>
> Does the winged life destroy;
> But he who kisses the joy as it flies
> Lives in eternity's sun rise.

2. The need to comprehend beauty. Beauty has its intellectual side, which is the more beautiful the better it's understood.

When the mind exercises its prehensility, it is natural for the fingers to take part, if only to keep the object in striking distance of the mind. Certainly owning a book or record permits one to study the work repeatedly and at one's convenience. The danger lies in mistaking ownership for mastery.

3. The need to distinguish oneself as a consumer. In capitalism there are first heroes of production and then (as Riesman has shown) heroes of consumption. These are people who spend on an heroic scale, perhaps, or with heroic discrimination. The collector may be heroic in either of these ways, but the true collector's heroism is closer to the ancient model. It is exploit, the dauntless and cunning overcoming of obstacles in pursuit of the prize. The prize iself is secondary to the pursuit (if this is true of men generally, as Pascal thought, it is truer of heroes). Clarence's collecting is of this heroic type. His eagerness to share his collection, which at first seems to contradict the whole idea of acquisition, is just the openhandedness of the hero who, having pulled off his exploit, is free with the proceeds. Clarence will lend records out or give them away, but never sell one—imagine Menelaus selling the spoils of Troy! Clarence loves to talk about his collection, and how he came by this disk or that autograph. Every item is a trophy.

There is a paradox here, too. The true hero of consumption is a rebel against consumption. By taking acquisition to an ascetic extreme he repudiates it, and so transplants himself to an older and nobler world. (In the same way the true hero of production, the chivalrous captain of industry or reckless entrepreneur, rebels against production.) To write such behavior off as conspicuous consumption is to miss its point. The prodigal son is not just a show-off.

4. The need to belong. Considered as a feeling, this need might be called nostalgia. When one feels nostalgia for a time one has lived in or wishes one had lived in, cultural objects are a fairly dignified tonic. What is really a wallowing in atavism can pass for the appreciation of timeless beauty. (In the same

way, the art lover with bad taste can justify it as an interest in bygone fashions.) Each object connects its owner with two eras, that of its creation and that of its acquisition. Clarence, who was a full-fledged nostalgiac even as a boy, learned in middle age a nostalgia much closer to the bone, a nostalgia for his "heyday." His records soothe both. They let him talk, too, both about the decades they were made in, which he may or may not have lived through, and about the adventurous years when he got them.

In this, if in little else, Clarence is blessed. He has a past to mourn. He has been spared the most common and most pernicious nostalgia, nostalgia for the here and now. For most of us feel that we are at home, and yet we don't feel *at home*. We think: I was born for an age like this, so why don't I belong? And in the frantic effort to belong we enlist our belongings. David Riesman, who interviewed Chicago teenagers in 1947, wrote:

> Like the "trading cards" which symbolize competitive consumption for the eight- to eleven-year-olds, the collection of records seemed to be one way of establishing one's relatedness to the group. . . . Tunes meant people: roads to people, remembrances of them. At the same time the teen-agers showed great anxiety about having the "right" preferences. . . . The cultural objects, whatever their nature, are mementos that somehow remain unhumanized by the force of a genuinely fetishistic attachment.

Actually, I doubt that these teenagers had reached the point of genuine fetishism, where objects are not roads to people but substitutes for them; but no doubt some of them would reach it, given time. When relating to the group becomes too difficult—because its standards are unjust, because it is unfaithful, or because it cannot be found—fetishism is the sensible alternative. This is where Clarence seems to have arrived, by a fairly circuitous route.

5. The need to impress others, or oneself. This can be simple philistine snobbery or something subtler, to which even a *Davidsbündler* is sometimes liable. Hillel the Elder warned against using scripture as a worldly crown. I think this was directed not only at show-offs, but at all intellectuals who like to feel the sweet weight of culture on their heads. The Aramaic word for crown, *taga*, also describes the calligraphic filigree with which scribes adorn certain letters in a biblical scroll. How many book collectors really go for the words and ideas and not rather the typeface, the odor of fresh ink or aging paper, the satisfying shape of a name—"Hillel the Elder," for example? The point is that one can have a sincere love of culture without having any interest in it. That kind of love is almost as well satisfied by owning records as by listening to them.

In a traditional culture whose tradition is intact there are certain vessels of unquestioned worth—scriptures, the canon, the basic repertoire—around which all other things are trained like capillaries around an artery. That is what distinguishes tradition from mere preservation; that is what permits discrimination. (A traditional culture in this sense may be literate or preliterate, but it can never be perfectly "organic" or "harmonious." If a society without dissonance ever existed, it would have no need of active tradition. In any case, "traditional" must be understood as a relative term.) When those main arteries rupture, value diffuses. Since nothing is sacred, everything is sacred. And anyone who wants to preserve the culture is faced with the choice of keeping nothing or keeping everything.

This dilemma involves the arts and the sciences alike. Facts are collected indiscriminately by the naive empiricist, who lives in fear of missing the one fact that will give meaning to the rest. His fear is justified; that fact will never be found. Meanwhile, classification gives a semblance of order to things. And meaning is left at the mercy of the last hidden mollusc on the last uncharted reef.

Though the master himself was innocent of it, one might trace this tendency back to Aristotle's school. His successor Theophrastus was a manic collector and classifier, and that habit of the Peripatetics came to dominate the science of late antiquity. The Alexandrians were the first scholars in the modern sense and had the first great library (the birdcage of the Muses). These philosophers were epistemic bag people. Our own bag people, lugging arcane cargoes through the inner city, sometimes seem like unschooled Peripatetics. The idea of hoarders on the move makes perfect sense: if you stay put you miss all the things that are where you are not. Of course, most bag people are people who have been driven from their homes by speculators, can't get welfare because they have no address, don't want to be shaken down in a city shelter, and are acting pragmatically under the circumstances. Some, however, have homes and incomes and behave in ways that are hard to understand from an economic point of view. I am thinking of the kind described by Bellow in *Mr. Sammler's Planet* in the person of Shula, Sammler's daughter, who "went to sermons and free lectures everywhere . . . the shopping bag with salvage, loot coupons, and throwaway literature between her knees. Afterward she was the first to ask questions." (Sammler too is a collector—that is the literal meaning of his name—a collector of ideas. But he fights this tendency in himself, sensing that the time has come to *select*.)

Clarence is a bag person. He is as peripatetic as his arthritis permits and he is unquestionably an intellectual, as perhaps many bag people are. (Momma: *Don't take all that junk. Pegeen Fitzgerald: He has a very inquiring mind.*) He collects facts as well as things. The facts are mostly trivia and the things, including his records, mostly junk, but that only proves he's a scholar. To be a first-rate scholar you must have a taste for all that is second rate, third rate, *n*th rate. For a scholar's collection is always comprehensive. Where practicalities limit comprehensiveness, the other great scholastic principle, whimsy, comes into play (according to Walter Benjamin, "everything said from the angle of a true collector is whimsical"). Once seized upon, however arbitrarily, a tangent must be followed to the end (*I collect anything with Clarence on it*). Note that neither principle—comprehensiveness or whimsy—has anything to do with what is good, or even with what you really like.

   True scholars, true collectors, and true bag people are caricatures of us all. We moderns have no safe principle of selection, so we collect. In a sense we collect *because* we're peripatetic; rootless, we pick up the forest and take it along.

Before records came along nobody talked about the music "industry." What the music industry makes is "product," a mass term referring to some number of "units." What the industry people do with product brings to mind the ancient discobolus: in the words of a Warner Bros. marketing executive, they "throw it against the wall to see what sticks."

   Some eight out of ten releases lose money for the manufacturer. His compensation comes from the monster hits, the records that really stick. The discobolus image is an admission that the company cannot determine which records will be hits—that the millions of dollars spent on market research and promotion cannot psych out the buyer. True, there are artists who almost always make money. And since hype does have some effect, a company's prophecy of success for a record can be self-fulfilling. But such assumptions are dangerous. That was one of the lessons of the slump of 1979, when a new Kiss album was, with much fanfare, shipped platinum—that is, a first run of more than a million units was sent out to the stores—and came back almost untouched.

If anyone can be said to control the record-buying public it is the radio deejay, or rather the program director. But the program director's job is to please a lot of the people a lot of the time. He plays the records that are selling or likely to sell, and the ones his listeners request. Although record companies can apply great pressure, they are somewhat hampered by laws against payola and against the control of radio stations and record companies by the same corporations.

Despite these plain facts, conspiracy theories flourish. According to a patrician Marxism that began with Marx and William Morris and was cultivated by the Frankfurt School (in particular by Marcuse and Adorno) the masses really do have bad taste, but not naturally. It is capitalism that stunts their palates, force-feeding them its swill until they like it, or imagine they do. Adorno made the application to music. He argued that classical music, because it reminds the dehumanized masses of their humanity, threatens the system and so is discouraged. But popular music, an opiate that dispels all realistic thought and reinforces the mechanized rhythms of the production process, is encouraged. By "popular music" Adorno meant everything from polkas to Charlie Parker.

American followers of the Frankfurt School, including almost all rock critics whether they know it or not, stop short of this. But they agree that popular taste has been corrupted; that is how they explain its divergences from their own. And they agree that it has been corrupted through the open conspiracy of record executives, marketers, promoters, retailers, program directors and hack musicians. If this conspiracy is too inept to fix the chart standings of specific records, it is at least able to sell styles and start trends.

In fact, the cabal cannot manage even that. Rock and roll was scorned at first by the major record companies. They paid for their priggishness while basement labels like Chess and

Sun made fortunes. Disco was discovered by alert independents like Casablanca. Once a bandwagon is underway the majors are happy to climb aboard—and elbow their way to the front—but they are rarely in the driver's seat. So it's silly to say of the listening public, as Adorno does, that "in this insistence on the fashionable standards it fancies itself in possession of a remnant of free choice." It *is* free—at least, its straitjacket is custom cut.

Before capitalism, the musician sang for his supper. He did his work in the presence of his patrons—noblemen, clerics, festive clumps of peasantry—and, as he satisfied, had his own needs met in return. Between this state and the present were many stages: subscription concerts, commissioned scores, subscription scores, paid public concerts, published scores, piano rolls. With the advent of records music's backward metamorphosis, from butterfly to chrysalis, was complete. Music is now fully a commodity, exchangeable for the universal commodity, money. The musician need never see the working man behind the money; the listener need never see the working musician behind the vinyl. Each is, in a modified Marxist sense, a fetishist.

When I buy a record, the musician is eclipsed by the disk. And I am eclipsed by my money—not only from the musician's view but from my own. When a ten-dollar bill leaves my right hand and a bagged record enters my left, it is the climax. The shudder and ring of the register is the true music; later I will play the record, but that will be redundant. My money has already heard it.

What I am caricaturing here is, I think, a fairly common mode of record buying. The buying is what counts, which is one reason why the record buyer is insatiable. The desire to buy does not always coincide with the desire to hear music. If I want to hear music, surely there is something on my shelf or on the radio that can satisfy me; if I want to hear a certain record I don't have, perhaps I can borrow it from a friend or a library. The desire to buy, on the other hand, explodes when my wallet reaches a certain critical mass, or when I'm anxious, or when I've worked hard at something idiotic and want a reward. Then money wants to be spent, and if I fancy myself a music lover it seems natural to spend it on a record. I could spend it on a concert, I suppose—but a record is tangible, like money.

For music to become so fully a commodity, having its most intense intercourse with money, seems odd. In our fond antithesis of God and Mammon, music belongs with God. This is partly because music has seemed so incorporeal, and partly because it has played a central role in religion and ritual. (A thumbnail definition of ritual: an action or set of actions, repeated at regular intervals or on recurring occasions, and following a set pattern that is seen as obligatory but is not justified, point for point, in pragmatic or scientific terms.) In traditional societies, music—often coupled with words, drama, dance—figures in all kinds of ritual. Like the sizzle of hecatombs, music soothes the gods. It is good for people also, harmonizing and uniting them. The young Nietzsche, writing of ancient Greek ritual, interpreted music as the voice of oneness: where Apollo's visual art teaches the principle of individuation, Dionysian music lets us melt into the one will.

As an element of ritual, music can unify the group either abstractly or for a specific purpose. One such purpose is war; the Hollywood image of warpath tom-toms is largely correct. Another purpose is work, or whatever brings sustenance. There are musical ceremonies before the hunt and after, at the feast; there are rain dances and harvest festivals; there are work songs and field hollers. Another purpose is procreation. "Social organization," writes the ethnomusicologist Alan P. Merriam, "is marked at almost every point by song: the life cycle includes birth songs, with special subdivisions for multiple births; lullabies; naming songs; toilet-training songs; puberty songs; greeting songs; love and marriage songs; family, lineage and clan songs; songs of social associational groups; funeral songs. . . ." Some of these songs may be customary, not obligatory, but still it is hard to get by without them. The gamut is summed up in the remark of a Sia Indian: "My friend, without songs you cannot do anything."

In the West music kept close to the knees of ritual well into the eighteenth century. Processionals, marches, wedding cantatas, funeral odes, passions, oratorios, sarabandes, serenades, requiems, coronation masses, anthems, battle hymns, chorales, masses *in tempore belli*: all functioned in specific, more or less ritualized situations. But it was a tendency of both Protestant and Enlightenment thinking to disparage ritual. Social life was to be streamlined, and ritual looked like useless baggage. As various activities were stripped of their rituals, music was often allowed to remain because it was soothing, or arousing, or otherwise useful. But music used in this way lost much of its magic. Played at a meal, a dance, a wedding or a war it seemed mere background—or worse, a crude attempt at strumming up a mood. It seemed vulgar. Thackeray gives a good idea of this in the installment of his *Book of Snobs* (a series that ran in *Punch* in 1846) dealing with parties.

> All this while, amidst the crowd and the scuffle, and a perpetual buzz and chatter, and the flare of the wax candles, and an intolerable smell of musk—what the poor Snobs who write fashionable romances call "the gleam of gems, the odor of perfumes, and the blaze of countless lamps"—a scrubby-looking, yellow faced foreigner, with cleaned gloves, is warbling inaudibly in a corner, to the accompaniment of another.

Clearly music was uncomfortable with blunt function. It needed ritual, even if it had to generate its own.

The public concert, invented in London in 1672, infiltrated

Europe slowly in the eighteenth century and rapidly in the nineteenth. Gradually the concert acquired its own rituals (applause, encores, respectful dress) and taboos (no humming, no talking, no eating). It was like a religious service, and the religion it served was music. Private recitals followed suit. Formerly the servant of the salon crowd, the musician (Beethoven, Chopin, Liszt) was now its cynosure. Music nearly replaced conversation as the reason for people to gather; soirées and their etiquette revolved around the piano.

Even where music still seemed to serve extrinsic pomp, the tables had often been turned. Mozart's Requiem, commissioned by a shady stranger, never performed its intended office. Mozart came to think of it as his own requiem, and so do we; and we think of it as a monument to the musician, not the man. The *Missa Solemnis*, too, was supposed to grace a ceremony—the installation of an archbishop—but Beethoven sabotaged that plan by chipping away in the name of art long past his deadline. Brahms wrote an *Academic Festival Overture*, but the festival in question honored Brahms with a doctorate, and the overture he wrote in thanks was first performed the following year, at a concert.

Music lives in time, unfolds in time. So does ritual. Both impose a common time on those present. Visual art does not; it lets the eye and mind set their own pace. Literature does not, certainly not when read silently, and even when read aloud it grants a certain latitude.

In Nara there is a temple with roofs so rhythmically arranged that they are called *kōreru ongaku*, "frozen music." Goethe called all architecture frozen music, and Schopenhauer agreed, saying rhythm does for time what symmetry does for space. Another way of putting this would be to say that music is the architecture of time.

Two different orders of time, a greater and a lesser, are embraced in music's architecture. The lesser order is the time that a given piece of music actually encloses and that, by

means of sound and silence, it divides and designs. Whenever
any number of people hear any piece of music played in any
way, they share, in this sense, a common time. The greater
order is a continuum that cycles through days, years, and
lifetimes. Music of various kinds played at various points in this
continuum helps to give it structure.

Ideally, the greater and lesser motions of time should
mesh, like the cogs and flywheel of an escapement. And in
traditional cultures this was often the case. But when music
began to develop as pure art—when, obeying an inner logic, it
burst out in the sublime hypertrophy that was Bach, Mozart,
Beethoven—then it lost its place. Just when music was achiev-
ing the perfect mimesis of life's rhythm, it lost its place in life's
rhythm.

This happened gradually, and for a while there were still
forms that clung to their place on the great wheel: think of
Monteverdi's Vespers, Telemann's *Tafelmusik*, Bach's cantata
for (say) the fourteenth Sunday after Trinity, Mozart's serenades, Schumann's *Spring* Symphony (just barely clinging,
now), Chopin's nocturnes. And some Eastern classical musics
kept an intricate connection with larger time—Indian music,
for example, prescribing specific ragas, modes, for specific
seasons and times of day. But in the West, by the early nineteenth century, traditional contexts had mostly given way to
artificial ones. Just as visual art lost much of its connection with
living space, coming down off ceilings and altars and settling
into frames and museums, so music moved into explicitly musical time periods, like that of the salon soirée or the Tuesday-
night opera. Meanwhile, popular music (ballads, sentimental
and bawdy airs) fell into periods deemed appropriate for "entertainment"—a concept that had grown up right alongside
"art for art's sake."

This was better than nothing. However ersatz, however
stratified, a musical architecture of time did exist in the nineteenth century. It was shattered by the phonograph. Before

the phonograph any playing of music (with the single exception of a musician's playing for himself) was perforce a social event. People had to get together—Prince Leopold of Cöthen with his court orchestra, Count Rasumovsky with the rest of his amateur quartet, young Bernard Shaw with a thousand other Wagnerites, a hundred instrumentalists, a dozen singers, a conductor and sundry stagehands. So people got together, and to simplify matters they got together at regular intervals. Such practicalities had always supported music's link with ritual. When the phonograph arrived, much of that scaffolding collapsed.

For music was now an object that could be owned by the individual and used at his own convenience. There was no need to cooperate, coordinate, or share with anyone else. Technically the musicians were still necessary; given the economics of production, so was the rest of the audience. But only technically. Once the record was owned they disappeared.

Now the *Symphony of a Thousand* could play to an audience of one. Now a man could hear nocturnes at breakfast, vespers at noon, and the Easter Oratorio on Chanukah. He could do his morning crossword to the "One O'Clock Jump" and make love right through the *St. Matthew Passion*. Anything was possible; nothing was sacred; freedom was (barring complaints from the neighbors and occasional desperate holding actions such as the Russian synod's 1912 ban on the recording of prayers) absolute. It was the freedom, once the cathedral of culture had been wrecked, to take home the bits you liked and arrange them as you pleased. Once again a mechanical invention had met capitalism's need to recreate all of life in its image. The cathedral of culture was now a supermarket.

But this *is* freedom, after all: liberal freedom really is freedom when you compare it to the various "higher" freedoms, whether fascist, communist or theocratic. In this century, nostalgia for cathedrals has led to the building of prisons—totalitarian states where music, which has a reputation as political dynamite, has been carefully controlled. The Soviets announced in 1928 that the importing or playing of American jazz was punishable by a fine of one hundred rubles and six months in jail; jazz became fully acceptable only when it lost its dangerous appeal and rock and roll acquired it. The Ayatollah Khomeini imposed similar strictures. So records have become, almost as much as books, a symbol of freedom. Before there was *samizdat* there was *Roentgenizdat*—underground recordings of jazz and rock on x-ray plates.

In Fellini's *Amarcord*, the narrator's infrangible leftist uncle is chased all over the village by Fascist police. Just when they seem to have lost him they hear, coming from the church steeple, a voice singing the "Internationale." They barrage the little steeple with gunfire, the voice stops, the old man's wife starts up a stricken wailing. But something has fallen to the ground. It is the fragment of a phonograph. The uncle has escaped. Isaac Babel's story "Gedali," on the other hand, finds the "Internationale" in power—and requisitioning the phonograph of a poor Zhitomir shopkeeper. " 'Hand over your phonograph to the State, Gedali . . . ' 'I am fond of music, Pani,' I say to the Revolution. 'You don't know what you're fond of, Gedali. I'll shoot you and then you'll know.' "

Totalitarianism has rarely found technology stacked against it, however. If, in the realm of sound, one gadget was a horsefly to the Behemoth, another quickly became its ally. "We could not have conquered Germany," said Adolf Hitler, "without the loudspeaker"—not only the public-address loudspeaker that wafted his words through the Kurfurstendamm but the radio loudspeaker that carried them into remote homes and beer halls. And it was not only words they carried, for the Nazis were great lovers and exploiters of music. It had to be Aryan, of course: "Judeo-Negroid" music was swept from the airwaves, which was no mean feat in an age of global swing. (Hitler was incensed to learn that "Ja, wir haben keinen Bananen heute," the smash hit of 1923 and a personal favorite, had been written by Jews.) The principle was simple. Radio puts its dispersed listeners under the spell of a shared event. The ritual aura of live performance—rhetorical, musical, what have you—is broadcast. This has nothing to do with radio waves or brain waves; it is a simple matter of simultaneity. The consciousness that at this very moment the band is playing, the Leader is ascending the platform, the crowd is bristling with jackknife salutes, and millions of your compatriots are poised as you are before the radio—this consciousness is enough to make the whole nation an arena. And the effect is roughly the same if the band is the Berlin radio orchestra playing Beethoven's Fifth Symphony (destiny knocking on every German door). Either way you have an architecture of time, or rather a cynical engineering of it.

It is noteworthy that radio rose to prominence and records went into decline during a worldwide economic depression. Those were the years when fascism became attractive, in part because it offered a kind of ritualistic solidarity. In America fascism did not become greatly attractive but radio did. The usual explanation is that people couldn't afford records, and of course that had a lot to do with it. But we know that before the Depression black workers would line up on Friday evenings, when the eagle had flown, outside record shops, and that they managed to support a flourishing "race records" industry. Poor people do buy records. After the Crash, though, poor and rich alike felt shattered, splintered, isolated. What they found in radio, I think, was the solace of solidarity and of predictable, structured time. When, in the mid-thirties, the shock had passed, records came back.

Both the good and bad effects of radio are reduced, in today's democracies, by the number and diversity of stations. Musically the only tyrant is democratic taste, which may be less oppressive to listeners than to offbeat musicians who want airplay. Elvis Costello's anti-anthem "Radio Radio" (*Radio is the sound salvation/Radio is cleaning up the nation. . . . Either shut up or get cut up, they don't want to hear about it, it's only*

*inches on the reel-to-reel/And the radio is in the hands
of such a lot of fools trying to anaesthetize the way
that you feel)* is much more totalitarian in spirit than the
policies it protests. On a dance floor, the effect of its hook is
galvanic in a knee-jerk way, though this way may be
part of the satire. In any case, the song had a good deal
of airplay.

Where radio unites, records fracture. They are well suited to a
society where everyone is off pursuing his own dream. If some
of us are content, like after-dinner nappers, to dream the same
dreams as our neighbors, others are hidden rebels; and the
latter category is the narrator of Ralph Ellison's *Invisible Man*.
Structurally the book is a sequence of dreamlike memories
spun off from a single Louis Armstrong disk. The framing
chapters find the narrator living rent-free and utility-fee-free in
a forgotten basement that is "warm and full of light."

> Now I have one radio-phonograph; I plan to have
> five. There is a certain acoustical deadness in my hole,
> and when I have music I want to *feel* its vibration, not
> only with my ear but with my whole body. I'd like to
> hear five recordings of Louis Armstrong playing and
> singing "What Did I Do to Be so Black and Blue"—all
> at the same time. . . . Perhaps I like Louis Armstrong
> because he's made poetry out of being invisible. . . .
> Invisibility, let me explain, gives one a slightly different
> sense of time, you're never quite on the beat. . . .
> Instead of the swift and imperceptible flowing of time,
> you are aware of its nodes, those points where time
> stands still or from which it leaps ahead. And you slip
> into the breaks and look around.

Invisibility, a condition of blacks especially but also of others
out of whack with society, is here seen to have its points. The

narrator has tried to live in mainstream American time, with its "swift and imperceptible flowing," but has found it a mindless torrent. The only relief is to "slip into the breaks and look around." Invisibility lets you do that. Private music, music no one else hears, reinforces your invisibility by giving you a private structure of time to set against public time.

Ellison's hero wants to end his hibernation and make another stab at fitting into society's time, perhaps by changing it—by giving it some of the structure his own dreams have devised. The book ends with a thrilling reference to the medium of solidarity, radio: "Who knows but that, on the lower frequencies, I speak for you?"

On some frequency, I think, he speaks for Clarence, who is in a way a white invisible man (*people . . . avoid me now . . . they just throw back their heads and cross to the other side of the street*). Clarence's history of suffering, however swollen by paranoia, has given him something of a hounded-race mentality (he told me that his name, in full Clarence Abram Browne, has been taken for that of a black or a Jew). In fact, many of the lines in the Armstrong song Ellison speaks of, lines (he does not quote them) like *Even a mouse/Ran from my house*, could have come right out of Clarence's mouth. This embittered hermit's life is not what he wants; it feels like exile. (He cannot afford a phone or a train ride. In answer to an exploratory letter, he wrote, *I am longing to see you. Please don't disappoint me. I get so lonely here.*) Both men rebel against time, using records as weapons; while Ellison's man uses the music itself to slip inside time and undermine it, Clarence is engaged in a massive holding action.

There is something of Clarence in each of us. If there were not, records would not be the prevalent form of music in our world. Music would not be a thing. We have let it become a thing because we all know that things are more dependable than musicians, or social life, or the Muses. Clarence puts it well: *Records are inanimate until you put the needle in the groove, and then they come to life.*

Chapter Three

Tomás

Tomás and I had a rendezvous at a thrift shop near my apartment. He was looking for a tuxedo. With practiced fingertips he raked the drab racks and, like a magician, pulled out a plausible suit. He disappeared, reappeared. "My dear, what do you think? The color is too blue. But it fits *perfectly*." Tomás's shoulders were broad, his waist small. He was working out three hours a day at the Columbia University gym. With his classic square-cut features and this new black-and-white, triangular torso—T-shirt beneath the tuxedo—he was elegant as a theorem of Euclid.

He put down a deposit on the tuxedo and a set of long underwear, and we left. At my apartment Tomás (whose name I have changed) put Mozart's C minor Mass on the turntable and sprawled on the couch, flexing his latest muscles while I made scrambled eggs. "My record of this is ruined," he said, "I don't know why. But I keep it because it's a beautiful record and my heart is with it and I'm going to keep it for the rest of my days. Otherwise I'd throw it as a Frisbee because it's not worth a fucking penny.

"As a matter of fact I'm *dying*," he said, attacking his eggs like a stevedore, "because for the first time since I've been in America I don't have money to buy records anymore. You remember at Harvard I used to buy at least ten or fifteen records a month, except for that one summer when I bought three hundred records in two months? I mean I worked eight hours a day just to buy records, because I spent three quarters of my salary on records and a quarter on food and entertainment. That was a special situation. And two recordings with Obraztsova have come out, the *Samson and Delilah* and the *Werther*, and both of them have been promised to be given to me for birthday or Christmas presents but they haven't come my way yet and I'm dying. And I wish I had my independence so I could just go to the record store and get them like I used to at the Coop. Those were—oh my God what days were those.

"It's the closest thing I have to consumerism. Like when many Americans go to Bloomingdale's and they spend the whole afternoon buying clothes and toiletries and they come home and they feel great and they feel realized as human beings. That's capitalism at its best. I'm not like that in most of my life. I'm not interested in things that rule my life and run it. But records, I think that is my weakness. Because I buy a record and it just makes me a different person for an hour or two. And I run home to listen to it and I play it and I play it and I play it and I play it until I'm sick of it. I had a record of arias by Obraztsova that I think was on my turntable for the whole summer. I got it in June and it was on my turntable until September. I've been listening to *Tristan and Isolde* now because I saw the concert with Bernstein, and I've been listening to the love duet—side number five—every night from seven o'clock until midnight. That is something that Salvador Dali does too, so I have some share with genius, my dear. Because he apparently has had side twelve of the *Götterdämmerung* on his turntable for the past thirteen years."

Tomás leaned back, looking content and contemplative. I

asked him whether phonographs had been common in Chile
when he was growing up.

"Oh yes," he said, "but my house was particularly . . .
My father loves classical music; he hates opera. My mother
loves opera, but only in the opera house, with the jewels and
furs. She had a record of tenor arias with Franco Corelli. But
my father was the record-player man; he has a large collection
of Beethoven and Brahms. The day I was born my father
played Beethoven's Seventh Symphony to celebrate, and he's
been playing it ever since.

"I remember hearing in primary school the Mozart Fortieth
Symphony and I fell in love with it. And I ran to my father and
I said, 'I have to have this record,' and my father said, 'Well,
you're very lucky. I'm going to Santiago tomorrow, so I will get
it for you.' I remember as if it had happened yesterday. All day
long waiting for it, all fucking day long waiting, and it was six
and it was seven and it was eight and it was nine and about
nine my father was supposed to have arrived. He didn't arrive
until ten-thirty because there was some kind of delay, and
there was the record and I enjoyed the joy of my life. I have
never been so happy.

"That was the first record I ever owned of my own. Once I
started getting heavily into opera, my grandfather was the one
who started buying me a collection. It was very limited in the
sense that if you wanted an opera you would buy the one that
was available; you couldn't choose the singer. I don't think
there was one single recording in Chile of Maria Callas in a full
opera. There was a lot of Renata Tebaldi. Birgit Nilsson was in
Chile what Maria Callas is now here. When I was twelve or
thirteen I wanted so badly to have her *Tristan and Isolde*, and
they only had the old recording with Flagstad. Finally I found a
friend of the family who was going to America, and he bought
me the recording. So I was already rather fanatical. I'm glad I
wasn't into Maria Callas then, because I would have had to
order from America every single recording."

I asked Tomás if any of his friends in school had shared his enthusiasms. "No," he said, looking wistful. "In high school I think I was the only one who liked classical music throughout all my generation. I remember listening to the second act of *Tosca*, which is really wild, and *really* I just wanted to share that with someone. My mother, who was the only person I could talk to about opera, liked *Tosca*, but not the second act. *She loves the first act*—all the mellow, lyrical music. But this big drama thing, I just wanted somebody to go wild over it. And when I found people at Harvard who loved the second act . . . But then I was just a very lonely lad.

"That was one of the greatest things when I came to America. That is why I was so anxious to meet anybody who liked classical music; that is how I met you."

In college I had an obnoxious habit of whistling, and it is possible that I was whistling something from Lucia's mad scene on the dinner line that day. Looking back, I can see no other reason why the person filling the silverware bins should have struck up a conversation about *Lucia di Lammermoor*. He had close-sheared curly black hair, a Latin aristocrat's face touched with melancholy acne, and a quick, refracted smile. Like me he owned a copy of the Callas *Lucia*; he, however, had worn out five previous copies, or so he claimed. That astonished me. I pictured a pre-Columbian phonograph with a jaguar's canine for a needle.

Tomás's major was physics but his passion was opera. His passion was such that I found it impossible to say that I really liked opera only a little, far less than instrumental music. Carrying my tray into the dining hall I hung my head slightly, like an imposter. Probably Tomás sensed this; our later encounters were amicable but accidental. We rarely mentioned Maria Callas.

"I came to America two months after Maria Callas gave her farewell concert to the world. I would like to have seen the woman; she happens to be somebody I admire beyond imagination. But I think we're lucky enough that she lived in a time that her recordings have been preserved. One of the wonderful things I got in America was access to this treasure. Maria Callas was one of these people who needed an audience, more than anybody else. Thank God in heaven we have her wonderful collection of pirate records. And I can sit in my house and listen to her. I have just about everything she ever did.

"At the opera, if there is a great diva—it has to be a diva in the true definition of the word, the opera singer who dominates with the charisma—you are transported. But today there are no great divas, except for Obraztsova. I have been to the Metropolitan Opera House six or seven times this season so far. Very dependable performances, but no divas, and I'm bored to tears. And I go wild when I listen to my recording of Obraztsova singing or of Maria Callas singing. So in a way the diva-ness comes through in records, too. In the quietness of my room, with my commodities, with my bed—it just suits me a lot better. Why bother to go out?

"When I listen to records I have my own world and I'm not disturbed by coughing and I'm not disturbed by the motherfucker sitting next to me opening candy, like happened Thursday at Carnegie Hall. Bernstein was conducting the slowest *Tristan and Isolde* you ever heard, and it was mortal silence. And here this bastard . . .

"I remember my first year at Harvard, and you know coming from Chile, the underdeveloped world, I had to go to the Boston Symphony Orchestra, the greatest orchestra in the world. So I'm going to Symphony Hall and one day it clicked: what the hell am I coming *here*? I'm not even enjoying it because it comes at the wrong time, because I'm tired, or because I just had dinner and I'm full. I mean, why this whole ritual of going to the concert hall? That's why I don't like formal religion: I like to establish my own rituals, but I don't like to go by other people's rituals. Because usually rituals are very complicated things. They have to suit you very well; otherwise it's a very violent experience, I think."

My first encounter with Tomás, in the dining hall, took place in our sophomore year. As seniors we got to know each other better thanks to a common friend, a woman who had undertaken to fill some gaps in my moral education. She took me to parties where men wore mascara, the music was like an iron fist in a velvet glove, and Tomás was in his element. Tomás, it turned out, was famous—not as a physicist or discophile, but as Harvard's reigning undergraduate queen.

Through our common friend we kept in touch after graduation, in New York. Tomás, studying high-energy experimental physics at Columbia, would drop by to display new muscles, complain of poverty and smashed romances, or cadge a meal. He would describe his nightlife (the drag show at the Anvil, dance-floor fellatio at the Ramrod) with such gusto that we wondered if his intention was to ensure that a meal cooked for two would feed three. But he would describe an opening at the Met in much the same way.

Now, however, he seemed a little disenchanted with disco and opera house alike. "I've always thought of disco as a very operatic form of expression. Opera is grand feelings, big acts, broad gestures. And disco is very much like that—in a very mechanic, a very plastic sort of way. You are bombarded from every side with lasers and lights and *very* loud music. For me it's not a big deal because I'm used to it; as a matter of fact I find it vulgar. But for the time that disco was what it was, it suited my needs very well. It was very operatic.

"I used to like the opera because of the staging. But the stage sometimes distracts. For bel canto the stage is complementary—this is going to sound outrageous, but the music is simpleminded, so if you can add a little watercolor painting in the background it will all mix well. But I think Wagner is much too overpowering. The music is so gorgeous that Wagner was made for records, it wasn't made for the stage—as much as that will outrage quite a number of people, even he himself, because he considered himself the *Gesamtkunstwerk*, whatever that was—the synthesis of music and drama.''

I asked Tomás: When you listen to opera on record, do you picture the action going on?

"Yes of course, but you know imagination is so much better. I hate porno movies for that reason; I prefer to read porno books. The imagination is a lot richer than reality—I think certainly *my* imagination.''

Tomás studied piano when he was five, then the violin, then the guitar, but found them all difficult to animate. "I think if anything I would have been a great opera singer,'' he said, "if I'd ever had a voice.''

Was he ever frustrated, I asked, at merely listening, at not being able to express himself?

"But I do it all the time! I mean, I express myself. I run around the room and I throw myself on the floor and I sing with the music and I gesticulate and I look at myself in the mirror and I have my show. If I'm very carried away by something I'll probably jump right off my bed and run to the center of the room and start doing it. If it's a man it's a man, if it's a woman it's a woman. Plus if I'm in a very camp mood I'll probably pull down my bedspread and put it on my shoulders and make a costume, you know?

"As a matter of fact, that is precisely one of the reasons I like records so much. In the opera house I'm confined to this little chair where I cannot even speak, I cannot say 'Come on, listen to the high C, it's going to be wild!'

"As you know, music for me is pure passion. I mean I can't rationalize why *Tristan and Isolde* . . . I could go on for half an hour talking about the myth, whatever I've read, but that is not the point. *Tristan and Isolde* for me is just a pure emotion. I sink into my chair and I, I, I am *glad*, you know, I mix with the music and I blend away and I disappear.''

Chapter Four

Ceremonies of a Solitary

T he novelist Compton Mackenzie, the first great amateur of the gramophone (as the British call it, distinguishing Berliner's disk player from Edison's cylinder player) spent most of his adult life on tiny islands that he leased or purchased. His magazine *The Gramophone* began publication in 1923 from his home on the island of Herm in the English Channel. A few years later, on nearby Jethou, the walls of his music room went up around a new Balmain equipped (as his wife put it) with "the largest gramophone horn then known to man." When his record collection outgrew Jethou he built a bigger house on Barra in the Outer Hebrides.

From that time to this, islands have been at the center of phonographic mythology. The BBC's long-running radio program in which celebrities choose the records they would take to a desert island has been copied by Radio Canada, *High Fidelity* magazine and the rock critic Greil Marcus. Some people may occupy themselves with the selection of books for a desert island, but that exercise has too little of paradox in it.

One knows very well what a water-damaged volume of Shakespeare would look and smell like as it baked in one's hands on the beach; but the idea of finding a phonograph with batteries or an outlet of the proper voltage is purely fantastic, and so excites the imagination. And reading is naturally a solitary act, which listening to music is not, or *was* not.

The paradox of music for a desert island is right at the heart of phonography. To take the sounds of a full-fledged culture, sounds made possible by the efforts of thousands of musicians and technicians over the course of centuries, and enjoy them privately in your own good time: that's the freedom records give you. That freedom is purest when you are farthest away from society, so that your selections can be plunked down on a tabula rasa. The turntable is ideally that. And it closely resembles the cartoonist's desert island, a flat disk with a spindly palm tree at the center.

The city is no place for *listening* to records. Half the time one has to use them as shields against other people's sounds. Music becomes a substitute for silence. (In the country, music is the fulfillment of silence.) One does not freely choose when to listen, or even what to listen to, since the trespassing bass of a neighbor's rock, rap or disco records can be countered only by its like. Gresham's Law operates; simple music drives out subtle. But then certain kinds of simple music, such as hard rock, are right for the city, being not so much a substitute for silence as a fulfillment of noise.

Even in a quiet apartment, one is somehow aware of a hundred competing time structures—the business day, the schedules of radio and television, the neighbors' lifestyles and *their* music. So even an empty, bone-white loft falls short of a tabula rasa. Stravinsky called music "the sole domain in which man realizes the present." But living in the present is (contrary to vulgar opinion) nearly impossible in a modern city, which always hungers for the future and eats the past. One reason for the vogue of headphones among city dwellers is the sense they give that one has escaped the city's voracity, because one is inside the music. The desire to be inside a record is made graphic by the desert island fantasy.

Nowadays "desert island" is a nice, Art Deco-flavored euphemism for "fallout shelter." (Ellen Willis, in Marcus's collection of rock essays, *Stranded: Rock and Roll for a Desert Island*, is fairly candid about this.) Music is a basic provision. In 1966 the *Wall Street Journal* described a corporate "alternate headquarters" where, behind 28-ton steel doors, "easy chairs and a red-and-gold couch invite comfortable listening to piped-in concerts." Talking Heads, in "Life During Wartime," glimpse the awful alternative: *I got some groceries, some peanut butter, to last a couple of days/But I ain't got no speakers, ain't got no headphones, ain't got no records to play.* When John Lennon was shot there was a run on Beatles records; one of those busy picking the bins clean told a TV reporter that he was giving up on this society and heading for the hills, but first he was stocking up on Beatles records. The irony would not have been lost on Lennon, who—though he could afford more islands than Mackenzie and more hills than this young man—chose to live in New York City.

There is a bit of the survivalist in every record collector. You want a good supply of canned music there in the cupboard with the dehydrated seltzer. But the motive is not wholly selfish. The collector wishes to preserve history while escaping it—to save history from itself. And the man who makes records may have a similar motive. Fred Gaisberg, the first great record producer, was particularly proud of recordings he made during and just before each of the World Wars—the recording of Dvořák's Cello Concerto made by Casals and Szell in Prague in April 1937; or the "swan song of the Vienna Philharmonic Orchestra under their old conductor Bruno Walter," a Mahler Ninth recorded in January 1938. Each was "something precious and rare snatched from that seething cauldron of Europe before the storm broke."

But if a record is a time capsule and a phonograph is a time machine, they are so in an unaccustomed sense. A record is a sculpted block of time, repeatable at the owner's whim. That block may have been carved from another time and place (though only live recordings are carved in one piece) and so may be a document or record of its quarry. But a record of music does not record historical time. It records musical time which, though it exists in historical time, is not of it. A violoncello is already a time machine, taking its listener to a place outside time. The phonograph is also a time machine of this sort, but with the difference that the listener operates it himself and can take a spin as often as he pleases.

Records, I said, shattered the public architecture of time. They have replaced it with a kind of modular interior design. The individual supplies himself with sculpted blocks of time and proceeds to pave his day with them. Each block is infinitely repeatable. Each is different from, but formally interchangeable with, every other.

Interior design is not taken as seriously as it should be in our culture. Like ballet it is the domain of women and homosexuals, ignored by high-minded cultural critics. That is because it trifles with art objects by sticking them on nonwhite walls, mingling them with profane things and making them answer to the needs of daily life. Unlike architecture, it seems to be less than the sum of its parts.

Most of these strictures can be applied to the interior design of time by means of records. While Albinoni and Donald Byrd seem to find fulfillment as wallpaper (to use Frank Zappa's term), Beethoven seems unhappy in that role. Yet he gets used that way all the time. How lamentable is this? Does everyday life inevitably cheapen art? Isn't art tougher than that—can't it, instead, enrich everyday life, even when perceived only glancingly (as, in fact, most people perceive architecture)?

And where did we get the idea that art never gains from rubbing shoulders with life?

We got it from the art-for-art's-sake movement of the nineteenth century. Western music, especially art music, was then distancing itself from everyday public life. At the same time, music had found a way back into everyday private life; for the piano, putting harmony and polyphony at the diligent amateur's fingertips, had made the solitary enjoyment of music a lively option. But it was *too* lively an option for the less diligent. And while the amateur pianist was free to insert music into his everyday life, there were certain limitations; it was difficult to play the piano while eating, shaving, writing, or falling asleep.

It is possible to play records while eating, shaving, writing, and falling asleep and for many people it is impossible not to. Proselytizing for recorded chamber music in the first issue of *The Gramophone*, Compton Mackenzie wrote:

> Personally, I should recommend taking one's musical exercises before getting up in the morning and before turning over at night; but I know that a great prejudice exists in England against lying in bed for any other purpose than sleep, and so I suggest that the morning music should accompany the shave. If you lather your face during the first two movements, you will get such a lather as only barbers know how to give; and if you start shaving to the third movement, you will find that the last movement will last long enough for you to put your shaving things neatly away.

One might think Mackenzie is here suggesting (however facetiously) the grossly functional use of music—the very thing *l'art pour l'art* had repudiated as bourgeois. Two points in his defense. First, shaving to music (especially a scherzo) is actually dysfunctional to the point of mortal peril, as Chaplin shows in *The Great Dictator* when he shaves a client in time to a

Brahms Hungarian Dance. Second, even as Mackenzie lay in
bed with Brahms and Schubert, younger Germans such as
Weill, Brecht and Hindemith were repudiating *l'art pour l'art*
as a bourgeois evasion and developing instead a theory of
Gebrauchsmusik. As the critic Paul Rosenfeld noted some
years later, *Gebrauch* can mean not only 'use,' but also 'custom' or even 'ritual.' So the compound word could be an
emblem of neo-medieval humility: the musician as craftsman,
fashioning music for specific functions on demand (Hindemith,
late-middle Stravinsky). It could be a brazen admission of agit-
prop intentions (Brecht/Weill). But it could also mean a return
to ritual, as in *Le Sacre*, *Les Noces*, or Weill's *Der Jasager*, a
Chinese parable of self-sacrifice that Brecht tinted red.

Ritual and function had grown apart in the West, and in
the *Gebrauchsmusik* movement we see an effort to reunite
them. A similar effort was underway in Soviet Russia, as another soon would be in Nazi Germany. But *Gebrauchsmusik*
was at least potentially *anti*totalitarian. For where totalitarian
ritual was manipulative and depended on the blindness of the
listener, *Gebrauchsmusik* tried to make the listener aware of
the music's mechanics and his own responses. This "aliena-
tion effect," as Brecht called it, assumed a certain sophistication in the listener. It could do so, I think, largely thanks to the
currency of records. Berliners of the twenties knew that a given
piece of music could be used in any number of ways. Anyone
who owned a phonograph could use music for whatever he
chose, in cheerful contempt of the composer's intentions, cultural conventions, and the sacred *Geist* or spirit of the music.
(Sophisticated Berliners were not taken in, one assumes, when
the Nazis celebrated their seizure of power in 1933 with a
command performance of *Die Meistersinger*. They knew that
this was not the fulfillment of the music's inner aspiration, but
just one of its many possible uses. But soon people would be
desophisticated by radio and by Goebbels's new tool, the wire
recorder, which would broadcast the Führer's voice from mov-

ing trucks. These devices could *impose* a context and a meaning.)

While the ideology of *Gebrauchsmusik* put great weight on community, its form implied that the individual was free to create his own ritual to suit his own needs. Not that anyone needed such dispensation; the freedom inhered in the medium. Mackenzie was not one to pant after the latest Continental breeze, yet we find him writing in Cobbett's *Cyclopaedic Survey of Chamber Music*, published in 1929:

> But what occasions there are for music of which few can avail themselves! It is easy to believe that he who has not heard a Mozart quartet played in the freshness of dawn has never enjoyed his music to the full, and since it might puzzle even a millionaire to rouse his private quartet at such an hour and make the players sit in the dews beneath his bedroom window, the gramophone becomes indispensable for such an occasion. . . . [T]he changing sky above the tree tops or the chimney stacks is enough for the eye, and in so many of Mozart's quartets the pattern of the music is the pattern of the dayspring itself.

Mackenzie, who was fond of quoting Robert Louis Stevenson's dictum that a yacht and a private string quartet are the only real advantages of great wealth, might have been interested to learn that Prince Nicholas Volkonsky, Tolstoy's grandfather and predecessor as lord of Yasnaya Polyana, awoke each morning to the strains of a Haydn symphony played beneath his bedroom window by an octet of serf-musicians, who then dispersed (Troyat tells us) "one going off to feed the pigs, another to knit stockings in the servant's hall, a third to spade in the garden." In Mackenzie's day it was harder to get good help.

*   *   *

By this point the student of Walter Benjamin will be on edge. Mechanical reproduction, he will object, destroys the ritual value of a work of art, its "aura." How can a cheap copy of art, like a poster or a record, figure in a ritual?

Benjamin's 1936 essay "The Work of Art in the Age of Mechanical Reproduction," which started many of us thinking about these matters, deals mainly with the visual arts, and backhandedly sweeps music along. But in the case of visual art there is only one dimension of reproduction, space. In the case of music there are two, space and time. And it is in time that the real miracle of loaves and fishes occurs. One minute Edison was shouting "Mary Had a Little Lamb" and the next minute, with his mouth shut, he was shouting it again. The first talking machine was miraculous even though there was no way to mass produce records (a singer would stand in front of a half dozen cylinder machines and sing the same number a hundred times, and the company would have six hundred cylinders to sell). Although the cylinder could not reproduce itself, it could reproduce sound; Emerson's prediction that we would "harness the echo" had come true within a generation. Berliner's disk made possible the reproduction of the record itself by stamping from a master. But Edison had stolen his thunder.

Photogravure reproduces an art *object*, proliferating it in space. This, as Benjamin says, cheapens its ritual value, which depends less on the observable qualities of the object than on its haecceity or "thisness," its unique identity. Phonography, by contrast, reproduces an art *event*, proliferating it in time. For a moment the analogy wants to keep going. Doesn't an art event, such as a concert, have a ritual value that depends on its uniqueness?

Strictly speaking, "event" is not a ritual category at all, precisely because it does imply uniqueness. To have ritual value an "event" must recur. In other words, it must not be an historical event at all, but an instance of something timeless.

Later I will emphasize that, in the great majority of cases, there is no original musical event that a record records or reproduces. Instead, each playing of a given record is an instance of something timeless. The original musical event never occurred; it exists, if it exists anywhere, outside history. In short, it is *myth*, just like the myths "reenacted" in primitive ritual.

Repetition is essential to ritual, and exact repetition is what it has always striven to attain. According to Hindu scripture, the inaccurate singing of a sacred raga could be fatal to the singer. The same held for off-key Apache shamans. In Polynesia the careless performer might be executed; on the island of Gaua in the New Hebrides (the musicologist Curt Sachs tells us) "old men used to stand by with bows and arrows and shoot at every dancer who made a mistake." The earliest musical notations were designed to preserve sacred formulae; some, such as Babylonian notation, were the secret preserve of priests and cantors. Max Weber ascribed these tendencies, and aesthetic stylization in general, to a concern for magical efficacy. If the death penalty for wrong notes is missing in Christianity, the concern for liturgical accuracy abides. As Henry Raynor writes in his *Social History of Music*, "The history of the development of Western notation is a history of the attempts of ecclesiastical musicians to ensure the accuracy of the rite."

Notation can ensure against lapses of memory, but not against slips of the tongue or the hand. Only recording— above all tape recording, with its absolving splices—can ensure absolute accuracy. Moreover, even an immaculate live performance will differ in some degree from the last immaculate performance. Only a record never varies.

Some people's private phonographic rituals are plainly religious, as when people play *Messiah* on Christmas day. I myself formerly, as an Orthodox Jew who lived in the city but believed that the proper spirit of the Sabbath was pastoral, used to listen on Friday afternoons after my shower to Klemperer's recording of Beethoven's Sixth Symphony, a record most persuasive of the blessedness of leisure. (When the Scherzo was being recorded Walter Legge, the producer, kept calling down from the control booth to ask if the tempo wasn't, after all, rather slow? Klemperer, in unusually good humor, would answer: "Don't worry, Walter, you will get used to it.") But most private phonographic ritual is secular. Composer's birthdays are observed in the obvious way. There is the custom of hearing *The Rite of Spring* at the vernal equinox. There is the anticustom of playing The Mothers of Invention on Mother's Day. A critic writes that for him Sunday morning would not be Sunday morning without Thelonious Monk.

People inclined to such observances may also observe taboos. If a record has its special place in your life, you don't cheapen it by playing it at random. If you care deeply about a composer, you don't ask him to accompany you to the bathroom—you take the pickup off for a minute. On the other hand, you don't take a symphony off in the middle, if you can help it; turning the radio off might be excusable, as the show will go on without you, but if you take the record off you boorishly disrupt the performance. (For practical people it's the other way around, because with a record they can always pick up where they left off.)

The physical act of playing a record can itself be ritualistic. My own ancient AR turntable needs to be spun a few times by hand before the pulley and gears will catch, and the tone arm has to be lowered preliminarily beneath the level of the platter to get the damping right. No one else knows to do these things. My Levitical knowledge makes me master of all phonographic rites conducted in my home. But even modern machines want a good deal of attention to their levers and knobs. In fact, the more state-of-the-art the machine, the more attention it wants. No serious discophile will put on an LP without cleaning it, and the most popular cleaning system involves, minimally, squeezing three drops of Hi-Technology Record

Cleaning Fluid on a velvety pad with walnut-grained handle, smearing the drops with the bottom of the squeeze bottle, holding the pad perpendicular to the record grooves, pressing the damp side of the convex pad against the surface of the record while making sure that the long axis of the pad is perpendicular to the grooves, turning the pad slowly on its axis so that the dry part is pressed against the record, raking the soiled pad with the bristled DC-1 Pad Cleaner, then wondering what to clean the Pad Cleaner with. The instructions are unctuously dogmatic on the "proper use of 3 drops" in annointing the pad. All this sounds toilsome but soon comes as naturally as laying phylacteries, and then one can hardly bear to put a record on otherwise. There is something soul-satisfying about a ritual that separates music from noise, culture from chaos. (On the other hand, lately I have been buying cassettes. I am no longer Orthodox, either.)

With records, I said earlier, one could make love while listening to the *St. Matthew Passion*. Unless he adheres to some kind of post-Zinzendorfian heresy, the phonographic ritualist will never do such a thing. But such things and worse are done. Benjamin Britten complained: "It is one of the unhappiest results of the march of science and commerce that this unique work [the *St. Matthew*], at the turn of a switch, is at the mercy of any loud roomful of cocktail drinkers—to be listened to or switched off at will, without ceremony or occasion." Not long ago I heard a late-night classical disk jockey purr, "I suggest that you get out your popcorn, or if you're older and more mature, your martini olives, and sit back and enjoy Bach's *St. Matthew Passion*." This from a disk jockey, who has taken it upon himself to suggest, if not exactly to construct, a public architecture of time. The private citizen can afford to be even more reckless, and often is. But if his recklessness is not mere callousness, it can be creative; and as Tomás observes, the great thing about private ritual is that it can be a medium of self-expression. Is it not wonderful that a post-

Zinzendorfian heretic should be able to make love to the *Passion?*

Tomás's private rituals involve acting out certain secular Passions—murders, suicides, love-deaths of one kind or another. (*Salome*, a favorite, is at once sacred and sexual, a true abomination.) Draped in his bedspread, Tomás reenacts the nineteenth-century mythology of love and death, which today survives mainly among gays.

For Tomás, music is not structure but "pure passion." And Tomás's repetitions of music are not so much architectural as obsessive or incantatory, in the manner of ecstatic religion. (Weber distinguished ecstatic religion from ritualistic, but there are many hybrid forms, such as Hinduism and Hasidism.) To call his activities obsessive is not necessarily to make a psychiatric judgment. We might just as well call the architectural ritualist compulsive. I would prefer to say that both use symbols to give the moment meaning. The ecstatic finds meaning in concentration, the architect in context.

What would Tomás do without his phonographic playacting—would he weep on the shoulders of strangers? Ravish little boys? Smash furniture as well as atoms? Become unable to smash atoms? One can only assume that without this disorderly conduct his life would be less orderly and less meaningful.

Meaning (like anything that has meaning) is not won once and for all. A little negligence and it slips away. The musical ritual that punctuates one's life can become merely syntactical, if one lets it. The record that has been on the turntable all summer may become a drug (*Repeat as Necessary* is a new wave rock album), or the appetite may surfeit, or the passion play may slide into camp. When exact repetition demands care, as in performance from notation or memory, meaning is hard-earned; but once earned it is not easily lost. When exact repetition is automatic, meaning comes easy and goes the same way. Mechanical reproduction makes private ritual convenient, but cheap.

In 1913 Claude Debussy wrote:

> In a time like ours, when the genius of engineers has
> reached such undreamed of proportion, one can hear
> famous pieces of music as easily as one can buy a glass
> of beer. It only costs ten centimes, too, just like the
> automatic weighing scales! Should we not fear this do-
> mestication of sound, this magic preserved in a disc
> that anyone can awaken at will? Will it not mean a
> diminution of the secret forces of art, which until now
> have been considered indestructible?

Debussy was talking about the Salon du Phonographe, a sort
of dandified, walk-in jukebox on the boulevard des Italiens
where, for a coin dropped in a slot set in the mahogany wall,
patrons could sit back in red-plush armchairs and imbibe their
selections through ear tubes. But he was also aiming, more
broadly, at the phonographs that Charles and Emile Pathé
were then busily planting in French homes.

Perhaps unwittingly, Debussy hits on a paradox. He says
records make music cheap, like automatic weighing scales (science crushing the "secret forces of art"). But then he lets slip
that the disk, too, has its magic. For technology often does,
certainly when new (in America, automatic weighing scales
also tell your fortune) and sometimes even when old (fire is
very old technology but can still fill us with awe). Debussy
might reply that this magic is extramusical. But so, often
enough, is the magic of live music. And this point would not
have been lost on Debussy, who despised virtuosos because
they tended to distort music (his own in particular) in the name
of magic.

We have all become like Prospero, able to conjure up
invisible musicians who sing and play at our pleasure. Part of
the fun is our sense of power. We can manipulate the poker-
faced, flawless Heifetz. We can shut up Streisand. We can

boost the basses and cellos in the Berlin Philharmonic, defying Karajan's meticulous balances.

In this the phonograph is rather like the rest of the "home entertainment center," which is a voodoo doll's house full of politicians, movie stars, dangerous romances and world-historical events—all in miniature, all manipulable. These facsimiles assure us that the world makes sense and we can manage it. (Of course, our management skills vanish once we step off the living-room carpet and we are smart enough not to point our TV remote control wands at teenage hoodlums as Peter Sellers does in *Being There*.) To pretend that this attitude cannot extend to high art would be disingenuous. Controlling cultural objects, like owning them, is a way of feeling cultured. (For that matter, what is ownership without control?) Besides, the manipulation of defenseless musicians has been a favorite sport not only of listeners but of record producers and even composers. An entire school of electronic music specializes in just this; an unusually candid example is Charles Dodge's *Any Resemblance Is Purely Coincidental*, in which a famous recording of "Vesti la giubba" by the first and greatest icon of phonography, Caruso, is made to take humiliating pratfalls. (Caruso, who drew caricatures of everyone in sight and who once, singing "Che gelida manina"—"What a frozen little hand"—to Dame Melba in a performance of *La Bohème,* pressed into her hand a hot sausage which in fright she flung into the air, would be in no position to complain.)

Our sense of power is far from complete, however. Unlike Prospero, we cannot see the spirits we summon, and that makes things a little spooky. Late at night especially, the record listener may feel oddly vulnerable and exposed (unlike the radio listener, who is constantly in touch with other living, breathing humans). He may even feel observed. His position is the opposite of the moviegoer's, who himself is invisible, an observant ghost. The moviegoer is a point in space; the record listener is immense, a world bundled up in nerves.

At the movies, the philosopher Stanley [...] served, we experience our own immortality. [...] we have become pure spirits, present but inv[...] ords, one might say, we experience the immortality of others. of the human musicians whose spirits we invoke. In primitive magic the spirits whose powers are enlisted are nature spirits or the spirits of the dead. There is an echo of this in phonographic magic, lending it a certain eerieness. Record listening is a séance where we get to choose our ghosts. The voices we hear come from another world—something voices are good at. So there is a certain bafflement: the voice seems to be coming from the medium, or the loudspeaker, but where is it really coming from? Sight, in the habit of tracing sound to its source, finds nothing but some wooden boxes and a spinning circle. At the end of the search for focus one finds a surd. The performer becomes (in the etymological sense) occult.

Many recording artists are dead, and all eventually will be. Even when they are alive, their submission to waxing (to use the old term) or to entombment in vinyl or polyvinyl chloride is an intimation of immortality, and therefore of mortality. That we control the spirits of dead musicians is morbid enough; that we control the discarnate spirits of living ones may be worse. An Eskimo accosted by the ethnomusicologist Christian Leden said, "My songs are part of my soul, and if the demon in the white man's magic box steals my soul, why, I must die." Béla Bartók had a similar reaction from a fifteen-year-old Turkish nomad; it is as much a commonplace of ethnography as the primitive fear of cameras, and as consonant with our own unspoken instincts. The record listener and the musician—like the stargazer and the star, like a man and his familiar ghost— do not inhabit the same world. This is the premise of their intimacy. And their intimacy is only closer when the ghost is heard but not seen, since it then seems that the two worlds are not tangential, but coextensive. But then the ghost has power over the man—as Hamlet's ghost has when, having gone

.derground, he cries "Swear!" As Ariel has when, singing 'Full fathoms five thy father lies," he leads Ferdinand by the nose. "This is no mortal business, nor no sound/That the earth owes. I hear it now above me," says Ferdinand. Above, beneath, somewhere, but not in this world.

The radio listener may seem more the spiritualist, pulling ghosts from the air. If so, he is like one who attends a séance out of curiosity and is satisfied to hear any voice at all from the other side. The record listener wants to contact only certain spirits. In fact records, not the radio, sometimes play a part in actual séances. Thomas Mann, who flirted with spiritualism at first hand before depicting it in *The Magic Mountain*, gives the phonograph a crucial role in the séances at the sanitorium. It is a cherished record of the soldier's prayer from Gounod's *Faust* that finally lures back the ghost of Castorp's gallant cousin.

That incident bears looking into. Castorp is nearing the end of his quest for enlightenment and of (the corollary) his infatuation with death. Opportunely a new toy arrives at the House Berghof: an up-to-the-minute deluxe electric-drive phonograph. Set in a great "casket" finished in dull ebony, it is accompanied by a bookcase full of "fat magic tomes." An orchestra playing Offenbach is heard, then a famous Italian tenor; then "the spirit of a world famous violinist played as though behind veils." The patients are amused; Castorp is enchanted, and becomes custodian of the instrument, which he plays late into the night, "alone among four walls with his wonder-box; with the florid performance of this truncated little coffin of violin-wood, this small dull-black temple. . . ." He can do so without fear of disturbing the other patients, for the vibrations "grew weak and eerie with distance, like all magic."

Among his favorite records is Schubert's "Lindenbaum," although he knows that his love for its pure beauty is at the root a love of death. Another favorite is *Aida*. Castorp is consoled by the beauty of the final love duet in the tomb, but recognizes that the facts of the impending situation (pit gas, hunger, putrefaction) have been aestheticized away. A third favorite is the song from *Faust* in which Valentine—whom Castorp connects with his soldier cousin Joachim, newly dead—asks God to look after his younger sister.

When a young woman at the sanatorium proves to have psychic powers and the other patients, already bored with the phonograph, begin to hold séances, Castorp is reluctant, sensing "that such experiences . . . could never be anything but in bad taste, unintelligible and humanly valueless"; but his empiricism triumphs. At the first session an invisible young ghost named Holger, who chances to be a poet, taps out hours of heavily perfumed seascape lyricism ("Ah, see the dim green distance faint and die into eternity, while beneath broad veils of mist in dull carmine and milky radiance the summer sun delays to sink!") that outpurples all the favorite arias of the day. At the second and last séance, whose atmosphere reminds him of a visit to a brothel in his student days (brothels, of course, were among the earliest establishments to adopt the phonograph), an attempt is made to materialize the shade of Joachim. Only when Castorp thinks to replace the light music that has been playing with the record of Valentine's prayer does the attempt succeed. But a single look into the eyes— sad, but not reproachful—of the tragicomically attired ghost is enough. Castorp will have no more of black magic. And he loses, abruptly, his love for the black "sarcophagus of music" and the black disk.

One might ask why the phonograph, being metaphorically a medium, should also serve as the tool of a medium in a séance. It could be a matter of sympathetic magic, like producing like. It could be that the spirits of world-famous violinists are adept at summoning other spirits (Kreisler summons Holger, who summons Joachim, no pun intended). This last suggests a more general explanation: a chain of magical effects in which it is hard to say where the magic starts or leaves off. Prospero's magic makes Ariel make music, which in turn (like an incantation) works magic on Caliban and the Mantuan castaways. We make magic when we work the phonograph, causing spirits to make music. That music—exactly repeated, like a magic formula—can work further magic. It can make us disappear (*I, I, I am* glad, *you know, I mix with the music and I blend away . . .*). It can bring us serenity or make us dance like David before the ark. It can cure us of madness, or insomnia, or make insomnia a state of grace, as Glenn Gould's recordings of the *Goldberg Variations* have done for countless modern Kayserlings. It can make beautiful women melt in our arms. Or, the horn anticipating Gabriel's, it can wake the dead.

Once, in the long slope of time after midnight, having put on a Bach suite for cello, I began to listen for the flavor. It was dark and pungent, the sort of stuff the dead might feed on. I thought of Odysseus visiting Hades, and how the blood he sprinkled drew the dead like flies. I thought of Orpheus, and of whom I might bring back from that place. I tried to think of something else.

Asked to nominate a revenant, a dear one whom Holger might collar, the prurient patients were mum. For "the calling back of the dead, or the desirability of calling them back, was a ticklish matter, after all." Presumably they know all our ugly secrets. To face the dead is to face oneself; we do both when we face music. No wonder we fear true music, late at night, as much as we fear silence.

Whoever is not afraid must find the spirit world manageable, either because he is a saint or because he is complacent. If a saint, we say no more of him. If complacent, he may be a philistine firmly planted in life, or an aesthete half in love with easeful death, or a Hans Castorp passing through each stage in turn. For the aesthete, death is where a thing of beauty is a joy forever. As youthful love finds fulfillment in the urn, music finds it in records. And unplayed records are the sweetest of all.

Settembrini, Castorp's Masonic mentor, must have fore-
seen the arrival of the phonograph when he warned his disci-
ple several hundred pages earlier, as they sat in the shade and
listened to the Sunday band, against the poppy charms of
music. "Music is to all appearances movement itself—yet, for
all that, I suspect her of quietism. . . . For you, personally,
Engineer, she is beyond all doubt dangerous. I saw it in your
face as I came up. . . . She is an old hand at using opiates."

Aldous Huxley, who had as good an ear as anyone for the
resonances of technology, also cast the phonograph as an
instrument of death and the hope of afterlife. In *Point Counter
Point* the world-weary cynic Spandrell, who is "not a man—
either a demon or a dead angel," plays Beethoven's "Holy
thanks-song of a convalescent" from the A minor Quartet—
music in which he finds the only proof of God, the soul,
heaven—and kills himself. "Long notes, a chord repeated,
protracted, bright and pure, hanging, floating, effortlessly soar-
ing on and on. And then suddenly there was no more music;
only the scratching of the needle on the revolving disk."

It is a melancholy fact that death sells records. The death of a
recording star gives him the kind of sales boost that the Nobel
Prize, a pleasanter apotheosis, gives an author; the death of an
author has no such effect on sales. A painter's death may do
his prices some good, but only because originals are for sale
and supply can no longer grow to meet demand. Records are
copies, like books, and their supply is in principle unlimited. So
economics does not explain this macabre phenomenon.

It is most striking in the realm of rock and roll. Otis
Redding died in a plane crash three days after recording "The
Dock of the Bay," and the song went instantly to the top of the
charts. Record companies capitalized on the deaths of Bob
Marley, Jim Croce, Joplin, Hendrix, Buddy Holly. Elvis Presley made a fine comeback when he died; so did the Beatles
when Lennon was shot. The Doors made a comeback in 1980,

ten years after the death of Jim Morrison. In that year Elektra Records reported larger sales for each of the group's twelve albums—a total of more than two million records—than in any year since their original release. The fires were stoked by a new album made with Morrison's help, in which new instrumentals were recorded over old tapes of the leader speaking his poems.

Classical record sales do not behave in quite this way, partly because they are more dependent on live concerts for advertising and promotion. Also, classical musicians tend to die quietly and at an advanced age. The rare exceptions (Dinu Lipatti, Guido Cantelli, Glenn Gould) have had considerable posthumous success. But even grand old men like Furtwängler, Beecham, and Casals have had worthy afterlives in the record stores, and many are still going strong. RCA, in particular, has found Caruso, Toscanini, and Reiner almost as dependable as Presley himself. This company seems to work its dead artists especially hard. Toscanini's harsh-sounding Studio 8-H recordings are electronically reprocessed for stereo effect and end up sounding even harsher; Caruso returns in better voice than ever, enhanced by the Soundstream computer process; Reiner's classic Bartók and Strauss are reincarnated in half-speed remasterings and on digital compact disks. Jazz musicians rise from their ashes as Bluebirds and popular artists are memorialized in a series of two-record crêches. All this shows a commendable sense of history but must be discouraging to young musicians. In a letter to Irving Kolodin, the producer Walter Legge said of RCA's "astonishing restoration" of the Mengelberg *Heldenleben*: "If only the record companies can so improve the riches they have in their archives with like skill they have the artistic capital to cut down on their spending on recording for years to come. . . ." He was evidently unperturbed by the prospect that dead talent might drive out living, just as recorded music drives out live.

Legge's EMI, with its American affiliate Angel, has long

had a reissue program that, though unflashy, is artistically the richest of all. Its early trademark "The Sign of the Recording Angel" was abandoned in 1909 and revived much later for the U.S. operation. That first emblem, a winged cherub sprawled on a record and using a quill to engrave it, suggests that the company's business is to determine what each musician's after-life shall be. EMI's present logo, which it shares with American RCA Victor, is the one derived from Francis Barraud's famous painting "His Master's Voice." Although folksy, the image has a certain weirdness. Look at it and imagine: What if the poor dog's master is dead?

Looking at Nipper has sometimes put me in mind of Mary Stuart's lap dog that—in a scrap of history I seem to remember, probably bogus—scampered under her skirts after her beheading. Less idiotically, I am reminded of a story attributed to Edwin Welte, inventor of the "reproducing piano." Shortly after Busoni's death his widow, sitting in a deck chair on an ocean liner and staring out to sea, heard drifting from a nearby lounge the sound of a piano. The playing was unmistakable. "Ferrucio!" she cried. "Oh, Ferruccio *mio!*"

What is pathetic in Signora Busoni's case, as in Nipper's, is the incomprehension. But such stories, like stories of Eskimo afraid they will lose their souls, bring us back to our own more primitive feelings. Setting aside (and it is about time) any hidden morbidity, the immense popularity of the HMV logo suggests the following things: That we feel like dumb animals before the phonograph, cocking our ears in consternation. That we are not masters of the voice, but the other way around. That the owner of the voice is dear to us, that we miss him and would like to see and sniff him. That if the disk is faithful to the master, we will be faithful to the disk.

I am not competent to figure out the iconography behind Barraud's image, but paging through Janson I see a dog in roughly Nipper's posture listening, along with divers other animals, to David and his psaltery in the Paris Psalter of the tenth century; I see a Byzantine Adam, his head tilted in deliberation, and a tree that curves toward him like a phonograph horn; I see a Fra Angelico annunciation with a kneeling angel whose wings have that same curve. In each case the listening figure is fascinated, but also a little anxious as to who or where his real master might be.

One would like to show one's fidelity, but a voice is not something one can hold on to. (If religion began with the hearing of voices, the making of idols must have followed hard upon.) The Bakhrushin Museum has a Chaliapin Pavilion where babushkas regularly come to "visit" the singer, to hear his sable voice on tape and bring him flowers. At Wave Hill, Toscanini's mansion in the Bronx, one can hear tapes of his radio broadcasts and other unreleased performances. "We're amazed," a curator said, "at the number of people who will sit staring at the tape recorder, and often applaud at the end."

Good thing Toscanini did not record in stereo. A single speaker, at least, is something to stare at. The kind with a horn is best, recalling the blossoming horns of the old talking machines, which in turn recall wind instruments that hide the player's face but project his spirit. You can stare into a horn and know that at some vanishing point beyond the visible concavity there is someone breathing. With a phonographic horn there is no evidential spittle or aroma (Satchmo said of Bunk Johnson that "he drank a whole lot of port wine. You could smell it coming out of his horn—but it sure sounded beautiful"; Nipper would have appreciated this), only sound, but the sense of direct projection is there nonetheless. With a single speaker, even a box with fabric on the front, it still lingers. Stereo, however, arrays the musicians before you in empty space. You can almost pinpoint them, but they're not there. Instead of projecting, they are projected—but invisible, "a ghastly band." The introduction of stereo did not simply double the listener's pleasure; it changed the phenomenology of the phonograph by adding a spatial, and hence a visual, aspect that at once clarified and confused. It was not simply a technical improvement, any more than talkies were a technical improvement on the moving picture show. That many listeners are still uncomfortable with stereo is evident from the way they place their speakers: pointlessly close together, or else on opposite walls. The latter arrangement is even more comfortable than monophony, as it creates no focus of attention, so no illusion of human presence, so no disillusionment. Headphones go one better, suggesting that the kingdom of music is within you. Both headphones and the opposite-wall setup are popular among rock listeners, who have no preconception as to how live musicians should be deployed. The exaggerated stereo effects used by rock producers serve not to project musicians in exterior space, but to direct listeners' attention to different zones of interior space. (This works because rock music is at once eagerly social and deeply solipsistic—a condition of adolescence—and the rock musician does not mediate as musician, but as alter ego.)

But every mode of record listening leaves us with a need for something, if not someone, to see and touch. The adoration of the disk itself is one response (though this, as we have seen, answers other needs as well). But as records tend to look alike and one doesn't want to get fingerprints on them, in practice one adores the album cover, and this impulse (together with the science of marketing) is behind the importance of cover design in the record business.

The books that have been devoted to album art reproduce mainly rock album art. While classical covers (like those of adult pop and jazz records) generally settle for a straight photograph of the performer, rock covers indulge in fantasy, dreamy or nightmarish or both. Mirrored here is a distinction between the typical classical listener, who expects the musician to mediate between the private and public realms of music, and the typical rock listener, who cohabits with the musician in a world of private fancy. For the classical listener, the adora-

tion of the cover becomes a kind of pure idolatry; for the rock
listener, a pilgrimage through the looking glass.

For the rock collector it is a point of honor to own both
jackets issued for *Blonde on Blonde*; the nude–United Nations
import cover of *Electric Ladyland* as well as the tamer domestic one; the full range of colors for *Some Girls* (which may
have been a device to quintuple sales among cultists). That
one of the greatest rock albums of all takes its nickname from
its snowy absence of cover art only proves the rule. The original design for *The Beatles*, the album everyone calls the
White Album, was banned and the Beatles would accept no
other. Anyway, inside there are portrait photographs and a big
scrapbook-style collage, representing two major schools of
rock art: the performer as pin-up (without his instrument) and
the performer as intimate (who sends you snapshots of his
private life). A third and preponderant school is represented by
the *Sgt. Pepper* cover: the star as fantast, dressing up in costumes the teenager can't afford (in either sense) to wear.

While the classical collector finds heavy shellac disks more
cherishable than any kind of cover, the pop fascination with
album covers has given them a status as art objects independent of their contents. The conceptual artist Cosmo scatters
albums, with their plastic shrink-wraps intact, around his apartment as sculpture. A colleague known as Collette makes montages of album covers and jewelry enshrined in plexiglass (a
second virginity). And children chew disks of bubble gum that
come with tiny album covers instead of baseball cards. Pauline
Kael has written of the movie *Cat People*, "Each shot looks
like an album cover for records you don't ever want to play."
That is an insult, as intended, but only because of the "ever."
For the highest praise of album art is that it finally renders the
record unnecessary, as a perfect idol displaces the god it represents. From the musical or Mosaic point of view, that is why
both are dangerous. They can become fetishes that make us
deaf to the voice. ("Ears have they but hear not. . . . They

that make them shall become like them.") It must be admitted, though, that if records are more reliable than musicians, album covers are more reliable still, especially on a desert island. In *Stranded*, Tom Smucker writes:

> If I'm going to be on an island without a working phonograph, or with one I can count on only until the batteries run down, then I'd like to be marooned with my beloved *Pet Sounds* by the Beach Boys, preferably in the original mono version with the pictures from their Japanese tour on the back. Gazing at it, I could recall every cut, I've listened to it so often. Just having it near, I would be reassured.

Fetishism, as the cherishing of some thing reminiscent or redolent of the loved one, seems the highest fidelity. But it is finally a kind of betrayal. The young moped-messenger in the film *Diva*, after secretly taping a recital by his adored soprano (who refuses to record because "music comes and goes—you shouldn't try to hold it"), snatches from her dressing room, as a prescient afterthought, her silvery gown. We see this Jules later in his garage-loft, slumped in a corner; her voice lights the vast space, her dress is wrapped shawl-like around him. His eyes make tears of joy and possibly of shame. Later he slings the dress around his neck like an aviator's scarf, hops on his moped and, cruising avenue Foch, finds a whore—black like his beautiful soprano—who will wear the dress to bed. When he comes home he finds his apartment wrecked, this signaling the start of his misadventures. It must seem like retribution. Because he loved her voice too well and not well enough, he was not satisfied with hearing her voice on occasion but had to possess it; not satisfied with her voice, he must have her garment; not satisfied with her garment he must have a proxy body in it. And so (like the Beatles fans who needed the proxy Beatles of *Beatlemania*) he betrayed her.

The great Regency wit Sydney Smith once claimed that music was "the only cheap and unpunished rapture on earth." Gorodish, *Diva*'s Zen superhero, knows better. When Jules protests that his musical piracy was innocent, meant only for his own pleasure, Gorodish admonishes him: *Il n'y a pas de plaisirs innocents.*

Chapter Five

The Social Record

One summer evening in 1910 Leo Tolstoy, whose grandfather had begun each day with an aubade played by his serfs, returned the favor by giving the peasants of Yasnaya Polyana a serenade. Calling them to assembly on the village green, the aged count showed them a box with a horn sticking out. He fussed with the box, and out of the horn came the sound of a balalaika orchestra. The muzhiks gaped. Then, at the Count's prompting, they began to dance a hopak.

The summer before, a moody youth named Sergei Prokofiev had written his girlfriend Verochka:

> Recently civilization has penetrated our wilderness. One of the peasants has bought himself a gramophone. And now every evening this invention of the devil is placed outside his hut, and begins to gurgle its horrible songs. A crowd of spectators roars with delight and joins in with their own false renditions of the songs, dogs bark and wail, the cows returning from the fields

moo and run in all directions, and someone in a neighboring hut accompanies in a wrong key on his accor-
dion. At first I closed my window and tried to play the
piano, but it was of no use. I had to run away on a
bicycle from this company.

A new invention, however private its true tendency, begins
life in public. The telephone, the wireless, the television, long
before they penetrated the average home, were used commu-
nally in saloons and parlors. The phonograph was no exception, though in its earliest form it offered a rather private sort of
public experience, as its wraithy emanations could be heard
only through rubber ear tubes. In the 1890s the Edison-Tain-
ter-Bell phonograph, flopping as a business machine, found a
career as a purveyor of unserious music and monologues,
employed by exhibitors at county fairs, hotels and music halls.
"It was ludicrous in the extreme," Fred Gaisberg recalled, "to
see ten people grouped around a phonograph, each with a
listening tube leading from his ears, grinning and laughing at
what he heard. It was a fine advertisement for the onlookers
waiting their turn." Soon Gaisberg was installing coin-oper-
ated phonographs in saloons, restaurants and beer gardens.
About the same time, Charles Pathé saw a busy Edison machine at the Vincennes Fair, and losing no time he and his
brother installed one in their *bar americain* near the place
Pigalle, casually inaugurating what was to become one of Europe's great phonograph and recording concerns.

At the turn of the century the phonograph, having
sprouted a horn and dropped its asking price from $150 to
$7.50, was a popular entertainer in France and America, while
in Russia Fred Gaisberg was acquainting the tsar's household
with the disk gramophone, setting the stage for the village
merrymaking that would delight Tolstoy and annoy Prokofiev.
Within the decade the phonographic raj had conquered even
India, in whose bazaars Gaisberg was gratified to see "dozens

of natives seated on their haunches around a gramophone, rocking with laughter" at Bert Shepherd's "Laughing Song." By the twenties, more and more households could afford phonographs of their own, and as the novelty effect dissipated so did the crowds. But the phonograph remained a fixture of private parties—in Waugh's London, Brecht's Berlin, Van Vechten's New York—and of speakeasies and whorehouses. In Baltimore, a kid named Eleanora Fagan was happy to run errands for the madam on the corner and her girls. "When it came time to pay me, I used to tell her she could keep the money if she'd let me come up in her front parlor and listen to Louis Armstrong and Bessie Smith on her Victrola. A Victrola was a big deal in those days." Eleanora was thus introduced to prostitution and jazz, and eventually settled on the latter career after changing her name to Billie Holiday.

If in the ghettos (despite the brisk sale of race records) phonographs were scarce in the twenties, in the thirties they were scarce everywhere. The Depression effectively set the clock back: while the wireless took over the home, the phonograph retreated to the high ground of public places. Records echoed in cellar clubs; in newly legitimate saloons, jukeboxes showed their Deco faces. In the subsequent steady boom of the record business, which has equipped most American homes with at least one phonograph, these have remained the dominant forms of public record listening. The cellar club became the discothèque, which became the disco, which seems to be seeking the cellar again. The jukebox was streamlined but remained the jukebox.

When records first began to be seen as home entertainment they were seen as family entertainment. Yet the picture of a happy clan clustered around the phonograph horn was surely more common in advertising than in life, and even advertising soon gave it up. The first cylinders and disks, with their Sousa marches, artistic whistling and Irish vaudeville, were alike digestible to the intellect of a child, the moral standards of a mother and the musical tastes of a stone-deaf grandfather. Very quickly, however, the natural fecundity of the disk asserted itself. Now Uncle could have his Caruso, Mom her Irving Berlin, and the black sheep could crib trumpet licks from his race records. Radio took over the role of family entertainer and then, as call numbers multiplied, passed on the part to television.

When a number of people (a number greater than two) assemble in someone's home for the sole purpose of listening to records, they are much less likely to be family than friends, drawn together by an elective affinity. Opera lends itself to this sort of thing (in college I knew of two circles that met regularly to hear Wagner, one led by a beloved professor of Greek, the other by a philosophy graduate student widely thought to be unbalanced) because there is a libretto to follow, which keeps the eyes busy. Otherwise, unless one turns out the lights or follows the score, one confronts the deep embarrassment of listening to musicians who aren't there. The embarrassment is present, if latent, even when one listens alone. It is one reason why many people, not all of them unmusical, find themselves fidgeting or rereading liner notes or paging through a magazine instead of listening as they had intended to do. But of course it's worse in company. Compare the movies: first there were moving pictures, and no one expected pictures to talk, but still the silence was embarrassing. To keep people's minds on the screen, to keep them from becoming self-conscious and losing interest in what they saw, music was needed; and by 1929, when talkies arrived, cinemas accounted for more than three-quarters of all paid musical employment in England, according to union statistics. There was nothing like this to meet our embarrassment before the talking machine. There still isn't. The ear is accosted, but the eye can wander and take the ear along. And in a group the eye is embarrassed wherever it turns—whether to the loudspeakers, or the space between them, or other eyes, or the interior of its eyelid (people will think you're asleep).

Things get worse when people imitate concert decorum, forbearing to speak at all. Even Toscanini, in the "concerts" he gave his friends at the villa on Lago Maggiore in the days after his wife's funeral, was more lenient. Samuel Chotzinoff, who handled the maestro for NBC, recalled:

> In the evening, after supper, we would all go up to his room, where his son had installed a powerful phonograph. I would pretend that we were all going to a concert and arrange a different program of records for each night. The maid would bring bottles of red syrup and glasses on a tray. Fortified with drinks, we disposed ourselves around the phonograph and listened to his records for an hour and a half, exclaiming "oh" and "ah" rapturously (and sincerely) at certain moments, greatly to the old man's delight. He himself sat upright in a chair and conducted the music with the vigor and passion he displayed at rehearsals and performances.

So here there was something to look at, as well. I doubt the red syrup was alcoholic; but it is noteworthy that, although drinks can be had at intermission in some halls, only at home is it generally possible to listen to classical music through an uplifting fog of liquor, cannabis, cocaine or what have you. While such an atmosphere might not suit the strict contours of Bach or Hindemith it might do very well by Berlioz or Wagner, recalling the opiated air they themselves breathed.

The situation of the jazz listener is just the reverse. In bars and nightclubs and dance halls teetotalling is deviant behavior, so live jazz has usually been heard through a filter of liquor or dope. But the phonograph and radio allowed us to listen to jazz analytically, and in this way (among others) convinced us that jazz was not just entertainment, but music. It was not always through sobriety that we were convinced to *love* jazz, of course; the author Claude Brown for instance, heard his first

Charlie Parker record while stoned and was instantly converted. With rock, one was advised to listen to the records under the appropriate influence: acid for acid rock, ganja for reggae, cocaine for Eric Clapton, heroin or morphine for the Stones. This removed embarrassment of a conventional sort and enabled groups of friends to listen to records without lapsing into small talk. In the sixties, sessions of this kind were a mucilage of the counterculture. If rock concerts and festivals were revival meetings, record listening was the regular sacred service. (This was one sign that rock had become an ideology, like bebop-Beat, not just a defiant or escapist mood that teenagers could summon up with records in their rooms or vent at a high-school dance.)

In the normal run of things, people *don't* get together to listen to records. But even if they don't listen, only hear, the host's choice of music can determine the tone of the evening. By setting the tone too high he will either insult the composer (Britten's complaint) or, if his guests have bigger ears than mouths, break up the conversation.

Because the host controls the music, he has a certain responsibility to it. Even if he simply turns on the radio he is choosing a station and a type of music; he cannot abdicate responsibility as the wealthy of eighteenth-century Italy did when they met every evening at the opera. "Not to attend opera," Henry Raynor writes, "was to cut oneself off from society." He cites the testimony of Dr. Burney, who on visiting La Scala in the 1760s found behind each box "a complete room . . . with a fireplace in it and all convenience for refreshment and cards." Following the pattern established in Venice a century before, a box and anteroom were rented in perpetuity, and it was here, not at home, that one did one's entertaining. The noise, Dr. Burney reported, was "abominable, except while two or three airs and a duet were singing"; while, in Naples, "those who are not talking, or playing at cards, are usually fast asleep." Today only a coatrack remains in most opera houses to remind us of former amenities, and we make at least a show of attention to the singers. But at home we can be as heedless as any rococo socialite.

It might seem small-souled to insist that music of merit never be squandered on casual ears. Is it wrong to hang fine art in the living room, where it is sometimes the foreground but more often the background? There is a difference, though. A painting waits for our attention. With a flick of the ocular muscles, visual background can become a foreground. Background music is not a backdrop but, as it were, another play acted out behind the one we are in. If we miss a few minutes, we lose the sense of it. At least, this is true of most Western classical music, which, with a few self-conscious exceptions, is dramatic in the sense that it develops over time.

Some of the most self-conscious exceptions were composed by Erik Satie, who had this problem among others in mind. Influenced by the aesthetic of Greek music, which could do its uplifting work subliminally, he wrote that

> we must bring about a music which is like furniture—a music, that is, which will be part of the noises of the environment, will take them into consideration. I think of it as melodious, softening the noises of the knives and forks, not dominating them, not imposing itself. It would fill up those heavy silences that sometimes fall between friends dining together. It would spare them the trouble of paying attention to their own banal remarks. And at the same time it would neutralize the street noises which so indiscreetly enter into the play of conversation. To make such a music would be to respond to a need.

Satie responded. So did John Cage, who after quoting this passage in his essay on Satie adds, "Why is it necessary to give the sounds of knives and forks consideration? . . . Otherwise the music will have to have walls to defend itself, walls which will not only constantly be in need of repair, but which, even to get a drink of water, one will have to pass beyond, inviting disaster." Instead of walls one might say, a frame. One might define art that should not hang in the living room as art that has a frame.

Someone might have answered Satie by saying that the need had already been met. Mozart, Handel, Telemann, Vivaldi and countless others wrote *Tafelmusik* for rich patrons which we can have for free. Satie might have answered, first, that this music is dramatic in structure, and framed—at least the good stuff is—and that its former use as table music only argues a tin ear in the people who sat at the table. Second, that time has framed it all, good and bad, just as antique furniture is framed. We can't put our feet up. Finally, how could Telemann have anticipated the sounds of *our* knives and forks, or the specific banality of our modern remarks?

All this helps to explain why Cage writes, "Records, too, are available. But it would be an act of charity to oneself to smash them whenever they are discovered." For as Cage says, elaborating the silverware theme, "It is evidently a question of bringing one's intended actions into relation with the ambient unintended ones." Records are too intended, and their intention comes from too long ago; they cannot come into relation with present events. Records are framed. (Speaking of framed, notice how records get it from both sides, from champions of Western tradition like Britten and from anarchists like Cage. Yet Britten has recorded more of his own works than almost any other composer, and even Cage has his half-column in the catalogue.)

Still, there are moments in company when records come into their own, exquisite moments (a trifle decadent, like any blending of high pleasures) when wordless voices encircle the conversation and draw it down with them into deeper regions.

As Ives's Second Quartet reminds us ("String Quartet for four men who converse, discuss, argue [politics], fight, shake hands, shut up, then walk up the mountain side to view the firmament"), chamber music can have the give-and-take of good talk. The music, to affect the conversation, need not have the same topic, or any topic, only a related topology. Then the talk, in turn, affects the music by lending it a topic. These moments are serendipitous and no host can plan them. The best he can do is choose a record cannily, with a finger on the pulse of conversation; choose it not as background music, not as a concert selection, but as a guest that slips in unannounced and is soon noticed for eloquence.

In his casual power over our minds, in his conjuring of melodious ghosts, such a host is like Prospero. Prospero's magic made his stay on that island more pleasant, but found its real purpose when his guests arrived. With music and words they were led maieutically to the truth. Is that the secret fantasy of the record listener, in his double-locked desert island? That if only the stiff-necked would listen to these records they would hear how the world should be ordered?

I said earlier that in traditional societies music is part of life; that in the West it became detached; that it was let back in by the phonograph as it were through a back door. This schema ignores the distinction, explicit even in primitive cultures, between sacred music and secular. Sacred music is performed only on its proper occasion and exactly in the manner prescribed. Secular music also has a context, but singing it out of context is just eccentric, not sacrilegious, and the singer is free to adapt and invent. With the phonograph, music of every description—sacred, secular, art, entertainment, scavenged from cultures present and past—is injected into everyday life. In terms of context nothing is sacred; all music is secular. But in its manner of performance all music is sacred, because the phonograph always plays it exactly the same way.

So records bring music back into everyday life, where secular music once was, but in a manner appropriate to sacred music. The paradox tightens when we remember that in traditional cultures sacred music is supposed to be performed or directed by professionals (priests, shamans, religious and musical virtuosi). Secular music may have its minstrels, but in general is the province of the layman (even of the "unmusical," if the culture has that concept; some cultures, like the Venda described by John Blacking, consider all humans musical). Records can be played by anyone, but the music on them is played by professionals in temples far away. The upshot is that the music we relax with, which formerly was free, demotic, and participatory, is now stiff, slick, and hieratic—that is, framed.

What goes for our play music goes for our work music, since they tend to be identical. I once visited a direct-mail marketing house where dozens of young women sat at tables around a central radio, stuffing envelopes as breathy voices urged them to work that body, shake that booty, push, push, and so on. Muzak, which is programmed by human-factors engineers to produce maximum worker efficiency, is also dance music, though tamer and aimed at an older audience. Back in the thirties Compton Mackenzie wrote, "There was a time when dance music was played by the BBC under the impression that people danced to it. That delusion has long been cured. Dance music has become the staple noise emanating from a loudspeaker." He attributed this to the "hunger . . . for a rhythmic accompaniment to the unrhythmic noise of contemporary life." Adorno, recognizing that contemporary life is rhythmic in its way, was more subtle: "It is true that some of the bodily functions which the individual has really lost are imaginatively returned to him by music. Yet . . . in the mechanical rigor of their repetition, the functions copied by the rhythm are themselves identical with those of the production processes which robbed the individual of his original bodily functions." Of course, modern dance music has been fertilized by ethnic rhythms that are as far as possible from the mechanical. So the fault may lie less with the music than with its medium. Even the most organic rhythm can be killed by endlessly exact repetition.

But I am not speaking here of Muzak, whose arrangers are able to mummify the liveliest of originals. Bing Muscio, former president of Muzak Corp., who came to the firm from a manufacturer of air conditioners, said that his product should be heard but not listened to. Designed to flatten work efficiency curves, Muzak is programmed by a Teleprompter computer in fifteen-minute segments. A segment holds five selections, each more "stimulating" (in terms of tempo, rhythm, and orchestration) than the last. There are different programs for offices, light industry, heavy industry, and public places (where the emphasis is on "well-being" rather than efficiency). From its plant in Westbury, Long Island, the company sends out tapes that play in factories and rest rooms from Finland to Argentina, to some hundred million nonlisteners a day. That makes it the largest "network" in the world. Here is architecture of time on a titanic scale—the free-world equivalent of totalitarian radio. Generalissimo Franco used to have Muzak tapes from Westbury played over Radio Madrid. But then Muzak was conceived by a brigadier general who wanted to pump it into the trenches of the First World War and it had its first great success in the munitions factories of the Second.

William Schuman was maddened by it on a Metroliner train. "I couldn't work. I couldn't think. . . . My whole life is music, and I don't like to see it destroyed by omnipresence." The pianist Gerald Moore "begged my pretty American air hostess on one occasion to switch it off, and this she did most obligingly with a, 'Not musical, eh?' "

Of course, Muzak is not work music for musicians, but for workers. If good music were played in factories, either it would distract the workers or they would have to learn to ignore it.

Surely people should not be taking good music for granted. Should they, then, be taking bad music for granted? It may be a false dilemma. Where a task is mechanical, good music may not speed it up, but it will make it infinitely more bearable. "We want to help people to get through their workday," says Muzak's director of research. But that is what good music would do. Muzak, by contrast, is meant to speed the worker up and keep him running at an even speed, like a machine.

In some cultures work music is music one sings while working: grinding songs, harvest songs, building songs, sea chanteys, field hollers. When the worker is exuberant, the song recycles his exuberance. When he's bored, it entertains him. It thus reinforces the natural rhythm of the workday. Muzak comes from outside the worker. It smothers his exuberance, prods his exhaustion, and flattens the workday.

Intellectual work is another matter. When it was disclosed that Jimmy Carter was in the habit of reading two or three books concurrently while listening to classical music, the vagaries of his administration might have been foretold. Later, Helmut Schmidt complained that his best ideas got lost in the background music of the Oval Office. It is a very subjective thing, but I think most people would agree that analytical work and the assimilation of information are hindered by music, unless the music is either simple or familiar. Creative work, on the other hand, can benefit from music in a number of ways. Compton Mackenzie, in his day a celebrated novelist, found that records of chamber music occupied the regions of his mind not engaged with his writing and so kept them from distracting him with thoughts of their own. In Vermont, Edward Hoagland needs no electricity, but in New York City he puts "trumpet voluntaries on the phonograph in the morning, organ fugues after supper, and whale songs or wolf howls in the silence at night." Ann Beattie says she always plays music while she writes, and the record she's hearing often ends up in the story she is writing (at times, I think, the story grows out of the song). I sometimes play music hoping that it will color my phrases in certain ways—that Bach will lend them power, Mozart grace, Elvis Costello truculence. And music can be useful even when it distracts. Glenn Gould spoke of practicing Beethoven's Sonata Opus 109 when he was nineteen and getting stuck on a passage in the last movement that was "a positive horror"; three days before the recital he was hopelessly blocked. "So I decided to try the Last Resort method. That was to place beside the piano a couple of radios, or possibly one radio and one television, turn them up full blast. . . ." That, and concentrating on the left hand, because the problem was in the right, did the trick. It is an extreme case of something we have all experienced.

Creative work is the exception in our world, and work that was once creative in the plain sense—making things—is now a matter of "getting through the working day." But it might be argued convincingly (though not to the average plant manager) that in default of a work-chant tradition, good recorded music might be a good way to make the worker feel human. He might even prove it by singing along from time to time (since by good music I don't just mean fugues). In the very long run he might prove more productive than the worker aurally programmed to work like a machine.

Muzak is a quiet challenge to the sonic order of a free society, which is properly an equilibrium of diversities. There are louder challenges. The maddening neighbor—every urbanite has one—whose volume knob is moved by no entreaty is probably just a jerk, but it is possible that on some level he is an insurgent. Insurgence often seems to be the point of the immense stereophonic radio-cassette decks that are lugged around the cities by lower-class youth; and this is not just paranoid projection on the middle-class observer's part. Watch what happens on a subway train or residential street when someone reacts to the music with visible annoyance, or asks that it be turned down. If the boxman is not outright defiant he will show at least a certain tickled contempt, a spirit of *épater le bourgeois*. Not that he will cite Dada manifestos. More likely he will speak, in fully bourgeois terms, of his rights. And this will seem flatly absurd (like the argument of the immigrant who, having cut in front of my mother on the supermarket check-out line, said this was a free country and he could do what he wanted). But in fact he will have hit on one of the built-in contradictions of our system, which in its general form worries liberal social theories from Locke to Rawls. For they are all based on the individual pursuit of happiness, and leave no room for such happinesses as cannot be pursued by the individual alone, or *en famille*, or in limited voluntary association with others. Everyone has the right to arrange his own life, but no one has the right to arrange the life of the community. And no one has the right to make himself architect of public time; not even the public has that right. So no one has the right to *live in* public, architected time, because there isn't any to live in. But for some people happiness would be exactly that.

On a summer Sunday in Central Park it is sometimes hard to escape the feeling that an all-embracing P.A. system has been set up. At every turn another radio plays, tuned to the same station. "As if supplied with this jazz from a universal unfailing source, like cosmic rays"—so Bellow's Sammler thought. When the sun sets the radios go their separate ways, but that radiation still unites them.

Sammler has divined the essential form of black and Hispanic music. It is stuff—mystical, unfailing, unifying stuff. The varieties of this stuff are called by mass terms: jazz, swing, soul, salsa, funk. Each of these has become in its turn the stuff of an ideology. Not long ago funk had its turn, and a few minutes of radio listening would turn up the syllable in a dozen contexts

(Defunkt, Confunkshun, Instant Funk, Funk Pump). The manic, encyclopedic ideologue of funk, the Rabelais of funk, is George Clinton of Parliament/Funkadelic. In his hands "funk" is noun, verb, expletive, manifesto, tetragrammaton, a word to conjure with. Here are some snatches of his lyrics: *Give up the funk, we need the funk. . . . Pledge groovallegiance to the funk/The United Funk of Funkadelica. . . . One nation under a groove/Gettin' down just for the funk of it. . . . Do you promise to funk/The whole funk and nothing but the funk. . . .* A representative record is *Mothership Connection*, which begins with Clinton's spoken introduction: *Good evening. Do not attempt to adjust your radio; there is nothing wrong. We have taken control so as to bring you this special show. . . . Welcome to station WEFUNK. . . . coming to you directly from the Mothership.* The use of radio format is not just a ploy to get airplay; there is a genuine radio mysticism here that, mingling with sci-fi motifs, takes on an almost messianic cast. *If you got faults, defects or shortcomings, you know, like arthritis, rheumatism or migraines, whatever part of your body it is, I want you to lay it on your radio, let the vibes flow through. Funk not only moves, it can remove, dig?* The chorus of one song runs, *You've got all that's really needed/To save a dying world from its funklessness.* The back of the jacket shows the luminous Mothership touching down on a refuse-strewn ghetto street. All this is campy and adolescent as can be, but in its way as earnest as Beethoven's praise of the *Götterfunken*. The Mothership's divine spark just happens to be electric.

With tempting dialectic, funk suggests the following: music, having started out as ritual, having then become a thing, now becomes a *thang*. The difference is profound. A thing is what you possess, a thang is what possesses you. A thing occupies space, a thang occupies time and preoccupies people. A thing, above all, is private; a thang can be shared. As thang, music is again communal and celebratory. Again it is spirit; again it is ritual (Clinton has costumes and a playful cult). But this is a synthesis, not a backlash, for instead of tribal uniformity or the imposed uniformity of totalitarianism there is a feast of diversity. A hundred flowers bloom, and not in fenced-off gardens either. *I got a thang, you got a thang, everybody got a thang./ Whyn't we get together, doin' our thang, in order to help each other?* In musical terms: *Who says a jazz band/Can't play dance music? Who says a rock band/Can't play funky/? Who says a funk band/Can't play rock?*

All this is a bit quixotic, of course. How are diversity and solidarity to be reconciled, in the musical realm or any other? This, in a nutshell, is the problem of community, and no one has cracked it yet. Clinton seeks a solution in understanding rather than bargaining, in play rather than business. It is not a foolproof philosophy (Milan Kundera's *Book of Laughter and Forgetting* convinces me that totalitarianism, too, can begin in angelic laughter). It is not a philosophy at all, merely a feeling. But it is appealing.

An occurrence on the Third Avenue bus, late one Saturday night. Two black youths get on with their box, keeping it turned way up. Several middle-aged, middle-class whites look annoyed but don't dare speak up. There is tension aboard; at each stoplight the breathy voice and thumping bass seem to romp provokingly up and down the aisle. Suddenly a party of Brooklynish, thirtyish whites sitting in the back start to clap and sing along. For a second the tension thickens (is this a takeoff or a getting down?) and then instantly dissipates (it doesn't matter!) and the black youths are smiling, the middle-aged whites are smiling, and the bus appears to have become a tribal village on wheels.

Even if scenes like this are taking place all over the country, which I doubt, they may be misleading. To begin with, what most boxes emit is either disco or rap. In general, neither of these has the élan of funk; disco is too bland, rap too strident. But the real problem may be the medium.

Consider this TV commercial for a line of portable radios.

A black couple sits on a stylized Harlem stoop, wishing they had some music. As if in answer there descends from the heavens a giant portable radio. From the radio emerges, first, the music of Earth, Wind & Fire, and then Earth, Wind & Fire itself, the members of the band, boogying. The conceit seems innocent until one notices what these musicians are playing: not instruments, but portable radios. Commercials, even in their wildest flights of Escheresque fancy: are calculated. This particular commercial has its grip on two deep facts, the mechanical quality of the music (it does not seem to be made by people—though this band may be the wrong one to accuse) and the solipsism of the listeners.

One damp afternoon some summers ago I stumbled on a jazz concert at the bandshell in Central Park that featured some popular hard-bop-going-on-fusion musicians. It was being broadcast live on WRVR and had managed to lure to the band shell's muddy vicinity a sizable audience that was mostly young, middle class, and black. Some of the younger and less middle-class listeners were carrying radios and some of the radios were on, tuned to WRVR's broadcast of the concert. This was odd, for though the sightlines to the stage were ragged the sound was loud and clear—unless you were standing near one of the radios.

Chapter Six

The Cyrano Machine

A Trobriand Islander told Malinowski, "The throat is a long passage like the *wila* (cunnus) and the two attract each other. A man who has a beautiful voice will like women very much and they will like him." The ethnographer, who had heard many stories of seduction by song, observed that "in the Trobriands, as with us, a tenor or baritone is sure of success with women." Not every man can be so lucky; not every man can have a velvet throat or the knack of unpacking his heart in lyrics. Failing that, he must find either a Cyrano to stand in the shadows beneath the balcony, or a phonograph.

The role of proxy troubador that Rostand gave Cyrano was an apt one, for it appears to have been the historical Savinien Cyrano de Bergerac who first conceived of the phonograph. In a science fiction novel published in 1656, *Histoire comique des états et empires de la lune*, he described the inhabitants of the moon, their peculiar speech—a wordless but articulate music—and their books.

At the opening of the box I found something in metal almost similar to our clocks, filled with an infinite number of little springs and imperceptible mechanisms. It is a book indeed, but a miraculous book without pages or letters; in fine, it is a book to learn from [in] which eyes are useless, only ears are needed. When someone wishes to read he winds up the mechanism with a large number of all sorts of keys; then he turns the pointer towards the chapter he wishes to hear, and immediately, as if from a man's mouth or a musical instrument, this machine gives out all the distinct and different sounds which serve as the expression of speech between the noble moon-dwellers.

Cyrano seems to have in mind an elaboration of the music box of his day, but several elements point forward to the early phonograph. His box is a windup mechanism with a pointer something like a tone arm or needle. It is equipped with "ear pendants." Above all, it is a talking machine—a talking book, as Stevie Wonder called one of his own records.

Rostand presumably read some of Cyrano's works, and his play was published in 1897, just when the Pathé brothers were hitting their stride; but it would be far-fetched to suggest that he sensed a connection. Still, contemporary portraits confirm the great nose, and Cyrano really did fight duels over it. Surely the pathos was there, the pathos of a poetic voice that is better off disembodied. Cyrano would have been a natural for making records (as his fictive friend Christian, with the good looks and no talent, would have been a natural for playing them). He seems to have wished that women and men of the future could know him, not by his face or his black-and-white words, but by his voice. For in his lunar Utopia, with its talking books, "you have continually about you all great men, living or dead, and you hear them *viva voce.*"

As a youth in Naples, Enrico Caruso "was frequently called upon to offer a serenade to young ladies on behalf of their unmusical fiancés" (according to Howard Greenfeld). After 1902 he was able to do this more efficiently with the aid of the machine Cyrano had conceived, and for many years his voice was the voice of the talking machine. But it was above all in popular music that Cyranos proliferated. *I'd like to thank the man who wrote the song/That made my baby fall in love with me.* This lyric has been said to sum up the subjective economics of pop music. We need add only that the performer, too, gets his share of thanks. "The popular song, like an unseen Cyrano, provides love phrases for that speechless Christian, the Public. And the Negro, a black Cyrano, adds lust to passion." Thus Dr. Isaac Goldberg, writing in the Harlem Renaissance vein of the twenties. He credits the importance in pop music of such "oppressed nationalities" as the Negro and the Jew to their reputation for "passions less bridled than those of the . . . Anglo-Saxon." But this neglects the role of the phonograph. It was the phonograph that allowed the Jew, with his cartooned Cyrano nose, to sing his heart out without offending the gentile eye. That goes double for the black Cyrano, whose original in literature is Othello. How did the Moor cause Desdemona "to fall in love with what she feared to look on," if not by singing the blues?

My story being done,
She gave me for my pains a world of sighs;
. . . And bade me, if I had a friend that loved her,
I should but teach him how to tell my story,
And that would woo her. Upon this hint I spake:

and proposed marriage, catching Desdemona's hint but missing her society's—that in the natural order of things the Moor should content himself with playing Cyrano to a white suitor.

Things have changed some since Othello's day, but not much. Miscegenation is still frowned on, and the black musician is still supposed to be invisible. (Most rock video channels show white bands almost exclusively, whereas rock and roll radio has been relatively integrated almost from the start.) But what progress has been made in this century can be attributed in part to records. On records the black musician was no longer a minstrel with shining eyeballs, but simply a musician. A Ma Rainey record looked just like a Patti record. If invisibility betokened the fallen estate of the black man, it was also his main chance to conquer. And that is just how the black sensibility did—to a degree—conquer America.

If one's intention is to seduce, it is convenient that Cyrano be not only unseen, but out of the way entirely. A machine accomplishes this trick. Moreover, in any conjunction of man, woman, and machine the machine lends its operator a quantity of sexual horsepower. But this particular machine has a sexual imagery of its own that is hard to miss. The spindle, tone arm, and needle are plainly phallic ("ploughing the furrow" is a sexual metaphor that goes back to Sophocles) while the moonlike disk is feminine. With its concentric circles, it is the front view of a cartoon breast (connoisseurs of Westminster Gold album covers may remember a photograph of a woman hiding her nakedness behind twin disks). In each of the years 1957 to 1961, coincident with the rise of rock and roll, there was at least one *Playboy* centerfold with records as props. However crude, such analogies should not be ignored. Curt Sachs cites Richard Thurnwald's report that "in New Guinea, sacred bamboo flutes, up to six meters long, are actually used as penes for ritual cohabitations with the chieftain's wife; they are played in the forest while a widow is compulsory [sic] sleeping with a relative . . . and girls are deflowered in front of them in the ceremonial house of the village." It is doubtful that a tone arm has ever served as phallus, but the metaphor goes deep.

If the record and the record player take definite sexual roles, the rest of a stereo system is androgynous, like a car. Its power and size suggest virility, but it tends to be gentled and manhandled and spoken of as a she. This ambivalence goes back to the old phonographic horn: the trumpet, Sachs tells us, is primarily masculine (in some cultures "women who happened to see a trumpet were often put to death"), but a more cavernous or flowery horn takes on feminine meanings. Then there is the feeling that a man's mechanical and sexual skills are related, both having to do with making something hum. Robert Johnson, the Delta bluesman whom many rock musicians honor as a first ancestor, recorded in 1936 a song called "Phonograph Blues."

Yeah but she got a phonograph, but it won't say a
  lonesome word.
  (Repeat)
What evil have I done, what evil has the poor girl
  heard?
Yes but I love my phonograph, but I broke my winding
  chain
  (Repeat)
And you've taken my loving and given it to your other
  man.

We played it on the sofa
We played it 'side the wall
But my needles have got rusty, and it will not play no
  more.

It is not always clear which part goes where, but you get the general idea. One might dismiss this as another instance of the endlessly inventive innuendo that runs through the blues, in songs like "Feed Your Friend With a Long-Handled Spoon" and "It's Tight Like That." But that genre, even when it treats of impotence or infidelity, is essentially comic, while "Phonograph Blues" sounds stricken. Johnson never gives the impression of picking metaphors at random, and he evidently took sex seriously (as did his girlfriends, one of whom is supposed to have poisoned him fatally when he was twenty-one). But the metaphor could hardly have been random in any case, since the phonograph had already become the faithful ancilla of love, both amateur and professional. David Niven had discovered love in the arms of a West End prostitute while "Yes, We Have No Bananas" dinned in his ears; Billie Holiday had discovered jazz in a brothel; the pianist Olga Samaroff had learned from a Turkish officer that her records were played often in his father's harem in Constantinople; Garcia Marquez's hundred years of solitude had been interrupted by foreign harlots with their "magic mill"; and Christopher Isherwood had written in his "Berlin Diary" of a certain Frl. Kost who, asked how she spent her time with a Japanese client innocent of German "when they were not actually in bed," responded, "Oh well, we play the gramophone together, you know, and eat chocolates, and then we laugh a lot. He's very fond of laughing. . . ."

Why was the phonograph so useful to harems and brothels? To harems, perhaps because musical eunuchs were no longer easy to come by. To brothels, because music alleviates embarrassment but musicians (males at least) may augment it. Jelly Roll Morton recollected how in New Orleans he "worked in all the houses, even Emma Johnson's Circus House, where the guests got everything from soup to nuts. . . . A screen was put up between me and the tricks they were doing for the guests, but I cut a slit in the screen, as I had come to be a sport now, myself, and wanted to see what anybody else was seeing." It must have been grand to hear Jelly Roll himself play his "Animule Dance," or Tony Jackson his "Naked Dance," but obviously the johns would have been more comfortable with records, if there had been any jazz records then.

Frl. Kost provides a fine counterpoint to Johnson. They both think of sex and record-playing as species of talk, but Frl. Kost describes the comedy of fractured communication, Johnson the tragedy (*it won't say a lonesome word*). Frl. Kost suggests the pathos of the proxy sex object, Johnson the pathos of the proxy seducer (*You've taken my loving and given it to your other man*).

The risks are fairly symmetrical. Whoever uses records to seduce risks becoming a mere body, as the beloved goes on dreaming of Caruso or Eddie Fisher or Madonna. But the people who make the records spend so much time in the studio and on the road, trying to seduce the world, that they risk losing the beloved to simpler lovers (as Caruso lost Giachetta to his chauffeur). Such risks lend verismo to arias like "Vesti la giubba," and furnish endless matter for the blues.

Think of Don Giovanni. A typical night's business brings the Don and Leporello to the street outside Donna Elvira's. The master wants to go after the lady's maid, so he swaps cloaks and hats with his man. Leporello will divert Donna Elvira, but only after the Don, standing behind him in the shadows, serenades her. What a fine rococo variation this is on a theme that Rostand will simplify—Cyrano ventriloquizing for a dummy pretending to be Cyrano! But nowadays it's commonplace. A man will dress and talk like pop stars, play their records for women, and rather enjoy the charade (*La burla mi da gusto!*) even if down deep he feels used, a mere *buffone*. He will gladly change places with his master (even feign his master's voice) up to a point. Then he has the satisfaction of watching the Don dragged down by jealous women, vengeful men, and his own demons, and of singing along with the gossip columnists: *Questo è il fin/Di chi fa mal.*

When the twelve-year-old Mendelssohn offered to play for

Goethe the most beautiful music in the world, and sat down and played the minuet from *Don Giovanni*, the old sage ought to have been shocked—this being the background music for an attempted seduction, or rather rape. But much beautiful music is used that way. The moral here is that it's harder to use it that way without the phonograph. The Don is a capable amateur, but when he has his hands full he needs the help of professional musicians. Some help they are—a scream or two and they stop playing. Records are useful, then, even to people who can do their own serenading. Stokowski himself, in whose honor Philadelphia's music school came to be called the Coitus Institute, was a great believer in the records of Bela Babai, "the most erotic gypsy-style violinist."

Seduction can be romantic—what is more romantic than a serenade?—but suggests calculation. Even someone honestly in love must feel a little devious when, that first evening, he or she chooses the moment for turning the lights low and putting on soft music. The moment always teeters on the brink of bathos and sometimes falls in (as when Woody Allen in *Play It Again, Sam* casually gestures with an album and the record goes sailing across the room, or when Dudley Moore in *Bedazzled* has to get up off the rug to nudge his broken record of Brahms). In the true romantic situation, music spontaneously kindles or fans a mutual passion. It tends to be live music, or maybe the radio or a jukebox; the private phonograph is too human to be spontaneous. Perhaps a certain bit of music becomes "our song," like the Vinteuil sonata in Proust. Then the phonograph becomes an engine of sentiment, able to make the theme song well up behind scenes of passion, reminiscence, or reconciliation. But it has its drawbacks. Unlike a movie's soundtrack, real-life recorded music does not well up from nowhere. While radio offers serendipity ("They're playing our song"), putting on a record is a conscious gesture subject to mawkishness and irony. When a bellows of this size is turned upon a flame, it is liable to blow it out.

Unlike singing or tickling the ivories, playing a record turns "our song" into a rigid semantic unit whose statement cannot be modified to match new complexions of feeling. On record our song is framed, which means we are framed—framed as in an old photograph, the way we were or are supposed to have been. And framed as by false evidence, in the form of a recording that pretends to say exactly what we mean.

Stanley Cavell has written that we do not become involved in movies, "we involve the movies in us. They become further fragments of what happens to me, further cards in the shuffle of my memory, with no telling what place in the future." This is true of records, with the difference that records are shuffled not just in memory, but in the actual present, and they are shuffled at will. It's easy to cheat, easy to keep playing aces which at length must lose their value. So there are two reasons for protecting one's records with rituals and taboos: their inherent value and the value they acquire from significant fingerprints. I knew a couple whose anthem was a seventeenth-century setting of verses from Canticles. In the synagogue that scroll is chanted once a year; to this couple, Helmut Rilling's record of the chaste, ecstatic setting by Heinrich Schütz was so sacred that they played it just about that often. And this was their favorite record.

Records figure in the sex act before, during, betwixt, and after. The latter function was immortalized by Eliot:

When lovely woman stoops to folly and
Paces about her room again, alone,
She smoothes her hair with automatic hand,
And puts a record on the gramophone.

Two gestures of order and reassurance: as her hand soothes her hair, the tone arm soothes the grooves. As music soothes the waves—for the next line, "This music crept by me upon the waters," is from Ferdinand's wondering speech on hearing

Ariel's music ("Allaying both their fury and my passion," he goes on, "with its sweet air"). The phonograph reassures, but spuriously. It does not wait "upon some god o' the island." It is just an automatic hand.

Perhaps the phonograph helps us make sex itself mechanical. If it does play this role, it ought to play it most visibly on the dance floor, center stage of our mating ritual. Let us have a look at the prephonographic situation. In traditional cultures courtship is a family affair, and the dancing of young men and women (often without contact between them) is guided by society. By Jane Austen's day this has not changed much, except that an overwhelming concern with money and class makes the ballroom floor a huge Monopoly board. No one pays any attention to the musicians.

Now think of the Big Band years here in the States. Whitney Balliett writes: "There were lots of hustling black jump bands then (Sibbey Lewis, Erskine Hawkins, the Mills Blue Rhythm Band), but none of their recordings capture what they sounded like in front of dancers. They were driving and free and exultant. They were showing off for the dancers, and the dancers, in return, showed off for them. It was a fervent, ritualistic relationship that made the music as close to visual as music can be."

What is going on here will be clearer if we remember almost any dance floor scene from the Hollywood comedies of the twenties, thirties, or forties. The man and woman are just that—adults—and their romance is either independent of family and society or in opposition to these. But a sort of ideal society is implied, as in classic comedy (Cavell has drawn the parallel with Shakespeare). It is a society of autonomous individuals and their deep elective harmonies; it is represented, a few feet above the dance floor, by the band. A black band more forcibly suggests the pull of unhypocritical sex, but even a sweet white band suggests it somewhat. And all musicians are assumed to be free spirits, unafraid to solo but glad to harmonize. When they show off for the dancers, the musicians are celebrating this ideal society. When the dancers show off for them, they are proving their fitness for it. They are showing their virtuosity as couples in a universe of couples (the universe of Scott and Zelda, Nick and Nora, Hepburn and Tracy, Bogart and Bacall). No wonder the relationship is "fervent, ritualistic."

Enter the fifties. The jukebox, already common, now practically defines a kind of dance music. Rock and roll, however, is not the music of adults but of adolescents. They don't fantasize about nightclubs when they dance to recorded music, and they can't begin to imagine an ideal society. Their music celebrates the state of transition, of transportation, with no particular place to go. It is all about wheels, rolling stones, clocks, disks.

> Up to the corner and round the bend
> Right to the juke joint you go in
>
> . . . .
>
> Feeling the music from head to toe
> Round and round and round you go.
>
> Hail, hail rock and roll!
> Deliver us from the days of old!

Thus Chuck Berry in "School Days." There were songs about live bands, too, but these did not represent an ideal society so much as an ideal peer group. A band's relationship with the dancers might be fervent, even ritualistic, but without the promise of a larger society there was no resonance. There was uncertainty, stridence (why this insistence that Beethoven roll over?), a fear of becoming too pooped to pop. The presence of live musicians could even make the dancers a little uncomfortable, because it raised vexing questions: How old are they? Do they think we're punks? Do they think I look like a jerk when I'm dancing?

The heady new wine of sixties music needed bottles—records—to contain its bouquet. Audiences used to the painstakingly tousled productions of Phil Spector, Berry Gordy, or George Martin could not be expected to find local bands danceable. But popular recording stars were so popular that they were always booked in large auditoria, not dance clubs. People danced to records, at discothèques and parties. In the late sixties there was a vision of an ideal society, but it was vague, and its vagueness was expressed in the dancing; no one really knew any steps. While no one would join the revolution if dancing were forbidden, the revolution made dancing seem a little less important. Fewer songs were written about it. There were quicker avenues to sex.

Disco brought dancing back, but only by abolishing the musician. It often transpired that a popular disco group could not appear live in any venue because it did not exist; it consisted of the studio musicians available for various sessions, a lot of equipment, and a producer. On occasion the fiction was dropped and the producer (Cerrone, for example) issued albums under his own name. But anonymity was preferred. The music was a sanitary product, untouched by human hands.

In a disco the dancers showed off, all right, but only for one another. There was no ideal society, no ideal peer group even, only an idealizing of the existing society, peer group, and self. All human predicates except body tone and wallet bulge were drained away. Sexual competition was as fierce as ever, but the class insignia of Jane Austen's ballroom and the witty semaphore of Leo McCarey's gave way to designer labels. (There really was a disco song, "The Greatest Dancer," in praise of a man who wears the finest designer clothes, from his head to his toes, Fiorucci, something, Gucci . . .)

It is an odd progression. Rock and roll had a boy's fascination with mechanical and rotary motion—rolling, spinning, twisting, screwing—that dancing to records doubly satisfied. Rock moved outward to embrace all life and preserve it in vinyl. Disco was a fake synthesis of the two trends, an electronic simulation of the organic. The syndrum mimicked the human heart, the "sweetener" mimicked strings, and the deejay, armed with beat-per-minute figures, calculated the stimulus progression as cannily as a Muzak computer—more cannily, because he could gauge the dancers' responses. Is this the kind of give-and-take Balliett saw in swing ballrooms, except that the musicians have given way to a single metamusician? Yes, if you think it irrelevant that the metamusician is in a control booth.

When discos went new wave, many began offering live music part of the time. Rock and roll revivalists approved the trend and spent a lot of time looking for danceable bands. But in practice when bands played, even obscure ones, people crowded the dance floor in front of the stage, hopping up and down but rarely dancing. Most people danced only during intermissions, when records were played.

People seem more comfortable dancing and courting to mechanical music. The charitable interpretation of this is that it lets them be alone with each other. The other interpretation is that it lets them be alone.

Chapter Seven

Glenn Gould

My generation might be forgiven for harboring a grudge against Glenn Gould, since he left the concert stage before we had a chance to hear him. In fact, we were too busy listening to his records to mind. His records proved to us that classical music was not all sentiment and decorum, dressing up for concerts and pleasing one's teacher; that it could be sharp-boned and lonely, giving the same ecstasy as a chemistry set, a chess game, or rain rushing the breach of a car window. And his writings, if we had noticed them, could have given us a little more of that ecstasy, along with some hints on how it might be understood.

Before Gould's death I had read only some of his liner notes and a charming sketch in *High Fidelity* about his favorite records. I knew that he had stopped concertizing, but I had no idea how elaborately he had worked out the reasons why. It was only an obituary by Edward Rothstein that alerted me to this, and to Geoffrey Payzant's superb *Glenn Gould: Music and Mind*, whose bibliography helped me hunt down the essays I wanted to read. Being well into my own book by then, I was a bit dismayed at how many of my pet ideas Gould had expressed earlier and with more authority. Since then Tim Page, a music critic and friend of Gould, has had the good sense to collect nearly all Gould's published writings—essays, reviews, profiles, satires, liner notes and anomalies—as well as interviews with Gould by Gould, Page and others and snippets from Gould's enormous output for radio and television.

Gould had a horror of art as it exists now, art red in brush and baton. His most fascinating essays sketch an alternative world in which, by the grace of electronics, "the audience would be the artist and their life would be art." Although it sounds eccentric, his thinking stems from sturdy local tradition—from Marshall McLuhan and the theologian Jean Le Moyne, from the hard pews of Protestant Toronto, from the whole feral, cabin-febrile North. Scattered in a vast, cold country, Canadians are as grateful for technology as Americans were a century ago, and perhaps as suspicious of art.

But Gould's view of art goes back to a man he never mentions, Plato. "The purpose of art is not the release of a momentary ejection of adrenaline but is, rather, the gradual, lifelong construction of a state of wonder and serenity"—except for the chemical, the sentence could almost be Plato's. To Gould, the catharsis that was Aristotle's prescription seems much too dangerous. But something not unlike this is the regimen of the concert hall, where the audience becomes a mob, the artist a demogogue or a martyr or a clown. Better is the physically distant, intellectually direct relation of artist and listener made possible by records. Best of all is the situation in which the artist disappears and the listener, shaping the music to his environment and his "project at hand," becomes the artist. When music becomes more fully "a part of our lives," it will "change them much more profoundly."

Where Plato in the *Laws* has his citizens organized in choirs, each constantly chanting the song of virtue, Gould

wants them to stay home and play creatively with their phonographs. The intention is the same, but typically Plato puts his
faith in government, Gould in technology. Following Le
Moyne, Gould argues that "the charity of the machine," by
"distancing" us from one another and from the natural conditions that force us to compete, brings us closer to divinity. "A
war, for instance, engaged in by computer-aimed missiles is a
slightly better, slightly less objectionable war than one fought
by clubs or spears."

This is a question of taste. Probably more of us would
join Gould in preferring records to the lions-and-Christians
atmosphere of the concert hall. On the other hand, some
musicians find that concerts concentrate their minds wonder-
fully. And blood lust is only one of the needs that concerts
satisfy; there is also the need for public ritual and for a public
architecture of time.

For this "high drama of human communication" Gould
has no patience. "Art on its loftiest mission," he says, "is
scarcely human at all." I like this; I scent in it not only Plato but
the dank, heady odor of Schopenhauer, another ancestor
Gould doesn't mention. But it hardly follows that "the minis-
trations of the radio and the phonograph" will help "each man
contemplatively create his own divinity." In theory, a comput-
erized tape recorder may offer more opportunities for creativ-
ity than the kind of recorder people played in the Renaissance.
One might, as Gould suggests, construct one's own "ideal
performance" from several recordings of a work or from a
"kit" of the artist's alternate takes. In practice, though, most
people will just sit back and listen, or at best string together,
with all the artistry of sausage-packers, cuts from their favorite
records. For every Wendy Carlos there will be a thousand
Walter Mittys. My point is that in making certain high terrain
trivially accessible, technology does not always impel us to go
higher. So it's understandable that Cage, who starts from a
Thoreauvian mysticism similar to Gould's, comes to a different

conclusion: "Remove the records from Texas/and someone/ will learn to sing."

Gould argues that when, at last, everybody is an artist, the artist will be a nobody, a specialized cell in the great electronic network. This ideal of medieval anonymity for the artist is fantastic; it would have been fantastic in the Middle Ages. Even then the artist did what he could to keep his name alive despite the indifference of church and court. But church and court wanted servants; the public of the electronic age wants stars. To blame this, as Gould does, on promoters and publicists is unfair. The impersonality of the electronic media is what makes the public crave "personalities": "distancing" is what makes closeness, however bogus, a crying need. It was Gould's practical grasp of this fact that made his own oddball career possible.

It may be that some classical musicians will successfully follow his example, marketing themselves as personalities without appearing in person. But the economics of recording are not charitable to serious musicians, so most will probably have to keep concertizing. And Gould, in his heart of hearts, may not really have expected all the young musicians to follow him into the studio, any more than Thoreau expected America to follow him into the woods. His recitals had set an example for younger pianists, but the purifying of performance that he had begun could be completed only by an act of negation. One could even say, without irony, that Gould served the concert stage best by leaving it: as he wrote of Schoenberg, "whenever one honestly defies a tradition, one becomes, in reality, the more responsible to it."

But one never knows, or one knows only later. History may conclude that Gould was the one sane musician of the century; and his colleagues who work the continents like traveling salesmen, unpacking their hearts from Altoona to Vancouver, may seem as pathetic to our grandchildren as the bowing and scraping geniuses of the eighteenth century seem to us. In this sense, Gould may prove to have been our Beethoven. However that may be, it is too bad that Gould's morbid interest in the death of live music should have drawn attention from his tidings that a new art, the art of recorded music—what I call phonography—had been born. Gould was right to believe that the center of musical gravity was now the spindle hole. He was right to insist that recorded music be viewed not as a reproduction of the concert but as an independent art, as distinct from live music as film is distinct from theater.

Yet even this battle was perhaps being fought—by Gould, John Culshaw, and a handful of others—on the wrong turf. It had already been won in the realm of popular music, where a concert is often a promotional appearance in which one attempts to mimic one's records. Concert music, on the other hand, belongs by definition in the concert hall. And most of its repertoire is written out note for note, leaving the phonographer only so much leeway. One of the effects of recording is, of course, to break down the walls—all music is leveled on the flat, flat disk. Still, Gould was an odd apostle of phonography, for as a classical pianist he could not construct records as ambitiously as people like Stokowski, Stockhausen, Phil Spector and Frank Zappa could. His contrapuntal radio documentaries—above all the trilogy *The Idea of North*, in which three or four people who never met in life may talk all at once over a basso continuo of surf—were his only real efforts at "composing" on tape. But Gould was well equipped for his role as phonographer by a Platonic conviction that truth in art must take a back seat to goodness, or to a truth that is formally and morally higher. The splice was Gould's noble lie.

Gould did not use the splice, as most pianists must, mainly to correct mistakes. He used it to weld numerous takes, all correct, each different, into a structure that would stand up to repeated listening. He did not fear the "non-take-two-ness" of concerts any more than the next pianist, but abhorred it as "antimusical." This too is a matter of taste. Some performers are more unnerved by microphones than by faces. Some positively need an audience (when Pachmann recorded, Gaisberg "marshalled into the studio a score of our prettiest typists"). Some play better in long takes than short ones (although the old saw that a splice is always detectable was blunted by an experiment Gould did in which musicians and engineers had worse than random success in guessing where he had spliced his records). In the end, there is no escape from performance; even a writer alone with his pencil is performing, and might as well be on a high wire for all the security he feels. We all deal with this as we can. But to dismiss Gould's thinking as a rationalization of his neuroses—to say that he squirted ink as camouflage, like a squid—is foolish. Of course he listened to his entrails. So does any thinker worth a damn. "You don't feel," Gould asks, "that a sense of discomfort, of unease, could be the sagest of counselors for both artist and audience?"

Gould was not comfortable with everything and anything electronic. In his central essay "The Prospects of Recording" he quotes Father Zossima's "astonishing preview of electronic culture": "There are those who maintain that the world is getting more and more united . . . as it overcomes distance and sends thoughts flying through the air. Alas, put no faith in such a bond of union." Through simultaneous transmission, Gould says, the art of an often isolated land such as Russia— "a splendid Shangri-La for the most extraordinary artistic experiments"—becomes "rather too accessible." "We set aside our touristlike fascination with distant and exotic places and give vent to impatience at the chronological tardiness the natives display." So Gould, who admires Mussorgsky as well as Schoenberg and Strauss and Bach for their calm disregard of the *Zeitgeist*, finds McLuhan's concept of the global village "alarming." But as luck would have it, the homogenizing force of radio and television meets its match, Gould says, in the staying power of records. Because they survive to be played again, records breed tolerance and even eccentricity.

Oddly, he is also happy about background music, with its "exhaustive compilation of the clichés of post-Renaissance music." Because it "attempts to harmonize with as many environmental situations as possible" and "can infiltrate our lives from so many different angles," background music makes even modern idioms "an intuitive part of our musical vocabulary." So twelve-tone music, shunned in the concert hall, has crept into the public mind through the back door of the B-movie, and in this Gould finds hope for Schoenberg's vindication.

It is true that background music gives the listener "a direct associative experience of the post-Renaissance vocabulary," and a smattering of non-Western vocabularies as well. The problem is that the associations are all wrong. Muzak is nowhere near as neutral as it pretends. Workplace Muzak adds rhythmic and harmonic spice at intervals to pep the workers up. Public-place Muzak instills a feeling of flush, acquisitive well-being. Sound tracks are even worse. We associate atonality with horror and anxiety; this may help a score like *Wozzeck* to succeed but dooms much of Schoenberg and Webern, whose attempts at serenity seem guilty by association. In the same way, the language of Debussy comes to express only sensuality, the language of Mozart only old-world grace, the language of jazz only insouciance. Each language is reduced to a couple of phrases, and with our huge vocabulary we cannot say anything, we can only quote. The alphabet soup that the mass media (including records) make of good music quickly spills back into the world of good music. Soon our best composers find that they cannot speak, or can only speak in quotes, ironically or pathetically. I am not sure that this is the inevitable result of records and radio and the vast vocabulary they force on us—although it does seem to have appeared, for example in Stravinsky and Weill, almost as soon as those media appeared. But certainly it is what happens when mass culture dominates those media. So I am less optimistic than Gould, and much less optimistic than Varèse or Stockhausen or David Amram, about the prospects of a world music. "No more walls" is a fine slogan, but not if you want to build a home.

Gould, however, was the rare bird that could nest happily in the chaos of the airwaves. He often kept the television and radio going—both of them—while he wrote or played. He had the art of fugue, the art of finding freedom in the arms of necessity. And he seems to have felt the wrangling channels of the media as a kind of great fugue. What he loved about fugue was its "intense subjective concentration upon the concerns of the moment"—not this fugue or that fugue but *the* fugue, the endless process, which the individual tunes into or out of at will. Edward Said has connected Gould's "contrapuntal vision" with that of Mann's Doctor Faustus: the fugue as will-to-omnipotence, as a way of playing God. Of course Gould had that will in him, but his whole philosophy rejected it. And the fugue was not a way of asserting that will, but of transcending it. His way was not Leverkühn's, but Bach's—the way of the mystic, the mouthpiece of the Lord. Gould did not play God. God played him.

Chapter Eight

Phonography

The word "record" is misleading. Only live recordings record an event; studio recordings, which are the great majority, record nothing. Pieced together from bits of actual events, they construct an ideal event. They are like the composite photograph of a minotaur. Yet Edison chose the word deliberately. He meant his invention to record grandparents' voices, business transactions and, as a last resort, musical performances. The use we put it to now might strike him as fraudulent, like doctoring the records.

One might compile a whole lexicon of deceptive phrases connected with the phonograph. When we hear a familiar voice on a record and say, "That's Bing Crosby's voice," do we mean his actual voice or a copy? We say, "Hey, is that a phoebe? No, it's Mort. Very funny, Mort." Then Mort says, "That's the sound of a phoebe," and we agree. We can say that Mort and the phoebe make exactly the same sound; or that Mort when asleep makes exactly the same sound as a pneumatic drill. Any two sounds that sound exactly the same are the same sound, even if they come from wildly different sources.

This goes for the synthesis of sound as well. If you hear a Moog-synthesized clarinet you can say "That's the sound of a clarinet" but not "That's a clarinet." And it certainly goes for the phonograph. If you hear a sound and say "Is that a clarinet I hear in the next room?" I can answer, "No, it's a record." If you say "That's the sound of a clarinet," I can only agree. How could I call it "the sound of a record"? There is no such thing.

Or is there? "How would you like to hear music at home the way the engineer hears it in the studio? The Magnavox Compact Disc. . . . It's like being in a recording studio." From a traditional point of view this advertisement is astonishing. The ideal is no longer live music, but some technologic Platonic form. But this makes perfect sense in terms of phonography, particularly the pop variety. Rock music in concert tends to sound like a crude impersonation of a record.

One is supposed to judge a stereo system by comparing its sound to live music. If the music one listens to is pure phonography—a pure studio product—that is impossible. One must either rely on laboratory measurements, or follow one's tastes without regard for accuracy. The first course is unsatisfying; the second is general among pop listeners and is said to have produced a vogue of "artificial" sound—excessively bright, with an emphasis on the extreme treble and bass—among speaker manufacturers. But if producers use these as studio reference speakers, then these are the proper vehicles of their sonic intentions.

Even in the classical sphere, live music is only one touchstone of recorded sound. Fidelity itself is a vexatious concept. A producer might attempt to make a record in Carnegie Hall that, when played back in Carnegie Hall, would fool a blindfolded audience. To do this he would have to remove most of the hall's natural resonance from the recording, lest it multiply itself and muffle the music. The resulting record would sound dismal in a living room. The orchestra would not sound like an orchestra, because it would lack the associated ambience. Yet it would be faithful, in a sense, to the original. On the other hand, a record that captures all the resonance of Carnegie Hall may overwhelm the average living room. So most studio recordings try to strike a balance.

In Conan Doyle's story "The Adventure of the Mazarin Stone," Holmes leaves a couple of suspects to their own devices in one room, telling them he is going to play the violin in the next. As the strains of Offenbach's "Barcarolle" drift in, they discuss their caper and bring out the loot for inspection; whereupon Holmes leaps from concealment, revolver in hand. "But, I say, what about that bloomin' fiddle! I hear it yet," the brawn of the operation exclaims. "Tut, tut! You are perfectly right," says Holmes. "Let it play. These modern gramophones are a remarkable invention."

This is not the most elegant of Conan Doyle's devices, and when we think of the Edwardian gramophone it seems idiotic. But the common ear of the day really was gulled by records. Under the right circumstances, with the right music, the effect was *trompe l'oreille*. In 1913 Edison staged a series of Tone-Test Recitals designed to prove that "the Edison Diamond Disc's re-creation of the music cannot be distinguished from the original." Audiences would first hear Maggie Teyte herself singing "Believe Me If All Those Enduring Young Charms," then her phonographic replica, and evidently many agreed that "there was no difference between Miss Teyte's voice and the New Edison RE-CREATION of it." Yet decades later Beecham could say, "Improvement in the gramophone is so imperceptible that it will take quite 5,000 years to make it any good." Today's digital sound leaves some listeners pinching themselves, convinced they're in the concert hall, while others are horrified. Each side has a battery of laboratory tests to cite.

...lity of recorded music has been a subjective mat-
... has been more so. Menuhin says the old shellac
...... nattering to violinists, varnishing over the scratches
and squeaks. Cynics may think he is trying to varnish over the
loss of his technique; but Fred Gaisberg long ago noted that
"the velvet tone of Kreisler's violin, for some unknown reason,
was best in those old records and has never been recaptured
by the electrical process." He added that "in some ways
acoustic recording flattered the voice. A glance at the rich
catalogue of that period will show that it was the heyday of the
singer." When in 1928 an electrically amplified phonograph
was introduced to Compton Mackenzie's island, his wife
"found this new noise quite unbearable, though it was the
latest thing and first-rate of its kind. . . . Amplification spells
vexation . . . but I soon got used to it, and even enjoyed it,
which may or may not be a good thing. The Editor was enthu-
siastic . . . but I sometimes came in and caught him playing
that old Balmain." In 1930 Mackenzie wrote of the new micro-
phone-made records, "I do not believe that any audience
could sit still and listen nowadays to hours of electrical recording and remain sane." In fact, the acoustical phonograph did
have a sound, warm and wooden and all its own. It was an
instrument in its own right. Accurate or not, that sound was
what people had come to expect from a phonograph.

But the unperfected electrical record also had its charms,
even the very worst examples, such as Toscanini's output from
Studio 8-H. Until the forties he could not conceive how the
phonograph could give anyone pleasure. His son Walter recalled the Maestro's annoyance: "That must be a flute, because a violin cannot do that. But—it does not sound like a
flute!" Convinced that records could never sound good anyway, he was the victim of vile engineering, which he often
aggravated (according to B. H. Haggin) by choosing a musically perfect but indistinct take over a less perfect but clear
one. Yet the sound that emerged even from 8-H, and certainly

from Carnegie Hall and Philadelphia, bore his stamp. For those of us too young to have heard him live, that sound has its own austere beauty. Haggin says his live sound was "radiant," but on record it is nothing like the sun; it is a perfect play of light and shadow, but without color, like a very bright moonlit night. (The sound matches those Hupka photographs on the earlier reissues, the molten white face against black. The face and the sound, so strikingly matched, make him one of the icons of phonography.) To what extent was this the live sound of his orchestra, and to what extent the artifact of incompetent engineers? I can't know and don't really care, any more than I care about the colors of the blouses and smocks of Cartier-Bresson's peasants.

There are two ways to make a record seem "alive." One is live recording, which sometimes conveys a real sense of occasion, through the spontaneity of the music-making and through accidents of ambience (as tawdry as coughing, as serendipitous as church bells at the start of a Richter Debussy recital). But sometimes a live recording sounds embalmed; whatever animated the concert seems to have escaped. The other way to make a record seem alive is to step up the use of studio techniques. Aggressive mixing and overdubbing, especially in rock, can give a sense of conscious intelligence and so of life.

These polar approaches have their counterparts in the cinema. Live recording is analogous to filming a stage play. True studio recording is like movie-making as we usually understand it, and as Walter Benjamin has described it: ". . . In the studio the mechanical equipment has penetrated so deeply into reality that its pure aspect freed from the foreign substance of equipment is the result of a special procedure. . . . The equipment-free aspect of reality here has become the height of artifice; the sight of immediate reality has become an orchid in the land of technology."

Even "live" recordings are not tamper-proof. The liner

notes to Odyssey's reissue of *Oedipus Rex* under Stravinsky applaud his "wise decision to incorporate the author's voice and to make of this first recording an authentic historical document." In this case history has been doctored, for "the present recording was taped in . . . Cologne, in October, 1951. M. Cocteau's speeches were dubbed in from a Paris performance eight months later." So authenticity, too, is a tricky concept and gets trickier by the moment as Bernstein overdubs his live Beethoven cycle from Vienna—so live that it ran on television—in the manner of a pop musician.

I want to explore further the parallel with film, which is the linchpin of my argument for calling phonography an art. But first let me deal with a weaker alternative claim, namely that phonography is merely a medium.

People call television a medium, film an art form. One reason may be that it is possible to broadcast a film on television without exercising any artistic judgment. You can't film a play without exercising some artistic judgment, at least in the matter of camera angles (and if you hold the same angle, full stage, for the whole thing you don't get a filmed play, you get a sedative). Similarly, you can't record a concert in a professional way without exercising artistic judgment. There is an illusion that you can, because sound is less directional than sight, its limits less rigid. But in fact a recording engineer or producer who doesn't know the score—where the kettle-drums enter, where the trumpets release—cannot do an adequate job.

These things are relative, and insisting on one's classifications is like making a sand castle and standing guard over it. Artists use the word "medium" to describe very specific vehicles, like gouache or the string trio. And the word "art" is best used in the singular, if at all. Once you break art down into arts you are playing with derivations, historical gossip, which Muse slept with whom. Still, it may be useful to pursue certain analogies. Phonography is to radio as film is to television. Call the first in each pair an art, the second a medium. The medium draws on the art and on other arts, and on other cultural activities as well. Likewise, the magazine and the newspaper are properly called media, since they draw on the arts of fiction, poetry, and so on.

Prokofiev, one of the first composers to notice the creative possibilities of the microphone, had his eyes and ears opened for him by Sergei Eisenstein. Working on the score for *Alexander Nevsky*, he saw that Eisenstein's Mannerist camera angles might have tonal equivalents. Even the imperfections of recording equipment might have their uses: for example, the crackle produced by overload.

> Since the sound of Teutonic trumpets and horns was no doubt unpleasant to the Russian ear [the composer wrote], in order not to miss the dramatic effect, I have insisted that these fanfares be played directly into the microphone. Also, in our orchestras we have very powerful instruments, such as a trombone, and in comparison the more feeble sound of a bassoon. If we place the bassoon right near the microphone and the trombone some twenty meters away from it, then we will have a powerful bassoon and in the background a barely audible trombone. This practice can offer a completely 'upside-down' means of orchestration, which would have been impossible in compositions for symphonic orchestra.

Three microphones, a number unprecedented in Russia, were used in recording the *Nevsky* score. Prokofiev put the brass and the chorus in separate studios and at one point divided the orchestra into four groups, variously aligned with respect to the microphones. Declining the baton, he took to the control booth, where he would kibitz the mixer and occasionally take his place. Eisenstein later praised Prokofiev's "tonal 'camera-angles,' " meaning his orchestration—but the director must have been aware that much of the real orchestration had been done not on paper, but in the studio. He wrote: "The moving graphic outlines of his musical images which thus arise are thrown onto our consciousness just as, through a blinding beam of a projector, moving images are thrown onto the white plane of the screen."

Like film, phonography is a collective art, even if record jackets are less generous with the credits. Some contributions are deliberately disguised, like the top notes of Flagstad's Isolde, sung by Elisabeth Schwarzkopf, or the left hand of George Frayne's piano solo on a certain Commander Cody album, played by Roger Kellaway. But for the most part the small army of engineers, studio musicians and assistant producers that takes part in a typical recording is simply ignored. (A record is twelve inches across at most and should not look like a big production. Since it is experienced in private, the appearance of intimacy should be maintained.) In charge of this small army is the producer, who is the counterpart of the film director.

In the classical field there have been three distinct generations of producer. The type of the first generation was Fred Gaisberg, who began his recording career in Washington at the age of sixteen, playing piano behind the likes of John York Atlee, the artistic whistler. He became an assistant in Berliner's laboratory and soon thereafter was sent out to conquer the world—England, Italy, Russia, the Far East, whatever was out there—for The Gramophone Company. Short, mustachioed, infallibly gregarious, he charmed the world's great artists into performing for his machine, which he sometimes brought to their apartments. His conception of his role was not grandiose. He was an engineer and a businessman, charged with getting the best musicians to record and seeing to it that the disks were without serious blemish. But he was proud of having documented so many legendary musicians, proud of having made legends of some (such as Caruso) and proud too—although he would never have presumed to call himself an artiste—of having given his artistes an occasional bright idea. It was he who commended the "Volga Boat Song" to Chaliapin, "and together we conceived the idea of beginning the number softly, rising to a *forte* and fading away to a whisper, to picture the approach and gradual retreat of the haulers on the river banks." And it was Gaisberg who made the fruitful May-September match of Yehudi Menuhin and Sir Edward Elgar.

After Gaisberg came Walter Legge, an Englishman so obsessed with perfection that many pronounced his name as if it were German—a forgivable error given that his wife was Elisabeth Schwarzkopf and his "musical alter ego" Herbert von Karajan. Legge was the Franklin D. Roosevelt of producers, expanding the powers of that office from passive administration to artistic activism. "I was the first of what are called 'producers' of records," he wrote, and elsewhere explained:

> My predecessor in the recording world was Fred Gaisberg. He believed that his job was to get the best artists into the studio and get onto wax the best sound pictures of what those artists habitually did in public, intermittently using his persuasive diplomatic skill as nurse-maid and tranquilizer to temperaments. Having watched him at work, I decided that recording must be a collaboration between artists and what are now called "producers." I wanted better results than are normally possible in public performance: I was determined to put onto disc the best that artists could do under the best possible conditions.

For Legge there were three reasons why a record could be better than any live performance. The first was that the artist could keep at it, or be kept at it, until he got it right. When the young Schwarzkopf first auditioned for Legge in Vienna he "started her to work on a very difficult little Hugo Wolf song, 'Wer rief dich denn?' bar by bar, word by word, inflection by inflection, a song demanding changing emotions often on one syllable, one note: it was the beginning of the way we were to work together for the next twenty-nine years. . . . After an hour-and-a-half, Herbert von Karajan, who was sitting with me, said, 'I'm going. You are a sadist.' " Yet Karajan himself was as eager a masochist as Schwarzkopf, and his phonographic marriage with Legge as successful, to some ears. Legge was not a great enthusiast of cosmetic splicing ("tape has produced false standards"), preferring to work his artists until a perfect take of a section emerged.

The second reason records could be better was other records. When Legge got Schwarzkopf to London he put her on a superrich diet of historic disks, and she, who had never owned a phonograph, now hungrily gobbled up "Rosa Ponselle's vintage port and thick cream timbre and noble line; the Slavic brilliance of Nina Koshetz; a few phrases from Farrar's Carmen, whose insinuations were reflected in Schwarzkopf's 'Im Chambre separée'; one word only from Melba, 'Bada' in 'Donde lieta.'. . ."

Karajan had this habit from the start. "He is like a magpie," Legge wrote, "when he comes to the house to stay. He goes through all the piles of new records, takes them up in his room and plays bits through. 'Listen, what do you think of this?' 'Have you heard Munch's tempo for that bit of *La Mer*? Quite extraordinary. We must try that out some time.' "

Such eclecticism might be fatal to a performer who did most of his work in the concert hall. But in recording one has the opportunity to regard one's own work with this same detachment. An undigested hash of other people's interpretations will be audible as such to the artist himself, as it might not be in concert. Although his recording of a symphony is assembled from dozens of takes, he can sit back and judge the total effect. On the other hand, his ears may come to hear a succession of polished blocks as a structure. Gould, who wrote admiringly of the terraced, baroque thing that a phonographer like Robert Craft makes even of romantic music, was a great fan of Karajan and Schwarzkopf. To my ears, Karajan's records and live performances often seem contrived, like furniture expertly joined and polished. But artists of later generations, trained to the phonographic teat, have followed his example. If you want to make a definitive recording, this is one way to do it. (The practice is not universal. Jan DeGaetani told an interviewer: "I *never* listen to a record while I'm working on a piece—point of honor! I don't want to pick and choose ideas I like, I want to develop those ideas out of me.") Opinion is divided about Schwarzkopf also, although no one has ever accused her of making a sound she did not fully intend to make. (At a master class I attended, to a student who was pleased that something he had done "sounded free that time," Schwarzkopf said: "You are not free when singing lieder.")

Finally, Legge believed that records could be better because artists could have the benefit of Legge's artistic judgment, not only in shaping their own efforts but in the final product shaped from those efforts. Of his classic *Tosca* with Callas, Gobbi and de Sabata he recalled, "We used miles of tape, and when the recording was finished I warned de Sabata that I needed him for a few days to help select what should go into the finished master tape. He replied, 'My work is finished. We are both artists. I give you this casket of uncut jewels and leave it entirely to you to make a crown worthy of Puccini and my work.' "

Musicians were not always so appreciative. *Immer war Undank Legges Lohn*—"ingratitude was always Legge's lot"—is a paraphrase of Wagner that recurs often in Legge's memoirs and letters. It may be more than consonance or self-pity that makes Legge identify with Loge, who is the god of fire, that leaping medium of the divine will. Fire keeps Brünnhilde in ageless sleep—as the phonograph's spark keeps Ponselle, Lehman, Callas—so that she can jump generations and be the mistress of men born after her. Legge accomplished this for many, including his wife. While there may be a smidgin of perversity in that, it is what every painter, poet and director tries to do for his model or his muse. Yet Legge, like Loge, rarely gets the homage due an artist or even a great craftsman. The invaluable servant of the gods, he is hardly ever recognized as one of their own. But he has his revenge, for if his fire is what preserves the gods it is also what ruins them. In the age of the phonograph there are no legends, just audible facts; and there is no Valhalla, just a shelf that gets more crowded each day.

In later years, when straitened budgets and the spirit of democracy had squeezed Legge out of the studio, he worried that he and John Culshaw had no successors. But Culshaw, much the younger man, was in a sense Legge's successor, and as different from Legge as Legge had been from Gaisberg. Although admired for the size of his undertakings, in particular the Solti *Ring*, Culshaw was condemned by some for a production technique that brazenly (by classical-music standards) pulled out the stops of the studio apparatus. Where Gaisberg was content to take a sound photograph, Legge to extract the impossibly perfect performance, Culshaw wanted to make something entirely new: a record that was deeply and unabashedly a record.

His 1968 recording of *Elektra* with Nilsson and Solti became a *cause celèbre*, not because it was much more radical in its techniques than his other records but because it involved him in controversy with Conrad L. Osborne, the formidable opera critic of *High Fidelity*. To Osborne's ears, the album's graphic stereophony and "radio mellerdrammer sound effects" added up to a manifesto. "What it says, in effect, is that this recording stands in relation to a live presentation much as a movie stands in relation to a stage original: it . . . must be conceived in its own terms." But a real translation of this sort requires wholesale rewriting, which filmmakers are permitted but record producers are not. Instead of monkeying with the microphones, which is all he has left to monkey with, the producer should reproduce the audible half of the opera house experience as faithfully as he knows how. If this does not content him, let his company commission "an important composer to write a stereo opera—an opera conceived for phonograph listening exclusively." But existing operas, whose very sanity rests on the conventions of the stage, should be left alone.

A record—Culshaw responded—is heard in the home. It cannot duplicate the experience of the opera house, nor should it. At its best, the operatic recording offers an entirely different experience, one that is more intimate, more direct in its psychological grip. Not only can it make opera compelling to people who never go near an opera house; it can realize "the score in all its complexities," textural and emotional, more fully than is possible in an opera house. Like most composers since Wagner, Strauss "consciously or unconsciously, was looking to a future when opera would be liberated from the confines of inherited tradition and architecture. . . . We didn't want to make a nice comfortable recording for the canary fanciers to chatter about: we wanted it to hurt in the way Strauss meant it to hurt, and involve in the way Strauss meant it to involve."

The contest was a draw, as it had to be, since highly personal habits were at issue. Evidently Osborne when listening to an operatic recording liked to imagine himself at the Met; Culshaw liked to imagine himself "in the imagination," a mythic zone where emotions are so strong that speech emerges as song, murder as rhapsody. Where would the composer prefer to find his listener? Most operatic composers could not have posed the question. Britten, who recorded his own operas with

Culshaw, presumably sided with him, as I suspect the young Strauss would have done. In any case, it seems to me that recorded opera is a less artificial art than live opera. Not more pure, though; we do not listen to records in an imaginative vacuum, but in the rooms where we live our lives. Records take opera out of the realm of pasteboard convention and set it down beside the sofa, near the kitchen, not far from the bedroom, where its gruesome or inane devices resonate in strange ways.

Gaisberg, Legge, and Culshaw were active mainly in Europe. On the whole, the American classical recording community has been in the Culshaw camp for some time; indeed, the rolling dice in Goddard Lieberson's 1951 recording of *Porgy and Bess* antedated the taking of similar chances in European studios. And Lieberson went beyond Culshaw, by commissioning from Noel Coward a phonographic version of his musical comedy *Conversation Piece,* which Columbia released in 1951 ("I must beware of this modern medium/Long-playing records *can* spell tedium"). In orchestral music American producers, such as Columbia's Andrew Kazdin, have used closer miking than the Europeans, spotlighting the instruments; the stereo image is more graphic and there is less ambience, although echo may be added selectively. To European critics the results seem either clinical or souped-up, but in any case artificial. Americans respond that "enhanced" balances are justified by the lack of a visual element: when concert audiences are tested, positioned Janus-wise, those facing the stage say the balances are fine, while those facing away say they can't hear the second violins.

Such matters as recording balance may seem trivial from the point of view of art. What difference can they make to the whopping power that marks a great performance, that only the artist himself can provide? One might as well ask what difference the hull can make to the movement of a ship. Matters of balance were important to Prokofiev and Stokowski, and both knew that at least half the action was in the control booth. Balance affects the listener's perspective, determining how and where the music shall draw him in. On some interpretations of music, the very ethics and metaphysics of a piece may depend on its balances.

The concerto affords a good example. This most overtly social of musical forms seems to have something to do with the relation between the individual and society. The soloist is the hero, obviously. Does the audience identify with the soloist, the orchestra, or both?

A concerto heard in the concert hall is like a crowd scene in the theater. We are invited to look at the hero through the eyes of the crowd. The soloist is a public figure; we hear his statements as public pronouncements, with an element of show. We see the virtuoso fingerings and are stimulated by their riskiness; in this, says Glenn Gould, we are as childishly sadistic as the crowd at a circus. When one does identify with the soloist, as eventually one does, it is by detaching oneself from the audience. A kind of analogy is worked out: he is alone in a crowd, I am alone in a crowd, we have something in common. Or he is in danger, I have been in danger, I feel for him.

On record, the concerto is a very different affair. It is like a crowd scene on film: we see the crowd through the hero's eyes. Immediately we are free to identify with the soloist's meditations—and they do seem to be meditations, not pronouncements. But this is less true if the recording balance between the soloist and the orchestra mimics the concert hall, with the soloist placed well back so that he is almost one of the orchestra. When a critic insists on this, it is as if a film critic should insist that all crowd scenes be shot from a middle distance. The result is neither the easy identification with the soloist that true phonography permits nor the more painful, perhaps more authentic sympathy of the concert hall listener for the soloist he can see.

In the classical field, the producer's authority is limited not only by the performer who has to approve the final mix, but by the composer who has written notes on paper. The popular composer, although more likely than the classical composer to be alive, is less likely to expect what he has written to be respected—if he has written it down at all. It is in the popular field, then, that the producer comes into his own. If the classical producer is like a film director who faithfully translates stage works to the screen, the popular producer more closely resembles the typical film director, who works from a sketchy script that he changes as he goes along. In the popular field, written notes or chords are about as important as written recipes in your *bubbe's* kitchen. The real cooking is done in the studio.

The genealogy of the popular producer is not easily untangled. It is hard, first of all, to find a single, distinguished founder of the line—unless this would be Edison, who was distinguished for half-deaf but delicate ears and fierce bad taste ("Who told you you're a piano player?" he is supposed to have asked Rachmaninoff). But it was Edison and his assistants who first talked bankable artists into standing in front of a horn and repeating a single number hundreds of times, while they fussed with the apparatus; and this was the original role of the producer. This evolved into a job like Gaisberg's, as much entrepreneurial and technical as artistic. But it was not until the early thirties that a figure of Gaisberg's stature appeared in the popular field. This was John Hammond, whose field trips in America, like Gaisberg's in Europe, turned up treasures: Bessie Smith, Count Basie, Teddy Wilson, Billie Holiday, and later Aretha Franklin and Bob Dylan. Gaisberg, however, recorded mainly written music, which in a sense was already recorded. What Hammond pursued was music in full flight—an oral tradition whose essentials could not be written down, and so could not be recorded at all except by means of the phonograph.

Pete Seeger (also signed by Hammond) used to repeat a saying of his father, the musicologist Charles Seeger: "A folk song in a book is like a photograph of a bird in flight." And this would apply even to a folk song recorded by the melograph, a fundamental-frequency analyzer invented by Charles Seeger that gives a much more accurate description of ethnic music than Western notation can give; it would apply even to a folk song recorded by the phonograph. An ethnomusicologist is concerned with the whole flight of a tradition. But Hammond, whose job often resembled the fieldwork of an ethnomusicologist like Charles Seeger or Alan Lomax, was concerned not with the whole flight, but with instants of rare beauty. What he was looking for was not the typical blues or jazz performance, but the exceptional one. By finding and stimulating these exceptional performances and making them permanent objects, he and his good colleagues turned folk music into art music. And his bad colleagues, by taking the typical and making it rigid, turned folk music into popular music.

At first it was not producers who did this but composers, arrangers, music publishers, performers, and the whole *brigade de cuisine* of Tin Pan Alley. It was not until the fifties and sixties that producers began to take a hand in shaping popular music. Sam Phillips, a middle-aged white engineer recording B. B. King, Howlin' Wolf and Junior Parker in his Memphis studio, wished he "could find a white artist who could put the same feel, the same touch and spontaneity into his songs." "He knew what he wanted to hear," Conway Twitty confirmed, "and everybody that walked into his studio—no matter what kind of music you sang—he'd push you in a certain direction." When Elvis Presley walked in he pushed him in the direction of up-tempo Negro blues, and the result was rock and roll. This, presumably, was an idea whose time had come and would have come with or without Sam Phillips. But the

Detroit Sound of the next decade was in large part the creature of producers, and could not have been created anywhere but in the studio. Berry Gordy, an automobile factory worker and song writer who started Tamla-Motown with $700 borrowed from his sister, applied the methods of the production line to music with great success. Gordy and his staff producers (among them Brian Holland, Lamont Dozier, Smokey Robinson and Harvey Fuqua) took eager inner-city talent, fed it with songs and studio arrangements, and drew forth a sleek sound that appealed both to blacks who aspired to suburbia and whites who wanted to escape it. This "Sound of Young America" was sufficiently well groomed that a teased accent or the hint of a moan could be thrilling. In its exploitation of the intimacy of the microphone, the glamour of high frequencies, and the dreaminess of an undifferentiated instrumental background, Motown was a true studio product, even though most of the featured artists were popular stage acts as well. And as such it was able to bring together listeners who would never have been found within earshot of the same stage.

Although technically an "independent," the Motown organization was in some ways similar to a Hollywood film studio, with a standardized production style. The first *auteur* among producers was Phil Spector, a singer and songwriter who moved into production in midcareer (at the age of twenty). The record company he founded in Los Angeles relied on a single arranger, a single chief engineer, a small team of session men, and a single producer whose name was featured on the record labels and embedded in the name of the label itself. In Philles' "little symphonies for the kids" groups like the Crystals, the Ronnettes and the Righteous Brothers were set adrift in a sea of kitsch—violins and saxophones, thunder and rain. In its urgent solipsism, its perfectionism, its mad *bricollage*, Spector's work was perhaps the first fully self-conscious phonography in the popular field. Like Glenn Gould, Spector was a recluse and eccentric; like Walter Legge he married his own creature, Veronica of the Ronnettes; and if these are blasphemous comparisons, they do point up certain phonographic traits.

Most of Spector's output was perfect trash, but his influence on his musical betters was immense. Frank Zappa (who had heard Varèse as well) and the Beatles (who probably had not) took up the construction of records where Spector left off, expanding from singles into albums and elevating kitsch into Dada. Spector later worked with the Beatles, together and severally, with mixed success. In their prime, the Beatles had their own ideas and needed a producer who would carry them out. (George Martin, who produced most of the great Beatles albums, was a superb engineer and practical musician, and his experience in doing comedy albums for the Goons must have been helpful in giving dramatic continuity to LPs like *Sgt. Pepper.*) Zappa was his own producer almost from the start.

The self-produced artist, the third type of producer in the popular field, is now the preeminent type. Several of these emerged from the Motown factory, notably Smokey Robinson, Marvin Gaye and Stevie Wonder, while the neighboring worlds of soul and funk yielded Curtis Mayfield and George Clinton. White musicians were slower to learn the studio ropes. Zappa was the pioneer, taking production credit on all but the first of his records; the credit on *Hot Rats* reads, "This movie for your ears was produced and directed by Frank Zappa." Like Chaplin, Orson Welles, or Woody Allen, each of these artists is at once author, actor and *auteur*. Some have gone further in this direction than any major filmmaker, playing all the parts on a record at once. If for Paul McCartney or Tom Fogerty this is a trick, for Mike Oldfield and Stevie Wonder it is a natural means of self-expression. Most of the men I have mentioned also produce other artists' records. They are often adept at helping an artist find his own voice, either because they tend to work with artists for whom they have some stylistic sympathy or because they know when an artist needs to be left alone. It was Zappa who, as producer, gave his friend Don Van Vliet the freedom he needed to make the first real Captain Beefheart album, *Trout Mask Replica*. And Brian Eno may be better known for the bands he has produced, such as Talking Heads, than for his own records.

There are other kinds of producers. There is the free lance known for a certain marketable sound, which for a price he will apply like a sauce to the work of a gamy band. There is the technician, neatly doing the bidding of technically ignorant pickers. There is the staff producer in the Motown tradition, cutting raw talent to fit the company last. There is the survival of Spector's type in the disco producer, whose "groups" may exist in name only, their identities diffused in a pool of studio musicians. And there is the survival of Sam Phillips's type in men like Jerry Wexler of Atlantic, who took Aretha Franklin from hapless Columbia, set her down in a Muscle Shoals studio, and tossed her "I Never Loved a Man (The Way I Love You)" as one tosses a lighted match at petroleum.

But finally it is the artist-producer, the musical creator whose impulse is to create records, who plays the central part in the development of phonography as an art. This is true even when the artist is not technically the producer; it is true in every field of music.

What are the causes of this impulse to create records? Let us take the hardest case first. The work of the classical composer is usually complete on paper. Money and fame he can win (if at all) by the operation of his pen, and by getting famous performers to play and record his works. What incentive can he have for recording them himself?

Marks on paper can be misinterpreted. A composer with unorthodox ideas about rhythm and sonority, whose work does not rest snugly within the German tradition of ideal music but has a strong sensuous element, will not want to give his performers too much rein. So it's not surprising that composers of the Russian and French empirical tradition have shown a lively interest in the phonograph. I mentioned Prokofiev. Rachmaninoff recorded much of his work, Ravel some of his. Strauss and Elgar, who committed much of their work to disk, were not French or Russian but *were* explorers of orchestral color. Stravinsky, the first composer to undertake the recording of all his own works, wrote that his records for Columbia "have the importance of documents which can serve as guides to all executants of my music."

When the composer is the performer, what the recording records is nothing less than the composer's intentions (assuming he's a good performer). He becomes a phonographer; if he is not composing in the recording studio, he might as well be. He is free to disregard his own markings but compelled to specify them—to indicate phrasing, dynamics, and the like by demonstration rather than description.

But such a composer still writes and publishes his music, which he would not do if he thought no one could read or reproduce it. His desire to guide future executants of his music suggests a belief that there will be such executants, and a desire that there should be. From São Paulo to Tokyo there are pianos and orchestras, all more or less interchangeable. They can all play Beethoven, and with a few extra instruments they can all play Stravinsky. The common language is strained and stretched, but it holds. And the common language is a marvelous thing. It lets us talk to Bach, just as the language of mathematics lets us talk to Leibnitz; and the fact that we play Bach on a modern piano or cello is as trivial, from this point of view, as the fact that we do calculus with a computer.

But suppose one's interest in music were less abstract, more sensual; or, on the contrary, so abstract that one chafed at quarter notes, semitones, and the historical accidents that are the instruments of the orchestra. Suppose one wished to make music as directly as a painter paints. A painter would be outraged if he were asked to create a work by listing the coor-

The Recording Angel

dots and the numbers of standard colors, which we could then interpret by connecting the dots and coloring by number. But that is what a composer is asked to do.

It is possible that Stravinsky, if he had kept on the path suggested by *Le Sacre*, would have been the first to demand this painterly freedom and obtain it in some new form of phonography. He was, as I said, concerned to record his intentions on disk, and in 1925 he wrote a piano piece, the Serenade in A major, expressly for recording (Leoncavallo had written the song "Mattinata" for a record in 1904). More to the point, he wrote music for piano roll in which as many as thirty notes were struck at once. And mechanism (puppets, clockwork songbirds) is an explicit theme in his work.

As a neoclassicist, however, Stravinsky became more interested in narrowing and refining the range of sonority than expanding it. So the task of finding a painterly, even sculptorly freedom for music fell to a man who drank with Modigliani at the Closerie des Lilas, who introduced Cocteau to Picasso and who all his life was, as he said, "rather more closely associated with painters, poets, architects and scientists than musicians." In Edgard Varèse a number of powerful influences converged, among them the Romanesque cathedrals of Burgundy, where he grew up; the rugged organum of Pérotin, probably first encountered at the Schola Cantorum in Paris; the acoustical experiments of Helmholtz; two small sirens from the Marché des Puces with which he conducted his own experiments; the early works of Stravinsky; the definition of music by the Polish philosopher Hoene-Wroński as "the corporealization of the intelligence that is in sounds"—a definition, Varèse said, "which started me thinking of music as organized sound instead of sanctified and regimented notes."

Among the older musicians impressed by this handsome rebel was Debussy, whose open ear ("I conjure up all the music that there is," he is supposed to have said, "and then I leave out whatever fails to please me") made him, along with

Berlioz, the primary French influence on Varèse. Debussy objected to mechanical music but willingly recorded his own music on piano rolls, and a letter to Varèse helps explain why: "You are quite right to take up the piano . . . one is so often betrayed by so-called pianists. . . . You have no idea how my piano music has been distorted, to the point that I scarcely recognize it." In 1907 the pull of Strauss and Busoni brought Varèse to Berlin, where both men befriended him. To Busoni, Varèse was attracted less by the legend of his pianism or the reality of his music than by his vision of what music might become. In Paris, Varèse had read Busoni's *Sketch of a New Aesthetic of Music*, "and when," he recalled, "I came upon 'Music is born free; and to win freedom is her destiny,' it was like hearing the echo of my own thought."

In his book Busoni deplored the straightjacket that notation, the tonal system, and his own keyboard instrument had forced on the "infinite gradation" of sound. "For our whole system of tone, key, and tonality, taken in its entirety, is only a part of a fraction of one diffracted ray from that Sun, 'Music,' in the empyrean of the 'eternal harmony.' " "Every notation is, in itself, the transcription of an abstract idea. The instant the pen seizes it, the idea loses its original form." As a first step toward the infinite, Busoni proposed a system of whole tones divided into sixths, and suggested that the newly invented Dynamophone of Dr. Thaddeus Cahill, which he had read about in an American magazine—a primitive electric synthesizer on which "the infinite gradation of the octave may be accomplished by merely moving a lever"—might serve as a first instrument of the new music.

In Berlin, Varèse visited Busoni often, to speculate on the future of music and have his own music criticized, and the pianist—who might have fit Romain Rolland's description of Varèse as "a kind of young Beethoven painted by Giorgione," except that his eyebrows were milder and his gaze troubled, not fierce—was "as fructifying to me as the sun and rain and fertilizer to soil." Varèse was surprised, though, to find Busoni's "musical tastes and his own music so orthodox." It was as if Busoni felt the sun of "absolute music" but could not bear to look on it, as Varèse with his eagle eyes could do. Busoni did practice some of the radical things he preached, but not the ones that interested Varèse; and since Busoni's idol was Mozart, his music often sounded tamer than it really was. His antirealist theory of opera was better realized by Kurt Weill, a pupil in his private composition class, than by himself; his theory of absolute music, by his pupil Otto Luening and by Varèse.

In 1915 Varèse came to America in search of millionaires and scientists who would build him the new instruments he needed. "What I am looking for," he told the *New York Telegraph*, "is new mechanical mediums which will lend themselves to every expression of thought and keep up with thought." In the meantime he produced a series of works for existing instruments—instruments of the standard orchestra, and others that had never been heard of, in combinations and intensities that few listeners could stand to hear but that were heard, nonetheless, through the efforts of Stokowski and of the International Composers' Guild that Varèse founded. *Amériques* introduces a siren, a whip, and a "lion's roar," *Intégrales* Chinese blocks, sleighbells, chains, a gong, a tam-tam, and a slapstick. *Arcana* adds forty percussion instruments to a Wagnerian orchestra. *Ionisation*, dispensing with the orchestra, achieves sublimity with thirty-seven percussion instruments and nothing else. Having heard Dr. Cahill's Dynamophone in New York and having been disappointed, Varèse waited until 1933 to use electronic sound in a score. That score was *Ecuatorial*, in which the sound of two instruments built for him by the inventor Leon Theremin (replaced in a later version by Ondes Martinot) was juxtaposed, to magnificent effect, with a Mayan text chanted by bass voices. But this was still a far cry from what he had in mind.

"I find myself frustrated at every moment by the poverty of the means of expression at my disposal," he told an interviewer. "I myself would like, for expressing my personal conceptions, a completely new means of expression," he told another. "A sound machine (and not a machine for reproducing sounds). What I compose, whatever my message is, would then be transmitted to my listener without being altered by interpretation. . . . The principle is the same when one opens a book to read it." He proposed a musical laboratory in which musicians and scientists would explore the laws of sound and the possibilities of sonority, aided by "a collection of phonograph records as complete as possible, comprising the musics of all races, all cultures, all periods and all tendencies." The plan would be fully realized only with the opening of Boulez's IRCAM in 1977; the world of the thirties and forties had other priorities.

In 1937 Varèse stopped composing. In 1939, with the help of an engineer, he experimented with making electronic music by varying the speed of a phonograph turntable. That same year John Cage did the same thing in the first of his *Imaginary Landscapes*. Cage was composing, Varèse was not. "I do not write experimental music," Varèse once said. "My experimenting is done before I make the music. Afterwards, it is the listener who must experiment." Cage would later write that in some respects "Varèse is an artist of the past. Rather than dealing with sounds as sounds, he deals with them as Varèse."

The chance to deal with electronic sounds as Varèse arrived in the fifties with the tape recorder. When Varèse's approaches to the Guggenheim Foundation, Bell Laboratories, and various high-fidelity concerns had been repulsed, an unknown benefactor gave him a big Ampex machine. Instantly he set to work splicing together the electronic interpolations for *Déserts*, his work-in-progress for winds, piano, percussion and tape. At the invitation of Pierre Schaeffer, an advocate of *musique concrète* (the collaging of taped natural sounds, which

Varèse rejected as simple-minded, as he had rejected Futur-
ism), Varèse completed the tape sections at the laboratories of
French Radio. The first performance, with musicians of the
ORTF flanked by loudspeakers, was given in 1954 at the
Théâtre des Champs-Elysées and broadcast live in stereo.

By this time, Otto Luening and Vladimir Ussachevsky in
New York and Karlheinz Stockhausen in Cologne had produced several experiments in electronic music; but these were
experiments. Varèse, by contrast, had been making electronic
music in his head for half a century; the moment the tools were
put in his hands he knew what to do with them. *Déserts* expresses all the emptiness of those fifty years of history in a
language exploding with their fullness. And something like that
paradox is audible in the great electronic music produced
since, and in much of the great phonography. Stockhausen's
Gesang der Jünglinge of 1956 was perhaps the first worthy
successor of *Déserts*, and Morton Subotnick's *The Wild Bull* of
1971, commissioned by Nonesuch Records, perhaps the most
popular—both inspired, like *Ecuatorial*, by ancient texts. Like
Varèse's *Poème électronique* of 1956, these were works for
tape alone. Although audiences have on occasion been
obliged to sit in concert halls and stare at loudspeakers while
such works were played, most works for tape are meant to be
listened to on record or radio. Stockhausen has written:

> . . . I listen to such music best and my imagination is
> most free when I am alone, just listening, preferably
> with closed eyes in order to shut out the things around
> me too. Then the inner eye opens to visions in time
> and space which overstep what the laws of the physical
> world around us permit . . . . Electronic music has
> liberated the inner world, for one knows that there is
> nothing to be seen outside oneself and that there can
> be no sense in asking with what and by what means
> the sounds and acoustical forms are produced.

It should be noted that the *Poème électronique* was meant to be heard with the eyes open and looking at images projected on the many-domed ceiling of the Philips pavilion at the Brussels World Fair of 1958. Varèse's music migrated through four hundred loudspeakers, moving in space as he had wanted it to do fifty years before. The pavilion, on which Varèse's collaborators were Le Corbusier and Iannis Xenakis, was torn down after the fair. Varèse reconstructed a two-channel version of the *Poème* at the Columbia-Princeton laboratory, and this was released on record. In any case, records were of great importance in Varèse's career, particularly the LP of *Intégrales, Density 21.5, Ionisation* and *Octandre* recorded by Frederic Waldman under the supervision of the composer. This even found its way to La Mesa, California, where a thirteen-year-old named Frank Zappa stumbled on it while hunting for Joe Houston records.

Varèse's jagged tradition is not the mainstream of electronic music. That flows from the prettier creations of Luening and his colleagues, and it flows into the vasty pool of Muzak. As RCA's 1955 demonstration record did not fail to demonstrate, the natural voice of a synthesizer—the pure sine wave—is bland and simple, and the natural tendency of an audio engineer is to complicate it while keeping it bland. Alongside a version of Bach's Fugue in C minor, "synthesized in the style of a clavichord," that anticipates Wendy Carlos's version, there is a monstrous arrangement of "Blue Skies" overlaying dozens of redundant parts, each approximating the attack, decay, and overtone characteristics of some conventional instrument as blandly as a mannikin imitates a man. A typical instance of this tradition in "serious" music is Subotnick's 1969 Nonesuch commission, *Silver Apples of the Moon*.

Blandness of tone can be a virtue when the composer's interest is as mathematical as Charles Wuorinen's is in *Time's*

Encomium, a Nonesuch commission that won the 1970 Pulitzer Prize for music. One might argue that Wuorinen, Babbitt and others of the Columbia-Princeton axis are the legitimate heirs of Varèse's scientific concerns. But once these concerns are deprived of the urgency of myth, one can compose until one is blue in the face without convincing the average listener to share them.

Convincing the average listener is not one of Babbitt's priorities, as his 1958 article "Who Cares If You Listen?" makes clear (although the title was *High Fidelity*'s, not Babbitt's). Not incidentally, this article adds several to the list of reasons why contemporary composers might prefer phonography, especially the electronic sort, to concerts. First of all, the increased "efficiency" of modern musical language, where each " 'atomic' event is located in a five-dimensional musical space determined by pitch class, register, dynamic, duration, and timbre," demands "increased accuracy from the transmitter (performer)" and "creates the need for purely electronic media of 'performance.' " The main problem with concerts is not the performers, though. It is the audience. Even though advanced music, like advanced work in mathematics, philosophy and physics, is beyond the comprehension of the "normally well-educated" layman, " the amenities of concertgoing protect his firmly stated 'I didn't like it' from further scrutiny." The same layman "chancing upon a lecture on 'Pointwise Periodic Homeomorphisms' " would hardly get away with a pronouncement like that. Babbitt concludes that "the composer would do himself and his music an immediate and eventual service by total, resolute, and voluntary withdrawal from this public world to one of private performance and electronic media, with its very real possibility of complete elimination of the public and social aspects of musical composition." (If this sounds a bit like Gould, in one respect Babbitt is more realistic: he expects the composer to support himself not with recording royalties, but with a university post.)

Although Babbitt gives the impression that he uses records to escape an audience, he actually uses them to reach one—*his* audience. Qualified listeners are few and far between; by selecting his records they select themselves. The record listener can listen repeatedly. He need not hand down a verdict at first hearing by applauding or failing to applaud or hissing. He communes with the composer one to one, at an intimate distance; whether or not this is, as Gould says, the best way to commune with all musicians, it is a good way to commune with musicians like Babbitt. And modern composers who hope for a wider audience than Babbitt's know that records are their best hope.

Another thing the record listener can do is read the liner notes carefully, in conjunction with repeated listenings. The "efficient" language of modern music often needs glossing, which modern composers are often happy to provide. Liner notes reveal processes the naked ear might not detect; the more a piece depends on process or concept, the more important liner notes become. Sometimes the liner notes *are* the music, as in Alvin Lucier's *I Am Sitting in a Room*: the composer reads a text explaining the process, which is a matter of playing back and rerecording this explanation until the resonance of the room makes it unintelligible. When the music is pure concept, like Cage's *4'33"*, liner notes are needed but a record is not.

In general, modernist composers who want to make masterpieces—pieces, for that matter—believe in records. Stravinsky, Schoenberg, Varèse, Babbitt and Boulez are good examples. But modernist composers who think of their work not as thing but as process, involving chance operations, or improvisation by the performers, or ritual, or a "happening," are less comfortable with records. Cage condemns them. Stockhausen is ambivalent, as he is about so many things. He claims that he is not like Boulez who, "intent on living on in his works . . . strives toward autonomy . . . and . . . constantly tends to build up 'great works' from his store of experience and knowledge." Stockhausen's modest wish is to found a new oral tradition. Although his scores are often "open," the recordings he makes with his own ensemble are meant to narrow the range of future interpretation. Both Cage and Stockhausen were pioneers of electronic music, but both have devised means of variation and improvisation in the use of electronic equipment and of prepared tapes—for example, the use of the microphone and the electro-acoustical filter "as a musical instrument" by live performers in Stockhausen's *Mikrophonie II*, or Cage's manipulation of electronic controls in accompaniments to Merce Cunningham's dances. Stockhausen was the first composer to produce "scores" of his purely electronic works, which meant they could be realized independently and maybe a bit differently in another laboratory.

The composer's relation to recording is further complicated when he thinks of his music in terms of ritual, as Partch, Orff, Britten and sometimes Stockhausen have done. All of these composers have made or supervised recordings of their work. Britten to be sure, has complained that records short-circuit the traditional ritual of music in church and concert hall. But, his collaborator Culshaw argues that Britten's church operas ("in their original setting, the audience can almost touch the performers") are, like Stockhausen's *Gruppen* and Culshaw's own recording of *Elektra*, part of a rebellion against the proscenium arch. In other words, the dry husk of concert and opera ritual is being replaced by new (or renascent) forms, and one of these is the private ritual of records.

The case of Partch is more complicated still. Half his work in composing was the building of new instruments—freewheeling, sculptural variations on the marimba and the gamelan, producing weird microtones and swoops. Many of these instruments are one-of-a-kind. Since Partch's exorcistic, often parodistic rituals cannot be performed without them, they are in a sense ritual objects. The reproduction of their sound, whether it dissipates their ritual aura or not, is the only way Partch's music can be be widely heard. And this, as I said, is an important function of phonography: the transmission of music that falls outside the common language of the orchestra.

Conlon Nancarrow's *Studies for Player Piano* are another good example. Here is a medium of a kind that Mozart and Stravinsky toyed with, but Nancarrow is the first good composer to give his life to it. Mozart's three works for barrel organ "cannot be played on the piano without faking," as Geoffrey Payzant points out; some of Stravinsky's cannot be played even with faking; but just thinking of playing Nancarrow's rattles the brain. In composing each of his Studies he spends months punching carefully calibrated holes into paper rolls. For many years his works could be heard only by pilgrims to his home in Mexico City, where his two souped-up Ampico player pianos reside, or maybe on tape at a rare modern-music concert. (The expedient of reproducing the rolls themselves for playback on other player pianos, although logical, would not be practical.) Now these vertiginous, gelatinous marvels, whose unfolding is like the quick and dirty life of cells, can be heard on record.

As much as Partch's chromelodeon or Nancarrow's Ampico, the clavichord of Bach and the viol of Purcell fall outside the common language of piano and orchestra. We can play Bach and Purcell on modern instruments, and it is good that we can; but as we dig deeper into the past of music, that contortion feels more and more awkward. As the harmonic language becomes less familiar we become more apt to think of the music as sound, and more anxious to hear the sound of the original instruments. Now, if we had to depend on the proliferation of viols and clavichords, shawms and sackbuts in the small towns of the world, few of us would ever hear old music as it was meant to be heard. But we have records. The original-instrument movement is just as phonographic as the

new-and-original-instrument movement. It is the other side of
the coin. So one is not surprised to find in a 1955 essay by
Varèse his wish "to see revived the instruments for which
Monteverdi, Lully and their predecessors wrote." What are all
these original-instrument recordings, after all, if not wish-fulfill-
ment dreams dreamt by the phonograph? The ideal original-
instrument recording of a Bach cantata is the one Bach would
have made in the Thomaskirche.

Wandering America in the nineteen-teens, Jelly Roll Morton
sojourned in Houston. He was not sorry to leave, he later told
Alan Lomax, inasmuch as "there wasn't any decent music
. . . only jews-harps, harmonicas, mandolins, guitars, and fellows singing the spasmodic blues—sing awhile and pick
awhile till they thought of another word to say." Decent or not,
this is how country blues was generally sung up until the twenties, when it began to be recorded. Blues was an oral tradition,
like folk balladry or ancient epic. And it was even more open-
ended than these, because it was essentially lyric. If a blues
told a story it was not a legend, but something that had lately
happened and that accounted for the song's mood. The metaphors, the contumely, the plangent picking could go on as
long as the singer's invention held up.

When Morton played and sang a blues, the harmonies
were carefully distributed over determined measures for a determined number of stanzas. An insufferable classicist, he
knew the blues as an aspect of New Orleans jazz, in which
Creole and Negro traditions had joined to produce music at
once explosive and contained. When about 1908 Morton began "to write down this peculiar form of mathematics and
harmonics that was strange to all the world," the forms of jazz
solidified further. But no one—not Morton, and certainly not
W. C. Handy—wrote down the rural blues. Its forms solidified
only in the process of recording.

The "race records" market was discovered in 1920 when

Mamie Smith stood in for Sophie Tucker at an Okeh session, had an unexpected success, and was called back to record "Crazy Blues." Mamie Smith, Ida Cox, Alberta Hunter, Ma Rainey and Bessie Smith were vaudeville singers who did twelve-bar, somewhat citified country blues with the backing of a jazz pianist or a small band, and who on stage ended a number when they had sung all the relevant verses they could remember or invent. (Louis Armstrong, who recorded with Bessie Smith, said she "always just had her blues in her head, sometimes made them up right in the studio.") Confronted with the time limits of recording, many blues singers responded, Martin Williams writes, "by simply stringing together four stanzas on (more or less) the same subject; others . . . attempted some kind of narrative continuity." But a few singers "do more; they give each blues a specifically poetic development which takes subtle advantage of the four-stanza limitation and creates a kind of classic form within it." And so the ten-inch, 78 r.p.m. disk gave birth to the classic blues. Roughly the same thing happened to true rural blues after 1925, when Paramount first recorded an itinerant picker from Texas named Blind Lemon Jefferson. The "spasmodic blues" quickly got a grip on itself, and in a little over a decade the four-stanza form had attained the poetic density of Robert Johnson's "Hellhound on My Trail."

Blues remained an oral tradition, but the tradition was vastly expanded. Whereas Bessie Smith had needed to go on the road with Ma Rainey in order to learn from her, Victoria Spivey and Billie Holiday and Mahalia Jackson could learn from Bessie Smith by staying put in Texas or Maryland or Louisiana and playing her records. In the same way Johnny Winter could learn guitar from Robert Johnson when Johnson had been dead twenty years. And the tradition was no longer in unremitting flux: one could step into "Backwater Blues" twice, a dozen times, and find greatness in the nightmare equilibrium of Smith's calm voice and Fletcher Henderson's seasick piano (neither of which could be preserved on paper). Such permanence meant that blues could be viewed as art, and with the Harlem Renaissance underway it was. It also meant that later blues musicians were less free to use formulaic phrases as elements of a common vocabulary, because many formulas were now identified with classic records. Instead of simply using a formulaic guitar lick or metaphor, one had either to quote its canonic form or consciously vary it. Depending on who was doing it, that kind of conscious variation kept the blues straining in two opposite directions, toward high art and toward kitsch. One might say "toward jazz" and "toward pop," but that would not be fair; the tension continues *within* jazz and *within* pop.

Although blues provided matter for Tin Pan Alley (and received some worthwhile things in return) almost from the beginning of the century, it was not until the fifties that blues became the basis of popular music. The country blues that had moved to the city and discovered electricity was a clear and compelling form. It was ripe to be taken up by people like Presley and Chuck Berry, who pushed it toward kitsch, and by people like the Beatles, Dylan, and Zappa who pushed it, clumsily and with much backsliding, toward self-conscious art. In rock and roll the last traces of a true oral tradition disappear; the game of canonic variation—variations on the canon of "classic" records—is in full swing. (The logical extension is dub music, in which one invents multitrack variations on a single cut.) And the object of the game is the making of records—for some it is a matter of mass production, for others of patient, even obsessive construction. To say that rock is petrified blues is a bad pun, but not a pointless one.

The effect of records on jazz has been a bit different. Jazz was never folk music. From the start it was a very sophisticated, very urban sort of entertainment. From the start its audience was white as well as black. And almost from the start its audience, white and black, suspected that it was something re-markable, with a tincture of the demonic or the angelic that set it apart from all entertainment previously known. Since, how-ever, it was partly improvised and could not in its essence be written down, and since one usually heard it while under the influence of alcohol, lust, or gaming-table greed, one could never be certain about it the morning after. The musicians, of course, knew exactly what they were doing. They were very proud—as emulous as Greek heroes, and as mercenary. But before the twenties it could not have occurred to many of them that what they were doing might be something more than entertainment.

Given the opportunity to make a record, a jazz musician might be flattered. He would surely appreciate the money (not knowing how small a part of the likely profits it represented). He might jump at the chance to become famous beyond the range of his own travels, beyond even the range of legend. If, like most jazz musicians, he lived in a sort of musical Wild West where he was always subject to challenge by the new gun-slinger in town, he might welcome the chance to set down his achievement once and for all.

In 1917 the first jazz records appeared. They were cut by a white group, the Original Dixieland Jazz Band. (According to Johnny St. Cyr, Freddie Keppard had the chance to record first but refused, saying "he wasn't gonna let the other fellows play his records and catch his stuff." The story rings true: Armstrong recalled that in New Orleans Keppard "used to keep a handkerchief over his valves so nobody could see what he was doing.") In 1923 Jelly Roll Morton and King Oliver started recording, and two years later Louis Armstrong, who had played second cornet in Oliver's Creole Jazz Band, began his series of Hot Five records for Okeh.

Records and radio were the proximate cause of the Jazz Age. Because of them the white audience was no longer lim-ited to gamblers, gangsters and doomed young musicians (I

mean outside New Orleans; in New Orleans jazz had long
been played at genteel fraternity dances). Intellectuals and
society matrons who hesitated to seek the music out in its lair
played the records. Distinguished composers in Europe heard
the records and understood that the popular transcriptions of
"jazz" and "blues" and "ragtime" they had seen were wan
facsimiles. In the pages of *The Nation* and *The New Republic*
the latest Armstrong records were analyzed by classical-music
critics like B. H. Haggin. It was not that being on record con-
ferred respectability; since Edison's day plenty of junk had
been recorded, and its junkiness had only been confirmed
by repeated listening. But it turned out that the best jazz
was anything but junk. As Haggin later wrote, recording
"makes it possible to hear and discuss" improvised jazz performances "as one does a piece by Haydn or Berlioz." And
the respectability achieved by the records was passed
along to the live music, so that by the end of the twenties
black jazz bands could he heard in the stuffiest hotel ballrooms.

All this is well known. But I will argue that records not only
disseminated jazz, but inseminated it—that in some ways they
created what we now call jazz. It is important to remember, first
of all, that numbers were often "composed" just before a
recording session. As record companies did not like to pay
royalties unless they had to, published tunes were avoided;
but if one of the musicians came up with a tune, that came
under his flat fee. So even regular performing bands, when
they recorded, often put aside their well-worn, worked-out
routines and threw together fresh ones. A skeletal tune, all ribs
and riffs, left plenty of room for powerful new muscle. Armstrong said of Oliver, "When he started makin' records, he
started bein' a writer. Ha ha ha!" The same was true of Armstrong and several of his Hot Five players. Classics like Oliver's
"Snake Rag" and Armstrong's "Cornet Chop Suey" were
concocted in this way.

Oliver's Creole Jazz Band records are densely and somewhat rigidly contrapuntal in the New Orleans style, with infre-
quent breaks and less improvisation than we like to think.
Armstrong's Hot Five sides move with startling rapidity from
this style to what we now think of as jazz—music with a
four-four swing and long, improvised solos that lag behind
and dart ahead of the beat like street urchins at a parade.
Most of those solos are Armstrong's; the rest of the Hot
Five, although top-flight New Orleans men (except for Lil
Hardin Armstrong, who was none of these things), barely
keep up.

The Hot Five was almost exclusively a studio band. Armstrong played with and led various Chicago dance bands in
those years, but it was only in the studio that he could experiment freely with the light-textured, daringly improvised music
that was in his head. The very first cut, "Gut Bucket Blues,"
shows Armstrong's keen sense of the medium. As the players
solo he introduces each by name, urging each to "whip that
thing" or "blow that thing"—evoking both a presence and a
place, New Orleans. The flip side, "Yes, I'm In the Barrel,"
begins with a riveting three-note riff, anticipating the sort of
"hook" that will later be standard equipment for a pop single.
In case this fails to catch us, Armstrong plays a swaggering
minor-blues oration over it, daring us to try and turn him off.
We can't, and in any case it's too late. In an instant the key has
turned major and the whole band is in step, playing with a
buoyancy that carries all before it, with Ory's slide trombone to
nudge the laggard. The dark drama of the prelude is back
within two measures and keeps coming back, as in a march
under heavy clouds; if Dodds's clarinet solo dissipates it somewhat, Armstrong's lead condenses it again. The style would
almost be pure New Orleans were it not for the dominance of
Armstrong's lead. That dominance is far greater on records
made a few months later, such as "Heebie Jeebies," which
contains the first recorded scat and was Armstrong's first hit,

and "Cornet Chop Suey," in which Armstrong surrounds his wife's white-rice solo with exotic breaks.

Armstrong was a shy man. Part of the attraction of his first Chicago job, James Lincoln Collier suggests, was that he "would be nestled down behind the large and forceful figure of Joe Oliver." Although by 1925 he was getting used to asserting himself onstage, he did so more by singing and clowning than by seriously playing his horn. In the recording studio, Armstrong was insulated from both the danger of failure and the lure of easy applause. The atmosphere was casual; producers assumed, as Collier puts it, that black music was "crude stuff" and "required few niceties of direction." So here, as Ellison might say, Armstrong was really invisible, and freely "made poetry out of being invisible"—"never quite on the beat." And here it was easy for him to deploy the full weight of his horn.

And he may have sensed that it was not only easy, but necessary. The ensemble music of New Orleans was fine so long as people could see the band, could see who was playing what and when, could watch the bustle of the stationary parade. Records were different. Of the records Armstrong had played on so far, those on which he accompanied Bessie Smith had been more compelling (and had sold better) than the ensemble records of Oliver and Fletcher Henderson. Perhaps Armstrong had learned that a powerful personality could hold a record together, welding a succession of pretty sounds into a compelling whole.

The principle involved here is not limited to jazz; in a sense, it is the same principle that suggests a forward balance for the soloist in a concerto recording. In a wider sense, it is the same principle that required, for phonography to get off the ground, figures like Armstrong and Caruso—figures I call icons of phonography.

Any new art, but especially one that is also a new medium, relying on technology to bridge distances in space and time, needs icons. For if the audience is being given something, it is also being deprived of something: a human presence. What I mean by icon is someone with a personality so powerful that he seems to be present when he isn't; someone so in command of his art that he turns its disadvantages into advantages; someone, preferably, whose person has the look of cartoon— a masklike, symbolic quality. The great icon of film was Chaplin. With him film ceased to be a novelty or a dumb mimic of drama. Its two great disadvantages, the lack of sound and the lack of live actors, became advantages. A child could draw the Tramp from memory; an intellectual could find in the Tramp the soul of cinema, which was the soul of machine-age man.

Similarly, with Caruso the phonograph ceased to be a toy, although it remained a blind and short-winded mimic of opera. But even that blindness could be an advantage—surely the easy caricature (sometimes self-drawn) of Caruso that the record listener knew was more endearing than his short, fat self in some ridiculous costume. And the phonograph's limited playing time meant that one heard only the juicy arias, not the dry recitative. Caruso had, in Gaisberg's words, "the one perfect voice for recording," and his mild hamminess helped make up for the lack of visible gesture. In 1924 Compton Mackenzie wrote:

> For years in the minds of nearly everybody there were records, and there were Caruso records. He impressed his personality through the medium of his recorded voice on kings and peasants. . . . People did not really begin to buy gramophones until the appearance of the Caruso records gave them an earnest of the gramophone's potentialities. . . . There are three things in this life that seem to store up the warmth of dead summers—pot-pourri and wine and the records of a great singer.

With Armstrong the phonograph began to do a job more remarkable than storage. It ceased to be a mimic; if anything, live music and paper-composed music would now mimic records, especially Armstrong's. Anyone could imitate his ballooning cheeks and gravelly voice, and any critic could recognize in him the voice of the phonograph, the voice of invisible man. So it is no accident that when one thinks of a stack of old 78's one thinks first, depending on one's predilections, either of Armstrong or of Caruso.

But the most powerful creative influences on a new art are not always the most powerful personalities in this sense. In film Eisenstein made his effect not by self-projection, but by painstaking and daring construction of the film object. In phonography Jelly Roll Morton played a similar role. His pianism on the classic Red Hot Peppers records of the twenties shows discretion remarkable in a man who wore a diamond in his tooth and claimed to have invented jazz. What is even more remarkable is his construction of dazzling phonographic montages in whole takes, without the aid of tape—as if Eisenstein had done the steps scene in *Potemkin* without a splice. That these masterpieces were, except for their skeletons, really composed in the studio is made clear by the recollections of the Red Hot Peppers themselves (who were not a permanent performing band, but simply the best New Orleans men available for a given session). Morton's records rely less on the power of his personality than on the power of his constructions: the dazzling succession of riffs, breaks, and bittersweet harmonies is what carries the listener along. Future phonographers, in popular and classical music as well as jazz, would need one power or the other to succeed.

Morton embodied the phonographic impulse in one of its purer forms. "There is nothing permanent in the entertainment business," he told Alan Lomax. To Morton not even records seemed permanent. But at least they were hard evidence of his greatness. They could be perfect, as a stage show rarely could be; and Jelly Roll was a perfectionist, as dandy in his art as in his dress. Although he composed on paper and believed that his "little black dots" contained the secret of jazz, he knew that to bring his music to life he needed musicians, New Orleans improvisers who knew what to put between the written notes. His genius as a phonographer lay in making his musicians put their musical imaginations at the service of his own—in making them spontaneously prove, like reagents in a flask, his calculations. The Red Hot Peppers records are the prototype for a school of phonography that includes Ellington, Monk, Mingus, Zappa, Miles Davis, and the Beatles—master builders who would mean much less to us if their work had been done only on paper.

When splicing did become a possibility, jazz musicians resisted it; as improvisers they believed, even more passionately than old-fashioned classical musicians, in the spontaneity of the long take. Bands like Basie's and Ellington's achieved great fluency onstage, which they duplicated in the studio. What critics have called the greatest jazz album ever made, *Kind of Blue*, consists, according to Bill Evans's liner notes, of first-take improvisations on sketches that Miles Davis had put before his players only moments before; Evans likened this virtually "pure spontaneity" to that of Japanese ink drawing. Ornette Coleman's *Free Jazz* was an even bolder experiment, a collective free improvisation recorded in one thirty-six-minute take (here a record validates "experimental" music by recording the results). On the other hand, some of Monk's mock-Gothic constructions were impossible for his superb players to achieve without splicing. And now Davis himself, like many younger jazz musicians, uses the multitrack techniques of pop without qualm.

Jazz people love and hate records. Like anglers, they talk about the ones that got away—the legendary players like Buddy Bolden, the glory days ("Joe Oliver's best days are not on records," said Armstrong), the sudden numinous solos that were not caught. They sometimes complain that on record their improvisations sound fossilized. "I have always found it difficult to listen to my past recordings," Stan Getz said. "They have felt too close, too painful and too frustratingly irrevocable." But Earl Hines recalled that when "Weather Bird" first came out, "Louis and I stayed by that recording practically an hour and a half or two hours and we just knocked each other out because we had no idea it was gonna turn out as good as it did." In general love has the upper hand, partly because records are the only solid proof of a jazz musician's greatness—or, for that matter, of the greatness of jazz. They make jazz "legitimate," in part by giving scholars and critics something to cite instead of swapping nightclub stories. In André Hodeir's *Jazz, Its Evolution and Essence* "the words *work* and *record* are used interchangeably," and this is common practice. In jazz the record is the work. Even in bebop, which made a cult of spontaneity, records were respected as permanent works of art; Charlie Parker's alternate takes for Savoy have come to be as treasured for their endless invention as Picasso's studies and series. In every sense, records are the conservatory of jazz: its school, its treasure-house and thesaurus, its way of husbanding resources.

The first great icon of classical-music phonography was a performer, Caruso. The first master builder was also a performer, Stokowski, whose interest in sound, at once sensual and scientific, set him apart from the other great conductors of his day. That interest was expressed early in experiments with the traditional seating plan of the orchestra (some of which, such as moving the second violins from stage right to stage left so that their sound holes faced the audience, are now standard practice). Naturally the sound of the early phonograph appalled him, and at first he refused to record. ". . . And then once in the night, I woke up and I thought to myself: how stupid of you! You should record this way although it is bad and you should try to make better methods of recording."

In 1917 he took ninety of his Philadelphians to Victor headquarters in Camden, New Jersey, to record two Hungarian Dances of Brahms. Encouraged by the "awful" results, Stokowski began experimenting: doubling the strings with winds and brass, deploying baffles, turning the French horns around so the bells faced the recording horn. The sound improved, although slowly—of the 450 sides he made by the acoustic process, Stokowski approved only sixty-six. In 1925 he became the first conductor to record electrically. In 1929 he began broadcasting, and at the first rehearsal was shocked when he noticed the mixer and learned his function: "Then you're paying the wrong man. He's the conductor and I'm not. I don't want this to be broadcast under my name if I'm not controlling the *pianissimo*, the *mezzo forte*, and the *fortissimo*." After several attempts to work the dials himself while conducting, he settled on making the engineer a member of the orchestra, to be cued as he would cue the first bassoon.

Reorchestration was common practice in early phonography; without it half the parts would have been inaudible. Gaisberg confessed that in operatic selections "there was no pretence of using the composer's score; we had to arrange for wind instruments entirely." The only string instrument audible in an ensemble was the specially designed Stroh violin, with its built-in horn. But Stokowski did this sort of thing better than anyone else and kept doing it when electrical recording made it seem unnecessary. If the medium no longer needed crutches, he would give it wings.

As far as Stokowski was concerned, "black marks on white paper" were the merest of guides for the interpretive imagination. "Methods of writing down sound on paper are tremendously imperfect," he said in 1931. "I believe the composer of the future will create his harmonies directly in tone by means of electrical-musical instruments which will record his idea exactly. Over sound films of the future I believe we will be able to convey emotions higher than ever thought—things subtle and intangible—almost psychic in their being." In 1952 he said,

"The composer usually has to wait for somebody else to play his music. Someday, like the painter, he may be able to work directly on the materials of sound, on the recorder for example." It may be that he took these ideas from Varèse, whose music he had championed; in any event, despite some talk of creating an all-electric orchestra, Stokowski never had much to do with electronic instruments. (He did broadcast the *Incantation for Tapesichord* of Luening and Ussachevsky on the 1953 premiere of his *Twentieth-Century Concert Hall*—a concert hall, he said, that was "in your living room or your automobile—perhaps even a secluded spot in the woods somewhere.") But his experiments with the recording of conventional instruments were historic: for example, the stereophonic recordings he made a quarter-century before stereo. These were the first fruits of a collaboration with Bell Laboratory engineers that began in 1930 and was still going strong in 1940, when Bell engineer Harvey Fletcher recorded a Stokowski performance in Philadelphia on three-channel film, played it back—with Stokowski working volume, tone and balance controls—before a distinguished audience in Carnegie Hall, and made a new stereophonic record of the "enhanced" result. In this way Stokowski could conduct and mix the same performance, as he had tried to do while broadcasting; and when, a decade later, magnetic tape had made this easy, he would insist on doing it—even when he had to do it, in deference to union rules, by putting his hand over the engineer's.

One of the guests at Carnegie Hall was Rachmaninoff, who groused that there was "too much 'enhancing,' too much Stokowski." That was not an uncommon reaction to his records. But as Glenn Gould noted, "no one denied that, for some mysterious reason, his innumerable recordings tended to *sound* better than those of most of his colleagues." This in spite of the fact (or perhaps because of it) that after he left Philadelphia his recording orchestras often comprised only thirty musicians.

In 1959 Gunther Schuller produced a Stokowski recording of Khachaturian's Second Symphony. In the mixing studio, Schuller recalled, Stokowski "sat down at the board with all of those knobs and dials, and started doing the most *incredible* things in terms of balances. He was practically recomposing Khachaturian's piece. Mind you, the orchestra had played it as written with all the correct dynamics"—as, presumably, they had played it at the concert a few days before. "But when we got into the mixing studio—my Lord—flutes became twice as loud as brass sections; he was bringing out the viola's inner parts *over* the melody in the violins and other strange distortions. And yet in that piece, looking at it charitably, he gave the final product a kind of raw, animalistic excitement. He made the music bigger than life."

Schuller might have objected more vigorously if the composer being recomposed had been Bach. In any case, what Stokowski was doing was true phonography. Making soft instruments louder than loud ones, for instance, was just the sort of effect, impossible in concert, that had so excited Prokofiev. Of course Prokofiev was Prokofiev and could do what he liked; Stokowski was not Khachaturian. That is the problem with the phonography of "concert" music. A quantity of moral scruple should inhibit the phonographer who claims to be performing someone else's work—a larger quantity, perhaps, than inhibited Stokowski. It may be that if a few frank words on the order of "transcription" or "symphonic synthesis," which Stokowski did use sometimes, were used more often, the moral question would subside. Certainly many composers were happy to be "recomposed" by Stokowski, either because they liked the sounds he made or because his records sold. The records of Beecham and Toscanini were as important in establishing the new medium, but Stokowski's blazed a path for the art.

Stokowski was both an icon and a master builder. He was also what Mischa Elman called him in 1911 and everyone called him thereafter, a wizard. Not a pay-no-attention-to-the-man-behind-the-curtain sort of wizard (which in phonography is usually the producer) but the sort that draws attention to his wand. (I speak figuratively—Stokowski never used a baton.) The good thing about the word "wizard" is that it helps one understand why phonography often appeals to extroverts as well as introverts among musicians.

We like to believe that virtuosos of the grand romantic type have a magic in their presence that records can never quite capture. Although it is not the sort of sentiment they tend to express on record jackets, the virtuosos like to believe it, too. Thus Artur Rubinstein speaks, in an interview with Glenn Gould, of the "emanation" that makes an audience "listen like they are in your hand" and that "cannot be done at all by a record." He and Gould are "absolute opposites," he says, for Gould claims that he can influence his listener in a healthier way through the distant, considered intimacy of records. And it is easy to slip from this to a general opposition: the romantic extrovert as recitalist, the cerebral introvert as phonographer. One finds charming confirmation of this in Gould's hermit habits, in Rubinstein's old-world fear of machines ("Even now, sometimes I get shocked when I get home and suddenly I hear a man's voice in my wife's room and I think 'She has a lover.' . . . But it is the radio, it is only the radio, and I am not quite used to it"), in Gould's good-natured spoof of Rubinstein's memoirs ("I had scarcely begun the first supper show of my gala season at the Maude Harbour Festival when, as was my habit, I glanced toward the boxes. And there, seated on one marked "Live Bait—Do Not Refrigerate," was a vision of such loveliness. . ."). But really the opposition is not so absolute. Gould, too, was a showman, and his preference for doing his show on records, radio, television and film does not disqualify him any more than it disqualifies Stokowski or Cecil B. DeMille. And Rubinstein made plenty of great records, including the Brahms F minor Quintet (with the Guarneri) that Gould professed to be "drunk on."

Still, the extrovert-introvert distinction has its uses. So does the parallel distinction between artists who project and artists who don't. In the early days of phonography, projecting was a necessity. One had physically to project sound into the recording horn, which was not easy. And one had to project emotion into that rearmost of balconies, the living room. Caruso and Armstrong both did both, brilliantly, in the recordings they made before 1925. Of course both played instruments—the voice and the trumpet—that were traditionally projective.

In 1925 electrical recording introduced a second possibility. A musician could make himself the object of the microphone, as great movie actors make themselves objects of the camera; and his inwardness could fascinate. Instead of leaping out at the listener this sort of artist seems to ignore him, and thereby draws him in. *Innigkeit* is a quality much prized by record critics. Concert reviewers, by and large, know better than to demand it; the principle that one who would be heard should whisper is not useful in a hall fifty yards deep. (Unless one means a stage whisper, than which there is nothing stagier.) But in the recording studio it is a very useful principle. Glenn Gould made excellent use of it, and the impression his records give that he is playing only for himself and old Bach is reinforced by his involuntary humming (which used to strike me as comical, but now sounds like the gibbering of a ghost). Projecting, he said, was the bad habit of using rhetorical flourishes to lasso the man in the rear balcony.

Gould's instrument is one that, with the lid up, can be quite projective, but it is also one that people often play for themselves. So inwardness may come more naturally to a pianist. Schnabel, the pianist whom the young Gould most admired, apparently managed to sound inward even in concert. My image of *Innigkeit* is Bill Evans hunched over his keyboard at the Village Vanguard; his meditative records bring the image back. But his colleague Miles Davis, whose instrument is the most projective of all—an instrument originally used to signal, to alarm—also sounds as though he were playing for himself. " . . . For myself and for musicians," he told an interviewer. For the rest of us his centripetal solos, which turn the melody around a few hypersensitive notes, are often hard to concentrate on, however taken we may be with the glorious sidemen or the subtle construction of his good records. (We may even feel that he uses the mute to keep his soul inside, away from us. In fact, we may feel that at times a deliberate shutting out of his audience makes his playing something other than inward.)

When we come to the voice we find, in the 1920s, a tradition of projection developed in opera houses and vaudeville palaces and encouraged by acoustic recording; and a quieter tradition surviving in folk music and barely surviving in chamber music. Electric recording brought about a great, creative flowering of this second tradition in popular music and in jazz as Billie Holiday, Bing Crosby, and Fred Astaire taught singers to make themselves objects of the microphone. Louis Armstrong did this when singing, especially when singing scat—those anti-words, with their blithe disregard of all communication theory. His abstraction of tunes and texts makes him seem abstracted himself, as if daydreaming. Lulled, the listener begins, as in "Lazy River," to "dream a dream of me, dream a dream of me." And one secret of Armstrong's formula from 1929 on is the way the projective trumpet reaches out and grabs the listener, the dreamy vocal draws him in, and finally the trumpet pushes him back into his own world, signing off with a high F.

It is not odd for a man with a guitar to sing and play for his own gratification, and the early country bluesmen often give this impression on record. Robert Johnson surely does, confirming the story that when some Mexican musicians came to hear him he first froze, then turned and sang facing the wall. So does his rock descendent Van Morrison (John Cale claims that when recording *Astral Weeks* "Morrison couldn't work with anybody, so finally they just shut him in the studio by himself . . . and later they overdubbed").

There is another mode, however, which in popular music and jazz may now be the most important of all, and which already has a serviceable name, cool. Neither appealing to the listener nor ignoring him, the cool performer speaks to him from somewhere inside the listener's head. The voice may be Olympian or diabolical, but it is always superior and always calm. It is often ironic. It knows the listener inside out. Cool fascinates, but not the way inwardness fascinates; the listener is not the observer but the observed. I am not sure who invented this mode, but I doubt it could have been done without the microphone; Bing Crosby, Fats Waller and Duke Ellington come to mind. It has been used effectively by T-Bone Walker, Chuck Berry, Miles Davis, Sonny Rollins, Dexter Gordon, Monk, Sinatra, the Beatles (especially Lennon), the Rolling Stones, Dylan, Zappa, Elvis Costello, Talking Heads—in short, by most of the great phonographers in popular music and jazz. In classical music it is much harder to identify. Among composers Satie, Weill, Stockhausen, Partch, Berio and Boulez seem to me cool at least sometimes; among performers Pinza, Richard Stoltzman, Weissenberg, and Teresa Stratas. It is hard to know how much of this is musical, how much mere image, but that conflation is one evidence of cool.

All three modes—the projective, the inward, and the cool—can be seen as responses to one of the paradoxes of the recording situation, namely that the audience is not there. This is just the flip side of the fact that, for the listener, the performer is not there, a fact I went on about in a previous chapter. In general, the paradoxes of making records are mirrored in the paradoxes of listening to them, which is why the artist's responses to the paradoxes are important from the point of view of aesthetics. If the responses were just contingent reflexes or defense mechanisms they might be interesting from the point of view of biology, but not of aesthetics. For what is most important about art is not how it is done, but what it does. (That is one reason why most of this book is written from the point of view of the listener rather than the phonographer, the other reason being that I am a listener.)

The life of the touring blues musician, Charles Keil has observed, furnishes all the loneliness and jealousy he needs to sing the blues authentically. It is a strong extract of modern life. The recording situation is an even stronger and more representative extract. The glass booths and baffles that isolate the musician from his fellow musicians; the abstracted audience; the sense of producing an object and of mass-producing a commodity; the deconstruction of time by takes and its reconstruction by splicing—these are strong metaphors of modern life. Their mirror images in the listener's experience are solitude; the occlusion of the musician; the use of music as an object and a commodity; the collapse of a public architecture of time and the creation of a private interior design of time. Since they contradict everything that music-making once seemed to be, they are paradoxes.

In response to these paradoxes, a set of formal and emotional patterns should by now have emerged that would be characteristic of recorded music as opposed to live music; these would be the modes and archetypes of phonography. Unfortunately, the task of nailing them down is too big for the present book. For now, I will only enlarge a little on a mode I think I can identify, the cool. It can be seen as emerging from several of the paradoxes of phonography. To the abstraction of the audience it responds by speaking as if to a single, utterly known individual, in the manner of a disembodied voice. To the reification of music it responds by creating a curious object. To the hardening of musical language it responds by juxtaposing phrases rather than using them; in place of rhetoric there is irony. (The same irony protects the phonographer from the irony of his unseen listeners, against which he would otherwise be defenseless—like the blind musician of folklore, whose descendant he is.) To the deconstruction of time, the cool mode responds with cyclical rather than linear or dramatic forms. A device that unites several of these responses is that of beginning and ending an album with items that are similar, perhaps similar in having a pointedly antique or naive quality. I find some or all of these responses in the Beatles' *Sgt. Pepper* and the White Album, Zappa's *Burnt Weenie Sandwich*, Lenya's German recording of Weill's *Threepenny Opera*, Thelonious Monk's *Monk's Music*, and Glenn Gould's first recording of the *Goldberg Variations*.

Chapter Nine

Nina

"Why don't you tell me what you want me to say," Nina said, "and I'll say it as best I can." She took a long drag on her cigarette and the smoke ascended endlessly. We were sitting on the rug in the middle of the room like children, with two vodka-and-tonics and a tape recorder between us. This studio apartment is very nearly a replica of Nina's childhood room, whose shell remains some seventy blocks uptown. The big brass bed and petite blond piano come from there, and possibly the two Firenze posters in their tall brass frames, a Renaissance prospect of terracotta rooftops and Masaccio's *Adam and Eve Driven from Paradise*. More recently acquired but matched to the blond piano are the butcher-block table, the chairs, and the bookcases with their navy-blue ranks of Oxford Greek and Latin texts and the brighter colors of critical tracts and paperback novels. Beneath the turntable is a single short shelf of records running from Gesualdo to Devo in no particular order.

I fed Nina (whose name is not Nina) a quotation from

herself. "When I play a record," she once told me, "it's as though someone else were expressing my feelings. When I play the piano, it's as though I were expressing someone else's feelings."

"Right," she said. "It still works that way. The great thing about playing records is that someone else is doing the work for you. Also, your repertory with records is so much larger because—let's face it—even if you're Horowitz there's a limited number of things you can play. Therefore, unless you were a great improviser and/or composer yourself, you would have to learn how to channel the full range of human emotions through the limited number of pieces you can play."

Nina took a deep breath of smoke. Her teeth have a patina. She used to complain that her nose is the nose of a Brueghel milkmaid. But she has the cordiform face, high firm cheeks and copious eyes of Claudette Colbert—eyes that will be glacial, then suddenly brim with childlike wonder, affection or mischief. She has that tough little rich girl look, the look that says to suitors: My heart belongs to Daddy, the son of a bitch.

"When I was studying playing I was always conscious of subjugating myself to the composer. Now, I remember playing the romantics and being told by my various teachers that they thought *the piece had a certain meaning*, so my job was to bring this out in such a way that the stupid audience could hear it. You sit down to play what is a faintly (your teacher decides) *troubled* nocturne—you know, maybe he didn't get the girl, or he's still trying, or he finds out she's a dyke or whatever—a little on the dark side. Well, you might have just gotten a raise and be in a very good mood, and yet you have to sit down and put across a heartbreaking version of it to a third party.

"That has nothing to do with self-expression, as far as I'm concerned. It just takes a gigantic amount of concentration and energy, and I ultimately found that very unfulfilling. And it's also why I now play almost nothing but Bach, because he leaves me the most room to say what I want. Even Beethoven—who needs it? If I feel like playing Beethoven I'll play Beethoven on a record player."

"But if you're not performing for your teacher or your audience," I said, "just for yourself, and you can decide whether you want to play the faintly troubled nocturne or the serene nocturne or the listless nocturne . . ."

"That's true. When I played a lot I did express myself this way. I have various neurotic rituals now that I'm trying very hard to exorcise in therapy, and every once in a while I say to myself: You always had depressions. What did you use to do before you did x—you know, drank, listened to loud music, ate cookies, or whatever. And I read my old journals and I see that what I did was play the piano, sometimes for seven hours a day. I was clearly getting something out of my system. The piano was in my room and it was my haven, my fortress against my parents and all the other ills of the world. The problem was I didn't play very well when I was doing it to emote. So I've always wondered why great artists always say that feeling the music is what makes them great. I think that's fifty percent true, and the guys who really play like automatons are not the great pianists. But you have to hit some kind of perfect compromise between emoting and executing. And I found that just too difficult, finally. You know, I either played rather badly and got stuff out of my system, or I played quite well and didn't. I just found I couldn't do it. And the less I played the more music I listened to and the more I got out of it."

Nina's speech is rapid and exact, with just a few more anacolutha than Plato allowed his Athenians. Her tone is passionate but evenly ironic, in a literary way. Though accentless, her English has the correctness and deliberate slanginess of a second language, which it is; until she was five she lived in Berlin. Her mother's people were Lutherans of Berlin, her father's

Jews of Hamburg related in varying degrees to Mendelssohn, Marx, and the Baal Shem Tov (although for the last two Nina's father has nothing but contempt). His uncle taught Greek in a *gymnasium* and was a friend of Freud. Brilliant, arrogant, brave (he served with U.S. intelligence in Germany during the war), Nina's father has Rudolf Serkin's hypertrophic forehead and intolerance of second-raters. As a specialist in foreign securities he was often abroad, and in any case wanted nothing to do with his children until they were old enough to discuss Plato. So when Nina and her kid brother left their grandmother in Berlin to live with their parents in New York, it was their mother they lived with, a beautiful blue-eyed dark-haired woman now stout, always stylish. She taught Nina the virtues of a European woman, with a twist of Berlin cynicism. The girl would have charm to burn—her mother would see to that; and her father would see to it that she knew six languages, among them music. Her early world was a carousel of lessons. Piano she began at five, at Mannes, and continued at Diller-Quayle. At the Lycée Française, at age six, she was briefly engaged to Yo Yo Ma. At Brearley she picked up Latin and Greek and her love of literature quickened. Twice she was admitted to Juilliard but backed out, choosing to pursue a broader *Bildung*.

Life in the Park Avenue apartment, with the Feininger oil and the delicate Lehmbruch, was not life as most Americans know it. Nina's parents were casually nudist and fond of drugs. On the other hand, their nice discriminations of class and decorum were purely bourgeois. Thus Nina's father boasted of his bouts with Japanese courtesans while his wife, though proud of her free and efficient Berlin lovelife and determined that Nina should imitate it, stayed faithful as a dog. Difficulties arose. Nina, barely adolescent, became her parents' unwilling internuncio. She grew up quickly and—at once coddled with fine wines and spurred like a race horse to excel, excel— became a wise child, sad. Under these circumstances she discovered that an endlessly repeated and refined page of Chopin could purchase an evening's oblivion.

When I met her at Harvard, where she studied literature, her terrible blue eyes declared: Art is better than life, and if you don't know it yet, wait a few years. As I did not choose to wait, we argued this point for some three years without much movement either way.

Now, anchored on the carpet, I brought up a related but somewhat less freighted issue: Eduard Hanslick's theory, elaborated by Susanne Langer, that music is not a form of self-expression at all. Since a performer cannot force himself to have the emotions a piece is supposed to be expressing, he can hardly be expressing himself when he plays. But to say that the composer expresses his emotions through the music is not very helpful either, since what his emotions are is anyone's guess. As Hanslick points out, the desolation of Gluck's "Che farò senza Euridice" can be transmuted, by changing a couple of words, into pure joy. We express emotion by yelling or crying, not by making music. What music does, according to Langer, is make a map of emotion. It works out by formal analogy the way our emotions move and behave. Music is a form of knowledge.

"That sounds like a great idea," Nina said. "In my mind I instantly say yes, and writing and painting and religion and all the other things. But I don't think that changes anything we were saying." She registered my surprise, but went on. "All I would be saying is, I ultimately found it good to map out my own feelings by choosing records, because I feel that certain guitar solos say it all for me at certain times. Because the map is so true. I have *no time* for that sensation when I'm executing it; the recognition is completely absent."

I said I thought Langer's theory complicated things. Why should looking at a map make us feel so good? If it's not self-expression, why does it have the same emotional effect? "I have every confidence," Nina said, "that some day they'll find the chemical that does it. This has something to do with being human. The ape will go *aaah* and we can play a guitar solo, right? There's probably a hormone for it or an acetate or something like that. We can sublimate and they can't. Dreams are maps too, with codes, and you can get up in the morning and read them"—she coughed profoundly—"and sometimes you feel better. I'm beginning to think that baseball does this for a large portion of the population. I think that you can really act out with those players and those moments of just *unbelievable* tension. And it *is* quite a beautiful thing—there's such a thing as a *perfect game*. . . ." We both smiled. "Perfect" has a big entry in Nina's lexicon.

"I was thinking," she said after a pause, "that the Walkman brought all kinds of interesting new issues to the fore. I talk about it a lot in therapy because it's such a powerful influence in my life. To me what it meant initially was that I could be a vegetable not just at home, but all the time. Like the heroine of my book"—Nina, when she is not at the copy desk of a business magazine or listening to music, is writing a novel—"her tragic flaw is that she spends too much time sitting around listening to live music and doing nothing else. So I got the Walkman and it just made me psychopathic, you know? Time disappeared and space disappeared and I could just do music all the time. And it knocked me out. So I would go in to Vivian and say, 'Do you think this is bad? Is this making me more robotic, not less so?'

"And she said to me a very interesting thing. She said that in fact the reason that box listeners and Walkman listeners find these things so pleasurable is not that it makes them more robotic, but that it makes them less so, because they have music to concentrate on instead of fulfilling certain forms. If you're walking down the street or riding a train or a bus, having a nice time listening to music, you are not going to worry about whether your shoes are scuffed, whether you're being polite to the bus driver, whether you're jostling the guy next to you. You'll be enjoying yourself instead. Now the ghetto blasters are slightly different because they can in some cases be used aggressively. But they're not always; I know a lot of people who have boxes just because they like to listen to music.

"And that made me feel a lot better. I thought, how interesting. And that fits in with my theory of music listening as self-definition and self-expression; it's your way of refusing to be a social unit for a little while, or any other kind of unit besides a listening, enjoying unit that thinks its own thoughts and maps its own emotions. Don't you think she's smart?" I made a noncommital sound and Nina went on, "I guess you just feel robotic when you're wearing them because you're so cut off."

"But what if you're just substituting one kind of robotism for another?"

Nina's eyes widened, taking on the look of injured, challenging innocence that eyes with contact lenses can take on. "What's robotic about listening to music?"

"It depends on the music. Disco is robotic. Most popular music is robotic."

"I'm sorry, I can't agree."

In college, when my nineteenth-century ears were just opening to jazz, Nina hit me with Aretha Franklin, Otis Rush, the Supremes, Frank Zappa and the Average White Band. Because I had heard her play Mozart on the piano, I gave these others the benefit of the doubt. At twenty I commenced my adolescence, and five or six years later it seemed to have run its course. I still listened to some popular music, but only some.

Nina said, "I think you've always invested the notes themselves with a lot of inherent stuff, like there's something in Mozart to get out of it. And I think that normally we project, more than anything else."

"So suppose people *are* projecting. Take the ghetto-blaster person or the secretary with the Walkman listening to the worst possible music."

"Yeah, so she listens to 'I'm Just a Woman in Love.' "

"She's mapping her life onto this really lousy music. Isn't she simplifying, romanticizing, and generally distorting?"

"Yeah. Art, remember? Remember?" Nina's eyes had widened again, this time with scorn. I had failed to remember that art is not life. "I'm sorry," she said, "but I think that what we all get out of this is largely—it's like eating baby food, you know? Predigested experience, and that's why it's so cathartic. Some guy went through this all for me and mapped this guitar solo that just makes my guts ache because I recognize it, and Zappa did the work. What could be better? What could be sweeter?"

Now she was on the firm ground of a favorite paradox: Art is the noblest thing there is, as noble as creamed carrots.

"All right," I said. "Wasn't there something to the Platonic theory that the kind of music you listen to makes a difference in the quality—or at least the tenor, the tone—of your daily life? And if you keep the radio on KKK, or whatever the latest trashy station is . . ."

"It's LIR and I listen to it twenty-four hours a day."

". . . It's kind of like living at McDonald's; and if you listen to WNYC it's like living at Versailles."

"I was going to say it's like living in—where do they broadcast those horrible university stations from? Mem Hall? Those unbelievably pretentious announcers. . . . My parents always listen to WQXR in the morning. This is a big mistake. They have programs for housewives called "Great Moments in Piano History." They play one movement of the *Moonlight* Sonata and then one movement of the *Pathétique* and then, you know, the first movement of the B-flat Bach partita because they're all chestnuts. This is *sick*, it's an *outrage* and it shouldn't be permitted. Honey, I will listen to seven hundred Crazy Eddie and Honda commercials before I'll listen to that.

Have you heard this great new wave song called 'Chalk Dust—The Umpire Strikes Back'? It's about John McEnroe at Wimbledon?" Snapping her fingers, she chanted a line: "*The ball's in/Everyone could see that there was chalk dust . . .* and in the end the umpire murders him on the tennis court. You can't tell me this isn't quality. It's timely, it's sprightly—it's a better way to start your day than some bozo trying to convince you that the *Moonlight* and the *Pathétique* are the same piece of music."

"But timely and sprightly are the qualities of magazine copy."

"Good magazine copy, yes?" Her inflection was mock Teutonic. She leaned back on her elbows like an interrogator and took a drag on her cigarette.

At Brearley, Nina had played keyboards in a rock and roll band that did the circuit of New York prep school dances. To begin each gig she would play a Bach prelude on the electric piano; that was the band's signature. I asked how she had lost interest in playing popular music.

"I think it was partly laziness. I was trained—I told you this—I just can't really play anything else, it just comes out sounding classical? It's really unpleasant: I often go to hear stride pianists or blues pianists and I watch what they do. I can see it, but when I get home I can't do it. But I have another question," she said, "about this Versailles business. I'm asking the questions here. What if you're just not that good a person? Maybe we just can't always live up to this level of stuff. Like I go through periods where I read a lot of Greek or I read nothing but Rilke, or I'll go on one of my Beethoven kicks. But I don't always feel that A-plus. I don't always feel that noble, and my emotions are mapped much more accurately, in fact, by Zappa guitar solos."

"And you don't feel that you could be ennobled by listening to something nobler?"

"But I don't want to be ennobled!"

That rang a bell, I said. Nina laughed tentatively while my head tilted back, fishing. Then I recalled that according to Adorno the refrain of the pop music listener is Brecht's line, "But I don't want to be human."

"Well, I don't want to be human. This is getting much too personal for me. Don't use my name. Call me 'a source.' 'The source continued . . .' "

I asked if she went to rock concerts these days and she said no, "because of the crowds and such, and also so much of the good stuff that's written now really is dependent on great studio technology. You can't get it onstage. On the other hand, I went to hear this reggae band the other night, and this is the type of performance where I think exactly the opposite would obtain. The stuff on a record would be deadly boring; the whole point was to be there and inhale all that garbage, and watch that guy falling down, and try to figure out his sermons on the mount.

"I thought of you this summer: I went to the ballet a few times"—Nina, who as a girl took lessons in this also, gives it the British inflection that makes it a contact sport like boxing and hockey—"and talk about catharsis! And I don't think that works on a TV. Ballet bores me on TV. You can't really see what these guys are doing with their bodies, how they're *killing* themselves before your very eyes."

In fact, I did want to talk about catharsis. What would happen, I asked Nina, if she were in a foul mood and someone put on some Mozart in C major?

"I'd just fall down and start laughing hysterically and go out to Saks and charge a dress. Instant cheer! I'd probably get very annoyed. I'd absent myself from felicity. Is that what you wanted me to say? I think that was the truth."

The question I was trying to raise was one that (to oversimplify vastly) divided Academics and Peripatetics: whether art acts by sympathy, infecting the listener with its own temperament, or by catharsis, meeting the listener's mood head-on and wrestling with it. Plato might prescribe Haydn or Count Basie for chronic anxiety; Aristotle, Mahler or Otis Rush. Mozart is a trickier prescription. I chose him as an example because his "cheerfulness" (when he is cheerful) has the profound grace that Plato would value. And while his "cheerfulness" is hardly ever, in his great music, unmixed with pain, it nevertheless can give the unreceptive listener (unreceptive because untrained, or just in a lousy mood) the impression that it is unmixed: instant cheer.

"How do you react to Mozart?" Nina asked. "He cheers you up, right?"

"If it's something blithely cheerful," I said, "I get annoyed. But if it's something that has a sort of deep cheerfulness, I don't."

"Deep cheerfulness," she said, "if you're in a rotten enough mood, can almost always be construed as gloom."

"Would the same apply to *playing* something cheerful?"

"You mean on an instrument? See, I think that has to change your mood—though you might resent it. But say you had to do it, to practice something. You're just not going to do it well unless you feel really cheerful. A lot of it is physiological, too. This is very California and 1980s, but there's a touch to Mozart, you can't play it from the shoulders. And if you feel really terrible and you have the whole weight of the world on your shoulders, I'm sure that the Mozart will wind up suffering from it—unless you can really listen and really get into it and change your mood and play thoughtful, cheerful Mozart.

"But you know, I play Bach mainly, and it's a great emotional leveler. All these pieces that change so much between the beginning and the end. Also, in those days minor didn't really mean minor, and major really didn't mean major; so you can read much more of your own stuff into a piece, because it's so much less easily identifiable as sad or happy, or even histrionic or nonhistrionic. Who's to say if the guy is being dramatic and emotional or if he's just playing a game where he's going to find out how many times he can use a G without using it in the same octave in five measures? But here's something really interesting: I don't really feel that way about *listening* to Bach. Like the unaccompanied violin sonatas—I just think they're real erotic, and I don't seem to listen to them any other way. I play them very rarely; something very peculiar must be going on with my hormones when I do.

"You know, I was thinking about this whole thing before you came, and I really think that the way I listen is very much defined by—and this is true of the heroine of my book, too—that failed-musician thing. It was a whole way of listening that very, very slowly developed after I left music school, and it replaced what playing music had been since I was three or four years old. Because music was always my emotional life; books were a mind thing. Music was what I did to get things out of my system. And I took pride in it, and it was fun to get better, and the music went through great changes. And then, you know, I just couldn't sustain that world. And I think I turned music listening into a similarly cathartic and creative act because I couldn't quite bear to part with the experience.

"I think that's why I wound up *practicing listening.* I don't buy records, and I'm not interested in new things any more than I was when I played. I played the same partita for four years, until I knew it so well and understood it so well that I was in complete control of it; and then I gave it up and turned to something else. I do the same thing with records now. I study them, and it has nothing to do with new sensations or entertainment.

"The first five weeks I listen to a record for overall melodic form. Then for five weeks I'll get obsessed with the rhythm. And according to how much there is to find and learn, that's how long I'll hang around and listen. I am still hearing things in 'Yo Mama' "—a Zappa guitar solo—"which I bought five years ago. This Police tape I think I've just about exhausted now, after six weeks."

"When you listen to piano records, do your fingers sometimes respond?"

"They do. And I often read the music. When I go on a Beethoven binge, I get a big kick out of lying around reading the score. I guess that's where they kind of intersect: reading the music and having somebody else play it for you."

"Still, isn't there something about being active—just as dancing is more cathartic than watching someone dance?"

"At a disco, maybe," Nina said. "But I think that was completely disproved this summer at the ballet."

"Well," I said, "you may have started with seventy units of nervous energy and gotten cathartized down to twelve, but this other guy, the dancer, started with a hundred and seventy and got cathartized . . ."

"All the way down to zero? Minus ten? Well no: according to my theory the poor bastard wasn't cathartized at all, he just tore a whole bunch of muscles and took speed and felt horrible. Dancers have awful lives."

"There are times, actually, since I started drinking more"—she hesitated—"that it really has become very scary to listen. This neurotic ritual of getting high and playing very loud music. There are so many days when I can easily and truly say that it's by far the finest moment of my day and the most enjoyable thing that I do. It's pure, it's perfect, it's endlessly repeatable. I mean, not only do I still feel that way; I feel more that way all the time."

"In that sense, would playing the piano be more like life, because it's . . ."

"Because it's hard . . ."

"Because it's hard and active and imperfect?"

Nina said, "Various boyfriends have always suggested that there was something very passive-slash-sexual about the way I enjoy listening to music." She had sometimes spoken of the physical effect music could have on her, how she would lie on the floor between enormous speakers and resonate like a drum. "And that doesn't really go with what I was saying before about its being a creative act. See, when this started I wasn't as conscious about the whole thing, not having a friend who was writing a book about records at the time. But when I was fifteen, yeah, it was definitely my sex life. My musical life then was playing the piano; my sex life was listening to music. It always sublimated something." She coughed delicately. "But that really did change when I stopped playing. I actually think I participate when I listen. I think it's vicarious performance."

Chapter Ten

Canned Catharsis

"Instrument" was the word enthusiasts used in the 1920s and 1930s when referring to their phonographs. It was artfully chosen. Grown men seriously interested in music did not want to be thought of as playing with toys. And the early phonograph was widely considered a toy, or at best a machine, and not the sort of thing with which a gentleman amateur of music ought to concern himself. It was understood as a sort of music box—a supremely versatile one that, in the words of a Berliner advertisement, "talks distinctly, sings any song with expression, plays the piano, cornet, banjo, and in fact any musical instrument with precision and pleasing effect"—but still a music box.

Compton Mackenzie was one of those who sought to remedy this error. In his writing the word "instrument" appears often and seems to come in two flavors, scientific and artistic. The phonograph is a scientific instrument for the reproduction of sound; it is also a musical instrument that the amateur must play, not play with. The second flavor is the more piquant. Of course, Mackenzie had to show that the phonograph was musical, a musical something. What else could it be but a musical instrument? But there is more to the word than that. In his memoirs Mackenzie remembered the days when "the road to the enjoyment of music was the piano, and the pianola was accepted as the mechanical aid which would open the door to a wider and deeper knowledge than could be obtained in any other way. Ernest Newman, the greatest musical critic of the time, had given the pianola his blessing and by ignoring the gramophone had implied his disbelief in its ability to serve as anything more useful than a rich man's toy." The young Mackenzie, who had given up on the piano after a few bleak lessons, pumped away on the pianola for some years, then gave his legs a rest by marrying a pianist. When finally he found his instrument it turned out to be the phonograph.

The progression from piano to pianola to phonograph may appear degenerative. Yet all three are machines. As Jacques Barzun has remarked, "the moment man ceased to make music with his voice alone the art became machine-ridden. Orpheus's lyre was a machine, a symphony orchestra is a regular factory for making artificial sounds, and a piano is the most appalling contrivance of levers and wires this side of the steam engine." In one sense the pianola is *more* mechanical than the phonograph, certainly than the electric phonograph: it is more machinelike, more rigid and insensitive to nuance.

In another sense, though, an instrument is mechanical to the degree that it performs musically important tasks for the player. The guitar takes care of intonation for you. The piano takes care of intonation and (to a degree) timbre. The Hammond organ takes care of intonation, timbre, and chording. The phonograph takes care of everything. Not that it takes no skill to play the phonograph—scientifically, it is a delicate instrument—but it takes no musical skill.

"If there is any such thing as sin, then it is a sin not to be able to play a musical instrument." So reflects the farmgirl in a

Halldor Laxness novel who has come to Reykjavik to study the harmonium. Our question is whether the phonograph offers a dispensation. If sin is the stunting of one's humanity, and man is a musical animal, we still have to decide whether a musical animal must make music or simply appreciate it.

Nowadays a "musician" is a professional and a "musical amateur" is someone who plays or sings. In 1800 whoever could sing or play competently was called a musician, while an amateur, true to his etymology, was a lover of music. (In French this is still the first meaning.) Etymologically the word was active, but one could love music actively in any number of ways: not only by playing an instrument, but by going to concerts and patronizing musicians.

In an age of gentle leisure, "amateur" was a compliment. Today, though the standards for its application have tightened, the word has become a put-down, the opposite of "pro." But the amateur is a very important character. His essential activity, which etymology reveals, redeems him and some of the world with him. Thoreau wrote in his journal, "I know of no redeeming qualities in me but a sincere love of some things. . . . Therein I am whole and entire. Therein I am God-propped."

Things like "the lichens on the rocks" were what he loved. He was an amateur naturalist, and an active one, yet he did not make nature the way an amateur musician is supposed to make music. He did, however, interpret nature; in his writing, he did recreate it. (And how can the interpretive musician claim to make music? On the ground that a moment ago there was empty air, and now there is music in it? Then anyone with a phonograph can make the same claim.) What he made were books, unnatural creatures that he often pretended not to love at all, and as they failed in the marketplace he reconciled himself to being an amateur at that, too. When most of the copies of his first book ended up stacked in his room he wrote:

I have now a library of nearly nine hundred volumes, over seven hundred of which I wrote myself. Is it not well that the author should behold the fruits of his labor? . . . Nevertheless, in spite of this result, sitting beside the inert mass of my works, I take up my pen tonight to record what thought or experience I may have had, with as much satisfaction as ever. Indeed, I believe that this result is more inspiring and better for me than if a thousand had bought my wares. It affects my privacy less and leaves me freer.

Here his pen was dipped in gall, but we are grateful that he went ahead and filled thirty-nine notebooks.

There is nothing eccentric even today about keeping a journal. But I cannot recall ever hearing the phrase "amateur writer." It sounds aberrant. Why do we speak of amateur painters and musicians and naturalists, but never of amateur writers? Probably because everyone is an amateur writer, more or less; in a literate society everyone can more or less write. Not everyone can play an instrument or sing a harmony part. But anyone can play a record; and it may be this new promiscuity of music that has forced us to restrict, by linguistic fiat, the number of her lovers, her amateurs.

But Thoreau's gibe about his nine-hundred-volume library suggests a deeper reason. His entry reads almost like a parody of the romantic individualism he had learned from Emerson, which sang the uniqueness of objects as well as persons—a parody of it in light of mechanical reproduction. Remember Keats's fear that he might "cease to be/Before my pen has glean'd my teeming brain/Before high-piléd books, in charact'ry/Hold like rich garners the full-ripen'd grain"? Thoreau, with nine years to live yet, is already buried under the "fruits of his labor"—"My works are piled up on one side of my chamber half as high as my head, my *opera omnia*." One book.

Printing enforced a distinction between the kind of writing

anyone can do (letters, diaries, grocery lists) and the kind writers do. What writers write gets printed. Someone who can't or won't get into print (and we always assume the first) is not an amateur writer, he is no writer at all. The ability to reproduce one's words becomes a proof of virility. The very notion of an amateur writer is risible. Thoreau knows it and feels it bitterly. But if now he calls the grapes sour, the continuation of his journal—past the failure of his second book, *Walden*, and on almost to his death—testifies to a true renunciation. Thoreau was an honest-to-God amateur who wrote for love of his subjects and his sentences. In another notebook: "I can express adequately only the thought which I *love* to express."

If it is true that only the individual is lovable, then the amateur and mechanical reproduction must always be at odds. Writing has long been a fiefdom of mechanical reproduction, but in music and the visual arts there is still plenty of room for the unique performance or object, and so for the amateur. People who play chamber music together in their homes or sing in church choirs are amateurs. People who make records are not. What about people who listen to records?

The best proof of love is the willingness to be bored. Learning to play an instrument is boring. Love for music can allay the tedium but not banish it. Finally the musician just accepts it, knowing that it will always be with him in some degree no matter how good he gets. But then, thumbing through bins of out-of-print records can be every bit as boring as practicing C-sharp minor scales. By this test the serious record collector would seem to be an amateur.

What about the notion that to love something is to know it? This is more than a biblical pun; some people are impelled to know the beloved inside-out. But many find the dark more romantic. Gertrude Stein, a very great amateur of painting, professed to know nothing about it. "She says it is a good thing to have no sense of how it is done in the things that amuse you. You should have one absorbing occupation and as for the other things in life for full enjoyment you should only contemplate results. In this way you are bound to feel more about it than those who know a little of how it is done." We might conclude that she loved books but only liked paintings ("I like to look at them," she said of Picasso's) but then again we might not.

Even if we agree that the amateur should know "how it is done"—the way a piece of music is put together, the way a performer takes it apart and reconstructs it—we need not require that he know how to do it. An ornithologist knows better than the birds how flying is done, but no one expects him to fly. Musicians are self-conscious birds; they have music in their muscles, but also in their minds. The mental side should be accessible with some study (more study, perhaps, than records alone can afford) to the nonmusician.

In the West we consider the kingdom of music to be less of the body than of the mind, and less of the mind than of the soul. Of course, a marching-band leader might think of music as invigorating physical culture, and that might explain the peculiar reservations expressed by John Philip Sousa, the first great recording star, with regard to his new racket. "With the phonograph," he said, "vocal exercises will be out of vogue! Then what of the national throat? Will it not weaken? What of the national chest? Will it not shrink?"

Our present concern, however, is the national soul. We have no instruments to measure it, to see if it has shrunk any in the Edisonian century just past. What we can do is examine the individual soul and try to get some idea of how music works upon or through it.

The first question we want to ask is one that (as I said in the last chapter) divided Academics and Peripatetics: whether music works by sympathy or by homoeopathy. Plato, articulating a

Greek prejudice, held that music acts on the soul by sympathy, directly impressing its character on the listener. Its character is that of the soul it imitates—for Plato and Aristotle share the Greek prejudice that music, like the other arts, is mimetic.

In Greece music was intimately bound up with poetry, so that it took all the tools of philosophical analysis to disentangle them—and Plato, for one, thought it better to leave them tangled. *Mousike* could refer to all the activities of the Muses. More specifically it could refer to two aspects of poetry: melody and rhythm. What we would call pure music—"the employment of the cithara and oboe [*aulos*] without vocal accompaniment"—was not uncommon. But Plato will not have it in his projected city, since "it is the hardest of tasks to discover what such wordless rhythm and tune signify, or what model worth considering they represent." This is in the *Laws*, a work of his old age; in the earlier *Republic* he allows shepherds in the fields a Pan-pipe (*syrinx*) to pipe on.

To be welcome in Plato's republic, poets must imitate (in direct discourse) only good men. Since the tune and rhythm "must follow the speech," the music's character, too, will be exclusively noble. So "the dirgelike modes of music," the mixed Lydian and the tense or higher Lydian, must go. So must the "soft and convivial" Ionian and Lydian modes. This leaves the Dorian and Phrygian modes, the one imitating "the accents of a brave man who is engaged in warfare or in any enforced business, and who . . . confronts fortune with a steadfast endurance and repels her strokes"; the other "for such a man engaged in works of peace, not enforced but voluntary." To accompany singing in these modes only the lyre and the cithara are needed, so harps, triangles, oboes and other polymodal instruments will not get past the city gates. As for rhythm, "we must not pursue complexity nor great variety in the basic movements, but must observe what are the rhythms of a life that is orderly and brave."

When all the elements of music "conform to the disposition [*ethos*]" of the good man's soul, the soul of the listener will follow suit. Hence "education in music is most sovereign, because more than anything else rhythm and harmony find their way to the inmost soul and take strongest hold upon it, bringing with them and imparting grace, if one is rightly trained, and otherwise the contrary."

It is ironic that the Socrates of the *Republic* should snub the oboe, for in the slightly earlier *Symposium* Socrates is eulogized as an oboist, like Marsyas the satyr. Like Marsyas, Socrates has the power to bewitch. "For the moment I hear him speak I am smitten with a kind of sacred rage, worse than any Corybant, and my heart jumps into my mouth and the tears start into my eyes. . . . I've felt I simply couldn't go on living the way I did." But Socrates is a "more wonderful" oboist even than Marsyas, for he needs no oboe—only words.

How is it that Plato, having treated his teacher to this well-shined encomium, later makes him spit it out? One answer is suggested in the encomium itself. "Socrates is the only man in the world that can make me feel ashamed. Because there's no getting away from it, I know I ought to do the things he tells me to, and yet the moment I'm out of his sight I don't care what I do to keep in with the mob." So the encomiast admits that the emotional effect of Socrates's words is evanescent, like any rage or fever. Its practical effect may be nil. And who is the encomiast? Alcibiades, who burst in on the party drunk as a lord (and heralded by an oboe) and who, as Plato's audience knows, will come to a bad end, disgraced in the Sicilian expedition and other fiascos. Ward of Pericles and pupil of Socrates, he will be a byword in Athens for beauty and brains gone astray.

Plato loves the Socrates pictured here, the pied piper of the agora. But he is starting to reject him, somewhat the way Nietzsche would come to reject the chromatic moralizing of Wagner. Already Plato has doubts about his teacher's career: need it have been so highly colored and so brief? It has been

observed that if Plato's state had ever gotten off the ground
the first index of outlawed artists would have included the
early Plato and maybe the historical Socrates—wholesale
dealers in irony, ambiguity, heartbreaking chromaticism. In the
Republic, Plato begins to purge his writing of the novelistic
felicities that had reached their height in the *Symposium*. Just
so, by silencing the oboe and the harp, he would "purge the
city which we said was so luxurious." Just so he would purge
music of modes that are convivial—*sympotikai*, suitable for a
symposium. "We are not innovating," says his Socrates, "in
preferring Apollo and the instruments of Apollo to Marsyas
and his instruments."

Aristotle in his *Politics* takes up the question of the moral
value of music where Plato left off. "When men hear imita-
tions . . . their feelings move in sympathy." "The objects of
no other sense, such as taste or touch, have any resemblance
to moral qualities," but even "in mere melodies there is an
imitation of character." Aristotle confirms Plato's account of
the emotions aroused by the various modes and rhythms. He
agrees that music is essential to moral education, especially in
the early stages, since "music has a natural sweetness." He
adds, "There seems to be in us a sort of affinity to musical
modes and rhythms, which makes some philosophers say that
the soul is a tuning, others, that it possesses tuning."

Aristotle would not have children taught to play the oboe,
the harp, the triangle, or other "professional instruments" not
"conducive to virtue," or to play or sing in sad or enfeebling
modes. But he does not join Plato in rejecting these modes
and instruments outright. For moral education is not the only
purpose music can serve. It can also provide intellectual pleasure, relaxation, and catharsis.

What is catharsis? Aristotle uses the word "without explanation," promising to gloss it in his lectures on poetry. But that
section of the *Poetics* (like the part that must have covered
music) is missing. Although it sounds like a rhetorician's coin-

age, *catharsis* is common Greek. It needs explanation only because its usage is common to the point of promiscuity. Catharsis can refer to the purification of the soul, the evacuation of the bowels, the clearing of a forest, the pruning of a tree, the winnowing of grain, menstruation, the cleansing of food, the cleansing of the universe by primordial fire, or the explanation—clearing up—of a concept like this one. Plato uses it for the purging of a decadent city. Aristotle, too, is concerned to purge the city but doesn't believe it can be done by fiat. All of us have unhealthy humors in us. They cannot be expelled from the city once and for all; they can only be stirred up and expelled periodically from each man's breast. Sacred rituals can do this; so can secular music and drama.

Feelings such as pity and fear, or, again, enthusiasm, exist very strongly in some souls, and have more or less influence over all. Some persons fall into a religious frenzy, whom we see as a result of the sacred melodies . . . restored as though they had found healing and purgation. Those who are influenced by pity or fear, and every emotional nature, must have a like experience, and others in so far as each is susceptible to such emotions, and all are in a manner purged and their souls lightened and delighted. The purgative melodies likewise give an innocent pleasure to mankind.

It follows that "all the modes must be employed by us, but not all of them in the same manner. In education the most ethical modes are to be preferred, but in listening to the performances of others we may admit the modes of action and passion also." Even the oboe, which according to myth Athena invented and then (because playing it uglified her face) threw away, is useful "when the performance aims not at instruction, but at the relief of the passions."

One might say that Plato uses a macroeconomics of the

emotions, Aristotle a microeconomics; but that is not the real disagreement. Plato, as much as his student, has his eye on the individual soul. It is just that he considers it more pliable, or perhaps tunable. The soul resonates in sympathy with the spirit of the music it hears. If it hears enough virtuous music it becomes permanently tuned to virtue. This means that one will tend to behave virtuously, not that one will *be* virtuous: that would require self-knowledge, a rarer thing.

Plato developed several models of the soul's operation, of some complexity; his theory of music is not based on a primitive feeling that like produces like. In fact, his psychology in the *Republic* is anything but mechanistic. His world is like an orchestra tuning up. To the untrained ear it sounds like a free-for-all, but the initiate knows that there is a perfect pitch to which this cacophony aspires, and he judges every object by its correspondence to the heavenly tuning fork. It is no accident that when an instrument is perfectly tuned to that standard it is also internally in harmony. When a man tunes his soul rightly he establishes a harmony of its three elements: the rational, the appetitive, and the spirited (*thymos*, an untranslatable word for the willful, proud, impetuous, fierce and noble in man, the warrior in him). Since this is what the very nature of the soul demands, it follows that "virtue . . . would be a kind of health and beauty and good condition of the soul, and vice would be disease, ugliness, and weakness."

For Plato it is in the natural order of things that desire, pride and related passions should be controlled by reason. Give a man good education and good music and his passions will fall into line. Aristotle is less sanguine: "For men are good in but one way, but bad in many," he says in his *Nicomachean Ethics*, quoting an unnamed poet. Virtue resides in the mean, which is a single point on a vast spectrum of error. Since the passions are the stuff of virtue, the idea is not to make reason crush them, but rather to let reason measure out each one— not too much, not too little. And the passions can't be calibrated once and for all; they must constantly be monitored and corrected by a kind of negative feedback. Sometimes pity or fear or enthusiasm will build up to unhealthy levels. To discharge them in action would not be virtuous and might be disastrous. To soothe them with temperate melodies would at best be a stopgap, like damming up steam that needs to escape. The alternative is catharsis.

Both sides of this ancient argument are still current, although rarely articulated. In America we have a pentatonic scale whose special function is Aristotelian: when we're blue, we listen to the blues. It's the hair of the dog that bit you, a sort of homoeopathy or immunotherapy. Diatonic music influenced by the blues is also used this way. When melancholy we listen to jazz ballads, with their poignant seventh chords; when anxious or antsy or angry, to bebop or rock. In each case we choose music that will confront our mood, contend with it, force it out, *express* it. But Platonic voices always protest that such music is too mournful, too sensuous, or too frantic and that, far from exorcising our demons, it exercises them. In the twenties jazz was called the devil's music. Now rock has that title, and every six months or so psychologists release a new study showing the unsettling effects of rock music on algebraic problem solving or the growth of tomatoes. (I am not making this up.) One recent study concluded that mental hygiene was best served by music in three-quarter time—like the waltz, which nineteenth-century moralists so detested. Swing, once subversive, is now so acceptable to Platonists that it serves as elevator music. The historical slippage here suggests that catharsis cannot be had either from music that one has not yet begun to understand or from music that one understands too well. The first can only annoy, the second sedate.

The role of understanding is most apparent in our response to concert music. Popular music (and to some extent jazz) tends to be emotionally stable, so that a given piece is all of a piece, like a lyric poem. A piece of concert music develops emotionally as it moves along; its moods change, and the mood of a section cannot be grasped apart from the whole. Unlike Greek modes or Indian ragas, our keys are meaningful (for most listeners) mainly in relation to the keys that surround them in the work. Our music has an emotional progress that we can hardly help thinking of as dramatic.

Aristotle in the *Poetics* shows how the plot structure of tragedy arouses pity and fear; perhaps the lost section would have told us what in the plot guarantees that they are purged. It might also have explained the role of music in the process (for tragedy, like most Greek poetry, involved music). But it is unlikely that the music itself, apart from its alternation of choral odes and trimeter, developed dramatically. The structure of European classical music does tend to be dramatic, though, as no less a dramatist and music critic than Bernard Shaw acknowledged in a postcard to his friend Elgar: "Why not a Financial Symphony? Allegro: Impending Disaster, Lento maestoso: Stony Broke, Scherzo: Light Heart and Empty Pocket, Allegro con Brio: Clouds Clearing." This is the model of a Beethovenian symphony in a minor key, with a finale or coda in the major—the nineteenth-century rationalization of tragedy. It might instead stay in the minor and keep the tragedy classically bleak. Or it might move to the major in a way that suggests not a happy ending, but resignation and a deeper redemption. A supreme instance of this is Mozart's G minor Quintet, which leads us through a landscape of almost unbearable sorrow and then, halfway through the last movement, takes us by the hand and makes us dance for joy to a tune that is a distant major-key cousin of the work's anguished opening theme.

Here is a direct way in which music can lead us from bad humor to good. But a classical tragic structure can do the same thing indirectly, by purging the bad humor and leaving a vacuum that healthy, fresh air will rush to fill. There are lots of other permutations, each in its own way unacceptable to the Platonist. Take Mahler: by pulling us along these vast metaphysical curves, does he pull us out of our self-pity? To some people it feels that way. But the Platonist says we are only sinking deeper.

It could be argued that Mahler's art lies in making structure irrelevant; that he needs so tremendous a structure precisely because he is looking for a single redeeming moment. And in fact catharsis doesn't always depend on a grand design. The experience can be concentrated. It can come from a moment's immersion in an urgent river of sound. Conversely, the sympathy theory does not have to be discomfited by Western musical form. It need only take a sort of Pythagorean view of form, seeing it as a linear dimension of harmony (as it was seen by the musicologist Heinrich Schenker), a matter of architecture rather than drama. Certainly there is a good deal of eighteenth-century music that seems emotionally static, or at best circular. It is difficult to find the standard ABA form enthrallingly dramatic (as Raymond Leppard has observed of Handel's arias da capo, "What do you do with a form that is basically, 'Part 1: I've killed my aunt; Part 2: But she was basically a very nice person; Part 3: I've killed my aunt'?" Compare Glenn Gould on the problem of repeats in Bach's partitas: "Saint George can only kill the dragon once"). On the other hand, ternary form does bear some resemblance to the archetype of comedy described by Northrop Frye, which has its own cathartic power. In general it is fair to say that the developmental forms of concert music (and of some non-Western musics, such as that played by the drum ensembles of Southern Africa) are more amenable to Aristotelian use, and short or static forms to Platonic. But the poise and pleasant antiquity of classical music make it, measure for measure, very attractive to the modern Platonist.

Let me return to a what-if I discussed with Nina. You are in a foul mood and someone puts on some Mozart in C major—not the *Jupiter* Symphony, but something blithely cheerful like the Piano Sonata K. 545. That very first sequence of scales is likely to test the patience of the most committed Platonist. *I'd probably get very annoyed.* Nina's response reminds me of something Beecham once said when Ethel Smyth chided him on an uncharacteristically frantic performance of *Figaro*:

> What with this heavy responsibility and that insoluble difficulty and the perpetual inrush of one thing on top of another, I was often in such a state of exasperation that I neither knew nor cared what I was doing. As for Mozart . . . don't you know how, when you are in that state, if the porter or the postman or some quite neutral person comes in, you can be quite civil and self-controlled. But if somebody you are fond of pokes a head round your door, you'd like to murder that person! Thus with Mozart. In such cases my feeling would as likely as not be "Damn and thrice damn Mozart."

When someone I am fond of walks in on my exasperation he is likely to try and recall me to my better self. But I have no desire to rejoin my better self, at least not yet. My savage breast refuses to be soothed, and every stroke rubs me the wrong way. And of course misery hates good company.

Now what we are talking about is not just "cheerful" Mozart but real Mozart, the full-grown, full-blooded Mozart in which sunlight and shadow are as inseparable as in a dappled wet meadow in May. It is too perfect. And in this sense Mozart is a paradigm of classical music. Most concert music written before the present century strikes the casual listener as a little too noble, too pure. As Nina put it, "I don't want to be ennobled." Her urban nervousness won't be Platonized away, and only sometimes submits to the fine alembic of a Beethoven sonata. The raw materials are too coarse, the premises too ugly. Most of the time punk rock works better, even for a woman who grew up playing Chopin on a blond piano.

Anyone who in the thick of this TV civilization can listen

constantly to Beethoven's quartets is either spiritually deaf or a saint. The music makes demands that under present conditions are simply unfair. For a modern catharsis *The Rite of Spring* (describing a rite not unlike the Dionysian mysteries Aristotle mentions) or Weill's *Mahagonny* seem more to the point—they have the nastiness, the meanness of spirit that we trust. Not all twentieth-century music has that quality; Webern and late Sibelius are so pure that one almost feels a need to prepare for them as for prayer. But those composers were hermits by inclination, and to hear their music we have to think like hermits.

It's not that this century is so much more horrible than past centuries (although at any moment it could be). The great cause of our unease is trivial, a by-product of democracy and electronics. Mass culture goes for the lowest common denominator, and this turns out to be much lower than the "lowest" element included. By any standard but sophistication American television is worse than anything America's various folk cultures had ever held up to inspection. American pop music is sometimes much better, but it can hardly extricate itself from the logic of television. Indeed, the demands of promotional video are likely to draw it much closer. New wave musicians are very conscious of the fact (they invented rock video) and exploit it with Brechtian relish. As children of Dada they share the objective of much modern art: to take what is ugliest in our experience and, by rearranging and distorting it, work a double alchemy, purifying both the object and the observer. Sometimes it works, sometimes not. The principle that if garbage goes in garbage will come out, although usually applied to computers, has some bearing on artists as well.

Plato wanted to supervise all artists and craftsmen so that "our guardians may not be bred among symbols of evil, as it were in a pasturage of poisonous herbs, lest grazing freely and cropping from many such day by day they little by little and all unawares accumulate and build up a huge mass of evil in their own souls." The modern artist believes that by manipulating symbols of evil he can redeem them. At least, he has to try—this cathode-ray pasture is all we have. But what if it turns out that in the course of our culinary experiments with weeds we are poisoning ourselves?

The case of pop music (and of avant-garde art music parasitic on it) poses in its prickliest form the general problem of Aristotelian listening. The problem applies to other kinds of music, as well. You can't get much more spiritual than Mahler, but how many hours of his music can you absorb before accumulating a lethal dose of *Weltschmerz*? Or much nobler than Schoenberg, but how much can you take in before you find yourself grinding your teeth?

Catharsis is a subtle process. It doesn't always happen when we want it, and we don't always want it when we think we do. Sometimes we secretly want to wallow. When I say, "Damn Mozart. I'm angry. I need something to get this out of my system, like Elvis Costello," I may actually mean, "I want to stay angry. I want to revel in spleen" (or melancholy, or lovesick lassitude, or whatever).

Amateurs of the phonograph know well the art of matching music to a mood. The mood may be nameless, but somewhere (in your collection, you hope) there is a record that perfectly expresses it. The sky is overcast, things have gone badly, you look forward to snow: Heifetz playing the Sibelius Violin Concerto. The smell of wet wool, uncomfortable memories: *Highway 61 Revisited*. You asked your husband to leave you and he obliged, you pace the house blankly, your son is getting restless, you are waiting to understand something: Bach's Cello Suite in G played on a child's toy phonograph on the floor where you sit. (The last scene, so European, is from Peter Handke's film of *The Left-Handed Woman*.)

This art can be honed to a morbid exactness, self-indulgent and sometimes self-defeating. Let's take a trivial paradox. Say that last night, in a troubled mood, I played the Tenth String Quartet of Shostakovich in hopes of some kind of catharsis or consolation. Tonight I find myself humming the second theme, with its perfect fifths and Old Believer gospel richness, and—on the principle that the phonograph is an extension of the vocal cords—I put the record (Borodin Quartet, good clean Socialist engineering) on again. Sure enough, I soon find myself in that same troubled mood, even though the problem that was troubling me last night has been solved in the course of the day. Is it possible the theme came back to me just because it was *catchy*? That would mean an obsolete mood can perpetuate itself by latching on to a durable tune.

Theodor Reik, the psychoanalyst who wrote *The Haunting Melody*, would say the tune haunted me because my problem lay deeper than I knew and had not really been solved at all. But surely there is a danger of wallowing in a problem. And there are activities related to wallowing but more respectable that can also be risky. Rather than catharsis, one may actually want consolation: this concept falls between our two Greek stools, because for the Greeks consolation was the province of rhetoric and philosophy, not of art. Brahms is the great consoler. He lets you feel good about feeling bad. Or one may want self-knowledge: not to purge one's feelings but to articulate them. It may be a mark of "serious" music that it offers this sharpness of focus, while most pop music exaggerates feelings and substandard jazz diffuses them. Articulation is not *incompatible* with catharsis; by the same token, psychoanalysis is not incompatible with cure.

One might argue that as the tragic hero (such as Oedipus) is purged when he recognizes his objective situation, so the spectator is purged when he recognizes his emotional situation. Nietzsche would say that the recognition goes deeper, that it is a recognition of a metaphysical unity in which the tragic hero's situation is also mine. But before we can apply any of this to music we need a clearer sense of how music "articulates" or "expresses" or "represents" the emotions, if it does.

In 1854 Eduard Hanslick gave a theoretical underpinning to his preference for Brahms over Wagner in *The Beautiful in Music*. He wrote:

> Only by virtue of ideas and judgments—unconscious though we may be of them when our feelings run high—can an indefinite state of mind pass into a definite feeling. The feeling of hope is inseparable from the conception of a happier state which is to come, and which we compare with the actual state. The feeling of sadness involves the notion of a past state of happiness. . . . On excluding these conceptions from consciousness, nothing remains but a vague sense of motion which at best could not rise above a general feeling of satisfaction or discomfort. The feeling of love cannot be conceived apart from the image of the beloved being, or apart from the desire and the longing for the possession of the object of our affections. It is not the kind of psychical activity but the intellectual substratum, the subject underlying it, which constitutes love. Dynamically speaking, love may be gentle or impetuous, buoyant or depressed, and yet it remains love. This reflection alone ought to make it clear that music can express only those qualifying adjectives, and not the substantive, love, itself. . . . A certain class of ideas, however, is quite susceptible of being adequately expressed by means which unquestionably belong to the sphere of music proper. This class comprises all ideas which, consistently with the organ to which they appeal, are associated with audible changes

of strength, motion, and ratio: the ideas of intensity waxing and diminishing; of motion hastening and lingering; of ingeniously complex and simple progression, etc.

Hanslick reminds us of the comically disparate interpretations that people will place on a single melody. Even vocal music that seems perfectly matched to its text would match an antithetical text just as well if we gave it the chance. "A melody, for instance, which impresses us as highly dramatic and which is intended to represent the feeling of rage can express this state of mind in no other way than by quick and impetuous motion. Words expressing passionate love, though diametrically oppposed in meaning, might, therefore, be suitably rendered by the same melody." Now Hanslick plays his trump: "At a time when thousands (among whom there were men like Jean-Jacques Rousseau) were moved to tears by the air from *Orpheus*:

J'ai perdu mon Eurydice,
Rien n'égale mon malheur,

Boye, a contemporary of Gluck, observed that precisely the same melody would accord equally well, if not better, with words conveying exactly the reverse, thus:

J'ai trouvé mon Eurydice,
Rien n'égale mon bonheur."

One might respond that this aria does tell us something about the union of opposites—not in music, but in the heart. Not just that opposed emotions may have the same dynamic, in some cold physical sense, but that they can actually *feel* frighteningly alike. Remember Mann's remark about our dead, that we don't really want them back? That seems to me to go to the heart of the Orpheus myth, with its unbearable reversals—now you see her, now you don't. But let us be more conventional about this aria. The words express regret, a sense of loss. Yet this specific kind of sorrow, which Hanslick would consider highly conceptual and inexpressible in music, contains remembered joy. It also contains a certain relief: now I can finally see her, in her temporal entirety, and sing perfect songs about her. Is it accidental that Orpheus is the hero of one of the first of all operas, Monteverdi's *L'Orfeo*? Anyway, haven't all the saddest songs a drop of joy in them, just because they are being sung? And are not all artists accomplices in their own sorrows, which are the precondition of their joy? (Adolphe de Leuven of the Opéra-Comique pleaded with Bizet and his librettists, "I beg you, do not let Carmen die. Death has never been seen on this stage." But Bizet loved Carmen too much to let her live. Don José's closing cry might be the author's epilogue: *C'est moi qui l'ai tué, ah Carmen, ma Carmen adorée.*)

A number of thinkers before Freud's time glimpsed the principle of ambivalence, but only the likes of Bach and Mozart were able to systematize it. Music is ambiguous not because it's vague, but because it is uncannily precise. I once tested Hanslick's example on someone quite innocent of Gluck and of Italian (the language in which the opera is generally sung) who guessed that the character was remembering something, regretting someone. Hanslick would probably credit this bull's-eye to the singing of Janet Baker; for he claims that while composition is an exercise of abstract imagination, performance allows for "a direct outflow of feeling into sound." He never explains this paradox.

Hanslick says that music is an acoustic phenomenon, a matter of physics, and so has only the resources to imitate physical states such as rest and motion, tension and relaxation. But the resources of speech are also acoustical, and much more limited, and yet sentences readily express or refer to emotions. The response to this would be that music has no semantics. The response to that would be says who? Deryck Cooke in *The Language of Music* has picked up and dusted off a Western tradition dating back to 1400 that makes of music "a language of emotions, akin to speech." Thus the progression 5-(4)-3-(2)-1 (minor) "has been much used to express an 'incoming' painful emotion, in a context of finality: acceptance of, or yielding to grief; discouragement and depression; passive suffering; and the despair connected with death" in music from Dunstable to Tchaikovsky. This code is a cultural artifact; other cultures have their own codes, which may be as general as the Greek system of modes (what we know of it) or as fully determined as the musical speech of Cyrano's moonmen.

But the code Cooke has broken is not a purely conventional one. Its "semantics" are rooted in the way the physical and dynamic materials of music—those Hanslickian materials which we can, as it were, visualize—depict the emotional life. Its conventions are less like the pure conventions of speech than like the subtle conventions of visual art. The subjective element is at least as strong as in abstract (but representational) painting.

Something like this is the approach Susanne Langer takes in her magisterial study of symbolism, *Philosophy in a New Key*. Of the many emotive theories of music advanced in the last few centuries hers is the most intelligent, and if she does not deeply disagree with what Richard Hooker wrote in 1594—that music uniquely represents "the very standing, rising and falling, the very steps and inflections every way, the turns and varieties of all passions whereunto the minde is subject"—she fleshes it out nicely.

"We can use music," she says, "to work off our subjective experiences and restore our personal balance, but this is not its primary function. Were it so, it would be utterly impossible for an artist to announce a program in advance, and expect to play it well." Music is not self-expression in the usual sense. Instead, "it expresses primarily the composer's *knowledge of human feeling* . . ." It is not precisely a language of emotion, as it has no vocabulary; but though denotation is lacking there is connotation to burn, the mark of true symbolism. Notes are not interchangeable with words like "anger" or "love," because "*music articulates forms which language cannot set forth.*" Naturally a melody admits of widely differing interpretations, "for *what music can actually express is only the morphology of feeling*; and it is quite plausible that some sad and some happy conditions may have a very similar morphology." In music there is no fixed denotation, but rather "a transient play of contents" much truer to our inner experience. Anyone in the market for an emotive theory of music can stop right here. But though the wisdom of centuries supports it, I am uncomfortable with this special status of music. It has to cramp the Muse, confining her to the inner world while her sisters range the inner and outer at will. "Music is our myth of the inner life," says Langer. Aren't all myths myths of the inner life, as well as the outer? They would hardly hold us as they do if they did not penetrate to the inner life. And they would not hold us, either, if they had no concrete contents (the plural is important) for us to hold on to.

There is something prissy and insulting in making the musician a species of psychologist. Dante was that, but he was also an astronomer, theologian, historian, political polemicist, metaphysician. Can we say less of Beethoven?

It is true that Western music reached its summit at a time and place of obsessive inwardness—Germany and Austria in the eighteenth and nineteenth centuries. Social life was stuck in its tracks, so people explored their insides. But alongside music it was not psychology that flourished (that happened later, when music was disintegrating); it was history, geography, natural science, and philosophy, above all metaphysics. There is another clue. Metaphysics grew from myth. Both grope for a layer of existence that is the foundation of every other, lending its deep structures to every other realm—the physical, the biological, the emotional, the social, the artistic. These clues point to Schopenhauer and to the final chapter of this book. For the moment we can accept under protest an emotive theory of music something like Langer's, the protest being that emotion is only one of the things music can represent, and perhaps a secondary one. We can also indicate the general terrain where a solution might be found to a puzzle that Hanslick poses and Langer avoids.

Hanslick says that what we commonly call emotions have concepts hidden in them. For example, "the feeling of love cannot be conceived apart from . . . the longing for the possession of the object of our affections." This puzzle does not yield to Langer's denotation/connotation surgery, nor to her opposing of "morphology" to the "condition" in itself. But suppose we admit the depiction of something external—a morphology, but not of the emotion itself. A gentle melody may or may not indicate "gentle love" (to use one of Hanslick's examples). But if there are two melodic lines in registers an octave apart, and neither is obbligato, then love is forcibly suggested, even if the melody is played by violin and cello rather than sung. The depiction of an external fact helps to define the inner one. Langer says a program is a crutch. I would say a program in this larger sense is one of the legs.

In any case, the view of music as a representation of "how feelings go" (Langer) does not prejudice the issue between Plato and Aristotle. Langer allows that music can have a contagious effect on the listener's mood and that it can be used by the musician as a means of venting his present emotions. She implies that these are degenerate cases. But it is not hard to see how on a higher level a musical representation of noble emotions might ennoble us or an image of good cheer cheer us, just as they might in a lyric poem. Likewise, a representation of our own present emotions might serve to purge them (the music burning them in effigy). It is often the vagueness of our mental states that is most disturbing, and the way they infiltrate and unman us, so that we can hardly distinguish them from ourselves. Music objectifies them. It lets us sever them, maybe jettison them.

In this respect the use of records for catharsis seems especially apt. Your nameless, restless mood evokes a certain record. As the record revolves it seems to reel the mood out of you like a fish. It reels it in, draws it into itself. The mood and the record are one, and when the record is over so is the mood.

This sounds like the best of all possible worlds—the articulacy of finished artistic expression, the ease of primitive emotional expression. Probing one's melancholy with Rubinstein's fingers is almost as easy as heaving a sigh. Remember Nina's dilemma. Either she played badly and got things out of her system, or she played well and didn't. The phonograph was her solution.

The other possible solution—to strike a balance between release and control—eluded her, probably because she played too well. Too well to be a happy amateur (". . . if you haven't got too much talent and aren't equipped with absolute pitch, playing is always a pleasure, particularly if you aren't playing alone," writes Josef Škvorecký in his novella *The Bass Saxophone*). And not quite well enough to be a great pianist, with a technique to match her passion. I suspect that most professional pianists find their equilibrium at a cooler emotional temperature than would suit her.

Presumably, most of us come to the phonograph not because we demand too much of ourselves but because we demand too little. Many of us might be happy amateurs if we were less lazy, and might have been less lazy in a less convenient age. Among amateurs the case that Langer considers degenerate is actually the norm: they express their emotions by interpreting, improvising, or even composing. It may be harder to do this with classical music than with folk or popular music, but it isn't impossible.

Langer makes the task seem harder than it is by distinguishing too rigidly between the expression of emotions and the exposition of our knowledge about them. In fact our emotions and our knowledge of the emotions interpenetrate, so that it is impossible to say which is manifesting itself in a given poem, prelude, or grunt. (*You don't know what love is/Until you've learned the meaning of the blues/Until you've loved a love you had to lose. . . .*) Knowledge filters feeling; feeling colors knowledge; past and present jostle each other.

John Dewey in *Art as Experience* gives a good sense of this interplay. In his lexicon "expression" is a term of praise, reserved for acts of artistry.

> While there is no expression, unless there is urge from within outwards, the welling up must be clarified and ordered by taking into itself the values of prior experiences before it can be an act of expression. And these values are not called into play save through objects of the environment that offer resistance to the direct discharge of emotion and impulse.

Emotional discharge is a necessary but not a sufficient condition of expression. "In an act of expression, things in the environment that would otherwise be mere smooth channels or else blind obstructions become means, media." For Dewey there is no expression without resistance. "Etymologically, an act of expression is a squeezing out, a pressing forth. Juice is expressed when grapes are crushed in the wine press. . . . Skin and seed are separated and retained. . . . It takes the wine press as well as grapes to ex-press juice, and it takes environing and resisting objects as well as internal emotion and impulsion to constitute an *expression* of emotion." Etymology is an uncertain guide; the earliest uses of the word do suggest a pressing out, but not necessarily a refining. Juice can be expressed, but so can "venym" or "the white of an ey." Indeed, what is expressed may be the baser part, as in purgation. Even the notion of external resistance can be done without, since we can think of the organism as "expressing itself," the resistance coming from within. (This is tricky, though, since even the language we think in is in some sense external.) But it is clear that expression requires some sort of resistance—or, looking at it from the other side, effort. And effort is exactly what the record listener escapes.

Not every record listener, though. For Nina, listening is active and effortful. It was effortful for Toscanini; B.H. Haggin tells how the Maestro would conduct his own records as they played, how "his hands involuntarily [began] to move with the music. . . ." Playing records tired him, he said. The anecdote reminds us that conductors do not actually play an instrument, any more than record listeners do. A musical ignoramus can "conduct" an orchestra if it's well trained and indulgent enough to ignore his flailings. But he can't express himself through the orchestra. By the same token anyone can play a record, but only the musically apt can listen well enough to express themselves. For the rest of us record listening is just too easy. It doesn't tire us.

There is, of course, a gross difference between the conductor and the record listener in the matter of self-expression. The one expresses himself in his choice of repertoire and in subtle gradations of phrasing, dynamics, balance, and tempo. The other expresses himself in his choice of repertoire, in his choice of recorded interpretations, and in simple modifications of volume and balance. Disregarding the last set of controls, which Glenn Gould hoped might one day be musically significant but which now are not, the difference boils down to this: the conductor must content himself with a limited repertoire but can make each piece his own, while the record listener has a practically infinite repertoire in which nothing is his own.

The record listener is a child of the supermarket. His self-expression is almost entirely a matter of selecting among packages that someone else designs. And he tends to think that these packages exhaust the possibilities. That kind of freedom can be tyrannical.

The repressive tendencies of Plato's musical doctrines are plain, and it is easy to see how a regime might think to control the minds of its subjects by controlling the music they hear. What is less obvious is that self-expression or catharsis can also be repressive if they are mass-produced. When there are records to meet every mood, from quiet desperation to rebellion, these antisocial affects can be reeled out and neatly packed away in cardboard jackets. Since their expression is prepackaged, no consequences are drawn. Robert Warshow has spoken of "that profundity where art, having become perfect, seems no longer to have any implications." There is such art, but not much of it. Our problem is that even a Helen Reddy record seems to have that kind of finality, simply by a trick of format.

Concerts can perform a similar trick. Their format is perfect for catharsis: you sit down and let the sounds squeeze you, you stand up and let out a burst of vigorous applause, and it's over. The soul has had its sauna. The doors close behind you and you return to the world of taxi meters. Concerts are useful in a society where the inner life needs periodic, safe ventilation. They are not too good for self-expression, either for audience or musicians, since programs are set and tickets bought beforehand. But since (as Aristotle said) we all carry around our little quanta of pity, fear, and other unsettling emotions whether they are unsettling us at the moment or not, the scattershot approach of public performance has its effect. Humors surface and are dispelled. Catharsis of a deeper kind is unlikely, though, for concerts are scattershot affairs in another sense: the edge of the music is deflected by other bodies, other minds.

It is easier to listen to great music in a concert hall than at home, for two opposed reasons. First, in a concert hall one has to listen because there is not much else to do. Second, the burden of the music is shared and so easier to bear, as a pulpit sermon is less onerous than a personal rebuke. One is not singled out; one is not called on to change one's life, any more than the fellow in the next seat. At home one must either ignore the music to some degree or else bear its full weight alone. J.B. Priestly once wrote that we should get down on our knees and thank the inventors of the long-playing record for letting us hear Schubert's C major Quintet in the solitude of our homes. And I do thank them, but at the same time I resent the burden they have placed on me. I am afraid to be alone with great music because I am afraid to be alone with my inner self, with my potential self, with (if you will pardon the expression, which my last chapter should explain) the self of the world.

It follows that I cannot find refuge from music in silence. Actually, the fear of music and the fear of silence are the same. Both can be allayed by talking, reading, or moving about. We all know this from experience, but Charles Lamb makes the best witness. "When I am not walking," he says, "I am reading; I cannot sit and think. Books think for me." He could not sit and listen to concerts, either: "To fill up sound with feeling, and strain ideas to keep pace with it; to gaze on empty forms, and be forced to make the pictures for yourself; to read a book, *all stops,* and be obliged to supply the verbal matter . . . this a faint shadowing of what I have undergone from a series of the ablest-executed pieces of this empty *instrumental music.*"

Thoreau, who liked to sit and think, often wrote of silence and music in the same sweep of the pen. "All sound is akin to Silence; it is a bubble on her surface which straightway bursts, an emblem of the strength and prolificness of the undercurrent. It is a faint utterance of Silence, and then only agreeable to our auditory nerves when it contrasts itself with the former. In proportion as it does this, and is a heightener and intensifier of the Silence, it is harmony and purest melody." (Here is the seed of a theory expounded by John Cage in *Silence.*) "I have been breaking silence these twenty-three years and have hardly made a rent in it. Silence has no end; speech is but the beginning of it. My friend thinks I *keep* silence, who am only choked with letting it out so fast. Does he forget that new mines of secrecy are constantly opening in me?"

The opaque soul feels differently. Music and silence are both supposed to be golden, but most people are terrified of their Midas touch. That is why both are hedged with ritual, or else trivialized—music to Muzak, silence to "peace and quiet," meaning a comfortable background hum. Otherwise they may gild everything, big and little, and that we don't want. We want to keep sex dirty, friendship efficient, work detached or crooked. We don't want to be so noble. Music or silence, either one heard clearly, would ennoble every thing or else explode it. By playing background music we kill both birds with one stone.

Yet the use of background music finds a noble justification in Plato. Plato counted musicians among the craftsmen by whose grace "our young men, dwelling as it were in a salubrious region, may receive benefit from all things about them, whence the influence that emanates from works of beauty may waft itself to eye or ear like a breeze that brings from wholesome places health, and so from earliest childhood insensibly guide them to likeness, to friendship, to harmony with beautiful reason." Music is aligned not with drama but with interior design, with vases and kraters and the ancient equivalents of wallpaper. It is part of the environment and can benefit us without our noticing it.

That music can work subliminally, Muzak proves; it can make one a "better worker" and therefore a "better citizen." As to profounder moral effects, I am not so sure that subliminal music can produce them. But then, what Plato wants music to induce is not virtue itself but a predisposition to virtue, a kind of emotional grace. Moreover, he speaks of music as a branch of education, a study to be actively pursued. While in the

Republic musical skill is commended as an aid to discrimination, both moral and aesthetic, in the later *Laws* active music-making becomes the crux of civic life. The doctrine that the just life is also the pleasant life (a true doctrine, Plato says, but useful even if false) is to be chanted like a spell "without intermission by everyone, adult or child, free man or slave, man or woman; in fact the whole city must repeat it incessantly to itself in forms to which we must somehow contrive to give inexhaustible variety and subtlety, so that the performers' appetite for their own hymnody and enjoyment of it may persist unabated."

Three choirs are to be established, of boys, young men and older men, sacred respectively to the Muses, Apollo, and Dionysus—for the wine of Dionysus will help the older men sing "with more spirit and less bashfulness." The audience is the impressionable young, but the young are also singing; and I suspect the real point is for the singer, whatever his age, to enchant *himself* with the fable of virtue. (As Solzhenitsyn once said, "Whatever you sing . . . you believe.") That is not what Plato says, though; he says that the performance should "both give the performers an immediate innocent pleasure and provide their juniors with a lesson in proper appreciation of sound character." The distinction is surprising, since it runs counter to our own prejudice that it's pleasanter to sit and listen, and more edifying to perform: it fits, however, the experience of the cantor who enjoys chanting the prayers but is too busy singing to meditate on them. In any case the distinction is incoherent by Plato's own lights. He says that the pleasantness of the choric songs will endear them and the virtues they represent to the hearts of the young, and that grown men trained in this way will have "correct feelings of pleasure and pain," being "attracted by the good [in music] and repelled by its opposite." It follows that good music will be pleasant *and* edifying for singer *and* listener. And no one is too old to be edified, for "education—this rightly disciplined state of pleasures and pains—is apt to be relaxed and spoiled in many ways in the course of a man's life." That is why Plato says of his musical spell that "the whole city must repeat it incessantly *to itself*" (my emphasis).

Though Plato now has kind words for Dionysus and for the nobler uses of enchantment, we must not imagine that the pied piper of the *Symposium* has come back. This second republic is hardly more tolerant musically, or otherwise, than the first. But Plato now seems to think we can absorb the influences of music in two apparently opposed ways: passively by living with it, or actively by performing it. The middle that is excluded is active listening.

Given Plato's sympathy theory, that makes good sense. When Nina is in a foul mood, she says, listening to C major Mozart only makes things worse. But playing Mozart on the piano "has to change your mood," as a matter of physiological necessity—if you want to play it well your back will have to straighten, the weight on your shoulders will have to lift. The transformation is unconscious, since your mind is on the notes, not on your mood. In an oddly similar way, cheerful background music can infiltrate and overthrow your ruling humor, slipping past its defenses. That is the hidden principle of Muzak. Workers who would never put up with the exhortations of a live brass band are whipped into productivity by an invisible one.

Because focusing on music as an outside force makes us want to resist it, active listening is the worst bet for Platonism. It is the best bet for the Peripatetic, though. While Aristotle's opinions on musical education mostly parallel Plato's, he is less concerned with skill in performance. Instrumental practice is good for children, who after all "should have something to do, and the rattle of Archytas, which people give to their children in order to amuse them and prevent them breaking anything in the house, was a capital invention, for a young thing cannot be quiet." But "when they are older they may be spared the execution; they must have learned to appreciate what is good and to delight in it, thanks to the knowledge which they acquired in their youth." The oboe, the Lydian harp and kindred sophisticated instruments that Plato rejects altogether, Aristotle accepts for professional use, since they "are intended only to give pleasure to the hearer, and require extraordinary skill of hand." The oboe, in particular, is so exciting that "the proper time for using it is when the performance aims not at instruction, but at the relief of the passions." Likewise, while "in education the most ethical modes are to be preferred . . . in listening to the performances of others we may admit the modes of action and passion also"— these being the modes that bring about catharsis.

Catharsis, for Aristotle, comes when we listen, not when we play. (Aristotle's reference to religious frenzy complicates this, but dancing and even singing might not interfere with one's own catharsis as playing an instrument would.) Nina would agree—at least, playing *well* does not give her the catharsis she wants, and listening well does.

What conclusions have we reached about the effect of records on the national (and international) soul? To begin with, it should be clear by now that music works by sympathy and catharsis, and has every right to work in both these ways. If music is to affect us by sympathy, we should either play it ourselves or let it sneak up on us, as background music. The danger of background music, which recording has made so pervasive, is that it will be used (by us or by others) to alter our mood in a cosmetic way, powdering over our deeper needs. It is true that active playing or singing can also be used this way, so that all that is accomplished is repression, in the psychological sense—and possibly in the political sense, if some philosopher-king or commissar is forcing you to play his song. But active playing can also heal, as when one plays a Mozart sonata and lets its grace fill one's body and soul. Unconnected to the body, records miss a key connection to the soul.

Catharsis, on the other hand, seems to depend on active listening, and here records come into their own. In some ways they are even better than concerts: they address us more intimately and they allow us more choice, so more self-expression. The problem is that our self-expression comes prepackaged; and we lose the desire to express ourselves the hard way, with our own arms and lungs. And despite Aristotle, despite Nina, my experience as a bad amateur is that that is the best catharsis. It will be a tragedy if, because of records, our standards become so inflexible that we cannot be happy amateurs. Then we will still be amateurs of music in the old sense—we will still love her—but as one loves a movie star, not a wife. We won't make love to her. And our souls will have shrunk.

Chapter Eleven

Saul

Saul's second love was his stereo system, a rambling Tiergarten of woofers, tweeters, and electronic crossovers that ruled the living room of his Forest Hills apartment. At the far end, where the windows must have been, there were bass enclosures like fortresses on which midranges, trebles and supertrebles perched like turrets. At the near end, to keep the room from listing, were terraces of electronics overgrown with knobs and bulbs. The turntable had two arms. From the intervals of wall, nudes in oil peeped out, rosey and abashed, selected for amplitude of thigh. There was no room for records; these lined the corridor on either side. At the ends of the corridor a bedroom and a kitchen were weightless as sparrow's wings on a great horned owl.

When I heard the system I was a boy, and it and Saul were in their late prime I had known him as long as I could remember. A crony of my grandfather's, he had given avuncular support to my hatching interests in all kinds of things, above all music. My grandfather is a man of few words and has not been known to read any book not written by a member of the family. Saul talks constantly, now in measured periods, now breaking into a Delancey Street canter. By us he is revered for his learning. He presided over my childhood like an owl, his dark eyes immense and benevolent behind the thickest lenses in creation; his nose hooked, his pate broad, his grin global.

His first love he encountered at the age of seven in his hometown, Vienna. He had wandered into a café where an all-girl band was playing. "The bass fiddle player," he told me solemnly, "was a statuesque redhead with cascading hair falling over her shoulder as her white, marblelike arm caressed the fiddle up at its top, and the other hand moved the bow up and back. And the sounds that came from those ladies! And her décolletage, of course, being she played in a café, was pronounced. . . ."

He discovered records at about the same time. "A friend of the family, an elderly gentleman, was a great lover of cantorial music, an aficionado, who had heard most of the important cantors in person and had a considerable record collection— shellacs, old, heavy, that he played on a Victrola. After you cranked it up some kind of a sound came out of the horn. Anyways, we would sit there and he would describe the cantor, the choir, and the synagogue, and the liturgy, and when he heard that a certain cantor would perform at a certain synagogue, he would take us to hear the actual performance of a particular piece of which he had a record by that cantor and choir."

The scion of rabbis, Saul was not encouraged to visit cafés. Even *Jewish* music was not thought a fit object for his intellect; in a bastion of rationalist orthodoxy like Saul's house, cantors were viewed as acrobats of the larynx. Was there a phonograph on the premises? "We didn't have a clock that gonged! No, the Victrola that I listened to belonged to a member of the family who was not a practicing rabbi, who was a lay person, and who, as I said, exclusively played cantorial records. I don't know that he had anything else." As far as the family was concerned, "there *was* no other music. If it wasn't played by klezmorim at a Jewish wedding and not sung at synagogue, it didn't exist." But Saul, wandering the city like a *Zigeuner*, knew very well that there was other music. And he knew that records were not just liturgical objects.

In 1921 his family left Vienna, sojourned in Holland, and settled in New York. He was nine. "I got killed. I almost got killed. Can you imagine in 1921 speaking nothing but German?" Actually, he was also fluent in Dutch and in Palestinian Hebrew and competent in Galician Yiddish, but none of them did him much good in the Lithuanian yeshiva he attended. In short order he mastered English and mended his Yiddish, then turned his attention to the objects of language, all the things in the world. What was not taught at the Yitzchak Elchanan Yeshiva he taught himself. "I was a voracious reader, so much so that my grandfather would come into my room two o'clock in the morning because he was annoyed that the lights were on. If I was reading anything which was not a *sefer*"—a holy book—"the lights got turned out."

As for staying up all night listening to records, that was out of the question. "That I could not do. I bought a portable phonograph that looked like a typewriter? Like a little suitcase, like a little satchel? And that I could squirrel under the bed. I could hide this little box, and nobody really bothered to ask me what was coming, what was going. But if I had turned— what do you mean at night? If I had turned it on *any* time I would have gotten thrown out." Records were not exactly *traife*, but "if you want to spend money you buy a book, something that you could refer back to and *learn something!* Because if a day went by and you didn't learn something it was a totally wasted day."

So Saul had this little satchel. "I didn't play it at home, but I was able to take it to parties or to gatherings, or just to sit and listen to. I had discovered—*jazz.*

"But I was still a neophyte, I didn't differentiate between Dixie and jazz and the pop music. However, I became a fan of Lester Lanin, who played sweet dance music with a decided beat. And as I remember, my earliest records had to have a *decided* beat." Saul gave each syllable a swing. "The more distinct the bass, the more distinct the rhythmic force of the recording. I didn't go for the instrumental soloists; I developed a knowledge of that much later. I didn't go for Paul Whiteman, because there was too much sound laid over too little rhythm. I was still going to school, and I would provide the dance music to all the little gatherings that we had *far away from home*— never the twain would meet. At that time I was beginning to lead two separate, independent lives: life at home, with all its constraints, and life outside. I discovered that there were some things in life that gave a great deal of pleasure. *Dancing* helped.

"Well, when I was living at home, one of my friends had his own apartment. He wasn't living away from home, the parents had a business on the ground floor, with the rooms in the back of the business. He had a small apartment above the store, which became his residence, even though he lived downstairs, he ate downstairs, his mother would come and clean up—but it gave us a place to hang out. *Now* I remember where the big radio was, where I kept my Victrola, and where we could actually have parties with music. There was an old piano there, and one of the group—we sort of mingled widely—one of the group was a Canadian boy who happened to be a musician, and when he would come up he would play the piano. So we were also exposed to live piano music.

"Then, I think about 1928, the electrical record came, and to me a whole new world opened. Because the beat that you got on the mechanical recordings, which was *imagined*, actually struck out and hit you over the head on the electrical recordings! The very first record that I bought electrically recorded was Al Jolson singing "Sonny Boy." That'll give you an idea of my taste. But it happened to have captivated me, it was so rich in contrast to what I had been listening to before. And of course after that I discovered Bunny Berrigan, Bix Beiderbecke, until I came to Eddie Condon, Louis Armstrong, and then the Swing Era. Well, then you really blossomed. I attended every performance of every band that came through New York. You name 'em, I was there. And began acquiring recordings of Glenn Miller, Benny Goodman, Tommy Dorsey, Jimmy Dorsey—some of the names are already past me— Artie Shaw, Larry Clinton . . .

"Now, the Never Blue Boys? The club, our cellar club!" Saul glossed impatiently. "I was in charge of the recordings. Then, in the late thirties I used to run big dances. Louis Armstrong with Fatha Hines and orchestra played for our dance! We paid them fifteen hundred dollars. He had just come to New York to play the Paramount with Bing Crosby in the movies. All right, we were charging a buck. We put twenty-four hundred people into that hall."

Into the cellar club?

"Oh no. By then I had become the president of the Orchard Street Boys, which was a very high-class businessman's organization, and every year we ran a benefit to distribute matzahs and Passover foods to needy families. I ran a dry goods store. I sold secondhand socks, whatever came along— you know what you sold on Orchard Street. We used to sell a dozen pair of socks for a dollar, men's socks. We used to sell *two hundred dozen* on a Saturday. Because it was less than wholesale; but being that we paid the bill immediately we got the discount, and that was our profit. So we could compete with the whole world. Those were exciting days." He told me a tale of high adventure about the time he and my grandfather bought several thousand beer bottles and couldn't get rid of them. Certain mysterious strangers finally bought the bottles and sold them at an enormous profit to the Pepsi company, which was going into the cola business and needed bottles in a hurry.

Those Depression days were exciting musically, too, and not only on the dance floor. "Radio. Before radio I could listen to a recording of Wagner or Beethoven and not really know the difference except that I enjoyed listening to it, it *sounded* good. Radio began to expose me to identity, because of course the announcer would identify the piece, the orchestra, the conductor, the singers. And then somewheres—I can't really pinpoint it in time—I discovered the Metropolitan Opera."

Saul mused, "You see I missed Caruso, and I missed Galli-Curci, so evidently it had to be in the thirties. I had Gigli and Martinelli and Lauri-Volpi; so that would be before the war, because once the war started," he chuckled, "we didn't have Italian tenors.

"Somewheres I must have been bitten by the bug, because I made up my mind I'm gonna go to the Met, I'm gonna hear the real thing. My first actual attendance was *Lucia* with Lily Pons. Now you know, Lily Pons was a beauty-ful thing on the stage—anyway, to this impressionable viewer she was—and she had a lovely voice, and a lovely quality. So I fell in love. This was the total spiritual discovery of something I didn't know existed. Oh, I'd heard some recordings, even though opera was not commonly played on the East Side; but this was a total revelation.

"My second opera I think was *Trovatore*; from then on it gets lost. I begin to pick up later, when I was really spending a great deal of time, especially in debut performances. I can rattle off a dozen: Richard Tucker. Di Stefano. Umm, del Monaco. Merrill. Roberta Peters, which was one of the most exciting debuts, because she was an unknown, and she was eighteen, and Zerlina got sick. And this nobody, out of left field, gets put on the stage, who didn't know where to stand! You know, up until that point I had never heard a young Zerlina. It was always an imaginary Zerlina, who sang all the notes in the right place, but it was never a young, nubile, desirable Zerlina"—Saul gave the adjectives breadth, and his leer had great dignity—"where you could understand why Pinza starts to drool. 'Cause when he drooled over the likes of Bidu Sayão you could understand it was make-believe, but this looked real. And then she opened her mouth. And she had a *fine* coloratura when she was eighteen. Well, we went crazy.

"Another exciting debut was Tucker, in *Gioconda*. Right at the early part of the opera there's "Cielo e mar," and we hadn't heard him, and you can imagine what an uproar there was. Another beautiful debut: Ferruccio Tagliavini. Of course, later on there where others, but then I was going so often and so regularly that I went through the roster completely. And that goes for the conductors, too: Fritz Busch, Thomas Beecham, Erich Leinsdorf. The famous Chicago conductor . . . Reiner, Fritz Reiner. George Szell. These were giants.

"For years I didn't pay to go into the Met. I knew an usher. Man who would stand outside with the black homburg and the tie? Irishman. I'd hang around in the lobby, he'd pick up the rope, I'd pass through, he'd close it. Course, we would present a gratuity sometimes, when there were not too many people around. And then of course I knew the ushers *in* the house, in the orchestra, so if the critics weren't there, I had a choice orchestra seat. One night I sat with Mrs. Kipnis—Alexander was singing, so I sat in his seat!"

Saul continued to reminisce, reeling out Leviathans that I had known only as tinny voices and tiny figures, flat like gold-fish. At length I asked about records.

"Records were a source of pleasure; they were also the basis of my later appreciation. I don't think that without rec-ords I would have been so serious a listener. Because eventually it was Carnegie Hall and the Philharmonic, pianists, violinists. It was because of the broadening that the records gave me that I began to look for other forms of pleasure, of enrichment.

"Now, in the early fifties you were already getting the London ffrr''—full frequency range recordings. *"That's* when I started really appreciating operatic recordings. But fifty, fifty-one, I still have nothing better than an Atwater Kent five-tube radio—big box, with the horrible sound, but to me it sounded beautiful. I then started hearing about something they called high fidelity, and I became very interested. And I started inquiring, knowing next to nothing about electronics. Because when we had that Kent tube set, who ever looked in the back? Now my first system—I'm trying to remember, there have been so many changes—my first system was a Scott tuner, monaural of course; a British amplifier with great giant cartridge transformers that weighed a ton, that were supposed to be rock solid, had total harmonic distortion of less than ten percent''— we both laughed—"I'm exaggerating . . . five percent, which was, you know, terrific. And I had a Scott preamp and I splurged for an Altec Lansing speaker, extended range single cone. The Voice of the Theater. Sweet sound.

"I then expanded with the Altec triaxial, and I changed the enclosures and all that. But subsequently, when I went on multipath amplification—you know, electronic crossovers—I had nothing but woofers, midranges, highs, and horns, and that's when my equipment was Marantz. So ultimately I had eight electronic crossovers, which means there were sixteen amplifiers''—he laughed—"naturally. And there was an array of speakers all around the room to go with the low basses, one being the big Wharfdale woofer and one being the Altec woofer.

"And mind you, this was a tube system, so periodically I would check hundreds of tubes on my tube tester and try to remember which tubes went to which unit. And the thing was spread out over two rooms on the floor, where you couldn't walk in and out because you might step on something.

"Becoming a Metropolitan Opera standee and spending as many as four nights a week, naturally you begin to differentiate. So naturally I kept up with the state of the art, up until the time that I became ill."

We went to see Saul in the hospital shortly after his operation. Being a high-school student, I was frightened by the quiet. When Saul did speak, he sounded like an old crystal set; the squeak that even now, at moments of self-mockery, breaks in on his baritone dates from that convalescence. Bemusedly he recited the things he was now forbidden, these being more or less everything he had lived for. We saw him next at our Passover seder, where he was accustomed to dish out great helpings of learning he had no use for and get veal, tsimmes, borscht and stuffing in return. This year he talked little and ate only fish, broiled dry.

What followed was still more unsettling. Saul was giving up everything—his books, his nudes, his job as a police statistician, his Met subscription, his records, and his system—taking his pension, and moving to Fort Lauderdale. That town had claimed many, my grandparents among them; but Saul? Fragments of the wreck floated out to me: a privately printed history of classical sex with citations from the Greek and Latin; an anthology of literary seduction; a score of opera recordings, including Kleiber's *Rosenkavalier*, Tebaldi's *Aida*, and a Fischer-Dieskau *Don Giovanni*.

That winter we went down to visit my grandparents, and to my joy I was billeted with Saul. He was staying in a motel efficiency, waiting for the electricians to finish with his condominium and for his wife to finish her career with New York Telephone and join him. We sat up late over a bourbon-and-branch, as Saul termed it. That bit of vernacular made me feel worldly, as did the dilute liquor; the spirit of Koheleth descended on the white plastic tabletop, the warm tumblers, and us in our undershirts. Saul's tongue was loosened. He was bitter.

For years now Lee, his wife, a short, large-headed, hesitantly smiling woman, had pestered him about his system. That monster in the living room was devouring their space, their time and their money. Did it sound *that* much better than a console? Lee shared most of his enthusiasms, his opera, symphony, and ballet subscriptions, but this hi-fi hobbyhorse of his was just too enormous—in effect, Trojan. The household had fallen to it.

For Saul it was all or nothing. Even before the heart attack, maintaining this system had begun to tax him—all those tubes, those exigent knobs. But how could he settle for less? To cut out a couple of crossovers and amplifiers would be like hacking off a limb. He would sense the numb spot, even if no one else could.

But now the handwriting was on the wall. Saul would never again have the energy his rig demanded. All right, he said to himself—to hell with it. Lee wanted it out? Out it went. It went, lock, stock and barrel, to Pittsburgh, to their daughter the psychologist and her husband. "And where do you think it ended up?" Saul asked me. "Gus couldn't handle it, he gave it to Carnegie Mellon, electric engineering. Oh, they loved it." Out went the records, most to Pittsburgh, some to me, a selection of rarities to the Library of the Performing Arts at Lincoln Center. A few hundred, fed to the incinerator, dispersed quietly in the skies over Forest Hills.

All or nothing. If his life was to be Spartanized, he would do it right. The doctor wanted him to take it easy? Lee wanted him to take her south? All right: they would leave this hive of culture and retire to Fort Lauderdale.

In recent years Saul's recollections have mellowed. They glide from Vienna to Orchard Street, from Carnegie Hall to Florida with equanimity. Tropic humors have softened his all-or-nothing stance. He attends the local concert series, has pieced a modest stereo together from odds and ends he used to keep in the bedroom up north, and buys an occasional cassette.

The conversation here drawn upon took place in my grandparents' spare room, the calm eye in a typhoon of relatives and television. A white plastic ceiling fan dreamed overhead; framed photos of earlier selves charitably ignored us. We sat like sages amid valises and damp towels, expanding as our bourbons sank. Saul began to talk about Ezio Pinza.

"The epitome, the very personification of Don Giovanni was only one man, and that was Pinza. I actually get a lump in my throat when I think of Don Giovanni in connection with anybody else but Pinza. When Pinza went into the musical comedy and no longer sang, for two years I could not attend a performance of *Don Giovanni*. For two years I could not attend a performance of *Nozze di Figaro*. Two roles died in my lifetime with Pinza. Because no one has been able to infuse the Champagne Aria in *Don Giovanni* with that tremendous life force, that tremendous verve, that great reaching for the fullness of every pleasure that life could give us—*now*, not later, not living for some future reward but getting it all right now—no one has been able to express it like Pinza did. In the 'Vieni alla finestra,' the balcony scene, Romeo couldn't out-Romeo Pinza. What female with any kind of warmth in her body could resist his serenade?

"Now, let us not forget another role of Pinza's that I don't think has been duplicated, and that is Mephistopheles in *Faust*. When he turns to Marguerite's neighbor, when he's trying to seduce her to get her out of the way of the main seduction, and she turns to him—unknowingly of course—and says, But I am a married woman, and he says, Don't worry, *we'll correct that*—not one person in the audience doubted that here was Death speaking in the most unctuous, in the most insidious kind of way, which was a secret between the audience and him but totally unknown to her. Now, nobody has been able to do that but Pinza.

"When you listen to Pinza, you can only describe his voice—now silken is too weak. Velvet. Plush. Incidentally, I also remember Pinza doing Sarastro in *The Magic Flute*. Now maybe his voice could not reach as deep as some bassos, but unquestionably you knew this was a glorious, a sublime person that you were hearing, and you forgot that it was Pinza; it was Sarastro, the great perfect dream of what man can achieve." Here was one of those astronomically rare alignments that fulfill a role as if for the first time, and it was Pinza's genius to pull this off regularly—like a full eclipse appearing several times a week, bull's-eye, over Thirty-fourth Street. "When there is that rare combination of all of the essentials of person and character and beauty and voice and image that you accept entirely as being true and real—those moments, whether in opera or in theater, are treasured. And if one is fortunate enough to have experienced them, to have been there when it happened, I guess that's what life is made up of. Of moments."

As Saul had waxed philosophical, I asked if his stereo system had been mainly a time machine designed to recapture those moments. "Oh no," he said. "It was not intended to recapture any of these, because it couldn't. It was parallel but separate. In other words, the pleasure I derived from recordings was independent of any pleasures I may have derived from the real thing. But I'm fortunate in having experienced so many real, that I can sort of trade off against what I enjoy from the recordings. Because it's the real that stay. They are indelible. I don't know if I ever had any indelible recordings, do you follow me?"

A paradox, I said.

"You know it's a strange thing. I find myself listening to a recording, and in some cases being familiar with the face of the artist that is doing the recording, but I don't see *that* face; I see the ideal face that I once was terribly impressed by in a live performance, where the person taking the character really fit the character. It is natural that when I hear some Zerlina on a record doing the 'Batti batti,' I can't help it, I remember Roberta Peters. It's inevitable. All other Zerlinas sing the role, but only one Zerlina actually lives the role. And that's Roberta Peters, that one time.

"Now Caballé, on the other hand, is an artist who when she attempts a role which incorporates a love interest is much more easily accepted with your eyes closed. The beauty of listening to a recording is you *dooooon't see.*" He rolled out the word like a window shade. "You only hear and feel."

If records had their place, but it was a modest one, what was the point of all that equipment?

"The ideal was to overwhelm me with the realism of imagining that it is a true reproduction of a live performance, which of course is very subjective and probably *un*attainable. But, in reaching out for the impossible dream, I kept adding and changing and improving and growing. To the point where it became—what shall I say—a travesty. Because no one in his right mind in a small apartment should have that much equipment. When this was shipped to Pittsburgh they hired a U-haul, and they barely got it in.

"And there was always the deep knowledge that nothing, nothing can come up to a live performance. Maybe that's because I did not live to the age of digital. I don't know. But I certainly didn't achieve it, with all my expense and effort."

Did he feel, I asked, like Moses on the mountaintop, barred from the promised land of digital technology? He quickly took up the theme. "So here I am sitting on this mountain, looking over this great expanse and knowing that somewheres over there yonder there is great new things that I'm not going to have *and who cares.* I'm not even reading up on the literature, because it is a mountain to which I do not aspire."

I asked if he could imagine any kind of digital or video or multimedia experience that might improve on live music.

"Nothing takes the place of real life."

Since when is opera real life?

"Opera is not real life. Opera is a heightened sense of the

emotion connected with life. Because who in his right mind could imagine someone in dire danger of his life stopping twenty-two minutes to sing about it? But I could imagine that a moment of emotion would take twenty-two minutes to describe itself."

Wasn't it possible, then, that just as the opera house heightens the experience of life, some electronic medium might heighten it further? He didn't think there were possibilities?

"Possibilities? If life survives, and continues, possibilities are unlimited. But you're overlooking the most important thing about live opera! The force, the tremendous energy that a group exerts on the individual. Otherwise you'd have no mob scene, you'd have no riot. It is a synergy. Durkheim laid down certain principles of social behavior, and they hold true as much today as in his time, eighty-five years ago. The group justifies the individual."

So why the obsession with high fidelity?

"Now wait a minute." Saul lowered his voice. "*It became an end in itself*. Like some people become stamp collectors? It isn't because they have an interest in lithography or political philosophy. Eventually, it takes over. It has a dynamic all its own. In retrospect, viewing it objectively, I may have been crazy! Becoming so totally involved in something which *did not give back what I put into it*. It had no connection with the pleasures and experiences of real life."

Real life meaning live music?

"Meaning going! seeing! hearing! feeling! Because there are some performances that you actually think you feel. Now, I'm not sorry for all the time and effort and energy and money I put into it, but I can't justify it, because I don't think it rewarded me to the same extent as standing in the snow on line to get in to hear Licia Albanese do Violetta.

"Now that we have been discussing it—and always when an idea is exposed to the light of day, it sort of hits you and says, 'This is not what you thought.' Because you never thought!"—a laugh, a squeak, an Orchard Street squawk of amazement—"you just went right on. So in retrospect, I may be beginning to question all that. But what good would it do me, since I can't start all over again and throw all that equipment out."

In 1950 or thereabouts, when Saul was investing in Marantz equipment, he came to know Saul Marantz. "And Mrs. Marantz, who ran the business. Saul Marantz was an engineer. He had one purpose in life: improved sound, to whatever capability was available. His equipment, I feel, was so majestic and so great for its time, because the *tolerances* were fantastic. And he took me around the factory. The space and manpower that he had assigned to performance and quality control! Everything, every wire that was put into his equipment was tested first for its specs.

"Mrs. Marantz wasn't crazy about Saul Marantz's attitude, because it was costing too much money, and giving less return than she would be happy with; in fact, eventually she sold out to Superscope. But I have the highest respect for that man. Because when I brought him back an amplifier that had a faulty plug, he almost fired half of his control. Who did this! Who approved this! *How* did this get by! He was ranting— sincerely, because to him perfection was the only way. Now, Herman Scott had two heart attacks! He was a perfectionist. But we don't have any more Herman Scotts or Saul Marantzes. Somehow or other in this life and in this world, in the state that we're in, there is no room for perfectionists. They are part of this small bunch of . . . Don Quixotes. And the world destroys them!"

But on what basis did they choose their windmills?

"Saul Marantz was an electrical engineer."

He could have made trigger mechanisms on atomic bombs.

"That strange combination of external forces didn't throw

him into that particular place at that particular time. This is where he found himself and this is where he expressed himself."

Could Saul's own quest—my Saul's—have been just as accidental?

"It might have been."

That was not what I wanted to hear. I offered another hypothesis. That of all operatic characters, Saul most identified with Don Giovanni. (This he conceded at once.) That this had something to do with the Don's philosophy. That audio engineers and audiophiles were not merely Quixotes, but Giovannis; that a certain deep sensuality drove the whole high-fidelity quest. That as a cognac maker continually blends and tests and savors, so the hi-fi perfectionist seeks an ideal sensuous moment in which everything goes right and a perfect sound is heard—a gleaming, spherical drop, a distillation of music. That this was a very specific quest, not interchangeable with the completion of crosswords or the piling up of bottlecaps to make a London Bridge.

Saul failed to take me up on this.

He said that it was a solitary quest. That it was subjective, "so right away you're in trouble, because you can't measure it, quantify it, or identify it. You are never at the point where you say, 'This is *it*.' Because there is always something coming up—not that you're asking for it. You would much prefer that everybody left things as they were, so that you could feel satisfied at the point you have reached. You see the whole history of mankind evolved because of this underlying force. But I'm not mankind! I'm just one little poysun!" His voice jumped like a jack-in-the-box.

Were there moments that justified the effort?

"Moments. Moments. But they were transitory. Because just at the moment when you felt secure, another external force said to you, 'Uh uh. Not yet . . .' But when it was good, it was very, very good. When I put a test record on and it said

'Thirty-five cycles,' and my speakers went"—he paused, listening for the tremor—"and when it said 'Twelve thousand cycles' and my ears started to ring—I knew that it was there, you know what I mean? I had: No hum. No surface noise. No distortion. With the controls and all of the variables that I could bring to bear on it, I could filter out or add or subtract, fine-tune each record to take care of its particular deficiencies. If in your second middle you weren't quite satisfied, you could attenuate or increase a particular segment that would go from five hundred Herz to a thousand Herz without affecting the two hundred and below. But you could also go crazy, which wasn't very difficult. Because sometimes I found myself sitting down and saying: Start all over. Because I lost myself some-wheres along the way."

A memory of Vienna. "There would be roving street bands that would play for coins, and they used to fascinate me. And I remember one day a gypsy ensemble—oh, about five pieces, with a bass viol and a cello and three violins—played in the street. Such sound as I have never experienced! And I fol-lowed them for the rest of the day wherever they stopped, not knowing what street I was on, what part of the city. . . . Of course eventually it got dark, they packed up their instruments and they departed, leaving me completely lost"—he grinned, his eyes gigantic behind the deep lenses—"a small child, not knowing where . . .

   "I found a policeman, who finally elicited from me my address; he took me on a streetcar, because it was no longer walking distance for either of us, and brought me home about eleven o'clock at night, at which time I payed dearly for my love of music." In broad shudders of laughter: "I got a beating that I'll never forget."

Chapter Twelve

Deus ex Machina

There was a time in my life when I needed a daily tenor sax fix. In a pinch, a four-measure break in a pop record would do; and it was remarkable that the oceanic power of the saxophone could be injected so quickly and deeply by means of the phonograph. The sound was a distillation, a serum. It was as if what Sonny Rollins called the "dignity of a big man with a big horn" were akin somehow to the dignity of a big stereo, careless of its power.

"Is it not strange," asks Benedick on hearing the fiddler, "that sheeps' guts should hale souls out of men's bodies?" We delight in the human ability to make something beautiful by scraping horsehair against intestines or spitting air through twisted metal. Instruments that are bitches to play, from which drawing a single clean note is like pulling a tooth, afford the keenest joy of all when played well; every note of the oboe, violin or French horn seems to recall the ordeal of its production and rejoice in its escape.

When such hard-won beauty runs a further obstacle course of polyvinyl chloride, laser light, copper, iron, cloth and wood and reaches our ears in one piece, our delight is that much greater. Like music, audio wrings beauty from an uncooperative medium. In that sense it is an art. And the art of phonography is music multiplied by itself.

The most famous duck of the eighteenth century was made of gilded copper. In a prospectus its maker, Jacques Vaucanson, promised that it would "drink, eat, quack, splash about on the water, and digest its food like a living duck," and by all accounts it did. Vaucanson's duck was the admiration of Europe, and still more marvelous were his musicians. Music boxes with moving figures mounted on them were a dime a dozen, but Vaucanson's automata actually played their instruments. His flautist played a real flute, stopping the holes with his fingers, and played well enough to excite the emulation of Jacquet-Droz and Leschot, the greatest music-box makers of the day. They conjured up a lady organist who played five tunes with her dainty hands as her eyes flickered and her bosom heaved with expression. Between numbers she curtsied. A clockwork-driven, pinned barrel determined her every move.

If these promising beginnings had been chased to their natural conclusion we might not have needed the phonograph. In time these creatures might even have learned to sing; for had not the statue of Memnon at Thebes uttered greetings to his mother, the dawn, every day without fail from the earthquake of 27 B.C., when he lost his head, until c. 170 A.D., when the prosy Romans had him repaired? Maybe not. But Roger Bacon was said to have made a talking head, and indisputably Josef Faber of Vienna made one in the 1860s, with ivory vocal cords and a rubber mouth malleable by means of a keyboard.

But icy fancy gave way to a cool reductionism. In the living room, instead of a curious mechanical orchestra we have a few plain boxes that can play any damned thing we please. The idiosyncracies of the musician's lips and limbs, each a fresh challenge to the eighteenth-century physicist's gay imagination, have been reduced to waveforms and numbers. Much the same happened in the visual realm, where "mechanical pictures," gorgeous moving tableaux, were replaced by the all-purpose "moving picture."

But I am getting ahead of myself. Long before the phonograph, the Enlightenment strain in the quest for mechanical music met a medieval one, grotesque, involuted, nurtured in Black Forest hamlets and the garrets of London and Prague. (Salzburg had a barrel organ in 1502; Henry VIII had "a virginal that goethe with a whele withoute playinge uppon"; the Striking Jacks of Wells Cathedral go back to 1392.) Where these streams converged, as on the neutral ground of Switzerland's Jura Valley, the industry flourished. Until records and radio shut them up, music boxes were everywhere, in scent bottles, beer tankards, fans, chairs that sang when sat on, even bustles like Queen Victoria's which played "God Save the Queen" when she sat down. They were very large, like the coach Kuznetsov and Dubasnikov built in 1785 whose wheels powered a barrel organ, or the Gavioli Orchestrion of 1908 with its 112 notes and its dozen stops. And they were very small, like the pocket watches from which birds or dogs emerged to chirp or bark the hours.

Because they did not attempt to reproduce music, but made their own—however rinky-dink—they were embraced by musicians more readily than the phonograph would be. Leopold Mozart wrote eleven tunes for the barrel organ of Salzburg Cathedral. His son composed for mechanical organ, while Haydn programmed flute-clocks. Muzio Clementi in London built chamber barrel organs in the early 1800s. Beethoven reserved his most bathetic inspiration, the *Wellington's Victory* overture, for Maelzel's Panharmonicon; and Stravinsky evened the score at a stroke by swiping an organ grinder's tune for use in *Petrushka*.

Sir Thomas Beecham begins his memoir *A Mingled Chime*

remembering the music boxes with which his father's house was mined, so that "the visitor who hung up his hat on a certain peg of the hall rack, or who absent-mindedly abstracted the wrong umbrella from the stand, would be startled at having provoked into life the cheerful strains of William Tell or Fra Diavolo." Sir Thomas far preferred these "laughing cascades of crystalline notes" to the phonograph's "whirrings and whizzings." Music boxes were toys, "and none pretended they were anything better"—"they were lovely toys and harmless to offend the most fastidious ear. Hearing them render anything grave or monumental suggested tiny copies of Michael Angelo or John of Bologna done in Dresden or Chelsea porcelain, and if one could not help laughing, at all events the laughter was kindly and affectionate."

The modern equivalents of music boxes and automata have been laughed at, but seldom with affection. The phonograph is admirable when accurate and laughable when inaccurate. The robot, which we had imagined as a refined automaton, a statue that returned embraces, has turned out to be no such thing. In fact, the romance was over the minute Karel Čapek, smack in the industrial heart of the Hapsburg empire, coined the word "robot" from the Russian root for "work." The robot was the image of alienated labor, what men would become after a few years on the assembly line. It was the pipe dream of the master, the nightmare of the slave. Then it began to haunt the master (make your tools too sharp and they may turn on you) and secretly comfort the slave, who might soon have his own slave. Sure enough, the robots one meets today at world fairs and Japanese factories are offspring not of the automaton, but of the spinning jenny. ("The most ineffective kind of machine," Lewis Mumford writes, "is the *realistic* mechanical imitation of man or another animal: technics remembers Vaucanson for his loom, rather than for his life-like mechanical duck. . . .")

Why is it worse to be a robot than an automaton, worse to

imagine oneself a phonograph than a music box? The eighteenth-century music box, like the eighteenth-century man,
was endowed by its creator with a character. The phonograph,
like the mass man, has no character to speak of, or sing from.
It has no music of its own. It only reacts to the data fed it.

The parable of our condition which the phonograph en-
acts—this, and the feeling that music is the last place where
mechanism ought to poke its head—has made it a favorite of
satirists. Orwell could have written his "On a Ruined Farm
near the His Master's Voice Gramophone Factory" near some
other kind of factory, but he chose this one. René Clair could
have set À nous la liberté, the rambling farce that is said to
have inspired Chaplin's Modern Times, at some other kind of
factory; the plot drew on the exploits of the frères Pathé, but
they made motion picture equipment also. The assembly-line
antics would have been the same in any case, but a few crucial
images might have lost their point. When the jailbird brothers
arrive in the city where they will make their fortune, they hear
the lovely voice of a woman fluttering the curtains of an open
window; on further inspection there is only a phonograph, the
first they have seen. Later, celebrating freedom far from the
factory, they sprawl in a field of wildflowers, which sing to
them. The flaring petals vibrate like phonograph horns.

The focus is soft in this scene, the music daffy, and one
feels intensely the ambivalence that makes the whole film so
tricky. In Modern Times, satire and sentiment know a sharper
division of labor; so too in City Lights, but there the phonograph is again anomalous. The poor Blind Girl plays it while
pining for the Tramp, whom she imagines a dashing million-
aire. Here is a comic subject—the blind listening to the invisible—worthy of the elder Breughel, but Chaplin plays it for
tears. On the platter is his own hit-record-to-be, the lachry-
mose "Smile."

In Modern Times the Tramp becomes a machine only
briefly; he is more often a bit of raw material manhandled by

machines. The deeper outrage of being a machine, and a defective one at that, is better plumbed by the set piece near the end of *Limelight* with Chaplin as a violinist and Buster Keaton as his accompanist. The violin untunes itself, Chaplin's leg keeps changing its length, and meanwhile Keaton's music keeps slipping off the piano faster than he can scoop it back on, like a perpetual fountain of paper. In short, they cannot start. They are like a phonograph needle stuck in the very first groove. Robert Warshow speaks of "the deep, sweet patience with which the two unhappy musicians accept these difficulties, somehow confident—out of God knows what reservoir of awful experience—that the moment will come at last when they will be able to play their piece. . . . The scene is unendurably funny, but the analogies that occur to me are tragic: Lear's 'Never, never, never, never, never!' or Kafka's 'It is enough that the arrows fit exactly in the wounds they have made.' " Those analogies should not startle, for the scene is not only beyond satire, as Warshow says, but beyond the tragic and the comic. The tragic and the comic are masks we put on, but beyond both is the mask we are born with. There is nothing sadder or funnier than the body. It, despite all the wrigglings of the *Zeitgeist*, stays put. Even Kafka's line about the arrows is funny, yet it brings to mind his grim penal colony where the prisoner's crime is engraved on his back by the stylus of a giant machine—a machine that suggests the phonograph of Kafka's day, the kind that could record on a wax master and then play back the processed disk. Of course, the story is not about records; it is a vision that the body instantly acknowledges, whatever the mind might make of it. Asking what it means is like trying to read one's own back.

Feeling like a record is even worse, in some ways, than feeling like a phonograph. There is something viciously circular in the life of a record. As a record you make the machine do your bidding, dance to your tune; but the tune was ground into you by a machine in the first place. The parable is not only of technological man but of any man with a body.

Machines are projections. The clockwork flautist is a dream of decorum. The robot is a nightmare of endurance. As Lewis Mumford has written, "men become mechanized, they themselves are transformed into mechanical, uniform, replace-able parts . . . before they take the final step of inventing machines that take on these duties." We create a thing in our own image, then are shocked that we resemble it.

Automata have charmed composers into writing for them and also about them, but in nineteenth-century music that charm gradually goes awry. Beethoven in the Allegretto of his Eighth Symphony seems (scholars disagree about this) to be poking good-natured fun at his friend Maelzel's metronome. The old organ grinder in Schubert's "Der Leierman" seems to have become his machine; although no one ever listens, his stiff fingers never stop their grinding. The alternations of piano and voice, each stunted both rhythmically and melodically, convey the weird kinship of man and machine. Offenbach's Hoffmann falls for a living doll who can sing and dance, and whose melody charmingly spoofs the mechanical antics of bel canto sopranos. When devilish forces tear her limb from limb the scene is gruesome enough for Euripides but tasteful enough for the stage of the Opéra-Comique, as it is merely the disman-tling of a machine.

Things get still more complicated in Stravinsky's *Le Ros-signol*, a work begun in 1908 under the tutelage of Rimsky-Korsakov, whose feathery exotica it mimicked, and finished, after a break for *The Firebird*, *Petrushka*, and *The Rite of Spring*, in 1914. Critics find the styles of the first and last acts inconsistent, but the gulf that listeners other than critics have to leap to get from one end of the opera to the other is not so much stylistic as emotional.

The story follows closely a tale by Hans Christian Andersen in which a nightingale famous among the Chinese peasants is brought to the Emperor's court. Her song brings tears to his eyes, but his head is soon turned by a mechanical nightingale sent by the Emperor of Japan. The true songbird flies away, and the Emperor appoints the automaton as his bedside "first singer." In time the automaton falters, the Emperor falls ill, Death is at his bedside; when suddenly the real nightingale appears and charms Death into yielding up his prize.

The composer starts out with an affection for the flesh-and-blood nightingale and a contempt for the mechanical one in tune with his romantic text. Six years later his sympathies have shifted. He has discovered the pathos of the barrel organ and the anguish of the puppet, Petrushka. He has discovered in this puppet the very image of industrial man, and (turning another corner ahead of traffic) he has seen in mechanism the iron law of all life, from the prehistoric spring of Le Sacre to the winter of St. Petersburg and Paris. ("And though," Paul Rosenfeld writes, "no automata invade the stage in Le Sacre and the score is bare of the clockwork music of its immediate predecessor, it, too, with its dark and ferocious coloring, adjusts us to a mechanistic order of things. . . .") The two nightingales are birds of a feather. The Emperor might as well toss a coin.

To anyone who has heard a nightingale this will not sound far-fetched. The song is superb, but like many bird songs it is ratchety and often repetitive, so it sounds mechanical. There is even a characteristic low rattle exactly like the unwinding of clockwork. We want to think of birdsong as unpremeditated art, which it is; but music boxes do not premeditate either. Bird and box are both, in a sense, programmed. And anyone who watches birds knows the jerky, abstracted motions of the head that forcibly suggest automata.

It would be plausible, though gratuitous, to see in Le Rossignol an allegory of the phonograph, which was all the rage in the Russia of 1908. Maybe Stravinsky, an arrogant young mandarin like Prokofiev, hated the new contraption as much as Prokofiev did. We know that like Prokofiev he later came to respect it; maybe he changed his mind before 1914. In such a reading delicious ironies arise. The clockwork gift that the Japanese bear is bejeweled and bedizened like a prima donna. It is something to look at. The real nightingale is a drab thing, glad to be lost in the thicket. Like the phonograph, it is nothing to look at. Usually, like the phonograph's hidden musicians, it is heard but unseen. That is true of many songbirds; one of the things that keeps the birdwatcher in a state of wonder is the swift attack of disembodied song. Even in winter it may take time to find the telltale throat, and in summer woods it may take forever. (To be awakened by rills of sound and follow them outside, and stand stock still for half an hour while the damp leaves fuse with your bedroom slippers, and peer upward at the transepts of the trees radiant with sound is, to be sure, wonderful whether you find your wood thrush or not.) The disembodied nature of birdsong may be what makes it ripe for recording and for incorporation, in recorded form, into human music. In 1924 Respighi, another pupil of Rimsky, wrote a nightingale into the score of his *Pines of Rome*. Its recorded song would be heard in concert—coming from nowhere, as in a copse of pines—as well as on recordings of the work. A much later classic, the Beatles' White Album, has backup vocals by a blackbird, and middle-brow arrangers have worked birds to death.

However we read *Le Rossignol*, we know Stravinsky embraced mechanism. In 1927 he gave the mechanical a classical pedigree with *Oedipus Rex*; at the American premiere led by Stokowski, twelve-foot puppets loomed onstage (lest we feel superior to puppets) while soloists acted as ventriloquists and an unseen narrator spoke through a megaphone. (Cocteau, the librettist, also wrote a play that hid its narrator inside a giant phonograph.) Stravinsky's respect for mechanism is apparent not only in his written works but also in his recorded legacy, in which are fixed—more rigidly than in the pinned barrel of a nightingale—his own interpretations of his works. But his embrace of the iron law was not gleeful, merely clear-eyed. His pessimism was the narrow aperture through which a sharp picture could be taken.

Other Slavs before Čapek and Stravinsky had heard the rattle of the mechanical. The most terrifying scene in *Boris Godunov* is the one in which the chiming of a clock, with its infestation of moving figures, induces the tsar's hallucination of the murdered child. The clock rings a mocking change on the bells of his coronation. If those promised omnipotence, the clock relentlessly tells of fate's prepotence—the way it lets a figure glimpse the light, then swings it back into darkness.

The Clock Scene works frighteningly well on record; Chaliapin's tinny 1931 recording gives one the sense of trespassing in the tsar's apartments. And in general, motoric music, music with a steady, mechanical beat, works better on record than any other kind. When there is no live performer to fasten on, the mind tends to wander from recitative and wispy impressionism. A beat rivets it, rock steady. This helps explain why American popular songs have sloughed off the Broadway-style slow introduction. It helps explain the success of recorded jazz and rock (as Chuck Berry says, "It's got a backbeat, you can't lose it") and the rolling over of Beethoven in the LP era to make way for baroque concerti grossi. A beat is like a Kantian category, a matrix that lets us perceive things as things instead of chaos. Baffling sounds are more tolerable when they have that backbone, which is one reason why avant-garde jazz-rock commands more followers than avant-garde classical music (except for minimalism, which has easy harmonies *and* a pulse).

Still, it is not exactly a matter of a beat substituting for a face *faut de mieux*. The mechanical beat of rock and roll or

Corelli sounds right coming out of a machine. Do railroad cars sing recitatives? Do air-hammers rhapsodize? "Everything is what it is, and not some other thing," as G. E. Moore said, and a phonograph is not a person.

Taken to an extreme, as it was by the Futurists, the need for something mechanical in music becomes a need for noise. Marinetti, mistaking mechanism for something new, thought it demanded a brand-new aesthetic. But other composers understood that the new aesthetic would in some ways be a very old one. Stravinsky found the materials of his machine-age music in Russian folksong and in Gesualdo, while Varèse reached back to Pérotin. Even George Antheil sprinkled *chinoiserie* on his awful *Ballet mécanique*.

But bad ideas die hard if they are based on bad feelings. Today we have heavy metal music, whose appeal may be compared to that of a motorcycle accident. By embracing the machine with open arms and legs, one seems to expel the mechanical from oneself. As a centaur becomes a god above the ribs because he is all animal below, so the biker's upper extremities cruise in a region of pure freedom. But the compound is unstable and finally explodes.

Seeing the mechanical as something outside himself, man hopes to lose himself in it—literally, if necessary. "War is beautiful because it initiates the dreamt-of metalization of the human body," writes Marinetti. "War is beautiful because it enriches a flowering meadow with fiery orchids of machine guns. War is beautiful because it combines the gunfire, the cannonades, the cease-fire, the scents, and the stench of putrefaction into a symphony." (This is not so outlandish; even the peaceful Sibelius, losing forty pounds in the siege of Helsingfors, had to admit to his diary that "the crescendo, as the thunder of the guns came nearer, a crescendo that lasted for close on thirty hours and ended in a fortissimo I could never have dreamed of, was really a great sensation.")

The love of mechanism has its peaceful side, however. The

young John Cage, for instance, took to spare parts and junk like the inventor's son he was (his father had invented a submarine), using phonograph pickups and radio coils in Rube Goldberg concatenations to get the sounds he wanted. When tape came along he took to that also, splicing twelve hours a day for six months, serene as a sushi chef, to make one work. The machine gave Cage something he deeply needed: unconsciousness, unintention. (His father claimed to do his best inventing while asleep.) Machines are more like nature than we are. Left to themselves, they are all Zen masters. "Ancient painters," Shunryu Suzuki tells us, "used to practice putting dots on paper in artistic disorder. This is rather difficult. Even though you try to do it, usually what you do is arranged in some order." But for a computer this is child's play. To reach the rarefied plane of randomness one must either take soundings from nature or use a machine. Otherwise one's humanity gets in the way. ("Once," Cage writes, "I was visiting my Aunt Marge. She was doing her laundry. She turned to me and said, 'You know? I love this machine much more than I do your Uncle Walter.' ") Even when reproducing human music a machine can naturalize it, by flinging it a random distance from its intended context. In one of Cage's *Imaginary Landscapes* twelve radios randomly tuned play at once; we all do something similar when we casually spin a radio dial or a record.

One can never be quite certain one has arrived somewhere until one has seen a road map. When a state of mind is in question the dialectic is helpful, so let me compress these meanderings into a map of that kind. First there was the Enlightenment, which welcomed the machine as handmaiden of the senses. Then came the romantic reaction, in its liveliest form almost Luddite. The synthesis is modern aestheticism, which senses in machinery something crueler, nobler, more impartial, more interesting than man.

As in Adam's fall God died—at least, was obliged to step

aside and let this accidental god take the limelight—so in the fall of the machine, in the revealing of its power to do evil, man becomes small again; and what a relief that is. When all the forces of nature had yielded to manipulation, nothing was left that was awful enough to worship. Now, as a byproduct of that same manipulation, something truly awful *has* appeared.

These are large themes, which one could illustrate in a book on cars or bombs or whatever technological article one happened to find most appealing or disgusting. The phonograph is an arbitrary topic, like all topics. Some are obviously more urgent, but the urgent ones have already been darkened with excessive light. Maybe a trivial topic will cast a sharper shadow into the fluorescent haze. The phonograph does point up some of these conflicts unusually well; it is not any old machine, but a machine of music, the art to whose condition all others aspire, often with disastrous results. From all other arts the human element must be exiled by an act of will: by a commandment written in stone or by such a forced self-erasure as Ortega y Gasset reproved in modernism. In music, the human element is absent from the start, or rather is present only on loan. Absolute, nonprogrammatic music contains no images of man, and contains his emotions only where he chooses to find them.

When other arts take up the machine as a tool, they cling all the closer to man as subject matter. While painting was at its most nonrepresentational, photography stood staunchly by the human face and figure. The camera's work has to be mimetic, but why have there been fewer still lifes and landscapes than portraits, nudes, and genre scenes? And why did the lensless photography initiated by Moholy-Nagy and Man Ray never really catch on? Again, while drama and dance played with time and geometry, becoming as abstract as the nagging presence of human actors would allow, film remained tangled in plots and characters. Even the freewheeling conceits of Busby Berkeley merely reorganized the materials of daily life. The same can be said of Cocteau and Buñuel. Filmmakers who have experimented with true abstraction are not even avant-garde—they have left the regiment altogether.

Phonography has been different. Record makers have not shunned absolute music. In fact, much of what may be called phonography in the purest sense—music created in the process of recording, like electronic music or studio jazz—is absolute music. Records have enabled the typical listener to experience music, perhaps for the first time, as something absolutely abstract—abstracted from human experience and located in a region far beyond it.

Is that a correct way to experience music? The answer depends on your theory of music, which hangs in turn on your experience of it. But your theory of music must also jibe with your metaphysics. Schopenhauer's theory of music, to which the argument now leads us, was the lintel of a great metaphysical structure full of damp corridors that no one visits anymore. It was popular at one time for its weight and gloom, which answered a *fin de siècle* need, and for its odd but compelling explanation of the way one feels when listening to music. Nietzsche and Wagner both altered the theory to fit the supercharged music they favored. But it is only now, with the help of the phonograph, that we can clearly hear what Schopenhauer heard.

According to Schopenhauer, the world I perceive is merely a representation—*Vorstellung*, which has the physical sense of placing a picture before the mind. The world is something I construct with the aid of certain innate, automatic mental tools. These are "categories" modeled on those of Kant (although for Schopenhauer the category of causality includes all the others). Behind this picture show is the thing-in-itself, which according to Kant is unknowable; but according to Schopenhauer the thing-in-itself is known, and at first hand. It is the will, which I feel in myself and recognize by analogy in all other objects, quick and inanimate. The will is the raging, aimless river that runs through me and through everything else. It is refracted through the Platonic Ideas, reaching various stages of objectification in the rock, the oak, the rabbit, the man. These Ideas or perfect forms are refracted in turn through the principle of individuation—time, space, causality—into the numberless rocks, oaks, rabbits and men that I perceive.

In this way the will becomes an object to me, the subject. Even the will within me, which I know directly, can be an object to me: this happens whenever I explain my behavior in terms of motives, goals, emotions, or character. These are illusions, but so, in a deeper sense, is my direct experience of the will—namely, my feeling of free will. In harsh fact I am a puppet of the will, locked in a death struggle against all its other puppets. ". . . The will must live on itself, since nothing exists besides it, and it is a hungry will. Hence arise pursuit, hunting, anxiety, and suffering." Does all this turmoil add up to anything, as it might for Nietzsche or Darwin? No. The will remains a worm, hungry and blind. In its refractions it battles against itself like the ant-lion that has been cut in two.

Is there any escape? Only the saint escapes permanently, by denying the will to live. But a temporary respite, a "Sabbath of the penal servitude of willing," can be found in art. The artist's perception is not chained to his will. He looks upon an apple tree not as something to eat from or build with, but as something to look upon. So it is no longer an individual object useful or useless to him as an individual creature; it has become the Idea of its species. Art is a copy of that Idea (not, as Plato alleged, a copy of a copy). As artists "we *lose* ourselves entirely in this object, to use a pregnant expression; in other words, we forget our individuality, our will, and continue to exist only as pure subject, as pure mirror of the object. . . ."

Like most mimetic theories of art, this one seems to leave music out in the cold. If no Idea leaves its imprint in music, some still deeper track must be there; for of all the arts music speaks most powerfully. Schopenhauer reasons that it must be like the other arts, only more so—that "its imitative reference to the world must be very profound."

Now, having devoted his mind "to the impression of music in its many different forms," he reaches this stunning conclusion: ". . . Music, since it passes over the Ideas, is also quite independent of the phenomenal world, positively ignores it, and, to a certain extent, could still exist even if there were no world at all, which cannot be said of the other arts. Thus music is as *immediate* an objectification and copy of the whole *will* as the world itself is, indeed as the ideas are. . . ."

Music could exist *even if there were no world at all*. These words pull the earth from under us, as music itself often does: that metaphysical shiver we feel in Carnegie Hall, as if the red carpet had slipped away and left us hanging over the abyss, has nothing to do with the faint rumblings of the N and RR trains.

Both music and the Ideas are objectifications of the will. Although there is no resemblance between them, there must be a parallel. The deep bass, Schopenhauer says, is analogous to the lowest grade of Ideas, the brute mass of the planet from which everything else is generated. Between bass and soprano fall the ripieno or harmony parts, representing the intermediate grades of the will's objectification—minerals, vegetables, animals. And the melody is man: "It relates the most secret history of the intellectually enlightened will, portrays every agitation, every effort, every movement of the intellectually enlightened will, everything which the faculty of reason summarizes under the wide and negative concept of feeling." So music does express feelings, as everyone says it does; but it expresses "their essential nature, without any accessories, and so also without the motives for them."

Of all the parts only the melody is a significant whole, since only man has the connected consciousness that gives a life shape. As the shape of man's life is a restless transition from want to satisfaction, then back to another want, so the shape of melody is "a constant digression and deviation from the keynote in a thousand ways." Yet music gives us solace. It "floats to us as from a paradise quite familiar and yet eternally remote"; for "it reproduces all the emotions of our innermost being, but entirely without reality and remote from its pain." In real life, by contrast, "we ourselves are now the vibrating string that is stretched and plucked."

Now Schopenhauer's words as they float down to us begin to sound less remote, more familiar. Haven't Hanslick and Langer given us the meat of this theory without the scholastic garnish? Even the part about nonhuman nature can be expressed commonsensically: for example, Langer says that the rhythms of the inner life expressed in music may also be those of nature. Schopenhauer's doctrine can be seen as an ingenious but trivial specification, tailoring the harmonic theory of his day to its cosmology. Why not speak clearly, then, in terms of motion or force or unified field theory and forget this stuff about the will?

There are reasons. "Hitherto," Schopenhauer writes, "the concept of *will* has been subsumed under the concept of *force*; I, on the other hand, do exactly the reverse, and intend every force in nature to be conceived as will." The concept of force we know from outside, from perception; but the concept of will we know from within. "Therefore, if we refer the concept of *force* to that of *will*, we have in fact referred something more unknown to something infinitely better known, indeed to the one thing really known to us immediately and completely; and we have very greatly extended our knowledge." Of course, I am tempted to say that only I have will, while the motions of rocks and rabbits are the result of force. Even the motions of my neighbors seem to be determined by the forces of nature—lust, inertia, gravity, genetics. They seem so *predictable*. The point is, they can say the same about me. "Spinoza says that if a stone projected through the air had consciousness, it would imagine it was flying of its own will. I add merely that the stone would be right."

What difference does all this make to someone who just wants to listen to music, and who tolerates philosophy only if it lets him listen deeper? By means of music, Schopenhauer says, we philosophize without knowing it. The danger in making that philosophy explicit is not that we may do it too well, and so puncture the magic—we are centuries away from that—but that we may get it wrong. A narrow theory can pinch our ears and impoverish our listening. That is what psychologizing, man-obsessed theories of music do, and abstractionist theories like Langer's are only a little better. The first kind of theory ignores nature entirely or mentions her only when some joker writes *Pastorale* at the top of a score; which might make sense if we were dealing with a marginal art like cameo or petit point. The second kind of theory lets music embrace the whole universe, but only around the ankles; that is, at a trivial level of abstraction. All the microcosm and the macrocosm are allowed to have in common is a kind of mobile geometry.

Why are we moved at the sight of a fountain, at the water's yearning rise and dying fall? The answer is in the adjectives, of course; which is not to say that the fountain is just a metaphor. If it is a metaphor, it is the deep kind, not the skimpy kind that gets by on visual similitude alone. The fountain moves us not because it reminds us of how we sometimes feel, but because we know just how it feels. A spray of melody that rises toward the octave, falters before reaching it, and falls to the subdominant moves us in the same way. That phrase is not about fountains and not about human aspirations. It is about the energy more elemental than either that flows through both.

To take such a universal view of music is not exactly revolutionary. In fact, it is fairly reactionary. Pythagoras and Plato connected the harmony of the soul with that of the universe, and this understanding persisted right down to Shakespeare's time. It was then that the Great Chain of Being began to fray as levelers, bastards and pretenders set degree aside and untuned that string. In Schopenhauer, however, not only has the chain been naturalized, but all its moral luster has been scraped away. We see his pessimism at work, and his Vedic skepticism. The chain is really a snake snapping blindly at its own tail. This is not as pretty a view as Plato's; but from a strictly modern point of view, isn't this the way things are?

Without necessarily drawing his practical consequences, we are drawn to his view of the world. His understanding of music ought to be equally compelling. Not, perhaps, his labored correspondences between the graded Ideas and contemporary musical theory (he goes so far as to root the rule against parallel fifths in the nature of inorganic matter). That might work with Mozart, whose perfection could be said to reflect a momentary equipoise of man and nature, with man securely on top and nature graciously accepting his pathetic fallacy. It won't work with plainchant, Javanese gamelan music or a Charlie Mingus bass-fiddle solo. But Schopenhauer's central insight is much less culture-bound. He manages to explain how it is that when we listen to music most deeply we seem to trace with one hand the furrows of the mind, with the other the folds of the universe. In other words, music is not just about people. It is bigger than that.

How odd that for hundreds of years Western man should have thought otherwise. But then these were rough centuries, and naturally he was preoccupied with his own affairs. When he paid good money for a concert seat he had no intention of empathizing with vegetables or rocks, still less with the primordial will. He was there to have his own emotions stroked. Or maybe just to put in an appearance, since the concert was a social event. In the concert hall he sat among humans. There were only humans onstage. Nature and its noises were shut out, and there was not even an icon, as in church, to remind him of extrahuman zones. Even the instruments were anthropomorphic (the womanly violin family, for example). Music was made by people, for people, so it had to be about people.

In the nineteenth century only a mystic or a hermit could get past this way of thinking, someone like Schopenhauer or Thoreau. "I hear one thrumming a guitar below stairs. . . . I soar or hover with clean skirts over the field of my life." When we hear music "we put our dormant feelers to the limits of the universe. . . . No particulars survive this expansion; persons do not survive it." It is noteworthy that these and similar meditations are almost always, for Thoreau, set off by music that floats in from a distance or another room. That was how Thoreau took his music when he wasn't playing the flute in a forest clearing. Others might get the same feeling in a church, with the sound of the choir and organ diffusing from above. This rarefied sort of experience has been made available to us as a matter of routine by the phonograph.

The concerto, which served as an example earlier, should serve here as well. It is a form that seems to speak of the relation between the individual and society. More than etymology connects it to the concert hall and to the problem of how one may act "in concert" with one's fellow men. We have already seen how phonography can change the listener's viewpoint, so that instead of seeing the soloist from the midst of the crowd one sees the crowd through his eyes. But a further possibility is also introduced. The concerto may describe the hero's relationship, not to society, but to nature or the world as a whole. For example, the recording of the Sibelius Violin Concerto by Heifetz and the Chicago Symphony may bring to mind a man walking in northern woods at dusk: a sense of communion without consummation. In concert the very same notes can seem mawkish or clumsy, like a man unused to company. Again, the Beethoven concerto sometimes seems slow and awkward when exposed to the scrutiny of a crowd, while on record (Menuhin with Furtwängler, say) it relaxes, breathing fresh air. Both these concertos failed initially to get a toehold in the concert hall.

Similarly, there are symphonies and overtures and choral works in which we are intended to hear nature even as we stare at sixty or seventy representatives of society. Pastoral music of symphonic size is just one example of what composers may have wanted to do but couldn't until the phonograph came along. They may have wanted to create music without the mediation of interpreters. They may have wanted direct communication with the listener ("from the heart, may it go to the heart"). Their inner visions may have been too personal, or mystical, or nature-mystical to be transmitted in a concert hall, but too richly colored and vast for any medium but the orchestra. Historians connect the symphony orchestra of the nineteenth century with standing armies, nationalisms, and the earth-punishing motions of organized men. Yet Mahler's symphonies, scored for whole regiments, make the motions of the spirit—of one man or of the universe, but certainly not of a group. "Imagine that the Universe begins to sound and sing," Mahler wrote of his Eighth Symphony. "These are not human voices any more, but planets and suns circling." He is not the only composer whose orchestra grew as his vision became more hermetic. One could say that of Bruckner, Ives, Strauss, Berlioz, even Beethoven. It must have been painful for such men to know that their larger works, when they were performed at all, would be confused with such events as the Boston Peace Festival of 1869, which featured an orchestra of a thousand, a chorus of ten thousand, and a hundred firemen banging on anvils.

By the same token, much naively descriptive pastoral music and much program music of the swashbuckling open-air kind may have been conceived in reaction to the close, sentimental air of the concert hall, the drawing room, and the provincial palace. When patrons and subscribers would prate about noble affections, how on earth could one ventilate one's music? How could one show that it did not have the same subject matter as gossip? Maybe by making the flutes simulate a storm. That was not the real subject matter, either, but it was an improvement.

I am thinking of Beethoven, but a century later Debussy faced the same embarrassments. He conceived "a kind of music composed especially for the open air, on broad lines, with bold vocal and instrumental effects, which would sport and skim among the tree-tops in the sunshine and fresh air. Harmonies which would seem out of place in an enclosed concert room would be in their true environment here." It seems to me that the phonograph would have made things easier for these composers, as it has made things easier for their listeners. Debussy, to be sure, had mixed feelings about the Pathé contraption and in this same essay charges that military music among the trees "is like the strident notes of some huge gramophone." But Varèse was to hear the voice of his master Debussy in the new device, recognizing it as the medium of a music "of moving sonic bodies in space," a music equal to the universe.

Here as elsewhere the logical extreme of phonography is electronic music. Earlier I quoted Stockhausen's comment that when one listens to electronic music at home, eyes closed, "the inner eye opens to visions in time and space which over-step what the laws of the physical world around us permit; spatial perspective and the logic of cause and effect in temporal events are both suspended." Cause and effect and spatial perspective are aspects of the phenomenal world, foreign to the will. Stockhausen is here serving Schopenhauer, whether he means to or not. While the human origin of electronic music is a mystery which "there is no point in asking" about, that of ordinary recorded music is a certainty (more or less) which there is no need to think about. In either case you are free to fill your mind with the music itself—or the music with your mind.

When we hear music we expand to fill available space. This is one reason for the Gulliver feeling we get, a feeling of monstrous sensitivity—as though our nerves were stretched across the universe—and vulnerability. (Headphones give this feeling instantly, but in a somewhat different form. While it is hard to say whether my self has expanded or the world has imploded, the violent privacy of the experience makes the sense of implosion stronger. Because the music seems to be coming from inside me, it merges with my direct experience of the will. As a result, the music seems to express my feelings of the moment, even when by its nature it ought to be at odds with them. Another result is one Nina noted: I do not seem to be listening to the music so much as playing it.)

Maybe all art expands the soul. But not all art does it the way music does. For example, architecture should build the soul up, but because our eyes move cautiously across the great spaces we are humbled rather than exalted. The interior of a great cathedral makes us feel small; only when it fills with music does the spirit stretch to its dimensions.

". . . To the man who gives himself up entirely to the impression of a symphony," says Schopenhauer, "it is as if he saw all the possible events of life and of the world passing by within himself." De Quincey, under the influence of opium rather than metaphysics, seems to have felt something similar:

> . . . a chorus, & c., of elaborate harmony, displayed before me, as in a piece of arras work, the whole of my past life—not as if recalled by an act of memory, but as if present and incarnated in the music: no longer painful to dwell upon: but the detail of its incidents removed, or blended in some hazy abstraction; and its passions exalted, spiritualized, and sublimed. All this was to be had for five shillings.

But whether or not one actually "sees" an infinity of images or events, one often has the sense that an hour of music encapsulates a world. A record is a world; even its shape, unchanged from Berliner to the laser disk, suggests this. In rock and roll the spinning disk has other associations, mostly having to do with undirected motion, but there is also the desire to trace a mystic circle around one's own world. "I fled school for the sanctuary of my room," the critic Jim Miller remembers, "where I could summon a world with a choice of singles. That was what rock and roll meant to me."

Every disk is a microcosm, a twelve-inch or four-and-three-quarter-inch world. A shelf of records is a row of possible worlds. Take one out, put it on, and a world unreels, the world one has chosen to live in for the next hour.

How does the record shelf differ from the bookshelf above it? We often think of a book, too, as a world. But a novel, because it refers to specific items of the world's furniture arranged in a conversational grouping, is blessedly partial. It is a room we can escape to from the room we actually live in. It is "a world," but not a whole world, not a version of *the* world. So one can actually read a great novel by Balzac or Jane Austen or Flannery O'Connor as an escape, confident that it will not scrape the tender places of one's daily life. That kind of escape is not so easy with Berlioz, Haydn, or Billie Holiday. (Schopenhauer's explanation of this is different but related: the nonmusical arts let us escape the will by losing ourselves in pure appearance.) Books that try to present a whole world, books of philosophy and some books of poetry, too often lose their power to touch us. Music alone is at once universal and close to the bone.

Music worthy of the name is greedy, imperious, even when it has lyrics so particular that one could use them to address a letter. It either fits one's mood or contradicts it (or does both); it can no more ignore it than gravity can ignore a stone. When we speak of using music as an escape, we mean we want the gravity of our situation counteracted—not wished away—by the pull of music. We want to reach escape velocity. If it works we are in orbit, circling this world, subject to its deeper laws but seeing it from a higher perspective. Only a handful of books have a comparable reach (no one escapes in a trivial way to Tolstoy or the Vedas or Spinoza).

Suppose I am sitting in a room in no way remarkable, except that the Air from Bach's Third Orchestral Suite is moving through it. I am staring at a patch of rug and the foot of a chair, but absently; what I am really following is the tread of this melody, the walking bass that seems to traverse galaxies at a step. When a record is fitted over the platter, a transparency or slide is fitted over a segment of space and time. The effect is a double exposure. But if the music is worth its salt, it will assert itself as the true reality, and all the lovely furniture of one's room will seem (if one is aware of it at all) a mere picture, a veil of Maya.

Can any other "home entertainment" device pull off this trick—superimpose its own space on the space people live in? Television remains at all times a flat surface, or at best a box in which images dance and wrestle. Books have no relation whatever to the room in which they are read; their space is elsewhere, and we follow them there. Then there is radio, which at times is indistinguishable from the phonograph in this respect; but its real tendency is to conflate my space with other spaces in the world. If the phonograph opens the cramped urban cell into as many worlds as there are records, radio makes the whole world a cozy domestic scene.

In speaking of a double exposure I don't mean that our sense of music must be visual. I mean that it is not just aural; it is the sense of a presence, a reality. We may fill this in with imagined shapes, or we may not. Cavell writes, "Those who miss serious radio will say that, unlike television, it left room for the imagination. That seems to me a wrong praise of imagination, which is ordinarily the laziest, if potentially the most precious, of human faculties. A world of sound is a world of immediate conviction." He is talking about radio drama, but the same goes for music on radio or record. Whether or not imagination's crayon is applied, the reality is there.

An earlier form of this experience is described by Kierkegaard in the first volume of *Either/Or*, where the narrator is obsessed with *Don Giovanni* but would not spend a penny for a ticket. "I stand outside in the corridor; I lean up against the partition which divides me from the auditorium and then the impression is most powerful; it is a world by itself, separated from me; I can see nothing, but I am near enough to hear, and yet so infinitely far away." He does not even want (as Saul or Tomás might) to imagine the Don's appearance, for if one sees him, "one no longer hears him, and in that way he is lost." The Don is not a man but a universal force, "the exuberant joy of life," which animates the entire opera and is "absolutely musical." On a good day, Schopenhauer might hear the will in Don Giovanni.

The effect is not confined to indoor quarters. Thoreau says that music "paints the landscape suddenly as no agriculture, no flowery crop that can be raised." In fact, out of doors it more often paints than opposes what the eye sees. "The murmuring of the breeze," says Debussy, giving his recipe for music *en plain air*, "would be mystically mingled with the rustling of the leaves and the scent of the flowers, since music can unite all of them in a harmony so completely natural that it seems to become one with them. The tall peaceful trees would be like the pipes of a great organ. . . ."

Chairs and tables, no less than trees, are objectifications of the will. Even indoors, then, music should at least sometimes paint what we see, deepening its reality instead of contradicting it. Schopenhauer says that "we could just as well call the world embodied music as embodied will; this is the reason why music makes every picture, indeed every scene from real life and from the world, at once appear in enhanced significance, and this is, of course, all the greater, the more analogous its melody is to the inner spirit of the phenomenon."

Thinking for the moment in terms of analogies of tempo, let us test this. Just as any kind of movement on a screen will seem to synchronize with any music played behind it if there is even the vaguest similarity of tempo, so the music played in one's living room will match whatever goes on there. (John Cage's music and Merce Cunningham's choreography, created independently and then slapped together, are another instance.) But if there is no motion in the room, or the motion is at the far end of the tempo range, then one gets the sense of the visible world as Maya. Out of doors this outcome is possible but less common, since the out of doors can seem very nearly as large as music, its motions as graceful and various.

In "The World of the Phonograph," an essay that I read a page of and then put away for two years because it breathed too closely on what I was writing, Paul Rosenfeld tells of a summer spent in a farmhouse where the Orthophonic stood between a screen door and a window looking out on lake, mountain, and sky. Here he discovered the world of the phonograph, "a metaphysical world, very like the physical." In lines as purple as the ghost-poet Holger's he describes how in the chants of the friars of Solesmes he heard "faint opalescent light traveling in streaks across the gray evening clouds"; in the second act of *Tristan*, the womb of the creative earth, "hearth of somber flames"; in the entr'acte of *Khovanshchina* a level near that one but dark as the grave, bearing "the colossal tonnage of the mountains, and with it the world's tragedy." Bach's Toccata and Fugue in D minor had to do with "the angular lightning and the slanting rain," the mechanical play of elemental powers. Brahms was a regal sunset, Mozart a golden, Olympian afternoon, Beethoven "the variegated surface of the earth, a human motion as of a man who strode among the liquid trees, amid fresh winds." The phonograph let Rosenfeld juxtapose works of music with "the natural world that can interpret the experiences they express." Of course, the natural world includes man, and a window open on a city street might give similar insights; indeed, Rosenfeld's imagination was prodded by the human events of "that grave summer of 1931." The concert hall, however, is built to exclude all human events larger than a cough.

"Under the charm of the Dionysian," Nietzsche writes, "nature which has become alienated, hostile, or subjugated, celebrates once more her reconciliation with her lost son, man." But if music might exist without a world, surely it might exist without man. We ought to be modern enough by now to listen to music and hear a world in which the presence of man is contingent, even irrelevant.

Thanks to the atom bomb, we can hear the last movement of Vaughan Williams's Sixth Symphony as a peroration on the absolutely empty field of a future war. (The old composer's rumbling speech, so oddly appended to an early recording, may have been meant by Decca to relieve that emptiness.) But plenty of pre-atomic music can also be heard as nonhuman. Beethoven's outer-space music in the Ninth Symphony—the ascending minor thirds following the words "über Sternen muss er wohnen"—never sounds quite right coming from woodwind players in dinner jackets; it sounds right coming from the blankness of a loudspeaker, preferably one perched on high. But the movement as a whole, to which Nietzsche refers us for a vision of Dionysian ecstasy, remains willfully human. Elsewhere Beethoven, instead of willing away his loneliness, lets it conduct him to icy, untenanted landscapes. The beginning of the Ninth Symphony suggests the creation of the world, an event no human was around to get emotional about. The slow movement of the second quartet in Opus 59 is like a barren planet, unvisited even by the artist who describes it, scattered with ruined porticos and the insteps of statues—or so it seems to me under the influence of the phonograph.

The standard outer-space music of today is electronic, the phonograph finding its own voice. It ranges from video game blips to the astral extravaganzas of Stockhausen (the first electronic work to be commissioned by a record company, Subotnick's *Silver Apples of the Moon*, falls plunk in the middle of the range). Varèse planned a dramatic work about an astronomer who exchanges signals with Sirius and who, when set upon by the uncomprehending masses, is translated there by "radiation instantée." The basis of this story was an American Indian folktale whose hero Varèse connected with the *Übermensch* of Nietzsche.

Let us follow this trail a little farther. Richard Strauss, one of several gray eminences impressed by the young Varèse, wrote his own more direct treatment of Nietzsche's theme. This was not overplayed until Stanley Kubrick used it in *2001: A Space Odyssey*, another story about a man who leaves mankind behind. Immediately the opening fanfare became (Like Holst's *The Planets*) a standard audio demonstration piece. The drums and organ could be found in Mouret; what really counted was the sense of galaxies announcing themselves to their chosen one.

Intelligence from another planet is expected to manifest itself in simple geometric shapes. The monolith of *2001* is one such token; and it is easy to feel, as the mighty theme music springs from it, that the disk is another. As it happens, we have chosen the disk as our own envoy to the rest of the sapient universe, such as it may be. At the heart of the spacecraft Voyager II, as it hurries to its appointment unspecified light-years away, is a phonograph with picture instructions that an alien child could understand. On the turntable is a golden record encoded with human music—Bach, Chuck Berry, Balinese gamelan—and, somehow or other, photographs of life on earth. "Billions of years from now," Carl Sagan writes, "our sun will have reduced Earth to a charred cinder. But the Voyager record will still be intact . . . a murmur of an ancient civilization that once flourished . . . on the distant planet Earth.''

Officially, the medium was chosen for its simplicity and permanence (a golden record is permanent if you don't play it). Deeper reasons are suggested by the cover art of the book *Murmurs of Earth*, which shows the golden record afloat in space, at home among the other orbs. A record is a world. It is the world scratched by man in a form that may survive him.

Index

Á nous la liberté (Clair, 231

Academic Festival Overture (Brahms), 27

Adam and Eve Driven from Paradise (Masaccio), 161

Adorno, Theodor, 23, 78–79

"Adventure of the Mazarin Stone, The" (Doyle), 111

Aida (Verdi), 217

Albanese, Licia, 222

Albinoni, Tommaso, 46

Alcibiades, 182

Alexander Nevsky (Prokofiev), 115–16

Alexander the Great, 12

Allegro, L' (Milton), 13

Allen, Woody, 94, 127

Amarcord (Fellini), 30

Amériques (Varèse), 132

Amram, David, 108

Andersen, Hans Christian, 234

Angelico, Fra, 64

Antheil, George, 237

Any Resemblance Is Purely Coincidental (Dodge), 56

Arcana (Varèse), 132

Aristotle, 21, 102, 171, 181, 183–87, 190, 202, 206–208

Armstrong, Lil Hardin, 145

Armstrong, Louis, 32, 33, 64, 71, 141, 143–46, 148–50, 155, 156, 213

Art as Experience (Dewey), 200

Astaire, Fred, 3, 156

Astral Weeks (Morrison)

Atlee, John York, 116

Austen, Jane, 96, 98, 250

Average White Band, 167

Baal Shem Tov, Israel, 164

Babai, Béla, 94

Babbitt, Milton, 136–37

Babel, Isaac, 30

Bach, Johann Sebastian, 28, 53, 60, 73, 81, 106, 108, 129, 135, 139, 140, 153, 155, 162–63, 171–72, 188, 191, 195, 251, 253, 255

Bacon, Roger, 228

Baker, Janet, 195

Ballet mécanique (Antheil), 237

Balliett, Whitney, 96

Balzac, Honoré de, 250

Barraud, Francis, 63–64

Bartók, Béla, 57

Barzun, Jacques, 176

Basie, Count, 149, 171
Bass Saxophone, The Škvorecký), 199
Beach Boys, 67
Beatlemania, 67
Beatles, 45, 61, 66, 67, 127, 142, 149, 157, 159, 235
Beattie, Ann, 81
Beautiful in Music, The (Hanslick), 193–94
Bedazzled (Donen), 94
Beecham, Sir Thomas, 62, 111, 153, 189, 215, 229–30
Beethoven, Ludwig van, 13, 27, 28, 31, 37, 46, 52, 61, 81, 83, 163, 173, 187, 189, 190, 229, 233, 236, 246–48, 253, 254, 255
Beiderbecke, Bix, 213
Being There (Ashby), 56
Bellow, Saul, 21, 82
Benjamin, Walter, 22, 50, 113
Berio, Luciano, 157
Berkeley, Busby, 239–40
Berlin, Irving, 72
Berliner, Émile, 43, 50, 116, 175, 250
Berlioz, Louis-Hector, 73, 247, 250
Bernstein, Leonard, 36, 39, 114
Berrigan, Bunny, 213
Berry, Chuck, 97, 142, 157, 236, 255
Bizet, Georges, 195
Blacking, John, 78
Blake, William, 17
Blonde on Blonde (Dylan), 66
Bohème, La (Puccini), 56
Bolden, Buddy, 149
Book of Laughter and Forgetting, The (Kundera), 84
Book of Snobs, The (Thackeray), 26
Boris Godunov (Mussorgsky), 236
Borodin, Aleksandr, 192
Boulez, Pierre, 133, 137–38, 157
Boyé, Caspar Johannes, 194
Brahms, Johannes, 27, 47, 151, 154, 192, 193, 253
Branch, Elwood, 8
Brecht, Bertolt,47–48, 71, 170, 190
Britten, Benjamin, 74, 76, 121–22, 138
Brown, Claude, 73–74
Browne, Clarence Abram, 1–9, 18, 21–22, 33
Bruckner, Anton, 247

Buch der Lieder (Heine), 15
Buñuel, Luis, 240
Burney, Charles, 74
Burnt Weenie Sandwich (Zappa), 159
Busch, Fritz, 215
Busoni, Ferruccio, 63, 131
Byrd, Donald, 46

Caballé, Montserrat, 221
Caccini, Giulio, 195
Cage, John, 75–76, 103, 133, 137–38, 203, 238, 253
Cahill, Thaddeus, 131, 132
Cale, John, 156
Callas, Maria, 37–39, 119, 120
Cantelli,Guido, 62
Čapek, Karel, 230, 236
Captain Beefheart, 128
Carlos, Wendy, 103, 135
Carnegie Hall (New York), 39, 110–11, 113, 152, 216, 242
Carter, Jimmy, 80
Cartier-Bresson, Henri, 113
Caruso, Enrico, 16, 56, 62, 72, 89, 93, 117, 146–48, 150, 155, 214
Casals, Pablo, 45, 62, 191
Cat People (Tourneur), 66
Cavell, Stanley, 57, 95, 96, 251–52
Chaliapin, Feodor, 64, 117, 236
Chaplin, Charlie, 47, 127, 147, 231–32
Chopin, Frédéric, 27, 28, 165
Chotzinoff, Samuel, 73
City Lights (Chaplin), 231
Clair, Rene, 231
Clapton, Eric, 74
Clementi, Muzio, 229
Clinton, George, 83–84, 127
Clinton, Larry, 213
Cobbett, Walter W., 49
Cocteau, Jean, 130, 235, 240
Colbert, Claudette, 162
Coleman, Ornette, 149
Collier, James Lincoln, 146
Collette, 66
Commander Cody, 116
Condon, Eddie, 213
Conversation Piece (Coward), 122
Cooke, Deryck, 196
Cooper, Jackie, 4
Corelli, Franco, 37, 237

Cosmo, 66
Costello, Elvis, 31–32, 81, 157, 191
Coward, Noel, 122
Cox, Ida, 141
Craft, Robert, 119
Creole Jazz Band, 143, 145
Croce, Jim, 61
Crosby, Bing, 156, 157, 213
Crystals, 126
Culshaw, John, 105, 120–22, 138
Cunningham, Merce, 138, 253
Cyclopaedic Survey of Chamber Music
    (Cobbett), 49
Cyrano de Bergerac, Savinien, 87–89
Cyrano de Bergerac (Rostand), 88, 89, 93

Dali, Salvador, 36
Daniel, Oliver, 150
Dante, 197
Darwin, Charles, 241
Davis, Miles, 149, 155–57
Debussy, Claude, 55, 107, 130–31, 248,
    252
DeGaetani, Jan, 119
del Monaco, Mario, 214
DeMille, Cecil B., 154
De Quincey, Thomas, 249
de Sabata, Victor, 119
Déserts (Varése), 133–34
Devo, 161
Dewey, John, 200
di Stefano, Giuseppe, 214
Diva (Beneix) 67–68
Dodge, Charles, 56
Don Giovanni (Mozart), 93–94, 217, 252
Donizetti, Gaetano, 38, 214
Doors, 61–62
Dorsey, Jimmy, 213
Dorsey, Tommy, 213
Doyle, Arthur Conan, 111
Dozier, Lamont, 126
Dunstable, John, 196
Durkheim, Emil, 222
Dvořak, Antonin, 45
Dylan, Bob, 65, 124, 142, 157

Earth, Wind & Fire, 85
Easter Oratorio (Bach), 29
Ecuatorial (Varése), 132, 134

Edison, Thomas Alva, 16, 43, 50, 70, 109,
    111, 124, 144
Eisenstein, Sergei, 115–16, 148
Either/Or (Kierkegaard), 252
Electric Ladyland (Hendrix), 66
Elektra (Strauss), 120, 138
Elgar, Sir Edward, 117, 129, 187
Eliot, T.S., 95
Ellington, Duke, 149, 157
Ellison, Ralph, 32–33, 146
Elman, Mischa, 153–54
Emerson, Ralph Waldo, 15, 178
Eno, Brian, 128
Etting, Ruth, 9
Euridice (Caccini), 195
Euridice (Peri), 195
Evans, Bill, 149, 155

Faber, Josef, 228
Fabulous Phonograph, The (Gelatt), 16
Farrar, Geraldine, 118
Faust (Gounod), 58, 59
Fellini, Federico, 30
Firebird, The (Stravinsky), 233
Fischer-Dieskau, Dietrich, 217
Fisher, Eddie, 93
Fitzgerald, Eddie, 4–5
Fitzgerald, Pegeen, 4–5, 7, 21
Flagstad, Kirsten, 37, 116
Fletcher, Harvey, 152
Fogerty, Tom, 127
4'33" (Cage), 137
France, Anatole, 14
Franco, Francisco, 79
Franklin, Aretha, 124, 128, 167
Franklin, Joe, 3
Frayne, George, 116
Free Jazz (Coleman), 149
Freud, Sigmund, 164
Frye, Northrop, 188
Fuqua, Harvey, 126
Furtwängler, Wilhelm, 62, 247

Gaisberg, Fred, 45, 70–71, 106, 112,
    116–17, 120, 122, 124, 147, 151
Galli-Curci, Amelita, 214
Garcia Marquez, Gabriel, 92
Gaye, Marvin, 127
"Gedali" (Babel), 20

Gelatt, Roland, 16
Gershwin, Frances, 3
Gershwin, George, 3
Gershwin, Ira, 3
Gesang der Jünglinge (Stockhausen), 134
Gesualdo, Don Carlo, 237
Getz, Stan, 150
Gigli, Beniamino, 214
Gioconda, La (Ponchielli), 215
Glenn Gould: Music and Mind (Payzant), 101–102
Gluck, Christoph, 165, 194, 195
Gobbi, Tito, 119
Goebbels, Joseph, 48–49
Goethe, Johann Wolfgang von, 27, 94
Goldberg, Isaac, 89
Goldberg, Rube, 238
Goldberg Variations (Bach), 60, 159
Goodman, Benny, 213
Gordon, Dexter, 157
Gordy, Berry, 98, 126
Götterdämmerung, Die, (Wagner), 36
Gould, Glenn, 60, 62, 81, 101–108, 123, 126, 136, 137, 152, 154, 155, 159, 188, 201
Gounod, Charles, 58, 59
Gramophone, 43, 47
Great Dictator, The (Chaplin), 47
Greenfeld, Howard, 89
Gruppen (Stockhausen), 138

Haggin, B. H., 112–13, 144, 201
Hammond, John, 124–25
Handel, George Frideric, 76, 188
Handke, Peter, 191
Handy, W. C., 140
Hanslick, Eduard, 165, 193–95, 198, 243
Haunting Melody, The (Reik), 192
Hawkins, Erskine, 96
Haydn, Franz Joseph, 49, 171, 229, 250
Hebrew Melodies (Byron), 15
Hegel, Georg Wilhelm Friedrich, 15
Heifetz, Jascha, 55, 191, 246
Heldenleben, Ein (Strauss), 62
Helmholtz, Hermann, 130
Henderson, Fletcher, 141–42
Hendrix, Jimi, 61
Henry VIII, King of England, 229
Hesiod, 17
High Fidelity, 43, 101, 120–21, 136

Highway 61 Revisited (Dylan), 191
Hillel the Elder, 20
Hindemith, Paul, 47–48, 73
Hines, Earl, 150, 213
His Master's Voice (Barraud), 63–64
Histoire comique des états et empires de la lune (Cyrano de Bergerac), 87–88
Hitler, Adolf, 30–31, 49
Hoagland, Edward, 80–81
Hodeir, André, 150
Hoene-Wrónsky, Józef Maria, 130
Hoffmann, E.T.A., 15
Holiday, Billie, 5, 71, 92, 141, 156, 250
Holland, Brian, 126
Holly, Buddy, 61
Holst, Gustav, 255
Hooker, Richard, 196
Horowitz, Vladimir, 162
Hot Rats (Zappa), 127
Houston, Joe, 135
Howlin' Wolf, 125
Hunter, Alberta, 141
Huxley, Aldous, 61

I Am Sitting in a Room (Lucier), 137
Idea of North, The (Gould), 105
Imaginary Landscapes (Cage), 133, 238
Incantation for Tapesichord, (Luening and Ussachevsky), 152
Intégrales (Uarèse), 132
International Composers' Guild, 132
Invisible Man (Ellison), 32–33
Ionisation (Varèse), 132, 135
Isherwood, Christopher, 29
Ives, Charles, 77, 247

Jackson, Mahalia, 141
Jackson, Tony, 93
Jasager, Der (Weill), 48
Jazz, Its Evolution and Essence (Hodeir), 150
Jean Paul (15)
Jefferson, Blind Lemon, 141
Johnson, Bunk, 64
Johnson, Emma, 92–93
Johnson, Robert, 91, 141, 156
Jolson, Al, 3, 213
Joplin, Janis, 61

Kael, Pauline, 66

Kafka, Franz, 232
Kant, Immanuel, 240
Karajan, Herbert von, 56, 117–19
Kayserling, Baron Herman von, 60
Kazdin, Andrew, 122
Keaton, Buster, 232
Keats, John, 178
Keil, Charles, 158
Kellaway, Roger, 116
Keppard, Freddie, 143
Khachaturian, Aram, 153
Khomeini, Ayatollah, 30
Khovanshchina (Mussorgsky), 253
Kierkegaard, Sören, 252
Kind of Blue (Davis), 140
King, B. B., 125
Kipnis, Alexander, 215
Kiss, 22–23
Kleiber, Erich, 217
Klemperer, Otto, 51–52
Koheleth, 217
Kolodin, Irving, 62
Koshetz, Nina, 118
Kreisler, Fritz, 59, 112
Kubrick, Stanley, 255
Kundera, Milan, 84

Lamb, Charles, 203
Langer, Susanne, 165, 196–200, 243, 244
Language of Music, The (Cooke), 196
Lanin, Lester, 212
Lauri-Volpí, Giacomo, 214
Lawrence, Jerry, 4
Laws (Plato), 102–103, 181
Laxness, Halldor, 176–77
Le Corbusier (Charles Jeanneret), 135
Lectures on Aesthetics (Hegel), 15
Leden, Christian, 57
Left-Handed Woman, The (Handke), 191
Legge, Walter, 52, 62, 117–20, 122, 126–27
Lehman, Lotte, 120
Leibnitz, Gottfried Wilhelm von, 129
Leinsdorf, Erich, 215
Le Moyne, Jean, 102, 103
Lennon, John, 45, 61, 157
Lenya, Lotte, 159
Leoncàvallo, Ruggiero, 130
Leopold of Cöthen, Prince, 29
Leppard, Raymond, 188

Lewis, Sibbey, 96
Lieberson, Goddard, 122
Limelight (Chaplin), 232
Lipatti, Dinu, 62
Liszt, Franz, 27
Locke, John, 82
Lomax, Alan, 125, 140, 148
Lucia di Lammermoor (Donizetti), 38, 214
Lucier, Alvin, 137
Luening, Otto, 132, 134, 135, 152
Lully, Jean Baptiste, 140
Lyrical Ballads (Coleridge and Wordsworth), 15

Ma, Yo Yo, 164
McCarey, Leo, 98
McCartney, Paul, 127
Mackenzie, Compton, 43, 45, 47, 49, 78, 80, 112, 147, 175–76
McLuhan, Marshall, 102, 106
Madonna, 93
Maelzel, Johann Nepomuk, 233
Magic Flute, The (Mozart), 219
Magic Mountain, The (Mann), 58–61
Mahagonny (Weill), 190
Mahler, Gustav, 45, 171, 188, 247
Malinowski, Bronislaw, 87
Mann, Thomas, 58–61, 108, 194
Marantz, Saul, 223–24
Marcus, Greil, 43
Marcuse, Herbert, 23
Marinetti, Emilio, 237
Marley, Bob, 61
Martin, George, 98, 127
Martinelli, Giovanni, 214
Marx, Groucho, 5
Marx, Karl, 23, 164
Marxism, 23, 24
Masaccio, 161
Massenet, Jules, 36
Mayfield, Curtis, 127
Meistersinger, Die (Wagner), 48
Melba, Dame Nellie, 56, 118
Mendelssohn, Felix, 93–94, 164
Mengelberg, Willem, 62
Menuhin, Yehudi, 112, 117, 247
Mer, La (Debussy), 118
Merriam, Alan P., 25–26
Merrill, Robert, 214
Messiah (Handel), 51

Metropolitan Opera House (New York), 39, 40, 121, 214, 217
Mikrophonie II (Stockhausen), 138
Miller, Glenn, 213
Miller, Jim, 250
Milton, John, 13
Mingled Chime, A (Beecham), 229–30
Mingus, Charlie, 149, 245
Missa Solemnis (Beethoven), 27
Mr. Sammler's Planet (Bellow), 21, 82
Modern Times, 231–32
Modigliani, Amedeo, 131
Moholy-Nagy, László, 239
Molotsky, Irvin, 3
Monk, Thelonious, 52, 149, 157, 159
Monk's Music (Monk), 159
Monteverdi, Claudio, 28, 140, 195
Moonlight Sonata (Beethoven), 168, 169
Moore, Dudley, 94
Moore, G. E., 237
Moore, Gerald, 79
Morris, William, 23
Morrison, Jim, 62
Morrison, Van, 156
Morton, Jelly Roll, 92–93, 140, 143, 148–49
Mothership Connection (Parliament), 83
Mothers of Invention, 52
Motown, 126, 128
Mouret, Jean-Joseph, 255
Mozart, Leopold, 229
Mozart, Wolfgang Amadeus, 27, 28, 35, 37, 76, 81, 107, 132, 139, 167, 170, 171, 187–89, 195, 206, 207, 229, 245, 253
Müller, Wilhelm, 15
Mumford, Lewis, 230, 233
Murmurs of Earth (Sagan), 256
Muscio, Bing, 79
Mussorgsky, Modest, 106
Muzak, 78–81, 99, 107, 135, 204

Nancarrow, Conlon, 139
Nation, 144
New Republic, 144
New York Telegraph, 132
New York Times, 3
Newman, Ernest, 176
Nicomachean Ethics (Aristotle), 185

Nietzsche, Friedrich, 25, 182, 192, 240, 241, 254, 255
Nilsson, Birgit, 37, 120
Nina (pseudonym), 161–74, 188–89, 191, 201, 206
Niven, David, 92
Nozze di Figaro, Le (Mozart), 219

Obraztsova, Elena, 36, 39
O'Connor, Flannery, 250
Oedipus Rex (Stravinsky), 114, 235–36
Offenbach, Jacques, 58, 111, 233
Oldfield, Mike, 127
Oliver, Joe, 143–46, 149
"On a Ruined Farm Near the His Master's Voice Gramophone Factory" (Orwell), 231
Orfeo ed Euridice (Gluck), 194–95
Orfeo, L' (Monteverdi), 195
Orff, Carl, 138
Original Dixieland Jazz Band, 143
Ortega y Gassett, José, 239
Orwell, George, 231
Osborne, Conrad L., 120–22

Pachmann, Vladimir de, 106
Page, Tim, 102
Paradise Lost (Milton), 13
Parker, Charlie, 23, 74, 150
Parliament/Funkadelic, 83
Partch, Harry, 138–39, 157
Pascal, Blaise, 18
Pathé, Charles, 55, 70, 88
Pathé, Emile, 55, 88
Pathétique Sonata (Beethoven), 168
Patti, Adelina, 16, 90
Payzant, Geoffrey, 101–102, 139
Penseroso, Il (Milton), 113
Peri, Jacopo, 195
Pérotin, 130, 237
Peters, Roberta, 214–15, 220–21
Petrushka (Stravinsky), 229, 233
Pet Sounds (Beach Boys), 67
Pet Sounds (Beach Boys), 67
Phillips, Sam, 125, 128
Philosophy in a New Key (Langer), 196
Picasso, Pablo, 130, 180
Pines of Rome, The (Respighi), 235
Pinza, Ezio, 157, 215, 219–20

Planets, The (Holst), 255
Plato, 102–103, 163, 164, 171, 180–85, 190–91, 202, 204–206, 241, 244–45
Playboy, 90
Play It Again, Sam (Allen), 94
Poéme électronique (Varèse), 134, 135
Poetics (Aristotle), 183, 187
Police, 173
Politics (Aristotle), 183
Point Counter Point (Huxley), 61
Pons, Lily, 214
Ponselle, Rosa, 118, 120
Pope, Alexander, 15
Potemkin (Eisenstein), 148
Presley, Elvis, 61, 62, 125, 142
Priestly, J. B., 203
Prokofiev, Sergei, 69–70, 115–16, 123, 129, 153, 235
"Prospects of Recording, The" (Gould), 106
Proust, Marcel, 94
Puccini, Giacomo, 38, 119
Punch, 26
Purcell, Henry, 139
Pythagoras, 244–45

Rachmaninoff, Sergei, 124, 129, 152
Radio Canada, 43
Radio Madrid, 79
Rainey, Ma, 90, 141
Rasumovsky, Count Andreas, 29
Rawls, John, 82
Ray, Man, 239
Raynor, Henry, 51, 74–75
Redding, Otis, 61
Reddy, Helen, 202
Red Hot Peppers, 148–49
Reik, Theodor, 192
Reiner, Fritz, 62, 215
Repeat as Necessary (Edmunds), 54
Republic (Plato), 181–83, 185, 204–206
Respighi, Ottorino, 235
Richter, Sviatoslav, 113
Riesman, David, 18, 19
Righteous Brothers, 126
Rilke, Rainer Maria, 169
Rilling, Helmut, 95
Rimsky-Korsakov, Nikolai, 233, 235
Ring des Nibelungen, Der (Wagner), 120

Rite of Spring, The (Stravinsky), 52, 130, 233, 234
Robinson, Smokey, 126, 127
Rockwell, Norman, 8
Rolland, Romain, 131
Rolling Stones, 74, 157
Rollins, Sonny, 157, 227
Ronnettes, 126, 127
Roosevelt, Franklin D., 117
Rosenfeld, Paul, 48, 234, 253–54
Rosenkavalier, Der (Strauss), 217
Rossignol, Le (Stravinsky), 233–35
Rostand, Edmond, 87, 93
Rothstein, Edward, 101
Rousseau, Jean-Jacques, 194
Rubinstein, Artur, 154, 199
Rush, Otis, 167, 171

Sachs, Curt, 51, 90–91
Sagan, Carl, 255–56
Said, Edward, 108
St. Cyr, Johnny, 143
St. Matthew Passion (Bach), 29, 53–54
Saint-Saëns, Camille, 36
Salome (Strauss), 54
Salon du Phonographe (Paris), 55
Samaroff, Olga, 92
Samson and Delilah (Saint-Saëns), 36
Satie, Erik, 75–76, 157
Saul, 209–55
Schaeffer, Pierre, 133
Schenker, Heinrich, 188
Schlegel, Friedrich von, 14–15
Schmidt, Helmut, 80
Schnabel, Artur, 155
Schoenberg, Arnold, 104, 106, 107, 137, 191
Schöne Müllerin, Die (Schubert), 15
Schopenhauer, Arthur, 27, 103, 197–98, 240–46, 248, 249, 252
Schubert, Franz, 15, 58, 203, 233
Schuller, Gunther, 153
Schuman, William, 79
Schumann, Robert, 14, 28
Schütz, Heinrich, 95
Schwartzkopf, Elisabeth, 116–20
Scott, Herman, 223
Seeger, Charles, 125
Seeger, Pete, 125
Sellers, Peter, 56

Sgt. Pepper (Beatles), 66, 127
Serkin, Rudolf, 164
Shakespeare, William, 89–90, 96
Shaw, Artie, 213
Shaw, George Bernard, 29, 187
Shepherd, Bert, 71
Shostakovich, Dmitri, 192
Sibelius, Jean, 190, 191, 237, 246
Silence (Cage), 203
Silver Apples of the Moon (Subotnick), 135, 255
Sinatra, Frank, 157
Sketch of a New Aesthetic of Music (Busoni), 131
Škvorecký, Josef, 199
Smith, Bessie, 71, 124, 141–42, 146
Smith, Mamie, 141
Smith, Sydney, 68
Smucker, Tom, 67
Smyth, Ethel, 189
Social History of Music, A (Raynor), 51
Socrates, 182–83
Solti, Sir Georg, 120
Solzhenitsyn, Alexandr, 205
Some Girls (Rolling Stones), 66
Sophocles, 90
Sousa, John Philip, 71, 180
Spector, Phil, 98, 105, 126–28
Spector, Veronica, 126–27
Spinoza, Baruch, 243–44, 251
Spivey, Victoria, 141
Spring Symphony (Schumann), 28
Stein, Gertrude, 179–80
Stevenson, Robert Louis, 49
Stockhausen, Karlheinz, 105, 108, 134, 138, 157, 248
Stokowski, Leopold, 94, 105, 123, 132, 150–54, 235
Stoltzman, Richard, 157
Stranded: Rock and Roll for a Desert Island (Marcus), 45
Stratas, Teresa, 157
Strauss, Richard, 106, 121, 129, 247, 255
Stravinsky, Igor, 44, 107, 114, 129, 130, 137, 139, 229, 233–37
Streisand, Barbra, 55
Studies for Player Piano (Nancarrow), 139
Subotnick, Morton, 134, 135, 255
Sudhalter, Dick, 7–8

Supremes, 167
Suzuki, Shunryu, 238
Symphony of a Thousand (Mahler), 29
Symposium (Plato), 182, 206
Szell, George, 45, 215

Tagliavini, Ferruccio, 215
Talking Heads, 45, 128, 157
Tchaikovsky, Peter Ilyich, 196
Tebaldi, Renata, 37, 217
Telemann, Georg Philipp, 28, 76
Teyte, Maggie, 111
Thackeray, William Makepeace, 26
Theognis, 11
Theophrastus, 21
Theremin, Leon, 132
Thoreau, Henry David, 103–104, 177–78, 203–204, 246
Threepenny Opera (Weill), 159
Thurnwald, Richard, 90
Tieck, Ludwig, 15
Time's Encomium (Wuorinen), 135–36
Timon of Phlius, 12
Tolstoy, Leo, 49, 69, 70, 251
Tomás (pseudonym), 35–41, 53–54
Tosca (Puccini), 38, 119
Toscanini, Arturo, 62, 64, 73, 112–13, 153, 201
Toscanini, Walter, 112
Tristan and Isolde (Wagner), 36, 37, 39, 41, 253
Trout Mask Replica (Captain Beefheart), 128
Trovatore, Il (Verdi), 214
Troyat, Henri, 49
Tucker, Richard, 214, 215
Tucker, Sophie, 141
Twitty, Conway, 125
2001: A Space Odyssey (Kubrick), 255

Ussachevsky, Vladimir, 134, 152

Van Vechten, Carl, 71
Varèse, Edgard, 108, 127, 130–37, 140, 152, 237, 248, 255
Vaucanson, Jacques, 228, 230
Vaughan Williams, Ralph, 254
Victoria, Queen of England, 229

Vivaldi, Antonio, 76
Volkonsky, Prince Nicholas, 49

Wagner, Richard, 29, 36, 37, 40–41, 72,
     73, 119–21, 182, 193, 240
Waldman, Frederic, 135
Walker, T-Bone, 157
Wall Street Journal, 45
Waller, Fats, 157
Walter, Bruno, 45
Warshow, Robert, 202, 232
Waters, Ethel, 3, 7
Weber, Max, 51, 54
Webern, Anton von, 107, 190
Weill, Kurt, 47–48, 107, 132, 157, 159,
     190
Weissenberg, Alexis, 157
Welles, Orson, 127
Wellington's Victory (Beethoven), 229
Welte, Edwin, 63
Werther (Massenet), 36
Wexler, Jerry, 128
White Album (Beatles), 66, 159, 235
Whiteman, Paul, 212
"Who Cares If You Listen?" (Babbitt), 136

Wild Bull, The (Subotnick), 134
Williams, Martin, 141
Willis, Ellen, 45
Winter, Johnny, 141
Winterreise, Die (Schubert), 15
WLIR radio station, 168
WMCA radio station, 4
WNYC radio station, 168
Wolf, Hugo, 118
Wonder, Stevie, 88, 127
WOR radio station, 4–5
"Work of Art in the Age of Mechanical
     Reproduction, The" (Benjamin), 50
"World of the Phonograph, The"
     (Rosenfeld), 253–54
Wozzeck (Berg), 107
WQXR radio station, 168
WRVR radio station, 85
Wuorinen, Charles, 135–36

Xenakis, Iannis, 135

Zappa, Frank, 46, 105, 127–28, 135, 142,
     149, 157, 159, 167, 172–73
Zinzendorf, Nikolaus von, 53–54

FOR THE BEST IN PAPERBACKS, LOOK FOR THE

In every corner of the world, on every subject under the sun, Penguin represents quality and variety—the very best in publishing today.

For complete information about books available from Penguin—including Pelicans, Puffins, Peregrines, and Penguin Classics—and how to order them, write to us at the appropriate address below. Please note that for copyright reasons the selection of books varies from country to country.

In the United Kingdom: For a complete list of books available from Penguin in the U.K., please write to *Dept E.P., Penguin Books Ltd, Harmondsworth, Middlesex, UB7 0DA.*

In the United States: For a complete list of books available from Penguin in the U.S., please write to *Dept BA, Penguin, 299 Murray Hill Parkway, East Rutherford, New Jersey 07073.*

In Canada: For a complete list of books available from Penguin in Canada, please write to *Penguin Books Canada Ltd, 2801 John Street, Markham, Ontario L3R 1B4.*

In Australia: For a complete list of books available from Penguin in Australia, please write to the *Marketing Department, Penguin Books Australia Ltd, P.O. Box 257, Ringwood, Victoria 3134.*

In New Zealand: For a complete list of books available from Penguin in New Zealand, please write to the *Marketing Department, Penguin Books (NZ) Ltd, Private Bag, Takapuna, Auckland 9.*

In India: For a complete list of books available from Penguin, please write to *Penguin Overseas Ltd, 706 Eros Apartments, 56 Nehru Place, New Delhi, 110019.*

In Holland: For a complete list of books available from Penguin in Holland, please write to *Penguin Books Nederland B.V., Postbus 195, NL–1380AD Weesp, Netherlands.*

In Germany: For a complete list of books available from Penguin, please write to *Penguin Books Ltd, Friedrichstrasse 10–12, D–6000 Frankfurt Main 1, Federal Republic of Germany.*

In Spain: For a complete list of books available from Penguin in Spain, please write to *Longman Penguin España, Calle San Nicolas 15, E–28013 Madrid, Spain.*